CRITICAL ACCLAIM FOR JULIE MOFFETT!

A TOUCH OF FIRE

"A very enjoyable read...A definite keeper."
—*The Paperback Forum*

"Julie Moffett writes spirited, well-crafted historical romances that truly satisfy the reader..."
—*Romantic Times*

CORNERED BY PASSION...

"Well?" Miles prompted.

Faith felt her mouth go dry at the dark look in his eyes. With the ease of a cat stalking his prey, he had maneuvered her into a corner, leaving her little room to move without touching him. He smelled like soap, leather and horses and she could see that he had recently shaved.

"What I want is to be returned to where you found me—the Beaghmore Stone Circles."

Miles abruptly turned his body into hers, pinning her against the wall. Faith gasped in surprise as he braced his forearms on the stones above her head, his muscular thighs pressing against hers. He was so close. Faith could feel his breath on her cheek.

"Avoiding my questions will not work. I mean to discover what ye want from me, lass."

She could feel the heat from his body permeate the material of her nightgown. Her pulse skyrocketed.

"I want only to be released," she answered shakily.

"Are ye certain that is all?" he asked, sliding one hand slowly down the wall and onto her arm.

Faith shuddered as an electrical current seemed to jump between them. With a start, she realized it was desire she felt, raw and primal. Horrified that he might be able to see the need in her eyes, she jerked her head to the side.

"That's all," she whispered....

JULIE MOFFETT

A Double-Edged Blade

LOVE SPELL ⬧ NEW YORK CITY

LOVE SPELL®

March 2000
Published by

Dorchester Publishing Co., Inc.
276 Fifth Avenue
New York, NY 10001

ISBN 0-505-52369-8

DEDICATION

This book is for you,
Frances Hubbard Moffett,
my beloved grandmother who throughout her life taught
me dignity, respect and the joy of unreserved love.

And for you,
Alexander William Czechowski,
my son who teaches me daily how precious life really is
and how beautiful a child's smile can make the world.

I love you both.

A Double-Edged Blade

Prologue

*"There is no way of judging the future
but by the past."*
—An old Chinese proverb

The picnic began at midday.

*A red-and-white-checked blanket had been carefully spread
beneath a gnarled tree. A wicker picnic basket and several
colorfully wrapped presents lay on top of it.*

*A young family of three frolicked nearby on the sweet-
smelling grass. The sun shone gloriously and not a cloud
marred the blue canvas of the sky. There was a slight breeze,
but it was unusually warm for early spring in England.*

*A young girl with fair hair squealed in delight as her father
whirled her around. "Stop, Papa," she gasped, her head spinning dizzily.*

*Complying, he dropped her lightly on the grass. She col-
lapsed in a fit of giggles, her laughter rising to the treetops,
causing a pair of sparrows to flutter nervously in the branches
and fly away.*

"That's all for now," he said, ruffling her hair absently.

*The little girl smiled happily. Her father rarely showed her
this much attention. Sometimes she wondered why. Once she
overheard him telling Mummy that children were more trouble
than they were worth. She hoped she wasn't trouble. She had
tried so hard to be good.*

*Mummy said that Papa loved her, but she wasn't certain.
So today, on her eighth birthday, she was going to prove to
him that she was worthy of his attention and love.*

*"Papa," she said eagerly, tugging on his sleeve. "Play with
me more."*

"Enough, Faith," he said, looking down at her. His ex-

11

pression had changed. It was a subtle change, but the little girl noticed it nonetheless. "I'd like to walk a bit before lunch," he said. "It isn't often that I have a chance to be outdoors."

"Then I'll come with you," she replied quickly.

"Another time, perhaps. Today I'd like some time to myself."

"But it's my birthday."

"Don't whine, Faith. I said another time."

Faith felt the sharp, familiar pang of rejection. A lump surfaced in her throat as she watched her father walk away.

"I hate you," she whispered fiercely, clenching her hands into fists. "I'll hate you forever."

Bursting into tears, she leapt to her feet and began running in the opposite direction. Her mother called out to her, but she hardly heard.

What's wrong with me? *she thought, hot tears sliding down her cheeks.* Why doesn't Papa love me?

When she could run no longer she dropped to her knees, gasping for breath. Surprisingly, she had arrived at the lake—a place forbidden to her because she could not swim. Defiantly she stood, walking over the edge. Silently she dared her father to appear and chastise her. He did not.

Her anger began to fade in light of the beauty of the lake. The water shimmered in the sunlight like a brilliant jewel, its smooth surface broken only by a small silver fish that leapt up unexpectedly and splashed down a few feet away from her. Intrigued, Faith moved closer to the edge. The fish leapt up again. Leaning forward, Faith stretched out a hand in delight, hoping to touch it.

Her foot slipped. With a startled cry, she fell into the lake. To her horror, the water that only moments before had been beautiful and serene became cold and frightening. Spluttering, she tried to find her footing, but could not.

She opened her mouth to scream and the water rushed in. It pulled at her legs, sucking, clawing and dragging her under. She fought it, wildly thrashing her body, gulping desperately for air.

Unexpectedly her mother's arms—strong and secure—were around her, giving her a push toward safety.

"Swim, Faith. You can do it. Mummy knows you can."

The shove propelled her toward shallow water. Faith sobbed with relief when her feet touched the rocky bottom. She dragged herself to the edge, collapsing in a sodden heap on the bank. Shivering uncontrollably, she wrapped her arms around her waist and wept. The lake was calm.

"Mummy, where are you? Come back. Please, Mummy, I'm sorry. . . ."

"My God, what happened to you, Faith? Why are you in the water? Where is your mother?"

It was Papa, staring at her like a stern, disapproving judge. He had always been so strong, cold and distant.

"I'm sorry, Papa. Please . . . I didn't mean to." She looked at the place where she had last seen her mother. *"Mummy . . . is there."* Tears coursed down her face.

The look of disbelief and rage on her father's face was seared indelibly on her heart.

"Damn it, Faith, you were told never to go near the lake. Never! If anything has happened to your mother . . ."

He never finished his sentence as he stripped off his shirt and shoes and dived into the lake. But Faith knew what came next.

". . . it will be all your fault."

Mummy was gone and Papa would never love her.

It is your fault . . . your fault . . . your fault. . . .

Faith Worthington came awake with a jerk, her breathing coming in short, panicked gasps. Bolting upright on the couch, she groped clumsily for the lamp switch, blinking when the room flooded with light. When the familiar surroundings of her cozy townhouse came into focus she exhaled with relief, trying to slow the beat of her heart to a bearable rhythm. Unconsciously, her fingers curled around the worn cushions, as if trying to anchor herself to this world; the real world. She could feel the sticky wetness of sweat on her brow, the rapid flutter of her pulse.

"Relax, Worthington," she murmured, releasing her death grip on the cushions and leaning back on the couch. "It was just a dream."

Yet she knew it wasn't just any dream; it was *the dream,*

replaying the worst moments of her life over and over again. Like a stealthy assassin, it crept up when she was most vulnerable, twisting a knife of pain and guilt until it ripped her heart and left it bleeding, raw and exposed.

"For God's sake, ease up," Faith commanded herself sternly. Her heart rate slowed a bit, but the fear was still so tangible she could almost taste it.

Damn that cursed memory. Why wouldn't it rest in peace after twenty years?

Trembling, Faith ran her fingers through her pale blond hair, fighting back the nausea that churned in her stomach. Even now the memories haunted her. She could still hear the terrible sound of her father crying behind the closed door of his bedroom, inconsolable in his grief. He had been devastated by his wife's death and enraged by his daughter's disobedience.

It is your fault, Faith . . . your fault.

"No," she said aloud. Leaning back against the cushions, she drew a steady breath and pulled the green cable-knit sweater tighter around her slender shoulders. "I've got to put this behind me."

Now, of all times, would be the perfect opportunity to do it. Her life was finally coming together. She had a job she loved at MI5, the British internal secret service agency. As one of the few women undercover agents with an expertise in Irish political affairs, she was a much sought after commodity. For once in her life she was needed, valued and appreciated.

"Nothing is going to take that accomplishment away from me," she whispered fiercely. *"Nothing."*

She would not let guilt lead her down the same path to self-destruction her father had followed. Alcohol had not eased the pain and bitterness in his soul, nor had it helped him repair his disastrous relationship with his daughter. In the end, he had died alone—a disconsolate, unhappy man. And even though she was of the same flesh and blood, she was not like him. She was different. God help her, she had to be. Standing at his graveside, she had made a vow to bury the past with him and start her life anew.

It was long past time to do so.

Determinedly Faith forced herself to stretch, glancing at the antique clock on the mantel. It was half past seven; she had napped for two hours. That was far too long, given the work she still had to finish before her trip to Ireland in the morning. Bending over, she grabbed a hair clip off the cluttered coffee table and pulled her hair into a short ponytail at the nape of her neck. She would make herself some tea and get caught up on her reading. If she started now, she'd still have a few hours to bring herself up to date with the mission and finish her packing.

Feeling better now that she had a plan of action, Faith headed for the kitchen, stopping briefly at the hearth to rekindle the embers and add a few logs. Kneeling in front of the grate, she blew several times until the sparks finally caught and ignited the wood. As the fire began to crackle, Faith felt her spirits lift. Basking in the bright warmth of the fire, her initial reaction to the nightmare seemed foolish.

"Worthington, you're going mental at the tender age of twenty-eight," she muttered disgustedly. "A silly nightmare and you go to mush. Some agent you've turned out to be."

Standing, she vigorously brushed the dirt off her hands, chiding herself for such weakness. The mission to Ireland was an important one, and she had to be ready both physically and mentally. Putting her hands on her hips, she pursed her lips firmly and strode into the kitchen, purposefully leaving the images of the dark nightmare behind her.

The blazing fire hissed and crackled from the grate of the open hearth, sending a spray of sparks dangerously close to the wooden floor. Faith lowered the pages of the London *Times* momentarily to make certain nothing was on fire before shifting to a slightly more comfortable position on the couch. She had no wish to interrupt her reading to rise to fix the grate she had forgotten to close earlier. The article on Ireland was excellent. As soon as she finished it, she reached for the scissors and snipped it from the paper. She carelessly dropped the clipping onto the couch among a scattered pile of papers and files that had long ago spilled over onto the floor.

Yawning, she set the newspaper aside and leaned forward to take a sip of tea from a chipped cup that sat precariously near the edge of the coffee table. Cradling the cup in her hands, she leaned back on the couch and glanced about the room.

She felt safe and content here, surrounded by the things she loved most: her books and a rare collection of antique weapons. Her eyes rested on a French rapier circa 1630 that had been mounted next to an English broadsword and a pair of matching Highland dirks. The rapier had been her very first purchase, followed by the impressive Welsh shield that hung farther down the wall.

But her most treasured items hung over the mantel—an antique longbow made of yew and a leather quiver of seven intact arrows dated from fourteenth-century England. Pride shone in her eyes as she studied the finely crafted bow, admiring the sleek curves of the weapon. It was in magnificent condition. Although it had cost her an arm and a leg to purchase, the joy she had received in researching and studying the longbow had made it all worthwhile. She considered taking it down from the mantel to examine it when the sudden ring of the doorbell jarred her from her reverie.

"Oh, bother," she said irritably, looking toward the door. She wasn't dressed for visitors, clad only in a pair of ratty green sweats, thick socks and an oversized T-shirt with a jagged hole in its side. Her fuzzy green sweater had long ago been discarded and lay in a small heap at one end of the couch, beneath several newspaper clippings.

For a moment she waited, hoping the uninvited intruder would go away. When the bell rang again insistently Faith pushed the clippings off her lap and rose. Setting the teacup on the coffee table, she took one step before tripping over a stray book. With a cry, she stumbled into the coffee table, stubbing her toe. As she yelped in pain, the teacup went crashing to the floor, scattering tea and pieces of blue and white porcelain across the room.

"Oh, bloody hell," she exclaimed in pain, hopping about on one foot while clutching her toe. Glancing about, she looked for a handy rag but did not see one. Sighing, she left the mess where it was and went to the door, peering out through the peephole.

"Who is it?" she called out irritably, squinting through the hole. She could barely make out an indistinct form standing on her doorstep.

"It's me, Fiona. Christ, I've been out here in the drizzle for five minutes ringing the frigging bell. Let me in, will you?''

Faith immediately turned the deadbolt and unfastened the chain. Opening the door wide, she ushered her attractive young cousin inside. ''Fiona, this is an unexpected surprise. I wasn't expecting any visitors at this hour.''

''What do you mean 'at this hour'?'' Fiona asked, running her fingers through her fashionably short hair. ''Really, Faith, it's only half-past ten. The night is still young.''

Faith noticed immediately that despite the light rain Fiona looked impeccable, down to her carefully manicured nails. Her curvy, petite figure was set off to perfection by an expensive raincoat and a gorgeous silk scarf wound around her slender neck.

''I'm working.''

Fiona shook her head in despair, disapproving eyes taking in Faith's apparel. ''Must you do it in such a dreadful outfit? When was the last time you looked in a mirror? What if I had been one of those gorgeous young bachelors selling tickets to the prince's charity ball? I gave them your name and address, you know. Do you think they'd give you a second glance dressed like that?''

Faith crossed her arms against her chest stubbornly. ''There's nothing wrong with these clothes. They're comfortable. Besides, those bachelors are raising money for charity, not looking for dates. They don't care one whit what I look like as long as I buy a ticket.''

''You must be the only twenty-eight-year-old virgin in all of London,'' Fiona said, sighing in despair. ''How can you be so naive? Of course those gorgeous bachelors are looking for dates. That's the whole idea behind the ball.''

Faith's fair cheeks flushed crimson in embarrassment. ''Well, I wish you'd stop tormenting me about men. I'm happy just the way I am. I don't need sex or a man to fulfill me.''

''I'm not tormenting you,'' Fiona chided, deftly removing her coat and hanging it on a wooden peg. ''I'm simply extolling the virtues of love, romance and companionship. You might follow my example for once and give serious thought to your love life. I don't know what you would do without me. You wouldn't have gone on a single date last year if it hadn't been for my tireless efforts on your behalf.''

17

" 'Tireless efforts'?" Faith said incredulously. "Pestering me to death, you mean."

"Call it what you like," Fiona replied, smoothing her tailored red suit jacket. "At least it got you out of your flat."

"It was a bloody waste of time."

"I would hardly call it a waste of time," Fiona replied dryly. "You had one of London's most eligible bachelors panting at your heels. Peter Winthrop was quite smitten with you. If you had just given him half a chance, something might have come of it."

Faith shot her cousin a withering glare. "Peter Winthrop is a blithering idiot. He didn't even know the name of the current foreign minister, for Christ's sake."

Fiona's lips twitched slightly. "Well, I'm afraid Peter was a bit in his cups," she admitted, "although I might say you drove the poor man to it with heated discussions about politics, terrorism and literature. Must you always hold your dates to such high standards?"

Faith threw up her hands in exasperation. "He thought the Irish Republican Army was a punk rock band."

"Oh my," Fiona gasped in horror. "Off with his head, indeed."

A slight tinge of pink touched Faith's cheeks. "Very amusing."

"Oh, all right, all right," Fiona acquiesced, holding up her hand. "I officially call a truce. I did come here tonight with a purpose, and it was not to discuss the virtues of Peter Winthrop. I wanted to bring you this." She shoved a slightly soggy package into Faith's hands.

Faith looked at it in surprise. "What is it?"

"It's your birthday, you goose," Fiona answered affectionately.

"But my birthday isn't until next week."

"Well, I won't be here next week. Have you forgotten that I am going on holiday to Wales with Edward Hawthorne?"

"Hmm, yes. Soon to be the Earl of Hartwick, if I'm not mistaken."

Fiona smiled sweetly. "Can I help it if he is handsome, powerful and interested in me?"

"No, I suppose you can't," Faith admitted honestly, envious of the ease with which her cousin handled men. "You're lucky to have someone you really care about."

"Well, you could, too, if you'd just put a little effort into it." Fiona lifted her hand and tugged fondly on Faith's ponytail. "If you would let me, I could transform you into a stunning woman. A little makeup would enhance those positively gorgeous blue eyes of yours, and a more fashionable cut would do wonders for your hair. A trip or two to Madame La Salle's boutique for some new clothes that would flatter your figure, and you would be the envy of all of London."

Faith laughed. "Me the envy of London? With a body like mine? I'm still waiting for my curves to sprout. I've always been the ugly duckling cousin and you know it."

"That's not true," Fiona protested. "You just don't take the time to make yourself attractive. Besides, figures like yours are the rage in London these days."

Faith jammed her hands into the pockets of her sweats. "You know full well that all the makeup and clothes in the world won't change me. I am who I am. I've never been good at relationships, especially those with men. I have to learn to live with that."

Fiona's eyes softened. "I just want you to find a little happiness in your life. God knows, you deserve it."

Faith shrugged, a sad smile touching her lips. "I'm a firm believer that we all get what we deserve. I'll just have to wait and see about my allotment. Besides, how bad can it be? I have a smashingly pretty cousin through whom I can live out all my exotic fantasies."

Fiona smiled, linking her arm through Faith's. "Well, how about inviting this smashingly pretty cousin inside before she freezes to death in your entryway."

Faith laughed. "Sorry. After you." She swept her hand out toward the sitting room.

Fiona took two steps forward and nearly tripped over a half-packed suitcase. Surprised, she looked up. "Going somewhere?"

"Oh, just a short jaunt," Faith answered, deftly stepping between her cousin and the suitcase. "Nothing at all remarkable."

"Short jaunt, my foot," Fiona commented with a frown,

19

Julie Moffett

looking back and forth between the suitcase and Faith's face. "Undoubtedly you will be cavorting about in some mysterious location with unnamed companions clad in raincoats and fedoras. What the devil are you people called nowadays . . . 'spooks,' is it?"

Faith laughed lightly. "You've been watching too many spy films, Fiona. I am not a 'spook,' as the Americans would say. I happen to have a simple desk job at a rather discreet organization."

Fiona snorted inelegantly. "You've known me long enough to realize that I don't buy that nonsense about you having a simple desk job. You often disappear for days on end without any word whatsoever. Rather unusual for an analyst, I'd say."

"Don't be silly. I'm often out doing research."

"Oh, please," Fiona exclaimed indignantly. "I'm not bloody stupid, you know. But I'll let the matter rest. You already know how I feel about the kind of dangerous work you do."

Faith sighed inwardly. She could hardly disagree with her cousin—her work *was* dangerous. Yet she had never wanted to do anything else. Her father had spent his entire life working for MI5, first as an analyst and then, until his retirement, as a director. As a child, Faith had been both intrigued and jealous of her father's work. As an adult, she had secretly hoped that by joining the agency she would finally find a common ground on which they could meet.

But she hadn't been prepared for his violent opposition to her announcement that she wanted to join MI5. Instead of beaming with pride that his only daughter wished to follow in his footsteps, he had ranted and raved about the dangers and the unsuitability of women to such jobs. In fact, he had damn near prevented the company from hiring her. If it hadn't been for a very supportive professor from Oxford and her brilliant scholastic record, she might not have been admitted at all. Looking back on it with hindsight, Faith realized how pathetic she had been to hope for more with her father.

Still longing for Papa's love after all these years. Poor Faith, did you really think he would forgive you simply because you wanted to be like him?

"You worry too much about me, Fiona," Faith said, ignor-

20

ing the twist of pain in her stomach. "My job is rather boring, if you really must know."

"I'm certain I don't worry *enough*," Fiona said emphatically, heading for the couch. "But I suppose it's better that I don't know exactly what you do. No doubt it would give me something akin to heart failure." She stopped dead in the center of the room when she saw the scattered newspaper clippings on the couch, the chain gate left carelessly open at the fireplace and the broken teacup and liquid splattered on the floor. Turning, she put her hands on her hips in exasperation.

"For God's sake, Faith, why don't you get a housekeeper? This place is a mess."

Faith sighed, put her present on a table and moved past her cousin. "I know it's a bit untidy, but I didn't have time to clean today. And I wasn't expecting any visitors." She bent down and began picking up the jagged pieces of porcelain. "I have a lot of reading to catch up on before I leave tomorrow."

Shaking her head, Fiona bent down and picked up one of the clippings, reading the headline aloud. "*IRA Breaks Ceasefire: Will Peace Ever Come to Ireland?* Christ, couldn't you pick a happier subject?"

"Don't start lecturing again," Faith warned, crossing the room and disappearing into the kitchen. Fiona heard the water turn on and off before Faith reappeared with a wet rag. "Besides, I'm not reading it for pleasure," she said, bending over the spilled tea and rubbing vigorously. "You know it's my job."

"Then why don't you read this stuff at work? For pity's sake, I'd hardly say it is the kind of relaxing reading material one wants at home."

Faith looked up at her cousin, pushing a stray strand of fair hair off her forehead with the back of her hand. "I'm too busy at work to read. Anyway, it's quieter here, and I rarely have interruptions." She looked pointedly at her cousin, but Fiona only laughed at the unspoken accusation and perched lightly on the edge of the couch.

"Well, it's no wonder you can't get a date. You always have your head in a newspaper, you can't dress yourself properly and you're an impossible housekeeper. I won't even mention your culinary skills . . . or lack thereof. Instead of

21

spending your money on clothes or holidays, you spend your free time clipping depressing articles for work or decorating your flat with old rusted pieces of iron and metal.'' To emphasize her point, she dramatically waved her hand toward the swords on the wall.

''They are not rusted pieces of metal,'' Faith protested. ''They're antique weapons.''

''Whatever,'' Fiona replied before leaping from her seat to stomp on a few sparks that flew madly from the hearth. Sighing, she leaned over and pulled shut the chain door to the fireplace. As she straightened, a bright spark from the mantel caught the corner of her eye.

''What's this?'' she asked curiously, reaching up to the mantel and picking up a long, slender knife. The handle was remarkably small and Fiona's hand fit perfectly around it.

Faith came to her feet, putting aside the rag. Her eyes lit up as she moved closer to her cousin. ''It's a most curious piece, a seventeenth- or eighteenth-century dagger, probably made in Ireland. I saw it at an antique show last weekend and had this overwhelming urge to purchase it. The handle most certainly at one time contained precious jewels. If you look closely at the workmanship, you can see the effort that went into shaping the metal until it was just right. This kind of specialized detailed work on a small weapon wasn't common for England or Scotland at that time. Judging from the small size of the handle and the fact that it has a double-edged blade, it probably belonged to a woman.''

''Double-edged blade?'' Fiona said blankly.

''Men generally didn't use double-edged blades in those days. It was seen as rather unmanly; an insult to the owner's ability to fight as a warrior. Double-edged blades were made primarily for women who were seen as less able to protect themselves.''

''Fascinating,'' Fiona murmured, turning the dagger over in her hand.

Faith touched the blade lightly. ''Whoever the owner was, she appeared to have used it. You can see the tip has been bent back considerably, as if it hit against bone or something equally as hard.''

Fiona shivered. ''How utterly morbid. Can you really tell

all of that from simply looking at it?''

Faith nodded, still staring at the dirk. "With a bit more study, I could tell you even more. There is a small but unusual flaw in the metal near the hilt that makes the dagger very unique. It's almost as if the blacksmith was interrupted in the middle of the process. And you can see there was even some kind of engraving on both sides of the blade.''

Fiona squinted, holding the dagger closer to her face. "You're right. I do see something, but I can't read it. It must have worn off.''

Faith nodded. "It's a mystery. Although the writing is unreadable, this kind of engraving is very unusual for the period. I can't stop wondering who owned it and why she felt compelled to use it.''

Fiona quickly slipped her hand from the dagger, replacing it on the mantel. "Gads, an obsession with old weapons. Of all things to have inherited from your father, Faith.''

As soon as the words left her mouth, Fiona wished she could take them back. Faith stiffened visibly, the color draining from her cheeks.

"Oh, Christ, I'm sorry, pet," Fiona said quickly, laying a hand on Faith's arm. "I didn't mean to bring him up again.''

Faith exhaled, letting the tension flow from her body. "It's not your fault, Fiona. He's been dead for more than a year. I have to stop being so bloody sensitive whenever someone mentions his name.''

"I know," Fiona said quickly. "But one year really isn't that long when you stop and think about it. I mean, especially after what happened and all. . . .'' She let the sentence trail off lamely, realizing she was only making matters worse. An awkward silence ensued before Fiona sighed. "Curse my foolish tongue. Let's just forget I even brought him up. Why don't you open your present?''

Managing a smile, Faith nodded and walked over to the table to pick up her gift. She tore away the wrapping paper, tossing it carelessly to the floor. Opening the box, she lifted the lid and pushed aside the tissue paper before pulling out a small, gold-framed picture. It was an enlarged snapshot of herself and Fiona at a charity ball taken several months earlier. They had their arms thrown around each other's shoulders, their smiles bright and pretty. Faith felt a sweep of warmth go through her. Despite their obvious differences, Fiona was as close to a sister as Faith had, and the only family she had left in the world.

Fiona moved over to stand beside Faith, looking over her shoulder at the snapshot. "Not a bad looking pair, are we?" she commented with a grin.

"No, I suppose we aren't." Faith turned and gave her cousin a heartfelt hug. "Thank you for remembering my birthday. It's beautiful."

Fiona returned the hug warmly but started when she heard the clock on the mantel chime eleven. "Oh, bother. I promised to meet Edward at eleven. I must be off. You will give me a ring when you return from your trip?"

Faith nodded, following her cousin to the door. "Of course. Have fun."

After hastily donning her coat and giving Faith a quick peck on the cheek, Fiona paused in the doorway. "Still sisters?" she inquired, reciting the question the two had asked each other since they were children.

Faith nodded, giving the obligatory answer.

> *"My sister for always,*
> *Naught can us part.*
> *My sister forever,*
> *One bond to one heart."*

"Sisters for always," Fiona repeated softly with an affectionate smile, moving into the mist of the London night. "Have a smashing birthday, sweet," she called out from beneath the streetlight as she waved farewell before disappearing into the night.

Faith closed the door, a familiar twinge stabbing her heart. The sadness she felt after Fiona's buoyant visits often served to remind her of just how lonely she really was. All her life she had been a loner—painfully inadequate and awkward in her social dealings with people. Still, maybe Fiona had been right. Perhaps a little companionship wouldn't be such a bad thing. If only she knew how and where to find it.

A Double-Edged Blade

Faith walked back to the sitting room, added a log to the fire and returned to her spot on the couch. After she was comfortably settled she sighed once before picking up her newspaper and reading from where she had left off.

Chapter One

The Beaghmore Stone Circles
Republic of Ireland
April 30, 1996

Faith moved quietly in the darkness, taking the careful steps of someone well trained in night maneuvers. She was clad completely in black, her blond hair stuffed under a dark skull cap. The evening was unusually still; the only noise came from the cool spring wind, which produced a strange but softly forlorn whispering sound. Sporadic moonlight lit her way and bathed the Irish countryside in a soft, golden light.

Her heart was pounding with a rush of adrenaline. It surprised her somewhat; she always prided herself on her calm demeanor when she was on a mission. But tonight's activities held particular significance. If everything turned out as planned, MI5 would soon have one of the Irish Republican Army's most proficient assassins in their custody.

Faith summoned a mental image of the suspect, something she could easily do after many hours spent poring over his dossier. Padriac "Paddy" O'Rourke was a huge man with flaming red hair and a beard. Looking rather harmless, almost like a large teddy bear, it was hard to believe that he was suspected of assassinating more than ten people, including four British soldiers and two judges from Northern Ireland. He was the man most wanted by MI5, yet he was a frustratingly elusive fugitive. For five years he had avoided every trap the British had set for him. But tonight a new attempt had been arranged—a weapons exchange with an MI5 informant.

It had taken nearly two years of painstaking work that had almost been derailed when O'Rourke had insisted on the exchange taking place after midnight at a farmhouse not far from his boyhood home, O'Rourke Castle. Once stately and

26

majestic, the castle had reportedly fallen into ruin, and the O'Rourke family had been reduced to opening up the castle for tourists on the weekends in order to secure funds for repair. It was a bloody irony that the tour had allowed several British agents a useful glimpse into the ancestral home of one of Ireland's most infamous terrorists.

Although reluctant to permit O'Rourke to operate on such familiar ground, in the end MI5 had been forced to adjust. Every possibility had been considered, including roadblocks and sending in agents on foot to ensure that, once Paddy was in the vicinity, he did not slip through their fingers again.

The agents drew their locations by lottery. To her dismay, Faith drew the popular tourist site, the Beaghmore Stone Circles. Located about three kilometers from O'Rourke Castle atop a lonely hill, it was a convenient location for observation but certain to be far from the action.

Tonight, her birthday, was her first actual visit to the site. The area surrounding the stone circles was mostly farmland, and her feet were damp from a trek across the marshy ground. There was a small carpark near the site, but she had come on foot, away from the road in order to prevent detection. During her journey she had passed a few farmhouses and more than a few sheep, but all in all the site was in a fairly remote location.

Tonight the area was uncannily quiet. The stone configurations were visible in the moonlight, their unusual shapes casting shadows on the ground. Faith pulled a pencil-thin flashlight from the belt around her waist. Clicking it on, she quickly surveyed her surroundings.

"My God," she breathed, swinging the flashlight across the stones. It was an impressive sight. There were seven stone circles in all, six of them situated in pairs and ranging from about thirty to seventy-five feet in diameter. The pairs were arranged in a twin circle configuration, and a small runway of sorts led up to them in a straight east-southeast line. Another circle stood apart from the others, and Faith recognized it from her briefing papers as the famous Dragon's Teeth configuration, named so because sharp rocks stabbed into the ground within the circle and pointed upward to the sky. There were also a dozen round cairns, or burial sites. The literature she had read said human remains had been uncovered in some of the cairns.

Gooseflesh popped up across her arms and back. The photographs she had seen of the site had made it appear harmless enough in the light of day. But to be standing in the midst of the stones circles on May Eve and under a full moon was enough to make even someone as sensible as she a bit uncomfortable.

With a hasty click, Faith turned off the flashlight. Overactive imagination or not, there was definitely something eerie about this site; something she didn't care to dwell upon.

Swiftly, she took refuge in the shadows and sat down near one of the stone circles to wait. As time passed, she occasionally stood to flex her arms and legs, attempting to fight off a damp chill. Impatiently, she glanced down at the luminous dial on her watch. Fifteen minutes until midnight, and all appeared to be going according to schedule. The weapons exchange at the farmhouse would soon be taking place. Her radio was silent, which meant that no unexpected problems had arisen. She had seen only a few cars pass on the road below and there was no sign of trouble. The tension from earlier in the evening disappeared. She yawned, covering her mouth with the back of her hand.

Suddenly a crack sounded. Coming swiftly to a half-crouch, Faith placed her hand on the weapon beneath her jacket, her eyes scanning the dark for the source of the noise. To her astonishment, a magnificent stag suddenly stepped out of the shadows and into one of the stone circles. Stunned, she held her breath as his proud, antlered head lifted and then tilted, as if listening for something. For a moment he seemed to look directly at her before he turned away and dashed down the hill. Exhaling a deep breath, she shook her head in wonder. At that exact moment she heard a heavy footstep directly behind her.

Faith froze in fear for a split second before her training took over. Whirling around, she swiftly pulled the revolver from beneath her jacket.

She looked directly into a man's startled face. Recognition was instantaneous and frightening. Although Padriac O'Rourke was dressed in dark clothing with a black cap on his red head, the heavy beard and the large build were unmistakable. Why he was now at the Beaghmore Stone Circles and not at his rendezvous point she did not know. She only knew that the elusive assassin now stood in front of her, staring as if she were some kind of ghost.

Swearing, Paddy swung a meaty fist at her weapon. The gun flew from Faith's hand, sailing over her head and landing with a loud crack, presumably against one of the stones.

His violent movement jolted Faith from her shock. With a small cry, she whirled sideways, slamming her foot against his hip with a fierce kick. O'Rourke yelped in pain and stumbled backward several steps. The distraction gave Faith the few seconds she needed to throw herself sideways and roll into the shadows of the Dragon's Teeth stones. She immediately heard a bullet thud against one of the stones close to where she lay. With a sickening feeling she realized that O'Rourke was armed not only with a revolver but a silencer.

"Come on out now, English," he called. "I should have known this was a setup."

Her heart pounding like a sledgehammer, Faith slid noiselessly backward, giving a small prayer of thanks as the moon momentarily slid behind a cloud, darkening the landscape. The roll had torn the skull cap from her head, and her pale hair was like a beacon in the night. Cursing silently, she tucked as much of it as she could beneath her jacket and pressed against the ground. O'Rourke had fallen silent and she realized with a sinking feeling that he was stalking her. Coming to a crouch behind one of the thigh-high stones, Faith knew she had to act fast before he had time to plan his attack on her. With size and strength, not to mention a lethal weapon on his side, she was at a definite disadvantage.

Faith waited in silence, mentally calculating his position from where she had last seen him. When he finally passed her hiding place she leapt from the shadows, throwing all of her weight against the hand that held his gun.

Her bold attack took him by surprise. As he stumbled sideways, Faith dug her fingers into the soft flesh of his hands, trying to wrench the gun away from him. Grunting, Paddy tried to regain his balance, but Faith managed to knock his feet out from under him with a savage kick at the back of his kneecaps. Clawing wildly, O'Rourke dragged her down with him. Faith used this to her advantage by letting the full weight of her body fall directly onto his hand, hoping to jar loose the weapon.

A sharp spit sounded as the gun exploded upon impact and slid from Paddy's grasp and into the shadows. Terrified, Faith felt a burning sensation in her leg just as O'Rourke brought his hand up against her face, trying to push her away from him. She promptly bit his hand, drawing blood. Yelping in surprise, O'Rourke temporarily pulled back. Faith seized the advantage and jammed her elbow into his windpipe before bringing her good knee into his groin with a hard lunge.

Paddy howled in pain and rolled to one side, clutching his groin. Faith quickly got to her feet and out of his immediate reach. As her weight settled on her injured leg, an agonized cry slipped from her lips. Ignoring the pain, she threw herself toward the stones, where she frantically sought to find O'Rourke's gun. Out of the corner of her eye, she saw O'Rourke scrambling toward her. She nearly wept with relief as her fingers closed around cold metal. Whipping around, she pointed the gun at him.

"Freeze or I'll shoot," she shouted. "I mean it."

O'Rourke abruptly stopped his motion, looking uneasily at the gun. "Now, lass, I'd advise ye not to do anything hasty. Just take it easy."

Faith realized she was shaking violently. Her hand was trembling wildly, the gun wavering back and forth. O'Rourke took a cautious step backward as the moon slid out from behind the clouds, bathing them both in a golden light.

"Now, lass, I'd like to think we could make some kind o' deal. Why don't ye just lower the gun and let me leave? We'll simply forget we ever saw each other. I'll give ye my word as one professional to another."

Faith shook her head. "No deal, O'Rourke. Your word is worth nothing to me."

"Och, I'm wounded to the quick. Ye don't even know me and yet ye cast me in dishonor."

"I think it safe to say your reputation precedes you," she replied wryly. "Believe me, I have no intention of letting you walk out of here." Cautiously she reached down and felt her

30

thigh where the pain was most intense. Her skin burned as if it were on fire, but she didn't think the bullet had penetrated the skin.

O'Rourke crossed his thick arms across his chest. "Well then, I suppose we'll just stand here and stare at each other until ye pass out. I hit ye, didn't I?"

Faith braced her hand beneath her elbow and fought to keep her arm from wavering. "Sorry, O'Rourke, but you're a lousy shot," she said calmly. "The bullet only grazed my thigh. So I'd suggest that you sit down on the ground and keep your hands above your head."

"And if I refuse?"

"It may just give me the reason I need to shoot you. What the hell are you doing here anyway? It's almost midnight. You should be getting ready to make your weapons exchange."

O'Rourke grimaced wryly. "I'm embarrassed to say I nearly fell for your trap. Lucky for me, ye English didn't know I usually come to the Beaghmore Stone Circles before an assignment. It's for good fortune, ye see; a bit of the Irish superstition. It's why I set the exchange for tonight, seeing how it's May Eve and all."

Faith snorted. "May Eve? The night of great magic and mischief among the fairies? Christ, don't tell me you really believe in that rubbish."

"All the Irish believe. And why shouldn't we? Tonight it proved to be a rather beneficial belief for me."

She shook her head in disgust. "I'd hardly call it beneficial, being on the other end of my gun."

O'Rourke shrugged. "Perhaps."

"Perhaps, nothing. Now, sit down, nice and slow." He started to oblige, and she reached one careful hand into her jacket pocket for her radio.

At that exact moment, O'Rourke unexpectedly lunged toward one of the stone circles. With a rush of frightening clarity, Faith noticed the gleam of metal in the moonlight.

Her gun. She had forgotten about her gun.

Her breath froze in her throat as she aimed the gun and pulled the trigger. A single scream pierced the air, accompanied by a blinding flash of light. Horrified, Faith staggered backwards, shielding her eyes with the back of her hand. The

31

light disappeared and then there was dead silence.

For a moment Faith heard only the harsh sound of her own breathing and the thundering pounding of her heart. Spots of light danced in front of her eyes. Rubbing one eye with the back of her fist, she stepped forward.

She blinked once, and then twice, certain she was hallucinating. O'Rourke had vanished . . . literally. One moment he had been lunging for her gun, and in the next instant he was gone. Warily, she turned around in a circle, holding the gun out in front of her.

"Come on out, O'Rourke," she called. "It won't do any good to hide."

When there was no answer she moved forward, holding the gun steady in her hand. What she saw made her gasp in surprise. Lying untouched, just outside the Dragon's Teeth Circle, was her gun. Wherever O'Rourke had gone, he had not managed to take her weapon with him.

"What in the devil are you up to, O'Rourke?" she murmured.

She suddenly heard a faint crackle of what sounded like static electricity. The hairs on her arms and the back of her neck abruptly stood up. Cautiously, she reached into her jacket pocket and pulled out her compass. The hand was spinning crazily.

"An electromagnetic disturbance," she breathed. Any other time, she might have been fascinated by such a phenomenon, but now she had more pressing matters on her mind. Pocketing the compass, she stepped into Dragon's Teeth Circle, sidestepped one of the sharp stones and headed for her gun.

An abrupt wave of nausea slammed into her with the force of a tidal wave. Instinctively, she doubled over just as a brilliant flash of light exploded behind her eyes. Gasping, she clawed at her face, stumbling forward.

Her mind screamed at her to run, but her limbs refused to cooperate. With a supreme effort she tried to lift her hands but couldn't. Instead, the ground seemed to have been yanked out from under her. She lurched forward at a horrifying speed, as if being pushed from behind by a giant hand. Blinded and helpless, she was terrified; it was like being on a conductorless train completely out of control. She opened her mouth to scream, but no sound came out.

When she thought she could no longer stand the sensation her forward movement stopped. For a brief moment in time she had the eerie feeling that she was hanging precariously over the edge of a cliff. Then, with a sudden jolt, she felt herself falling, spiraling downward. Horrified, she summoned the last of her strength in a final, desperate attempt to save herself.

"Help," she screamed, the words torn from her throat before darkness rushed up to meet her.

Chapter Two

Castle Dun na Moor
Ireland
April 30, 1648

"The English be damned," Miles O'Bruaidar swore angrily, his tall, well-muscled body pacing back and forth in front of the enormous stone hearth. "God's wound, what brings the bastards out on such a night?"

As if hearing his question, a fierce wind howled outside the ancient stone walls of the castle, whipping past the enormous twin battlement towers and whistling across the wide, cobble-stoned courtyard. Rain slashed against the fortress, beating a relentless, stormy tune with its fury.

When no one answered Miles turned to face the small group of men that gathered around a polished, wooden table. "Are ye certain 'tis an English patrol, Furlong?" he asked again.

A short, stocky man with an enormous hawk nose and a beard looked up at his lord, nodding in grim response. "Aye, Miles, I am certain. I scouted the area myself. The patrol crossed o'er into Dunbar land about two hours ago. They appear to be running a course nearly parallel wi' the river. It looks as if they are on some kind o' scouting expedition, stopping frequently to make notes and study a map."

Miles resumed his pacing, the tightening of a muscle near his jaw the only indication of his simmering fury. He had known full well this day would come and that English patrols would invade his land—but to have it come so unexpectedly made his blood boil.

Curse their rotten English souls.

Miles scowled blackly, raking a hand through his hair. The English were spreading across Ireland like the plague. In order to slow their progress, he had built up a highly effective army

34

of Irish rebels who sustained a secret campaign of harassment against English soldiers and settlers. Nicknamed the Irish Lion because of his family's coat of arms, Miles had developed a network of friends who had managed to keep the settlers contained mostly to the north end of the island. Until now.

"God's teeth," Miles swore, bringing his fist down on the mantel with a loud crash, causing a few of the men to start in surprise. " 'Tis Cromwell again. Undoubtedly the English are impatient wi' their progress and are surveying the land. Yet 'tis too damn close to my land for coincidence. Apparently someone in Parliament has cause to question my activities. They are forcing my hand."

An angry murmur rippled through the dozen men seated at the table. There was no question that the elder Dunbar would fight any attempts to carve out a piece of his land, and Miles could hardly stand by and watch his neighbor and longtime ally battle alone against the English.

"What will ye do then, Miles?" The question came from a middle-aged priest clad in a long black robe and a wooden cross. His normally ruddy cheeks had paled at the seriousness of their discussion, his blue-gray eyes filled with concern. "Can ye no' lodge a plea wi' the governor?"

"I can certainly voice my objections, Father Michael," Miles answered, "but I fear 'tis little I can do if they will no' listen. I've known this day was coming, but 'tis been forced on me sooner than I expected by Cromwell's actions. Christ's blood, the man is the devil incarnate himself."

"Well, I won't let the English take a single rock from O'Bruaidar or Dunbar land," a voice piped up as a fair-headed lad leapt to his feet, proudly holding his hand on the hilt of his sword. "I'll fight each and every one o' those cursed Englishmen until they are all dead."

Miles stopped his pacing and regarded the boy with a half smile on his lips. Patrick O'Farrell, Miles's first cousin, was nearing thirteen and had all the bluster of a cock ready to fight. Brash and headstrong, Patrick possessed many of the same characteristics Miles had at that age. He looked upon the lad with all the fondness and exasperation of an older brother.

"Your offer is gallant, Patrick, but 'twill no' be necessary yet," Miles replied, ignoring his cousin's splutter of protest and returning to his seat at the table. "Furlong, how long do ye think 'twill take the patrol to reach the valley?"

Furlong pushed his greasy cap back on his head and absently stroked the side of his long nose. "An hour at the most, Miles. 'Twould be my guess that they'll camp in the protection o' the valley. 'Tis the logical place to wait out the storm."

"Aye, and the storm will no' abate for a time yet." All heads turned toward Shaun Gogarty, castle dwarf, gossip and bard. Raising his voice authoritatively, he added, "The clouds are positioned in such a way that the storm will remain for hours."

The men murmured, but no one questioned the dwarf's pronouncement. His uncanny ability to forecast the weather was well known and well respected throughout the region.

"Your insights on the storm are much appreciated, Shaun," Miles said with a brisk nod of his head. "But now we must determine a way to interrupt the patrol's mission and seize whatever papers and maps they have drawn. 'Twill force them to start anew and give us needed time to organize our response."

Shaun looked appalled at the suggestion. "Ye aren't suggesting that we ride out tonight in this foul weather?"

Miles shrugged impatiently. "Storm or no storm, I'll no' have an English patrol within striking distance o' my land. We ride for the valley at once."

"I must protest this course o' action," the dwarf proclaimed, sliding from the bench and straightening his short, squat body. "May I remind ye, my lord, that this is May Eve, the night o' great magic and mischief among the fey folk. 'Tis no' only unwise to travel out in such weather, 'tis madness. We would be risking no' only our lives, but our souls. Why, who knows what we will find? Och, I beg ye to wait till the morrow."

Miles shook his head firmly at the dwarf's dramatic plea. "We need the horseflesh, Shaun, and the poor weather will aid us in a surprise approach. We'll simply assume our usual disguises and relieve them o' their supplies. 'Twill put a quick end to their expedition, I expect."

"Do ye no' fear striking so close to home?" Father Michael asked Miles, worriedly fingering the wooden cross that hung around his neck. "What if they suspect that ye are the Irish Lion?"

"If we do not strike, they might be convinced that the Lion resides nearby. Nay, we must no' treat this English patrol any differently than the others. We'll ride."

"Miles, will ye let me go this time?" Patrick asked eagerly, leaping to his feet, his fair hair bouncing lightly against his shoulders. "Please, I beseech ye."

Miles crossed his arms against his chest, his massive shoulders straining against the fabric of his white linen shirt. Although tall and broad, his movements were that of a swift, graceful warrior. "Nay, no' this time, Patrick. I want ye to stay here at the castle wi' Father Michael and the others. But don't fash yourself, lad; 'twill be plenty o' opportunities in the future. Tonight I want only a few men and a fast ride."

Ignoring Patrick's cry of protest, Miles turned back to Furlong. "Have twelve o' the men saddle up," he said softly. "Will ye join us, Shaun?"

The small man harrumphed, shaking his head vigorously. "Me, out on May Eve in the midst o' a storm? I'd have to be daft."

"We could use your help," Miles replied. "There are few who are as skilled as ye wi' the bow."

The dwarf straightened his shoulders, puffing out his chest slightly. "Aye, 'tis common knowledge, that is. But I'm afraid I'll no' tempt fate this eve, my lord."

Miles shrugged. "As ye wish. I'll ask Dennis Callahan to ride in your place. He's a fair shot wi' the bow."

"Dennis Callahan?" Shaun screeched. "Why the lad couldn't hit the side o' the castle wi' a bow if ye pointed him in the proper direction."

Miles lifted an eyebrow expressively. "Well, if ye will no' agree to join us, Shaun, I'll have to take him in your place."

"But Dennis Callahan?" the dwarf protested, his bearded face flushing cherry red. Agitated, he began to pace the chamber. " 'Tis blackmail, this is. I suppose I have no choice but to join ye, if for no other reason than to save ye from the poor lad's disastrous aim."

Grinning, Miles rose to his feet. "I knew ye'd see it my way. Now don't fear the fey folk, Shaun. We'll protect ye.

Just prepare for a wet ride." Giving the dwarf a hearty slap on the shoulderblades, Miles exited the hall with Patrick on his heels, still pleading for a chance to join the men.

"A dangerous excursion on May Eve," Shaun mumbled morosely under his breath as the men left one by one. "Saints preserve me, what have I agreed to?"

"Still here, are ye, Shaun?" Miles asked, guiding his mount alongside the dwarf. He held a covered lantern in one hand and the reins in the other. "Haven't been spirited away yet by the *sidhe?*"

"Och, jest if ye wish, but 'tis no' wise to tempt the fairies so," Shaun muttered as he clung to the saddle that had been modified to fit his small, misshapen frame. Sheets of rain pelted his face, dribbling down his nose and disappearing somewhere in the thick hair of his beard. "Who knows what will befall the man bold enough to challenge the fey folk?"

Miles chuckled, drops of rain hitting his cheeks. "Pluck up, man. Even the fairies would no' be out on a night such as this. But I love a good Irish rain. It cleanses the soul, my da always said. Is that no' the truth, man?"

Shaun harrumphed grumpily. "The truth is that I'm soaked to the bone and soul-weary o' the deluge."

Miles leaned sideways in his saddle, putting a hand on the dwarf's shoulder. "Look, Shaun, I'm glad ye came wi' us. Your presence is good for the men, and for me, too. Ye know I need ye."

Shaun puffed out his chest proudly. "Well, o' course ye need me. Why else do ye think the fairies haven't got us yet?" He put his hand beneath his cloak and pulled out a ring of primrose.

Miles laughed, his teeth gleaming in the light of the lantern. "Well, hold on to it, man, and take heart; the rain can't last forever."

"In Ireland it can," Shaun replied, but Miles had already urged his steed on ahead to where Furlong had called a halt.

"Whoa," Miles said, abruptly bringing his horse to a stop next to the stocky scout. "What is it, Furlong?"

"I think we'll be coming upon the patrol any time now," the man answered, jamming his cap down tighter on his head.

"I'm going to ride out ahead to search for their camp. 'Tis infernal weather, but I'll find them. The English will be as miserable as we are in this rain." He rubbed his long nose thoughtfully, and Miles couldn't help but be reassured by the sight. Furlong's nose was legend in these parts for its uncanny ability to sniff out Englishmen.

Miles nodded as the scout jabbed his heels into the side of his steed, riding on ahead of the group. Whistling sharply to his men, Miles motioned for them to follow at a distance. Some time later they came to an abrupt halt when Furlong materialized near the top of a wooded hill, holding up his hand in warning. Miles carefully reined in his horse beside the scout, tracking the direction of Furlong's gaze. Someone was camped in the valley below, the glow of protected fires barely visible through the rain.

"Is it the English?" Miles asked softly, and Furlong nodded.

Smiling, Miles reached into a leather pouch attached to his saddle and took out a black linen hood. Pulling it over his head, he adjusted it until only his eyes, nose and mouth showed through. His men repeated this action until everyone was hooded and disguised.

With a jerk of his head, Miles motioned for the men to follow him. They stealthily made their way down the path into the valley. By the time the Englishmen finally noticed their presence, twenty-five mounted and masked men ringed the camp, pushing two soggy and rather embarrassed English sentries in front of them.

An English captain shouted and reached for his sword. But, in mid-draw, he found the side of an Irish lance pressed tightly against his chest.

"I'd advise ye no' to do that," Miles said from behind the hood. "Ye are trapped here, and the first o' ye that draws a weapon will see bloodshed."

The Englishman's hand dropped from the sword, his face a mixture of rage and fear. Other soldiers stood up slowly, looking around at the mounted men.

"We'll now be relieving ye o' your fodder, supplies and horseflesh," Miles said, moving his horse into the circle.

"Are you mad?" the English captain sputtered. "You'll

39

leave us with no means to travel and no food.''

Miles wheeled his stallion around, coming up directly beside the captain. "We could kill ye," he said mildly, and the captain felt a sudden chill go down his spine.

"N-no, that won't be necessary," the captain stammered. "T-take what you will; just leave us alone."

"Och now, I'd thought ye'd see it my way," Miles replied, a smile in his voice. With a quick flick of his hand, he motioned for his men to round up the horses and supplies. Then he slid from his mount, walking over to a pile of leather pouches protected from the rain by a large animal hide.

"They contain only papers," the captain said quickly. "Surely they are of no worth to you."

Miles did not bother to answer, instead opening a pouch, reaching inside and pulling out a fistful of papers.

"Och, what have we here?" he said, examining the papers with interest. "Maps and drawings o' Irish land. How fascinating." Walking over to the fire, he dropped a handful onto the flames, ignoring the weak protests of the captain. He emptied the remaining pouches in the same methodical manner, until the captain's shoulders slumped with discouragement.

Mounting his horse, Miles gathered the reins in his hands, turning the animal around. "Now, I'm advising ye no' to come this way again, or next time we'll be forced to kill ye. Ye may consider this a fair warning."

"Wh-who are you?" the captain whispered as the riders prepared to leave.

Miles leaned over the horse. "Go home, Englishman. Tell your superiors the Irish Lion will kill the next patrol who dares to pass this way."

Before the captain could close his gaping mouth, the Irishmen had cut free the horses and melted into the darkness as abruptly as they had appeared.

"One o' them escaped into the forest on horseback," Furlong said softly when they were safely away from the English soldiers. "Shall I go after him?"

Miles's eyes narrowed behind the hood. "We need all the horseflesh we can get. 'Twould be a pity to let even one get away." "Have the other men take the supplies back to the castle, and see that the horses are taken immediately to Armagh. Shaun and I will double back to find him.''

Furlong nodded and quickly relayed Miles's orders to the men. The men broke ranks, the larger group heading for home while Miles and Shaun spread out to search for the missing Englishman.

The rain had settled to a steady drizzle, but the wind blew in gusts, a chilling companion to Miles in his sodden clothes. He pushed his discomfort to the back of his mind, carefully guiding his steed through the dripping gloom of the forest, listening for any sounds that would give away his prey. Icy cold rivulets of rain slid down his face, but he shook the water out of his eyes with an impatient jerk of his head.

Suddenly Miles's horse whinnied softly, alerting him to the possibility that someone was near. It came from the direction of the ancient Druid stone circles.

''Och, so ye think to hide among the stones, do ye?'' Miles said softly.

Quickly, he slid off his stallion, resting his hand on the hilt of his sword. He took several stealthy steps, carefully parting the wet and dripping branches. Cold raindrops slipped down his face and chin, trickling into the top of his tunic.

Soon he came upon the Druid stones. A sudden flash of lightning streaked against the dreary blackness of the night sky. The distant boom of thunder followed closely, echoing eerily among the stones. Miles stopped for a moment, awed by the spectacular display of light and accompanying thunder. As he stood there in the shadows, he heard a new sound.

Crack. Crack.

Footsteps. Swiftly, Miles slid into the shadows, waiting and listening. He was certain they were the footsteps of a man. Perhaps he had found his English prey at last. A smile played across his lips as he pulled the black hood from his pouch and slipped it over his head.

Thump.

Noiselessly, Miles drew his sword from its sheath. He took one step before an agonizing scream split the air.

Cursing, he raced toward the sound. What he came upon caused him to stop in his tracks and blink in surprise. A motionless form lay facedown among the stones in the middle of one of the circles.

Holding his sword out in front of him in case this was some kind of trick, Miles cautiously approached the form, prodding it with his boot. When it did not move he pushed it over with his foot.

Miles's mouth dropped open in sheer astonishment. It was a woman! Sheathing his sword, he dropped to one knee, examining her for signs of life.

He breathed a sigh of relief when he saw her stir slightly. Concerned, he gently slid his arms beneath her neck and knees, lifting her into his arms. He had carried her a short distance away from the stones when she suddenly moaned, jerking her head sideways. Stopping, he glanced down at her.

Her eyes slowly fluttered open as a flash of lightning streaked across the sky, illuminating the area with a bright light. Miles had but a moment to look into the most beautiful blue eyes he had ever seen before she let out a bloodcurdling scream.

''By the Holy Rod o' Christ,'' he uttered, a split second before her fist slammed against his jaw.

Chapter Three

Faith moaned as she fought her way back to consciousness, employing supreme effort to force open her eyelids. Her vision blurred until a flash of light tore across the sky, illuminating a figure in a black hood. A sense of abject terror swept through her as she realized the figure was holding her in his arms.

Her first reaction was to let out an ear-shattering scream, followed instantly by an act of sheer self-preservation. Balling her fist tightly, she swung it at the man with all her might. As her fist hit squarely against his jaw, the man lost his grip. Faith tumbled from his arms, clawing at him for balance and ripping the black hood off his head. She hit the ground with a sickening thud and shrieked as a fierce pain shot up her injured leg. Groping madly at her belt for the gun, her hands came up empty. She slowly lifted them, gazing up at her captor.

"I'm unarmed," she said, her voice cracking slightly. "What do you want from me?"

"God's wound, woman, ye are a hellcat," the man replied furiously, rubbing his jaw. "First ye strike me and then ye claw yourself from my grip. Have ye lost your senses?" He pointed at the hood that lay next to her on the ground. "Och, 'twas it the hood that frightened ye?"

Faith looked at him in astonishment. His Irish brogue was so thick that she could hardly understand him.

"Wh-who are you?" she asked. She glanced about quickly, wondering if there were others with him. When she saw no one else she felt the squeeze of panic ease a little. One she might be able to handle even without a weapon.

His mouth curved into a smile, a small flash of white in the darkness. "Well, now that ye have unmasked me, I suppose I am forced to present myself. I am Miles O'Bruaidar, at your service, madame. I heard ye shout and came forward to assist ye in your distress."

43

"Assist me in my distress?" Faith repeated, wondering why he spoke in such a stilted manner. "Where am I?"

"Ye are on my land."

"Your land?" Faith repeated, fighting a strange feeling of disorientation. The last thing she remembered was the stone circles, O'Rourke disappearing and the strange flash of light.

Squinting into the dim light, she observed the outline of the man in front of her, noting that he was quite large, with exceptionally broad shoulders. Certainly not a man she was likely to outrun with a wounded leg, she thought wryly. He was dressed rather peculiarly, too, in some kind of strange black cloak that fell to his shins and fastened at the throat with a large brooch.

"May I be so bold as to ask what an English lass is doing alone in the forest at this hour?" he asked, taking a step forward. "How did ye become separated from the others?"

"Others?" Faith repeated in surprise. "What others?"

"I presume that ye are not traveling alone."

Faith glanced over her shoulder quickly. "Why do you say that? Have you seen someone else?"

"Is there someone else?"

Faith shrugged nonchalantly, thinking of Paddy O'Rourke. "Perhaps."

He studied her for a long moment, as if deciding whether to believe her. "I thought I heard footsteps before ye cried out for help," he finally answered, "but did no' see anyone."

"Really?" Faith murmured, wondering if those footsteps belonged to O'Rourke. Remembering her mission, she quickly reached into her jacket pocket for her radio. It was gone, either having been lost during her struggle with O'Rourke or confiscated by this Irishman while she was unconscious. Remembering that this stranger had been traipsing about the woods with a black hood on his head, Faith decided the second possibility did not bode well for her.

"Well, I certainly appreciate your assistance," Faith said calmly. "And I do apologize for hitting you. I'm rather opposed to being carried about by strange men, I suppose. But I really must be going. Do you think you might be able to take me to the nearest town? I must get to a telephone."

When he didn't answer Faith stared at him curiously. He

stood completely still like a dark statue for so long that she wondered if he had even heard her.

"Look here, Mr. O'Bruaidar, are you all right?" she finally asked.

"Am I all right? I fear 'tis ye who has hurt your head."

Puzzled, Faith reached up and gingerly felt her forehead and scalp for bumps. "I do have a pounding headache and my ears are ringing. But I don't think I have a head injury. I am rather cold, though."

"Aye, and 'tis no wonder, for ye are drenched. Here, take my cloak." He unfastened the brooch at his throat, shrugging out of his cloak and handing it down to her.

Faith took the cloak in her numb hands, realizing with a sense of astonishment that he was right. Her clothing was soaked and she was sitting in a muddy puddle. Stunned, she touched her face and hair, feeling the wetness. She had absolutely no recollection of it raining.

"My God," she whispered. "When did it rain? What happened to me?" Again vague recollections came rushing back: the blinding light, the weightless sensation and the hum and crackle of an electromagnetic disturbance. A cold rivulet of water rolled down her forehead, dripping off her nose. "How did I get here?" she asked. "The last thing I remember I was at the Beaghmore Stone Circles."

Miles bent over, gently arranging the cloak about her shoulders. Another flash of lightning lit the area, and Faith caught a quick glimpse of a handsome face with sharp, angular lines and a square jaw.

"I found ye lying senseless among the stones. I carried ye a bit before ye awoke. How badly are ye injured?"

She reached down to gingerly touch her thigh with her fingertips. "My leg hurts."

"Do ye remember why ye are clad in such strange garments?"

Faith looked down at her skin-tight, black standard issue MI5 pants and jacket, realizing that they probably gave away a lot more information than she cared to admit.

"My clothes . . ." she said, cursing herself for not being prepared as she grasped for a plausible explanation. "Well, I suppose they might seem a bit strange to you, but actually they are excellent for . . . ah . . . night hiking,'' she said, blurting out the first thing that came to mind.

"Night . . . what?"

"Hiking," Faith repeated with more enthusiasm. "Yes, that's it. It's a new fad in London, and I thought I'd try it while on holiday in Ireland. You see, night hiking requires one to traverse the countryside in the moonlight, enjoying the scenery of the forest at night. When I reached the stone circles, I must have fallen. Perhaps I did hit my head after all." She gave him a falsely bright smile when she saw his frown had deepened. "I apologize if I caused you any trouble. I suppose I won't be doing it again anytime soon."

"Did ye say night . . . hiking?" Miles repeated, his brogue sounding oddly strangled.

Faith lifted her hands helplessly. "I know it sounds bizarre, but the fads in London today rather defy a sensible explanation.''

"A sensible explanation?" he exploded before starting to pace back and forth in front of her. His boots made a soft squishing sound on the wet earth. "The only sensible explanation for an English lass dressed in a disguise and wandering about my land in the middle o' the night is that she is an English spy."

"A spy?" Faith repeated with feigned shock. "Me? Why that's ludicrous."

"Is it?" he said angrily, stopping to run his fingers through his hair. "By the rod o' Christ, have the English become so desperate that they are now using women to spy on Ireland? Why 'tis depraved and disgraceful.''

"Now wait just a bloody minute—" Faith started to protest when Miles rudely interrupted her.

"We don't have much time, lass," he said briskly. "What's your name?"

Faith looked up at him, surprised and not just a little worried by the crisp new tone of his voice. "My name?" she repeated dumbly. "Yes, well, my name is . . . Faith."

In a split second she made the decision that there could be no harm in using her real first name. In fact, if he meant to harm her or hold her hostage, it might be to her advantage if someone overheard him using her real name.

"For what cause have ye been punished? What's been done to your hair?"

"My hair?" she echoed in alarm, reaching up to touch the back of her head. Other than the fact that her hair was in an awful tangle and full of dirt, branches and twigs, it still seemed attached to her head. "What's wrong with my hair?" she asked defensively.

"It's been chopped off at your shoulders and hangs o'er your eyes."

"Chopped off?" she exclaimed. "I admit that it isn't in prime condition at this particular moment, but it doesn't always look this bad." He snorted in disbelief, and Faith felt ridiculously offended. "Well, it's no cause to be rude," she admonished, extracting a twig from her hair and casting it aside.

"Ye also seem a wee bit underfed."

"What?"

"I could feel the bones in your ribs and legs as I carried ye."

"Well, I never," she spluttered. "What does my figure have to do with any of this?"

"Did the English patrol do this to ye as some kind o' punishment?"

"Patrol? What patrol?"

Miles growled, stopping his pacing. "My patience is nearing its end, lass. Are ye wi' the patrol or no'?"

"Now, you listen to me, Mr. O'Bruaidar," Faith retorted irritably. "I'll have you know that my patience is rather strained as well. How can I know if I'm with *this* patrol if I don't even know who *they* are? Why does it matter? If there are Englishmen near, I ask you to take me to them."

Miles's eyes narrowed. "I hardly think ye are in a position to make demands, lass. 'Tis fairly obvious what ye are doing here clad in that disguise."

"I told you this isn't a disguise."

Miles's lips twisted into a cynical smile. "Och, o' course. Ye've been night . . . hacking."

"Hiking."

"Whatever. I'm afraid I am no' going to take ye to that patrol. I need to question ye a bit further."

Faith pushed herself to her feet, putting her hands on her hips. "Look, Mr. O'Bruaidar, this has clearly become an unfortunate misunderstanding. I assure you that I do not represent a threat to you or your land. In fact, just point me in the direction of the nearest road and I'll be on my way. I don't wish to trouble you any further."

" 'Tis too late for that, I fear."

"Are you saying you are going to prevent me from leaving?"

He nodded. Then, in one abrupt motion, he leaned over and picked her up, slinging her over his shoulder.

Faith cried out in surprise, digging her fingers into his shoulders. "What in the hell do you think you're doing?" she shrieked. "Get your goddamned bloody hands off me."

He paused for a moment, seemingly stunned. "God's teeth, where did ye learn such language? I've never heard such curses from the mouth o' a lady before."

"What are you, some kind of saint?" she hissed. "I said put me down this instant."

Miles grunted for an answer but did not comply. After a moment he began walking, ignoring her repeated protests.

Outraged, Faith thought about trying to grab a branch and use it as a weapon against him. But judging from the sheer size and strength of him, she knew he would be able to overpower her easily. Frustrated, she forced herself to swallow her humiliation at being carried like a lumpy sack of potatoes through the forest, her derriere awkwardly sticking up in the air. Gritting her teeth, she decided to simply bide her time until a suitable opportunity for escape presented itself.

The sky began to clear and the moon slid from behind a cloud, lighting their way. Finally Miles stopped, lifting her off his shoulder and setting her on the ground. To her dismay, he kept his hands firmly on her waist. Faith suffered the intimate contact, wondering if he was concerned about her injured leg or simply ensuring that she did not try to escape. Shifting her weight slightly, she bumped into his side.

"Ouch . . . oh . . . what's that?" Pulling away from him slightly, Faith pointed down at the offending object, which rested against his thigh. "My God, is that a sword?"

When he nodded Faith's eyes widened in astonishment.

"Do you always ride about with a sword buckled at your waist?" A sudden image of Sir Lancelot galloping across a green meadow flashed through her mind and an unbidden giggle escaped her lips.

"Would ye have me ride about unprotected, lass?"

"Well . . . I simply had no idea it was so dangerous in the Irish countryside. But a sword? Do you normally ride about with a black hood on your head for protection as well?"

Miles frowned. "That, I'm afraid, is none o' your concern."

"Indeed not," Faith murmured, now convinced that this man was deranged. Given what she had already been through this evening, she supposed it was just her luck.

Abruptly, he gave a shrill whistle, nearly causing Faith to jump from her skin. Turning, she was surprised to see a horse step out of the darkness, whinnying softly. Impressed in spite of herself, she looked up at the tall Irishman.

"How did you do that?"

The hard lines of his face softened. " 'Tis said that the Irish have a way with horses . . ." he replied with a trace of amusement in his voice, ". . . and with women."

Frowning, Faith tried to jerk from his grasp, but he held her firmly. "Och, ye have a temper on ye, lass. Ye'll also learn that the Irish have a good sense o' humor. Now keep still and I'll help ye bind that wound."

Keeping one hand clamped around the top of her arm, he reached into a leather pouch on the saddle and pulled out what looked to be a bandage roll. Holding the roll in his fist, he turned to look at her. "If ye try to run, I promise that ye'll not get far. Don't forget that this is my land."

Realizing that he was right, Faith nodded mutely. Miles released his hold on her arm and began unwinding the cloth strips from the roll.

"You don't need to do this," she protested. "It's just a scratch."

"Do no' be afraid. I'll no' harm ye." He knelt down in front of her, his hand holding firm against her hip.

She resisted the urge to jerk away and show him she was frightened. "I'm fully capable of doing this myself," she said as calmly as she could manage.

"Aye, I have no doubt that ye are," he replied, deftly pull-

49

ing aside the cloak to look at her leg. "Ye seem to be capable o' a great many things. But 'twill be difficult enough for me to bind your leg properly under these conditions. Don't move," he repeated sharply as she nervously fidgeted from one leg to the other.

"All right, just hurry up."

Resolutely, he grasped her thigh between his large hands. "Wh-what are you doing?" she choked.

Miles glanced up. " 'Tis a wee bit tender, is it no'?"

"It's fine," Faith snapped, her cheeks flushing crimson. "Let's just finish this as quickly as possible."

Miles returned to the task at hand, carefully winding the strips around her leg and fastening them together with a large knot. "There," he said, rising to his feet. "That should hold until we get ye to Molly."

"Molly?" Faith asked blankly.

"Aye, she is well known in this area for her healing skills. She'll see to it that your injury is properly attended." He turned Faith toward the horse. "Up ye go, lass. We'll be taking a little ride now."

He lifted her onto the beast before swiftly mounting behind her. Wrapping one arm around her waist, he urged his steed forward with a murmur and a slight pressure from his thighs.

"Where are you taking me?" Faith demanded, deliberately moving his hand from her waist and pushing it aside.

"Ye'll see soon enough," he replied, not touching her again. Moments later, the steed stepped over a fallen log, causing Faith to abruptly slide sideways in the saddle. As her injured leg slammed against the side of the horse, she cried out in pain.

"Good God, isn't there some kind of road we can follow?" she exclaimed, between anguished gulps of air.

"Do ye still wish to ride without my assistance?" Miles asked mildly.

With considerable pain and effort, Faith managed to straighten herself in the saddle. "Do we have much farther to go?"

" 'Tis no' far, but the way is difficult."

Faith gritted her teeth against a hot, stinging wave of pain that shot up and down her leg. "Then I accept your offer of assistance," she said stiffly. "But keep your hand still, and it's only for the duration of this ride."

Miles easily slid his muscular arm about her waist, holding her firm in the saddle. "I thought ye'd see it my way," he commented, and Faith was certain she heard a note of amusement in his voice.

They rode the rest of the way in silence. Faith clenched her teeth to keep from crying out in agony as her thigh bumped the saddle with every step. As soon as she was certain she could not bear the pain for another moment, the horse suddenly picked up the pace, as if sensing something. Moments later, they broke through the trees and into a clearing.

Faith's eyes widened as she caught sight of the looming castle. It sat on a small hill, its high stone walls rising steeply. Although it was dark, she could make out two formidable towers and several dark shapes resembling buildings of some kind.

"What castle is this?" she asked softly.

"Castle Dun na Moor," Miles answered, a trace of pride evident in his voice.

Faith racked her brain but could not remember any such castle in the area. Shrugging, she supposed there were many such private residences scattered throughout the Irish countryside.

They rode through a stone arch that seemed to serve as an entrance gate to the castle. Faith nearly fell from the horse in fright when several men materialized out of the darkness, coming to stand beside them. One of them asked Miles something in a foreign tongue and he answered fluently.

Curious, she turned her head slightly. "What language are you speaking?"

He looked surprised at the question. "Haven't ye heard anyone speak Irish before? 'Tis Gaelic we speak here, though most o' us speak English, as well."

Faith registered a moment of astonishment. "Gaelic? Why, I thought people hardly spoke it anymore in Ireland. Certainly not as well as you."

Miles chuckled, tossing the reins to one of the men. "I suppose, then, ye have a lot to learn about us, lass."

He slid off the horse in one fluid motion, barking something to the men and reaching up to help Faith off. Whatever he

51

said heightened the men's curiosity, for they jostled closer, apparently to get a better look at her. As her feet touched the ground, Faith gasped as her weight settled temporarily on her injured leg. Miles quickly put his arm around her waist to support her. She pulled away quickly, leaning against the horse for balance.

"Och, have ye never seen a *Sassenach?*" Miles said in English as someone bumped into him. "Come now, don't frighten the poor lass."

Faith glared up at him. "I'm hardly frightened."

"Aye, but ye should be."

Before she could say another word he swept her off her feet, cradling her like a child. This time he took care with her injured leg. The men snickered in amusement as she hissed in outrage, trying to pull herself from his grasp.

"Put me down immediately," she ordered.

"Ye are injured, lass," Miles answered firmly. "And I'll not have ye limping into my home."

Realizing that arguing would get her nowhere, Faith pursed her lips together tightly, lying as stiffly as possible in his arms.

They passed through a sturdy oak door and into a huge corridor. Men came from every side door to greet them. They spoke rapidly to each other in Gaelic, and again Faith thought it odd that they seemed to speak it so well. Not only that, but they were all dressed in old-fashioned costumes.

She looked about her rich surroundings in surprise as Miles carried her through the castle, greeting almost everyone by name. Her cheeks flushed pink in mortification as some of the men appeared to exchange ribald jests with him, but he didn't seem embarrassed in the least. To her chagrin, he even whistled cheerfully, as if he carried bedraggled women through the castle every day.

He finally set her down when they reached what looked like a sitting room with a cheery blaze in the fireplace. He had just helped her into a chair when a middle-aged woman burst into the chamber, making clucking sounds with her tongue.

"Miles, what is all this talk about finding a young lass?" she said, her mouth opening in astonishment as her gaze fell on Faith. "For the love o' saints, what have ye brought me, lad?"

"She's an English lass, Molly," Miles answered quietly. "I found her at the Druid stones. She's been injured."

"Blessed Virgin, what happened to her hair?"

Puzzled, Faith reached up to push the bangs from her forehead, wondering why everyone had such a bizarre fascination with her hair.

"I don't know," he answered, shrugging. "She won't say."

Turning in the chair, Faith looked up at him as he stood beside her, his thick arms crossed against his chest. Seeing him in the light for the first time, she realized her initial impression of him as a man of imposing size had certainly been correct. He was exceptionally tall and broad-shouldered, with muscular forearms and legs as large as tree trunks. His square, handsome face was tanned, as if he spent a great deal of time outdoors, and his jaw was covered with a day's worth of whiskers. His dark, thick hair was almost as long as hers and was tied back at the nape of his neck. He was dressed most peculiarly in a linen shirt open slightly at the throat and a pair of black breeches molded almost indecently to his legs, hips and thighs. And while Faith thought all of that was certainly strange, it was her first close look at his sword that caused her to blink in astonishment.

"My God, your sword," she gasped in surprise.

Bewildered, Miles looked down at his sword and then back at her. "Didn't we already discuss this once? What bothers ye now about my sword?"

"Do you realize that you have a genuine English backsword there? They are extremely rare. Where did you get it?"

"I assure ye, lass, I came by mine through honest means."

"Would you mind if I took a look at it?"

Miles's mouth dropped open. "Ye want to examine my sword?"

"I know it's a rather odd request, but I've never had the opportunity to see one of these outside of a museum."

"A what?"

"Please, I just want to take a look at it," she pleaded softly.

Miles frowned and then, sighing, drew his sword from the sheath. "Either I've gone completely mad or ye are the strangest lass I've ever met. Watch your fingers; the blade is sharp."

"Of course it's sharp," Faith replied indignantly, bending

53

over the magnificent piece. "And it's in beautiful condition, I might add." Her fingers lightly touched the blade and moved up to examine the ornate hilt and the small hand guard that protected the fingers during fencing. In her excitement, her fingers brushed against Miles's, sending a warm jolt through her. Abruptly she pulled her hand away.

"Do you have any idea how much this sword is worth?" she asked him in her sternest voice. "It would fetch more than a hundred thousand pounds at Sotheby's. I certainly wouldn't suggest wearing it and God forbid that you should ever actually use it. An antique piece like this should be mounted and preserved."

Miles's mouth gaped open incredulously. "Mount my sword?" he choked. With a low growl, he snatched it from her and sheathed it.

Molly quickly knelt in front of Faith, placing her hand lightly on her leg. "Mayhap we've talked enough about the sword. How do ye feel, lass? Does your leg hurt much?"

Faith stared at the chubby woman with graying hair. Her face was round and warm, her eyes a soft brown. She, too, was dressed oddly—clad in a long, pretty gown with expensive lace on the sleeves and bodice. Something was decidedly wrong with these people, Faith thought.

"My leg is fine," she replied. "Just a little sore."

"There's no need to be afraid," Molly said gently. "What's your name?"

"Faith."

"And your family name?" Miles spoke up impatiently. "I fear I neglected to ask ye earlier."

Faith shook her head. "I'm sorry, but no more information," she said quietly. "Not until I know exactly who you are, what you want from me and why you have brought me here."

"I'd advise ye not to raise my ire, woman," Miles warned softly, his green eyes hardening at her challenge. "Ye are in no position to make demands of me."

"And I'd advise you not to threaten me," Faith replied, meeting his look evenly. "I don't frighten easily."

Molly clucked disparagingly, shaking her head in disapproval. "Och, stop this posturing, ye two, and let me have a proper look at the injury.'' She pressed her hand firmly against Faith's bandaged thigh.

''Ouch,'' Faith cried out, pulling away. ''Must you keep probing it?''

''Tis tender, I see,'' Molly observed. ''I'll have to take a look at it. Can ye get out o' those . . . breeches?'' she asked, giving Miles a questioning look. Miles raised an eyebrow in response, as if to say he had no explanation for her odd dress.

''I'm not undressing in front of him,'' Faith replied, crossing her arms firmly against her chest.

Molly's lips twitched with a smile. ''Be off wi' ye, Miles. I'll tend to the lass.''

''She owes me a few answers first.''

''Give me time to clean her wound and give her something to eat,'' Molly pleaded. ''She looks famished.''

''Did you just say clean my wound?'' Faith interrupted hastily. ''Aren't you going to permit me to see a doctor?''

Molly looked at her sympathetically. ''Ye have naught to fear, lass. Many here say I have a gentle way with my hands. 'Twill no' hurt much.''

''Much?''

Miles gave a loud, exasperated sigh. ''What do ye expect, lass? That we take ye to court to have ye pampered by the king's own physician? By the wounds o' Christ, be thankful that I even allow Molly to minister to ye.''

''King?'' Faith echoed, looking at Miles in alarm. ''Did you just say king?''

''Are ye daft?'' Miles snapped irritably at her. ''Why do ye keep repeating everything I say?''

''Miles . . .'' Molly said softly, her eyes holding a hint of warning. ''The lass is injured.''

Miles dragged a hand through his hair in frustration. ''Och, all right, Molly. I'll grant ye a short time to take care o' her ills. But bring her to me in the library when ye are finished wi' her. And make haste. I'll no' be kept waiting.'' Turning sharply on his heel, he left the room, slamming the door loudly behind him.

''Miles is a man o' little patience,'' Molly said, whispering. ''Ye'd be wise to remember that, lass.''

Faith reached out and put a hand on the woman's arm.

55

"What is going on here? Where am I?"

Molly gave her a puzzled look. "Why, ye're at Castle Dun na Moor."

"No, I mean . . . where is the nearest town?"

Molly's brows creased in confusion. "Town? We are a day's ride from Drogheda, if that is what ye mean."

Faith blinked in surprise. Drogheda was a large port city on the eastern coast, somewhere between Belfast and Dublin. To her knowledge, the trip would take about an hour or so by car. "A day's ride? Don't you have an auto?"

Molly looked at her blankly and Faith sighed. Apparently, these people lived quite the rural life.

"Never mind," Faith said. "Actually, I wasn't thinking of a city as far as Drogheda. How about something closer, like Cookstown?"

"Cookstown?"

"You mean to say you've never heard of Cookstown?" Faith exclaimed. When Molly shook her head Faith frowned. As she was fairly certain that she and Miles hadn't traveled more than two kilometers from the Beaghmore Stone Circles, it meant she still had to be within a reasonably short traveling distance to Cookstown.

So why didn't this woman have a clue as to what she was talking about?

"Look, Molly," Faith said quietly, "you seem kind and I need your help. But you had better know the truth: Miles has abducted me and means to do me harm."

A horrified expression crossed Molly's face. "Mary, Mother o' God," she gasped. "Where have ye come by such a thought, lass? I've raised that lad, and in my whole life I've never known him to raise a hand against a woman, even if she is English."

Faith gripped Molly's hand, leaning forward. "Then help me now. Please, I beg you to permit me to make one phone call. I promise that no harm will come to you or your family."

Molly stared at her for a long moment before quickly pulling her hand from Faith's grip. "Ye are wi' fever, no doubt. And 'tis no wonder. What ye need is a strong cup o' poteen to bring ye back to your senses. Then we'll bind your wound." She stood, straightening her skirts. "Now just sit here, lass,

56

and I'll fetch a wee dram for ye, as well as some food. Then we'll see to that wound o' yours.'' She patted Faith's hand gently before turning to leave.

Faith blinked in astonishment as Molly closed the door behind her. Had everyone in Ireland gone raving mad, or was it just these people in this godforsaken castle?

Shaking her head, she made a swift survey of the room, hoping against odds that there might be a telephone at her disposal. She was not overly surprised when she did not find one. In fact, there was no television, no lamps, no light switches . . . no sign of any modern conveniences whatsoever. Yet the entire area was furnished with gorgeous antique furniture, beautiful paintings and tapestries and thick, expensive rugs. It seemed clear to Faith that the owners of the castle wished to impart a particular old-fashioned ambience to their guests.

Some other time I might have been impressed.

Groaning softly, she rose to her feet. She had no more time to wonder about these strange people and how they lived. She was finally alone and would not waste another moment of her good fortune. She limped to the window, favoring her injured leg. Pulling aside the drapes, she saw the first rays of dawn had already appeared in the sky, tinging the horizon with a faint pink glow.

Wearily, she paused, pressing her forehead against the stone wall. It had been one hell of a night. She was certain that by now her superiors would be frantically combing the countryside for her. She had to get word to them that she was all right.

Looking down, Faith judged the drop to the ground. It was a short one, but she couldn't make it with a sore leg. She would have to find something to help lower herself down.

A sudden gleam flashed in her eyes as she eyed a pair of long, thick cords that apparently served to pull the drapes from the window. Quickly, she untied them, binding them together with a knot. Then she tied one end to the sturdy leg of a heavy table and dropped the other out the window. Saying a small prayer, she carefully eased herself onto the windowsill and began the awkward climb down.

Reaching the ground safely, she took a moment to rest. Then, taking a deep breath, she began hobbling in the direction in which she had seen one of the men lead the horses.

Faith quietly entered the livery, thanking her lucky stars that only a young boy appeared to be in the stables. His back was turned to her and he whistled cheerfully while going about his business. Quietly, Faith sidled up to one of the still-saddled mounts and unwound the reins from a post. Stifling the groan of pain that rose in her throat, Faith pulled herself into the saddle. Wheeling the horse around, she heard the stable boy cry out in surprise.

Digging her heels into the side of the horse, she shot out of the stable. She nearly collided with Miles, who was just entering the stable. Screaming a warning, she swerved, missing him by inches. He shouted something angrily at her, but she ignored him, bending low over the mane of the horse and heading for the gate with increasing speed.

As she neared the stone arch of the gate, she heard someone shout. She shrieked in surprise as several men leapt out of her way. Praying she hadn't harmed anyone, Faith sped through the gate and out into the clearing. Inhaling sharply, she slapped the reins against the horse's neck, urging it on faster.

As she galloped across the clearing, Faith scanned frantically for the road but could not see it. She cursed under her breath, not understanding why it wasn't in plain view. Her eyes searched the horizon, but she could see nothing . . . not even a dirt trail. In fact, there were no signs of cars or any motorized vehicles whatsoever.

Swallowing back the panic that bubbled in her throat, Faith anxiously sought a solution. She realized that without a road to follow, her situation had quickly gone from precarious to disastrous. She couldn't force her mount through a dense forest she did not know and still manage to outrun her pursuer. Nor could she slip from the horse and hide herself in the forest. Her leg was throbbing and her strength had all but disappeared.

Desperate, Faith took a precious moment to look over her shoulder. Someone was following and, from what she could determine, was gaining on her. Turning back in the saddle, she yanked hard on the reins, bringing the horse to an abrupt stop just inches from the forest edge.

Moments later, her pursuer pulled up alongside her. Scowling fiercely, Miles angrily grabbed the reins from her stiff fingers. "Ye little fool," he snarled, slipping from his horse. "Had ye a wish to kill yourself?"

Faith simply pressed her lips together tightly as he pulled her none too gently from the saddle. "For God's sake, ye could have broken your neck, woman," he continued furiously. "What the devil got into ye?"

"Don't you dare touch me, you . . . lunatic!" Faith shrieked, jerking away from his grasp and stumbling away from him.

Miles grabbed at her from behind. Pushing at him, Faith fell backward, her momentum pulling him off balance and bringing him with her. Swearing softly, Miles twisted his body sideways, taking the brunt of their fall on his shoulder. Before she could roll away, he firmly pulled her on top of him, locking his arms around her waist.

"Let go of me," she hissed.

Miles released one of his arms from around her waist and gripped her chin in his hand. "Ye are the most stubborn woman I've ever met. Why do ye keep running from me, lass? I'm no' going to hurt ye."

"Then why are you holding me against my will?"

"I think we both know the answer to that question," he replied, turning her face from side to side and studying it.

"What are you doing?"

"I want to have a good look at ye in case ye try to slip away again."

"This is outrageous. Release me at once."

"A bit o' bossy goods, ye are. Ye are also rather bonny. But 'tis your eyes that make ye more than ordinary. They are exactly the color o' my Lough Emy. Magnificent."

Faith pursed her lips. "Forget it. Flattery doesn't work with me."

A twinkle flashed in Miles's eyes. "We'll see about that," he said. "Now listen to me, lass. I know ye are afraid, but I'll no' harm ye. I just want to know who sent ye here to spy on me."

"Spy on you? I have no idea what you are talking about."

Miles shook his head. "It'll no' help to lie to me, lass. But if ye tell me the truth, I'll make a deal wi' the English and trade ye for some o' my own men. 'Tis my belief that this would be the most suitable arrangement for both o' us."

"Trade?" Faith echoed in astonishment. "You want to trade me for some of your men? Are you mad? It doesn't matter who I am; the English won't trade for me."

"They won't?" Miles asked, raising an eyebrow.

"Of course not. I assume you are working for or sympathetic to the IRA, and that is why you are holding me against my will. Must I remind you that England doesn't deal with terrorists? We never have and we never will. You'd only be wasting your time."

"IRA? Terr—what?"

"Oh, for God's sake, don't play naive," she snapped. "It's no secret that England never bargains with those people who promote indiscriminate violence to further their cause."

For a moment he looked at her in shock. "Ye accuse *us* o' violence?" he roared so loudly, Faith's ears rang. "Ye, who come to Ireland to steal our land, mock our religion and kill our people? Have a care to speak such words in my presence, woman."

At his outraged stance, Faith's temper snapped. In the past twenty-four hours she had single-handedly confronted the IRA's most proficient assassin, been shot at, mysteriously knocked unconscious by some kind of electromagnetic disturbance and kidnapped by a half-cocked Irishman and his family. It was simply too much.

"How dare you imply that England is the source of the violence," she said indignantly, raising her voice a notch. "Indiscriminate violence cannot be justified no matter what the cause."

He looked so angry, Faith thought he might strike her. Instead, a long and heavy pause hung between them before he spoke.

"Ye judge us harshly, lass," he said, his voice holding a surprising note of regret. "If ye mean to blame the Irish for fighting to protect their land and heritage, then ye may well find us guilty. 'Tis most unfortunate that the fighting oft takes the lives o' innocent people. But no' one Irish life that has been lost, be it soldier or innocent, will have been given in vain." He exhaled deeply. "If ye mean to hold us accountable for what happened at Ulster, I'll be the first to admit 'twas a mistake. But a man can only be pushed so far before he loses his patience and balance. 'Twas the English who pushed us, altho' I'm no' proud to say what that forced us into doing.''

Faith's mouth dropped open. ''Ulster?''

Miles's brow drew together in a frown. ''I assume ye are talking about the killings o' the English settlers in forty-one. 'Tis what ye meant now, wasn't it, lass?''

''Forty-one?'' Faith gasped. ''Are you referring to the Ulster massacre of *sixteen hundred* and forty-one?''

''Woman, I've been more than patient—''

''No, you wait,'' she interrupted incredulously. ''Why in the world are you referring to an event that happened nearly three hundred and fifty years ago?''

Miles snorted angrily. ''Three hundred and fifty years ago? Are ye daft? 'Twas but a few years past.''

Faith felt her head begin to spin. ''A few years past?'' she uttered, looking at him in shock. ''What are you saying? That this is . . . that you think . . . that you are living in the seventeenth century?''

Miles gave her an equally odd look. ''What I think is mayhap ye hurt more than just your leg.''

''You can't be serious.''

''I assure ye that I'm completely serious. Are ye working for Cromwell or no'?''

''Cromwell?'' she exclaimed in horror. ''As in Oliver? Oliver Cromwell? By God, you *are* serious.'' Her eyes widened in shock. ''So, either you've a very convincing figment of my imagination or I'm having a most bizarre dream. Either way, this isn't real.''

Miles frowned. ''Are ye all right, lass? Ye seem a wee bit pale.''

''Of course I'm pale. You'd be pale, too, if you were having the most surreal experience of your entire life. The frightening thing is that in some extraordinary way this is all beginning to make horrid sense. It would certainly explain why you people are dressed in such clothes, why no one has heard of Cookstown, why no one can point me to a phone and why there isn't a paved road in sight. It would also explain why that child is dressed like that.''

''Child? What child?'' Miles asked, twisting his head and body to look above him. A young village boy was running toward them, waving his arms madly.

"That child," she repeated softly.

Miles swore softly, attempting to sit up. But Faith abruptly dropped her head on his chest, sending them both back to the ground with a hard thump.

"Christ's wounds, what are ye doing?" he exclaimed.

"The stone circles," she muttered to herself. "Maybe the electromagnetic disturbance created some kind of a time warp or time bubble. No, this can't be happening. Wake up, Faith. Someone please pinch me."

"Ye've no cause to be afraid, lass."

"Easy for you to say. You aren't real." She suddenly pushed up against his chest, looking down at him curiously. "Except that you *feel* incredibly real." Beneath her splayed fingers, she could feel his warm, muscular chest rising and falling and the rapid thud of his heart. She reached up and brushed her fingers against the hollow of his throat, feeling the scratch of his unshaved whiskers. "Yes, I'd say you feel quite real."

He looked at her intently, his green eyes darkening. " 'Tis other ways to assure ye o' that if need be." He lifted his hand, letting it rest suggestively just above her breast.

Faith flushed in embarrassment. For the first time she realized how intimately they were lying on the ground. One of her legs was nestled snugly between his muscular thighs and his arm felt like a band of steel around her waist. To her horror, she could feel something else of his, pressing firm and hard against her leg.

"Oh, God," she gasped. "This can't be real. It's just the creation of a very, *very* active imagination." She dropped her head back into his chest, squeezing her eyes shut. "Time to wake up, Faith," she said sternly.

"Need ye assistance, me lord?" a small voice asked.

Faith lifted her head abruptly. It smashed directly into the bottom of Miles's chin, slamming his teeth together.

"Saints above," he roared in pain.

"Sorry," Faith mumbled as Miles rubbed his jaw, a frown on his face.

"Has she harmed ye?" the lad asked Miles anxiously.

Miles scowled darkly. "Nay, the lass has no' harmed me,

and she herself is unharmed. We were but having a small . . . ah . . . discourse.'' He managed to sit up, still keeping Faith firmly on his lap.

''Then why is she clad like that?'' the child asked with wide eyes.

Faith met his gaze, studying the boy curiously. She judged him to be about eight years old. He was dressed in a filthy shirt that hung to his knees and a ripped pair of breeches. His feet were bare even though there was a slight chill to the morning air and the grass was damp from dew. He looked as though he hadn't been washed in a year and reeked with the horrid smell of grime and sweat.

''What are ye doing here, lad?'' Miles asked.

The boy fidgeted uneasily. ''Gathering kindling, I was, my lord, but I saw me a fox and chased it this way. Time passed quicker than I thought. Now the morn has come and gone and I'll likely receive a thrashing for no' bringing home the wood in time.''

Miles stood, bringing Faith upright with him. In the distance she saw several riders rapidly approaching on horseback. Miles's men, she assumed, arriving to save the day.

''What is your name?'' Miles asked the boy.

''Kevin, me lord.''

''Well, Kevin, I'll have one o' my men escort ye back to the village. 'Tis the least I can do for such a gallant attempt to assist me.''

''Ye w-will?'' the boy stammered, clearly torn between feelings of excitement and abject fear. ''B-but, me lord, 'twould no' be fitting . . . I mean, 'tis no' necessary . . .''

His words were interrupted by the riders who noisily galloped up. One of them slid off his horse. He was a squat, stocky man with a long nose and a greasy hat upon his head.

He saw Faith and gave a low whistle. ''Christ's wounds, Miles, what happened?'' he asked. ''Is this the English lass?''

''Aye, Furlong, 'tis her,'' Miles answered. ''I fear she tried to leave without saying a proper farewell.''

The man stroked his nose thoughtfully before pushing the cap back on his head. ''Didn't like your hospitality much now, did she? Why is she dressed in such odd garments? And what happened to her hair?''

Faith threw up her hands in exasperation. "That's it," she declared. "You can make fun of my clothes, but I'm not going to take any more criticism about my hair."

Miles shook his head solemnly at Furlong. "I fear the lass finds Irish manners lacking."

"That's not kidding," she murmured under her breath.

"Who's the lad?" Furlong asked, studying the boy.

Miles shrugged. "He says his name is Kevin. Mayhap ye'll see him back to the village. I told him 'twas the least I could do for his offer o' assistance."

"Offer o' assistance?" Furlong repeated with a raised eyebrow.

"Aye, he feared his lord was in danger."

"What kind o' danger?"

"From the lass here," Miles answered, his eyes twinkling. He took a step closer to Furlong and lowered his voice. "After all, she did have me on my back."

The two men snickered and Faith put her hands on her hips, frowning. "Very amusing, gentlemen."

Miles grinned, inclining his head toward Furlong. "Och, it appears the lass finds our humor lacking as well. What's a man to do?"

"Release me?" Faith offered hopefully.

Miles's expression sobered. "I'm afraid I can't do that," he said. "Ye'll have to return to the castle wi' me. Furlong, ye take the lad to the village."

"Wait," Faith said suddenly, causing both men to start in surprise. "Would it be possible for me to see this village, too? I assure you, I'll not try anything out of the ordinary."

Both men stared at her as if she had gone completely mad. Taking a deep breath, Faith tried again. "I'm serious in my request. I would like to visit the village. I give you my word that I will not try to escape."

Miles found his voice first. "Why do ye have need to see the village?"

Faith lifted her hands helplessly. "This is going to sound very strange, but I want to see for myself that all of this is real and that it's not just a figment of my imagination."

Miles frowned, studying her face for a long moment. "I don't understand, lass."

"I know you don't," she said softly. "But I assure you, this is not a ruse. You may bind me, if you feel it necessary. But I must see how these people are living."

Miles exchanged a glance with Furlong, who shrugged. Turning back to Faith, Miles crossed his arms against his chest. "All right, lass, I'll permit ye a look at the village. But ye'll ride with me."

Faith nodded in agreement. Miles mounted his horse first and then stretched out a hand to her. Biting back the urge to groan from the pain in her leg, she gave Miles her hand and he helped her into the saddle. As she settled herself, her thigh throbbed with a dull pain. Oddly enough, the discomfort seemed rather unreal and unimportant as compared to the events that were unfolding about her.

Could it be that I am actually existing in another century?

Fighting her panic, Faith gripped the saddle until her knuckles were white. Finally they reached a clearing. Faith saw several primitive huts scattered about the area. People moved briskly between the huts and the small campfires. Dogs and cats ran about freely, barking and chasing one another in circles.

Faith simply absorbed the sight, her mouth hanging open in astonishment. It looked exactly the way she imagined a seventeenth-century village would look.

I am living in the seventeenth century. Oh, my God, how did this happen?

Clucking softly, Miles urged his horse forward. People came out to greet them, showing obvious affection for the Irishman. Faith could only stare at it all in amazement. The place smelled to high heaven. Manure, rotting food, dog and animal excrement were everywhere. It took all the willpower Faith had to keep from gagging.

Men, women and children dressed in clothes that were little more than rags ran about the horses, happily exchanging jests with the men. They all seemed as curious about her as she was about them, but no one said anything aloud about her strange dress.

Instead, the focus of the attention seemed to be on the small drama unfolding between the young lad, Kevin, and a woman who was apparently his mother. The woman was dressed in a stained and ragged gown, her head covered by a dirt-encrusted kerchief.

"Kevin, ye wicked lad," she shouted at him as he slid off Furlong's horse. "Where have ye been?"

"I was just gathering the kindling, mum, when... when..." he mumbled, swallowing miserably, his face red with humiliation at the public scolding. "I'm sorry."

"The lad was assisting me," Miles spoke up. "I fear I'm the reason he is late wi' his morning chores."

The woman stared openmouthed at Miles before dropping into a deep curtsey. "Och, m' lord, why 'tis an honor to have our son aid ye. I only feared he had caused ye unnecessary trouble. The lad is a bit strong-minded, ye see."

"Strong-mindedness can oft be a desirable trait in a man," Miles replied, a trace of amusement in his voice. "Kevin is a good lad."

"Aye, o' course he is, m' lord," the woman answered, nodding her head vigorously. "I always said that, haven't I, Kevin, lad?" The boy nodded, looking at Miles with sheer adulation.

Curious, Faith turned her head slightly to look at Miles. He was grinning broadly, offering the young boy a wink. She had to admit she was rather surprised by his offer of cover for the boy, as well as the genuine affection and respect the people seemed to have for him. She supposed that was rather unusual for the times, whatever time that might be, given her understanding that the rich usually paid little, if any, attention to the poor.

"Now tell me what ye have need o' in the village," Miles called out. The villagers eagerly clamored around him, offering up suggestions. As their voices droned on, Faith began to feel oddly sleepy. Looking down at her leg, she saw that blood was seeping through her bandage in an ugly red stain.

"Dear God," she whispered, feeling sick. "What is happening to me?"

Miles heard her whisper and leaned forward. Seeing the spreading crimson stain on her leg, he swore softly before pulling her back against his chest. Abruptly pulling on the reins, he turned his horse around.

"Furlong will hear the rest o' your requests," he said

briskly to the villagers. "I must get the lass back to the castle."

With a jerk of his head, Miles indicated several of his men were to follow him. Quickly, they made their way into the forest. "I'm sorry, lass. I should have seen ye back to the castle at once. Why didn't ye tell me? I didn't realize your injury was grave." He kept her head cradled against his shoulder, gently pressing his hand to her cheek to keep her head from bouncing about painfully.

"It's not," she insisted. "It's only a scratch. But why did you do it?"

"Do what?"

"Lie for that boy."

Miles laughed. "Och, that. Well, I was a young lad once, too, and oft into mischief. There was many a time I had hoped for someone to rescue me from having my arse beaten black and blue. 'Twas the least I could do to reward the lad's anxiousness to protect his lord from danger."

"Were you in danger?" Faith asked, a note of amusement creeping into her own voice.

He looked down at her, his green eyes darkening for a moment with an emotion Faith couldn't read. "Perhaps in danger o' losing my better judgment."

His voice was unexpectedly seductive, and Faith felt a tingle of awareness in the bottom of her stomach. "I find it hard to believe that you weren't able to charm your way out of a thrashing," she said wryly.

He gave her a crooked smile, and a lock of his dark hair fell over his forehead. Faith could easily imagine him as a young, spirited, mischievous boy. "Och, I assure ye that my da did no' see me excused from punishment. I had my fair share o' tanned hides."

Faith laughed. "You are a strange man."

In a curious gesture of affection, Miles reached down to touch her cheek. " 'Tis the nicest thing ye've said to me since I've met ye, lass. Perhaps we'll get on, after all."

Faith groaned, closing her eyes. "Don't count on it, Irishman. Don't count on it at all."

Chapter Four

Miles carried Faith up a flight of stairs to a small but comfortable room. The coverlet had been pulled back on the enormous bed and a small fire burned cheerfully in the hearth. Gently, Miles laid her on the bed and ordered one of the servants to fetch Molly. She rushed into the room moments later, shaking her head in wonder.

"What did ye say to the lass to frighten her into trying to escape?" Molly chided him softly, as Faith moaned incoherently.

"What did I say?" Miles asked, turning around to face the woman, disbelief etched on his face. "The lass has done nothing but fight me ever since I found her. She struck me in the face when I found her, nearly rode o'er me with one o' my own horses and came damn close to injuring my favorite mare riding across the clearing as if the devil himself were after her. She's touched in the head, I'd say."

Molly shook her head disapprovingly. "Tsk, Miles, she is but a mere wisp o' a lass and deathly afraid o' ye. She was certain that ye wished to harm her."

Miles cursed softly under his breath. "If she is one o' Cromwell's spies, he must have put the fear o' the Irish in her. I do need information from her, Molly, but I'll raise no hand in harm against her. She'll have to remain my prisoner 'til I find out what the devil she is doing here on O'Bruaidar land."

Molly sniffed. "Well, spy or no spy, her wound will have to be cleaned and she needs some rest."

"She'll remain under guard," Miles said firmly.

Sighing, Molly nodded and then went to the door to usher in two serving girls, who nervously waited in the corridor.

"I'll need help unclothing the lass," Molly instructed as they circled around the large bed to do her bidding.

Seeing that everything appeared to be in order, Miles took

one last look at Faith's face before turning to leave. Pausing in the doorway, he heard one of the serving girls shriek in horror.

"What ails ye?" he asked, striding over to the trembling girl.

"Wh-what's that?" the girl whispered, pointing at Faith's black shoe.

Curiously, Miles reached down and carefully pulled the offending object from Faith's foot. Amazed, he took the shoe over to the hearth, examining it in the glow of the fire. He touched the rubber sole in wonder.

"Will ye look at this, Molly?" he whispered. "I've no' ever seen anything like it."

"I've no time to inspect her belongings now, Miles," she answered briskly, tugging Faith's pants over her hips and off her legs. "Although, 'tis God's truth that her disguise is rather odd. 'Tis some strange device on her garment as well." She pointed at the metal zipper on Faith's discarded jacket.

Faith moaned, lifting her hand weakly from the bed. Shrugging, Miles set down the shoe by the hearth and walked over to her. Faith's eyes fluttered open and she weakly tried to sit up.

Miles pushed her gently back against the bed. "Ye're no' going anywhere, lass. We'll just clean your wound and give ye a draught to make ye sleep."

"No, no," Faith moaned, her head moving back and forth on the pillow.

"Give me the draught," Miles ordered one of the girls, who hastily pushed a wooden cup into his hands and scooted as far away from the Englishwoman as possible.

Frowning, Miles lifted Faith's head, tilting it back slightly. "Drink," he commanded, pressing the cup to her lips.

Faith tried to move away, but Miles held her firmly. "Drink," he said again. "'Twill help the pain. Come on, now."

Reluctantly, Faith parted her lips, and Miles carefully poured some of the liquid down her throat. Faith coughed, tears streaming from her eyes.

"Bitter," she spluttered between coughs, "It's bitter."

"'Twill help ye rest," Miles promised, gently resting her

69

head back on the pillow. After a few moments Faith's eyes fluttered shut, her breathing becoming even and steady.

Molly resumed tugging on the pants until she managed to slide them off Faith's hips and down her legs. With a small gasp of surprise, she examined the wound.

"By God, Miles, look at her leg. 'Tis almost as if she has been burned."

"Burned?" Miles repeated, leaning over her shoulder to look at her thigh.

The skin on her outer thigh had been seared and was now red and swollen. Blood oozed in various spots from the wound. The serving girls peered closer at the oddity, gasping and murmuring among themselves uneasily, until Molly finally shooed them out of the room.

"The girls are skittish about the English lass, and 'twill no' serve us to have the servants passing on unfounded tales," she said, closing the door firmly behind them. "I'll tend to her myself."

Miles did not comment, his eyes still fixed on Faith's wound. "By the love o' God," he breathed. "What kind o' weapon would do this?"

Shaking her head, Molly crossed the room and bent over Faith again. "I don't know," she determined after a few more minutes of observation. " 'Tis the first time my eyes have seen such a wound."

"Indeed," Miles murmured. " 'Tis no modest feat that the lass suffered such an injury and yet nearly managed to escape from me. 'Tis a curious strength and courage she possesses."

"Perhaps. Or mayhap she is just frightened to death o' ye. Now help me lift her leg, Miles. I want to look underneath."

Miles dutifully lifted a shapely white ankle while Molly examined the other side of Faith's thigh. "It appears untouched," she said with obvious relief a few moments later. " 'Twill be but a matter o' healing."

Miles nodded, gently setting Faith's leg back down on the bed. He let his eyes travel up the length of her leg, stopping on an intriguing bit of silk and lace that hugged her hips, covering the soft curls of her womanhood. He had never before seen such undergarments on a woman, but he found the sight of the lacy material physically stirring. God's wounds, every-

70

thing about this woman seemed to interest him.

Dragging his eyes from her, Miles forced his mind on to other matters. For what purpose had she been sent to him? And why had she been injured while on his land?

"Who are ye?" Miles whispered while Molly quietly bandaged the wound. As Faith moaned in a restless sleep, Miles took her cold fingers between his hands.

"Beware, lass," he warned her softly. "Fight me ye may, but I mean to find out who ye really are."

"Ye have a visitor, Miles," Furlong said quietly, bending over to speak in his lord's ear.

Miles stared hungrily at the uneaten leg of venison on his plate before sighing and pushing himself away from the table. As he turned around, he heard a voice shout across the great chamber.

"By the wooden cross o' Christ, 'tis ye, Miles O'Bruaidar!"

Miles jerked his head around to see a familiar figure striding across the room toward him. The light streaming in through the open window outlined the visitor's broad shoulders, thick arms and sandy-colored mane of hair. He was dressed in a long plaid shirt of dark green and red, belted at the middle and exposing his knees as starkly bare.

"Ian Maclaren," Miles boomed back. The two men met halfway across the room and clasped hands warmly. "Thank God ye made it safely. How was your journey?"

The Scot flashed him a grin of dazzling white. "Pissin' wet, that's what I say. I'd forgotten how damp it gets in Ireland in the spring."

Miles laughed, the deep sound echoing throughout the chamber. "Damp? Can't ye see the sun is shining today? 'Tis a fitting welcome for ye."

"Aye, today it shines when I finally have a roof o'er my head for the first time in weeks."

" 'Tis good to see ye, Ian."

"Aye, 'tis good to see ye, too, friend. Altho' I wish it could be under different circumstances." The two men looked at each other knowingly, and Furlong withdrew quietly.

Miles led Ian to the table. They were barely seated when Molly rushed into the room, her eyes alight. "Ian Maclaren.

'Tis good to see ye again, lad. Are ye hungry?''

Miles laughed. "Need ye ask? Ian is always hungry. Bring him some food, Molly."

The matronly woman quickly disappeared, only to return moments later with a plate heaped with a leg of lamb, thick chunks of bread and a tankard of ale. She placed the food in front of the Scotsman, who smiled at her boyishly.

"Och, Molly, ye get more beautiful every time I see ye."

Molly crinkled her eyes, wiggling her middle-aged figure saucily. "Ye always did have fine taste in women."

Ian threw back his head and let out a great peal of laughter as Molly happily bounced off to the kitchen, a broad smile on her face. Miles took a bite of his biscuit, shaking his head.

"Aren't ye married yet, Ian?"

Ian tore off a piece of the bread and stuffed it into his mouth, an expression of mock surprise on his face. "Och, and who are ye to ask me such a question?" he said with his mouth full. "I dinna see ye with a wife yet. 'Tis all your fault, ye know. Ye set a sorry example for a lout like me."

"Och, I'll no' take blame for your sinful ways, Ian Maclaren. Besides, ye know wi' my questionable activities, I'm no' an attractive prospect for a lass. Still, I have managed to recently become betrothed."

Ian looked genuinely surprised. "Who is the lucky woman?"

Miles shrugged. "Arabella Dunbar. Her da and I share borders. 'Twas Dunbar's idea; he thought it wise to strengthen our alliance."

Ian lifted his mug to Miles in a congratulatory salute, and the two men took a large swallow. Setting his mug back on the table, Miles leaned over, lowering his voice. "Come now, Ian. What causes ye to leave Scotland and rush o'er to Ireland to see me? Could it be the rumors o' Cromwell that I've been hearing are true?"

Ian took another drink of the ale, wiping his mouth with the back of his hand. "Aye, and it causes me pain to tell ye so. Cromwell is said to be preparin' to come to Ireland by next summer." Ian leaned across the table, his voice lowering. " 'Tis said he's obsessed with avengin' the deaths of the English

72

settlers at Ulster. And he wants the head o' the rebel leader, the Irish Lion.''

Miles's hand curled into a fist. "God's breath, I knew it! That arrogant bastard thinks he can conquer Ireland. Well, he is wrong.''

Ian pushed his plate to the side, resting his thick forearms on the table. "He thinks he can rule Scotland, as well. Ever since King Charles signed a secret treaty wi' the Scots, Cromwell and the English Parliament have been in an awful rage. There are even whispers that Cromwell plots the king's death.''

Miles whistled softly under his breath. "Christ, the man is bold. Does he seek the throne?''

"I canna say. But I will tell ye for certain that sides are being drawn. Make no mistake about it, Miles, the Scots will raise arms to protect Charles and that treaty.''

Miles frowned before taking a swig of the ale and setting the tankard down on the table. "Ye didn't come all this way just to tell me that. Why are ye really here, Ian?''

The Scotsman leaned across the table, looking directly at Miles. "I think ye already know why. Charles believes, quite correctly, that if Scotland and Ireland are to resist Cromwell and the English Parliament, we'd be wise to do it together.''

"Don't ask this o' me, Ian.''

"I must. England is on the verge o' splitting apart. We have no other choice than to support Charles o'er Cromwell.''

Miles drew in his breath sharply. "Have care to suggest that the Irish would actively support an English king, Ian. King Charles has been no friend o' Ireland.''

"Aye, 'tis most unfortunate. He promises to sign a treaty wi' Ireland much like the one he signed wi' Scotland, if ye'll join forces wi' him in fighting Cromwell.''

Miles laughed, but there was no humor in his voice. "I place little faith in desperate pledges. Why has Charles really sought me out?''

Ian rubbed his knuckles wearily. "The King has asked me to seek out and persuade the Irish Lion to give his help.'' He pointedly glanced at the heavy signet ring on Miles's third finger. The firelight glinted off the golden crest of a lion emblazoned in the center. "I didna tell him who ye are . . . but I

73

told him I might be able to find ye.''

Miles's face hardened, the muscles in his jaw clenching. '' 'Tis bloody close to blackmail ye are treading, man.''

"Ye know I'd no' betray ye,'' the Scotsman answered quietly. "But 'tis no secret that Cromwell has promised Parliament the head o' the Irish Lion—your head, Miles. He has said quite clearly that the 'Irish problem' needs to be settled once and for all. If there is one thing Charles can be sure o', 'tis that ye are no friend of Cromwell's.''

Miles remained silent, the scowl deepening on his face. Although his hands lay loosely on the table, Ian saw them curl into fists of anger and frustration. "And what would Charles have me do?'' he finally asked.

"He wants ye to secretly gather support for him among Irish noblemen willing to fight on his side against Cromwell. The Marquis o' Ormonde, a resident o' Ireland and lifelong friend o' the king, has been entrusted to lead these men into battle. Ye would aid him in this task.''

Miles frowned. "Well, ye may as well know that I'm not the safest o' candidates to help ye, Ian. I have every reason to believe that Cromwell already suspects me. Last night someone sent an English patrol to survey land bordering my own. After a little midnight visit to this patrol, relieving them o' their papers and horseflesh, I stumbled across an English lass lying senseless on the ground. She'd been injured and left alone. Now, I don't know what the devil happened out there, but 'tis my best guess that she's spying for Cromwell.''

Ian drew in his breath sharply. "God's wounds, have ye questioned her?''

Miles ran his fingers through his hair wearily. "Aye, but she refuses to talk. And she is rather . . . odd. I can't explain it, but something about her is no' quite right. However, I am certain the lass is no' in this alone.''

Ian whistled softly. "Why do ye say that?''

"There was someone else wi' her . . . someone who slipped away,'' Miles answered, his eyes hardening. "I heard his footsteps in the forest shortly before I found the lass.''

Ian sat silently for a moment, contemplating Miles's words. "What are ye going to do?''

"I need answers from her, and I fully intend to have them.''

"And what o' Charles's request? Will ye help him?"

Miles drummed his fingers for a long time on top of the table, his brow furrowed in deep concentration. After several minutes had passed he stood, pushing himself away from the table.

"Curse it all, I must be mad to even consider such a proposition. Ye may be right that as the Irish Lion I've been successful against small groups o' soldiers that accompanied the first waves o' English settlers here. But to ask me to conduct secret diplomacy for an English king? 'Tis too bloody much ye ask o' me."

" 'Tis little choice we have, Miles. We must do what we can to stop Cromwell, no matter what the cost."

Miles exhaled deeply, halting in front of the mantel. "All right, Ian, I'll begin to inquire discreetly as to which o' the noblemen can be counted on if Cromwell makes a bid for the throne. On the morrow I'll send my young cousin, Patrick, to visit his uncle in Armagh, carrying a note o' inquiry from me. Ye've given me little choice. If Ireland chooses neither man, we doom ourselves to a fate in which no one in Europe will support us."

Ian stood, putting his hand lightly on Miles's shoulder. "I'll leave in the morn to pay a visit to the Marquis de Ormonde, and then I must return to Scotland. 'Tis my profound hope that Scotland will be able to defeat Cromwell and no' force ye into this choice. But I'll be honest wi' ye, Miles: I'm no' confident that we can. Cromwell is one lucky bastard and a damn good soldier. 'Twill be a most difficult fight if he makes an open bid for the throne."

Miles turned around to look at his friend, his green eyes somber. "Then we'll just have to do our best, Ian. 'Tis all our countries can ask o' us."

Chapter Five

Faith opened her eyes abruptly, her throat burning. Her first waking thought was that she was lying flat on her back in a strange bed. Disoriented, she pushed herself up on her elbows, wincing as the memories rushed back.

"So this wasn't just a dream," she murmured, examining her surroundings.

She spied a small bowl of water on the table near her bed. Dipping her finger into the bowl, she tasted the water, glad to discover it was fresh. Thirsty, she picked up the bowl and drank from it greedily. As her thirst abated, she pushed aside the covers, observing that she was dressed in some kind of long linen nightgown. Scrunching up the gown around her hips, she leaned over to examine her thigh. It had been bound rather skillfully and, from the smell of it, treated with some kind of sticky poultice. It ached, but not with the agonizing, burning sensation she had felt before.

Sighing, Faith leaned back against the pillows. Now that she was awake, she needed some time for reflection, to think about what had happened to her. A professional analyst by training, she was well versed in looking at all the pieces of a puzzle in order to form a complete picture. Now, as she analyzed all the aspects of her situation—even those that were remarkably strange—everything seemed to point to the irrational conclusion that she had somehow defied the boundaries of time and was living in another century.

"But how?" she whispered aloud, pressing her hand to her brow.

Simple logic and known scientific fact precluded such a possibility. As far as she knew, time travel existed only in theory and hypotheses. But how could she ignore the consistency of the dress, language and politics of the people she had met?

She exhaled deeply, dropping her hand from her forehead

onto her lap. She supposed these people could be acting, putting on an elaborate show for her benefit. But that wasn't logical either. Her capture had been accidental—not premeditated—and she sincerely doubted these people could have so effectively prepared for her arrival on such short notice. Especially not the inhabitants of the village. Besides, what would be the point? There were certainly other quicker, more effective ways to get her to talk. Pretending that they were from another century served no understandable purpose. She certainly wasn't going to spill her guts because someone waved a seventeenth-century sword at her and wore a pair of breeches.

Then could it be that she really had stepped through a rip in time, an opening born of the strange stone circles and an electromagnetic disturbance? Was she living proof that such travel was really possible? Things like this didn't happen to people like her. Or did they?

Rasp, rasp, rattle.

The soft noise at the door jolted Faith from her musings. Expecting someone to enter, she looked up, waiting. When the door did not open she frowned, her curiosity piqued. Pulling the covers aside cautiously, she lowered her bare feet to the floor and limped toward the door. Again she heard the noise, but at closer range Faith thought it sounded suspiciously like a loud snore.

Not knowing whether the door was bolted on the outside, Faith quietly placed her hand on the latch. In one swift movement she pushed down on the latch and pulled open the door with a hard yank. There was a shriek of surprise as a small form tumbled into the room and landed at her feet, looking up at her in astonishment.

Faith blinked once and then twice. The man sprawled in front of her looked like a real live leprechaun, dressed in a pair of black pantaloons and a long-sleeved white shirt with a vest of gold and green brocade. His shoes were black with gold buckles, and a small black hat with a plume feather sat askew upon his head.

Wondering if she had truly gone mad, Faith bent over to touch his hand to see if he was real or just a figment of her imagination. At her movement, his green eyes widened in fear.

In one startlingly fluid movement, he leapt from the floor, hastening to safety at the other end of the room.

"Cease your action," he cried out, dancing agitatedly from one foot to the other. "Bring no harm to this household, I beg o' ye."

Staring at the small, bearded man in amazement, Faith sought to find her voice. "Wh-who are you?"

The dwarf stopped his nervous movements and took a deep breath. "I am Shaun Gogarty, at your service, my lady." He bowed with a flourish but managed to keep his eyes trained warily on her face.

"What were you doing at my door?"

"I'm guarding ye," he answered proudly, puffing his chest out a few inches.

"*You* are guarding *me?*" Faith said in astonishment before she burst out laughing. Now she was certain that she had lost her mental faculties. Did they think she was so weak she could not overpower the small man and make her escape?

"I know what ye are thinking," Shaun said indignantly. "Physically I'm no match for ye, but ye'll no' be escaping from the window or the door. See for yourself, lass."

Curious, Faith limped over to the window, pulling aside the drapes. The sunlight was blinding, and she shaded her eyes, squinting down into the courtyard. A large man with a sword on his lap sat resting beneath a shaded tree. When he saw her in the window he lifted a hand in greeting. Angrily, Faith turned away and stiffly moved back to the doorway. Stepping through the still-open entry into the corridor, she saw two more men down the hall talking softly. When they saw her standing there they gaped openly at her. Remembering that she was clad only in some kind of nightgown, Faith marched crookedly back into the room, slamming the door loudly behind her.

"All right," she said, crossing her arms in front of her. "I can see I'm well guarded. What is your role in all of this?"

"My lord fears ye may have gone daft and might do harm to yourself," the dwarf answered calmly. "I'm to alert the guards to such a possibility."

"I might do *what?*" Faith gasped in outrage. When the dwarf calmly met her stare Faith clenched her hands tightly at

78

her sides and counted to three before taking a deep and calming breath.

"Let's get something straight here: I am not going to harm myself." Her voice rose a notch, matching the heightened flush in her cheeks. "And I am not daft. But if you must know the truth, I will tell you what *is* pushing me toward insanity—it's you people." With as much dignity as possible, she turned her back on him and made her way back to the bed. "Now, what do you mean to do with me?" she asked crossly, seating herself on the edge of the bed.

The dwarf shrugged. "Och, I don't know, my lady. My lord does no' consult wi' me on such matters." He cocked his head to the left and then to the right, staring unabashedly at her.

"Why are you looking at me like that?" Faith snapped. Self-consciously, she ran her fingers through her hair, realizing that she probably looked a sight. "Are you going to say something about my hair, too?"

"Well, begging your pardon, my lady, but I've never seen hair so short. And 'tis most curious how it falls across your eyes."

"I knew it," Faith exclaimed, throwing up her hands. "No one in this century has ever seen bangs."

The dwarf stroked his beard thoughtfully. "Would ye mind turning to the side?" he asked politely. "I'm wondering how a fairy lass looks in profile."

"A fairy lass?" Faith exploded. Seeing the look of fright on the dwarf's face, she took a deep breath to calm herself. "Look, Shaun . . . may I call you that?" When he nodded his head she continued, "I'm sorry to disappoint you, but I'm not a fairy lass, a spirit, a specter or any kind of mystical being. I'm just a flesh-and-blood woman."

"O' course ye are," he said soothingly.

She sighed. "In fact, I'm just a woman who desperately needs a bath. Do you think you could arrange that for me?"

"A bath? Are ye a witch then?"

"A witch?" she spluttered. "Didn't you hear a word I just said?" When he looked at her uncomprehendingly she hit the flat of her palm against her forehead. "Oh, send it all to hell and back, maybe I am going daft."

"Extraordinary," he murmured. "I didn't know fairies used profanity."

Faith groaned, putting her head in her hand. "Look, Shaun, regardless of what you think, I would really, *really* like to have a bath. Can it be arranged or not?"

The dwarf smiled knowingly. "O' course it can, my lady. I know fairies like water. Ye had only to ask."

Faith opened her mouth to protest but then snapped it shut, deciding a retort wasn't worth the effort. "Thank you," she said between gritted teeth. "Now where are my clothes?"

Shaun pointed at a chair, where a long-sleeved yellow gown, a white smock, several petticoats and a stiff white garment resembling a cross between a medieval torture device and a girdle hung neatly over its back.

Faith looked at the clothing in incredulous surprise. "I'm expected to wear ... *that?*"

Shaun looked genuinely worried. "If ye are displeased with the choice o' gown, I can have Molly fetch another one."

Seeing the concern on his face, Faith felt her momentary anger pass. "I presume that wearing my own clothes is not an option. Where are they, may I ask?"

Shaun shrugged, and Faith wearily rubbed her temples. "Well, if my choices are that gown or my birthday suit, I suppose I'll have to opt for the gown. When in Rome one must do as the Romans do."

"Begging your pardon, my lady?"

"Never mind. The gown looks suitable, although I should warn you that I'm not going to wear that torture device. Also, before you leave, would you be so kind as to direct me to the water closet?"

Shaun stared at her blankly, and Faith's eyes widened. "Oh no, you don't mean to tell me that I'm going to have to use a ...a..." Her sentence trailed off as her glance swept the room, alighting on a white and rose-covered chamber pot in one corner of the room.

"Madame?" Shaun inquired politely.

Faith closed her eyes, shaking her head. "Oh, my God, this just keeps getting more bizarre. You'd better hurry up with that bath, Shaun. I might have to drown myself."

The dwarf looked at her with such alarm that Faith frowned.

"It was a joke, for pity's sake. You know . . . a jest."

He looked somewhat relieved, although a bit doubtful of her wry assurance. Slowly he nodded his head. "Well, if that will be all, I'll send Molly and a serving girl to help ye bathe and dress. If ye require something further, please do not hesitate to ask for me." He moved to the door, pulling it open.

As he turned to leave, Faith rose to her feet, feeling a moment of panic. "Please . . . wait just a moment," she called out. The dwarf stopped in the doorway, turning around to face her.

"Aye, my lady?"

"Will you answer me one more question?"

"Certainly."

Faith exhaled deeply. "What day and year is it?"

A flicker of surprise flashed in his eyes, but he offered no comment. Instead, he gave her an engaging grin before sweeping his hand out with a flourish.

"Why, 'tis the third day o' May in the year of our Lord, sixteen hundred and forty-eight."

As soon as Shaun left the room, Faith returned to the edge of the bed, dazed and afraid. Her conversation with the dwarf had further convinced her that however inconceivable it seemed, she appeared to be existing in seventeenth-century Ireland. Exactly how she had come to be here, she could not yet determine. But she knew she must try to ascertain what course of action to take.

If the dwarf spoke the truth, she had been at the castle for two days, having walked into the electromagnetic disturbance sometime on or shortly after midnight on May Eve. Now if the year were indeed 1648, she had traveled exactly three hundred and forty-eight years into the past. From what she recalled of history at that time, it would be about eight months before Oliver Cromwell and the English Parliament beheaded King Charles I and plunged England into a bloody war with Scotland and Ireland. After a particularly savage campaign against both the Scots and the Irish, Cromwell would eventually gain control of both countries.

"Oh Christ," Faith breathed grimly. "Ireland is not the place I want to be during one of Cromwell's campaigns. I've got to figure out how to get back to my own time.''

She thought it seemed sensible to assume that if she could move back in time, she could also move forward. The only problem was that she didn't know all the variables involved in this process. Why had she traveled three hundred and forty-eight years into the past and not three hundred and forty-five? Why had she traveled into the past and not into the future? What else might have affected the travel—a particular day, a certain time, a special weather pattern? What if she walked back into the electromagnetic disturbance and found herself six hundred years into the future? Then what?

Even more importantly, if she had traveled back in time, had Paddy O'Rourke done the same? Could that be the explanation for the bright light and his abrupt disappearance? Yet if he had moved back in time—where was he? Why hadn't Miles found him lying next to her?

Pressing her fingers to her temples, Faith tried to calm herself. She had to figure her own variables and work through them. Although she had no scientific foundation on which to base her conclusions, she had already decided that it must have been the electromagnetic disturbance within the confines of the stone circle that had somehow propelled her into the past. If she discounted all other variables and simply assumed that time moved at the same speed, whether in the past or the future, then there might be a chance that she could walk back into her own time, having lost only a few days.

But this was a tricky supposition and Faith knew it. If she postulated that time travel was random, then the odd number of years she had traveled could be explained as mere coincidence. But how in the world could she explain the precise nature of arriving the same *day* and at approximately the same *time* as when she left? None of those factors indicated any randomness whatsoever.

Faith sighed deeply. She really didn't know what to think anymore. Perhaps if she could get back to the Beaghmore Stone Circles, where Miles had found her, she might be able to formulate a better hypothesis. Maybe the ancient circles held some clues. She supposed it wouldn't hurt to get a better look at them.

But getting Miles to take her back there wouldn't be easy.

He clearly believed her to be a spy—presumably sent by Cromwell. The irony of the situation was that she really was a spy—just from another century. Therefore, as it stood, she had no rational explanation for being on Miles's land in the middle of the night, clad in what he would undoubtedly believe to be a disguise. This, unfortunately, made her all the more vulnerable to whatever game he intended to play with her.

Faith tapped her fingers restlessly on her chin. Knowing full well the dynamics of Irish and English politics in the seventeenth century, she'd have to be very careful of what she said and did. England was teetering on the brink of civil war—with the Parliament just months away from beheading their own king. Talk about political eggshells. Until she could get back to her own time, she'd have to behave as unassumingly as possible; blend in with the other people.

Faith groaned, straightening her back to relieve the dull ache that had begun in her shoulders. Blending in was highly unlikely and she knew it. She stuck out like a sore thumb in seventeenth-century rural Ireland. Her English heritage aside, Shaun, the dwarf, already believed her to be some kind of fairy—probably because of her strange clothes and educated speech. She was also fully aware that in this century nonconformity and too much knowledge could easily be translated into witchcraft. Although Faith had no idea how the Irish treated those persons suspected of witchcraft in this time, she assumed it was no different than the English who, with rather great enthusiasm, either burned or drowned their accused. It was not a fate she intended to seek out.

There was a low murmur of voices near the door and Faith lifted her head as Molly entered, carrying a tray with fresh water and hot gruel.

"Praise the saints, ye are all right," Molly said with obvious relief in her voice. "Shaun said ye had awoke and were asking for a bath." Turning back to the doorway, she spoke to a young girl who hovered nervously.

"Aileen, send for my lord. Tell him the lass has come awake." The serving girl bobbed her head and disappeared down the corridor. In her place, Faith saw the man called Furlong step into the room. He was clad in a pair of breeches, stockings, a white linen shirt and a vest. His large, hawklike nose was partially shadowed by the greasy cap he wore low on his brow. He crossed his arms over his chest and stared at her silently.

"Another guard?" Faith commented wryly. "Do you fear I'll overcome all three of the others and make my escape?"

Molly fluffed up some pillows behind Faith's back. She was wearing an old-fashioned gown of gray with her hair drawn off her face into a tight knot behind her neck. "Don't pay any attention to Furlong. He'll no' bother ye, lass. We're just glad ye are awake."

"Was I really asleep for two days?" Faith asked. "What exactly was in that draught?"

"Ye were ill," the older woman answered, pulling aside the drapes from the window and tying them with a cord, allowing the sun to stream in. Faith noticed with some amusement that the cords had been shortened, presumably in case she tried to repeat her previous attempt at escape.

Standing, Faith walked over to the window and stared out at the courtyard below. Her guard was still there beneath the tree, only this time he was chatting with a young, pretty girl wearing a bonnet and carrying a basket full of flowers.

"What are you going to do with me?" Faith asked quietly. "You can't keep me here forever."

"Shouldn't ye be directing such questions to me?" a deep voice inquired solemnly.

Faith turned around quickly to see Miles standing casually in the doorway, a half smile on his face, his green eyes regarding her with amusement. His massive shoulders spanned the doorway and the long sleeves of his white linen shirt were rolled up to his elbows, revealing muscular forearms. He was appallingly handsome, Faith decided, even more so because he seemed to appear so without trying to emanate a sense of power and ruggedness.

"All right," she said calmly. "I'll direct my question to you. What are your intentions toward me?"

His mouth curved into a slow smile. "For now, they are honorable," he answered, the warm glint in his eyes making Faith's stomach flutter uncomfortably. "But only if ye agree to answer a few questions o' mine."

"Such as?"

"What do ye know o' Oliver Cromwell?" he asked sharply.

"He's an Englishman," she offered helpfully.

A dark scowl crossed his face and he suddenly moved into the chamber, raising his hand abruptly. "Leave us," he ordered the others sharply.

Molly took one look at Miles's face and, lifting her skirts, moved quickly from the room. Furlong followed her silently, shutting the door behind him.

Miles strode across the room to where Faith stood near the window, his expression tight with strain. "I think I've been more than patient, woman. I've seen to your wound and have no' harmed ye. Now 'tis time to tell me who sent ye."

Faith lifted her chin stubbornly, refusing to be intimidated. "Look, Mr. O'Bruaidar . . . lord, master or whatever it is you're called . . . I'm afraid this has been one big misunderstanding."

His anger evaporated as he looked at her mouth in rapt fascination. It was soft, wide and marvelously impertinent. He suddenly wanted very badly to taste it.

"Ye may call me Miles," he said shortly.

Faith glanced at him, surprised by the change in his tone of voice. "Well then . . . Miles, I have no idea why you would wish to keep me here against my will. I've told you quite honestly that I'm not spying on you."

"Who are ye spying on, then?"

"I'm not spying on anyone." *At least not in this century,* she added mentally.

A melancholy frown flitted across his features, and Faith raised her hands in exasperation. "What more do you want from me? I've told you the truth."

"About yourself or about Cromwell?" he asked, his gaze sweeping over her again. Christ's wounds, she looked incredibly desirable with pink cheeks and tousled hair. Even the thick woolen sleeping gown she wore did not detract from her attractiveness. Perhaps it was because he could see her bare toes peeking out from beneath the hem, reminding him that there was very little else under that gown. Desire ribboned through him, unexpected but not unwelcome.

"Well?" Miles prompted when she did not answer.

Faith felt her mouth go dry at the dark look in his eyes.

With the ease of a cat stalking his prey, he had maneuvered her into a corner, leaving her little room in which to move without touching him. He leaned lightly against the wall as if he didn't have a care in the world, the broad outline of his muscular shoulders straining against the fabric of his shirt. He smelled like soap, leather and horses, and she could see that he had recently shaved. She thought it odd, as most of the men at the castle wore beards, but it only served to make him stand out among the others.

He shifted his weight against her and she trembled, surprised to find his closeness both disturbing and exciting. There was a restless energy about him that made Faith think of a panther with muscles coiled and ready to strike.

"I know as much as you about Cromwell," Faith finally answered, her voice surprisingly calm. "He's a member of the English Parliament. Rather conservative on the religion front and a smashing good solider."

"Is he responsible for sending the patrols so close to my land?"

"What patrols? I don't know what you are talking about."

"Don't lie to me, lass. I know ye were wi' that patrol."

Faith's blue eyes flashed angrily. "Now you listen to me: I told you I wasn't with any patrol and I meant it."

Miles stared at her for a long moment. Surprisingly, her stubbornness only made her more exciting. He ached to kiss the spot on her neck just above the prim collar of her nightgown.

"By God, I've never met such an impertinent lass," he finally exploded. "Are ye this unyielding wi' all men, including your husband?"

"Husband? Good God, I don't have a husband. And I'm certainly not being unyielding. You are the one holding me against my will, may I remind you."

"Ye don't have a husband?" Miles repeated, surprised. "Are ye widowed?"

"No, I'm not widowed. And I can hardly see how my marital status has any bearing on this conversation."

"Ye are no' married nor are ye widowed," he said in wonder. "How old are ye?"

Faith's mouth opened in indignation. "Why, it's none of

your bloody business," she spluttered.

"Then how is it that a bonny, high-bred lass like ye has never been wed? 'Tis most curious."

"There is nothing curious about it at all. It is just the way I want it to be."

Miles shook his head in disbelief. "Everything about ye is a mystery. What do ye want from me, lass?"

"What I want is to be returned to where you found me—the Beaghmore Stone Circles."

Miles abruptly turned his body into hers, pinning her against the wall. Faith gasped in surprise as he braced his forearms on the stones above her head, his muscular thighs pressing against hers. He was so close, Faith could feel his breath on her cheek.

"Avoiding my questions will no' work. I mean to discover what ye want from me, lass."

She could feel the heat from his body permeate through the material of her nightgown. Her pulse skyrocketed.

"I want only to be released," she answered shakily.

"Are ye certain that is all?" he asked, sliding one hand slowly down the wall and onto her arm.

Faith shuddered as an electrical current seemed to jump between them. With a start, she realized it was desire she felt, raw and primal. Horrified that he might be able to see the need in her eyes, she jerked her head to the side.

"That's all," she whispered.

He studied her face, not moving an inch. Finally he spoke. "Molly says ye requested a bath. I will grant ye that. When ye are finished ye will come to the library. We can further discuss your request to return to the stone circles as long as ye don't continue to be so unyielding."

Before she could respond, he abruptly pushed away from her and strode to the door. Without another glance back, he exited the room.

Faith watched him go, leaning against the stone wall and fighting to control her trembling knees. She had never felt this kind of intense physical attraction for any man. It was a terrifying sensation. She tried to reassure herself that the attraction was some kind of temporary insanity, like the rest of what was happening to her. She could not let herself be intimidated by it.

"So you think I'm unyielding, do you?" Faith murmured, crossing her arms determinedly against her chest. "Well, let me tell you something, Miles O'Bruaidar; you haven't seen anything yet."

Chapter Six

Faith felt like a new person when she emerged dripping wet from the tub. In fact, it felt so wonderful to be clean that she managed to ignore the small, uncomfortable shape of the wooden tub, the lukewarm water and the coarse bar of soap with which she cleansed herself. Without antibiotics at her disposal, Faith had decided it was of the utmost importance that she wash the wound the best she possibly could in order to prevent an infection. Again, she said a silent prayer of thanks that she had only been grazed, although the bullet had made an angry burn and welt.

Although it was strange and somewhat discomfiting to bathe in the presence of Molly and the young serving girl, Faith was so glad to remove the layers of filth and grime from her body that she almost forgot they were there. She also had to admit that while it was a first, it was not altogether an unpleasant experience to have someone cater to her every need. Perhaps there was something to be said for an aristocratic lifestyle, she thought with a wry grin.

"Here, lass, dry yourself with this," Molly said, handing Faith a cloth as she shook the water from her arms and legs.

Faith took the linen cloth, shaking it out. It wasn't soft terrycloth, but she supposed it would have to do. "What did you put in the water?" she asked curiously. "I smell like a field of blooms."

" 'Tis just rosewater, my lady," the young serving girl answered shyly. "I hope it pleases ye." Twisting her hands together nervously, she quickly looked down at the floor.

Seeing the girl's lips tremble, Faith hastened to reassure her. "Of course it pleases me. It's just a bit . . . aromatic." Fleetingly Faith wondered whether perfuming bath water was done on purpose, seeing how deodorant had yet to be invented.

Both Molly and the young girl looked at her strangely. "My

lady?'' the serving girl inquired softly.

Faith exhaled deeply. ''Never mind. The scent . . . it's lovely.''

The girl breathed an audible sigh and Faith wondered about her age. She looked barely twelve with long red hair parted in the middle and arranged down her back in a single thick braid. She was exceptionally skinny, with long, bony legs and arms and a splash of freckles on her face, neck and hands. For a moment, Faith felt a stirring kinship with the girl. As a child, she, too, had been painfully tall, shy and awkward. Faith remembered well that, back then, a kind word went a long way.

''What's your name?'' Faith said softly, placing a hand lightly on the girl's shoulder.

''Aileen,'' the girl answered, keeping her eyes lowered. ''I've stoked the fire for ye and placed a comb on the bed. Is there anything further ye wish from me, my lady?''

Faith glanced at Molly, who shook her head mutely. ''No, thank you. I just wanted you to know your help is much appreciated.''

The girl flushed red at the praise, giving Faith a timid smile. Molly said something to her in Gaelic and she curtseyed to Faith and quietly left the room.

'' 'Twas good-hearted o' ye to speak kindly to the girl,'' Molly commented. ''She doesn't have many friends and keeps mostly to herself. She's raising a younger brother on her own as her mother died a few years back.''

Faith shook her head. ''I'm sorry to hear that. She seems so . . . young.''

''Young she's no'; she's nearly fourteen. Not a comely lass, I'm afraid, but she's dependable.''

Faith felt her own cheeks warm at the statement, recalling a time when similar descriptions had been applied to herself. Pushing the memory aside with a vengeance, she began to rub her skin until it was pink. Then she toweled her hair and patted dry the area around her wound.

After wrapping the cloth around her body Faith limped to the bed and sat. Dragging the wooden comb through her hair, she asked Molly for some clean strips of cloth to rebind the wound. Nodding, Molly reached into a small basket, withdrawing several pieces of the linen.

"Do ye get your fair coloring from your mum, lass?" Molly asked as she arranged the pieces side by side on the bed.

At the unexpected question, Faith froze, the comb stopping in her hair. "My mum?" she murmured softly, her face draining of color.

Molly looked up in surprise at the agonized tone of Faith's voice. "I'm sorry, lass. The question has caused ye pain. Please forgive my prying tongue."

Faith's eyes snapped back into focus. "No . . . no, it's all right. It's just that for the past few days I haven't even thought of her. Yes, my mum had blonde hair and blue eyes like mine. She was very beautiful. I often wished I looked more like her."

"She's passed on then, has she?"

"Yes," Faith answered, fully aware of the irony that her mother hadn't even been born yet. "I was eight years old." She resumed the steady strokes with the comb, weeding out the tangles.

"Well, ye were lucky to have known your mum at all," Molly said wistfully. "Mine died when I was just two years o' age. I don't even remember her."

"I'm sorry. Was she ill?"

"Nay, she was killed by two English soldiers who came to take my da away for refusing to pay the tax levied on them by the king. She tried to stop them, but they bayoneted her to death right in front o' us. Then they took my da away. I never saw him again. A neighbor found me crying on top of mama's body a few hours later and took me to Castle Dun na Moor. Seamus O'Bruaidar, Miles's da, was but a young man then, but he took me in and I was raised among the servants. Later, when his young wife died a few years after birthing Miles, I took it upon me to raise his son. I love that lad as if he were o' my own flesh and blood."

"I can see that this family has been very kind to you."

"Och, the O'Bruaidars are my family. 'Tis why I tell ye that ye have naught to fear from Miles. He is a good man and won't hurt ye. He wants only to help ye."

Faith couldn't help but smile at the woman's earnest words. "I suppose I'll have to take your word on that. Molly, may I

91

ask you something else? Where is the clothing that I originally wore here?''

Molly shook her head sadly. "I'm sorry, lass, but we had to burn your garments. The whole lot o' it was ruined, except for these.'' Molly walked over to the hearth and held up Faith's shoes.

Faith reached out and took them in her hands, setting them on her lap. A simple pair of standard MI5 black shoes with rubber soles—her only connection to the past. Or the future, she supposed at this point. It just depended on how you looked at it.

"What about the contents of my pockets and belt?" Faith asked quietly. Mentally checklisting the items, she counted her pen-size flashlight, her radio, a compass, a few breathmints and some tissues. She was also missing her watch.

Of course, there was the more serious matter of the gun she had been holding when she walked into the Dragon's Teeth Circle. For all she knew, it was still lying somewhere in the vicinity of where she had been rendered unconscious.

"Pocket?" Molly repeated questioningly.

Faith blinked. "Yes, pocket," she murmured, wondering if they had even been invented yet. "Well, you see, I had some special items . . . sort of inside my garments and attached to the leather strip around my waist," she clarified. "Did you happen to see anything at all before you burned my clothes?"

Molly shook her head. "Nay, lass, I didn't see anything."

"A pity," Faith commented, deciding that it was probably for the best. Other than the gun and the silencer, the items were all things that could be easily replaced when she got back to her own time.

If she got back to her own time.

"Well, let's bind your wound," Molly said briskly. Walking over to the small table, she picked up a wooden bowl and carried it over to Faith. Frowning, Faith stuck her finger in what looked like a lumpy, white paste.

"What's this?" she asked curiously, wrinkling her nose at the terrible smell.

" 'Tis a healing salve. 'Twill help ye, lass.''

"You can't be serious," Faith said as the gooey substance plopped off her finger and back into the bowl. "It smells dreadful. You aren't putting that on my leg."

Molly picked up the wooden spoon firmly. Before Faith could open her mouth in protest, she plopped a spoonful onto Faith's leg and began to smear it liberally around.

"Ouch! Now wait just a minute—" Faith gasped indignantly, but Molly calmly ignored her by holding her leg still and making sure the wound was well covered.

"Fear no', lass. I've been making use o' this salve since before ye were born," she said briskly, picking up a piece of the linen strip and winding it around Faith's thigh. "Now I don't know how ye got this wicked wound and I won't pry, but ye'll have to trust me. I'll no' hurt ye."

Faith clamped her mouth shut. Despite her initial wariness, the salve did feel cool and comforting. Exhaling in resignation, she leaned back on her hands, letting Molly finish the binding.

"All done," Molly said as she stood and critically surveyed her work. "Ye'll heal well, altho' I'm afraid the leg 'twill pain ye for a bit longer. But ye are young and healthy and 'twill soon be but a memory."

Faith stood, testing the firmness of the bandage. She was at once glad for the strong scent of the rosewater as it helped make tolerable the rather questionable scent of the poultice. Hobbling across the room, Faith approached one of the chairs and pointed at the stiff white device that lay over its back. "By the way, what's that?"

"Why 'tis your corset. 'Twill help shape your waist so that the hands o' a man can easily span it."

"God forbid," Faith muttered. "Leave it to a man to want such a thing."

"What?"

"Nothing; I was just wondering if I must wear such a thing."

"Why o' course ye must," Molly insisted, walking over to the corset and lifting it up.

Faith groaned when she saw the corset was heavily boned in the front with long lace bindings in the back. "Are you certain?"

"I doubt the gown will fit properly without it." Humming cheerfully, Molly set down the corset and held up the yellow gown. She held it up to Faith, eyeing the length critically. "I let it out for ye as ye are a good head taller than Moireen. 'Tis no' a perfect fit, but I fear 'tis impossible to make it any longer.''

''Moireen?''

''Aye, the gown belonged to Moireen O'Bruaidar, Miles's mother. Ye're nearly her size, but a good sight taller and thinner. Miles's da couldn't bear to part wi' any o' her things when she died, so I just packed them away.'' Molly sighed sadly. ''I miss her, ye know. She was a kind woman, the Lady O'Bruaidar.''

''What of the present lady of the house?'' Faith asked curiously. ''Doesn't Miles have a wife?''

''Nay . . . no' yet.'' The distasteful way Molly said the words made Faith start in surprise. But Molly simply pressed her lips together firmly and offered no further comment.

Faith reached out and touched the material of the gown, wondering what Moireen O'Bruaidar had been like. What did the mistress of a castle actually do in the seventeenth century?

''Come, lass,'' Molly said, pulling Faith from her thoughts and leading her to a chair near the fire. ''Let's dry that hair o' yours.'' She lifted Faith's hair off her neck, rubbing it briskly between a piece of dry linen cloth. ''Tsk, now why did ye go and cut your hair, lass? 'Twas it all part o' your disguise?''

''I wasn't in disguise. It's just the rage in London, I guess.'' When Molly gave her a blank look she laughed. ''Fashion,'' she explained further.

Molly shook her head disapprovingly. ''Well, 'tis an awful shame. Ye have the most unusual color I have ever seen. It reminds me o' the pale moon on May Eve. 'Tis quite fetching.''

''I was born on May Eve,'' Faith said, feeling both touched and embarrassed by the compliment. She rarely received such praise, and when she did she felt as flustered as the young serving girl, Aileen.

Molly looked startled by the information. ''Saints above. 'Tis blessed ye are then, lass. All those born on May Eve possess the magic o' the fey folk inside o' them.''

Faith smiled. ''Oh, I don't believe in such things. I'm not the superstitious type.''

" 'Tisn't important what ye believe, only what ye are." She resumed drying Faith's hair between the cloth.

Uncomfortable, Faith decided to change the subject. "Molly, this may seem like an odd question, but what shall I put on as undergarments? You know, around the hips . . . and such." Despite her best intentions, Faith blushed furiously as she pointed between her thighs, feeling ridiculously like a small child asking a naughty question.

"Och," Molly said knowingly, "I saw the odd undergarments ye wore earlier. They appeared terribly uncomfortable. We have naught like that, but I will provide ye wi' a chemise." She pointed at the white smock.

Faith stared at the baggy garment in amazement. "A chemise? That's all? Are you saying I will wear absolutely nothing under that chemise?"

Molly's brows drew together in a puzzled frown. "Why, whatever for? 'Twould surely be a nuisance when ye had need to make quick use o' the chamber pot." Seeing Faith's stricken look, she blinked in surprise. "Is it time for your monthly flux, lass? Is that what is bothering ye?"

"I . . . I . . ." Faith mumbled, caught in a horrible mixture of embarrassment and morbid fascination. It wasn't her time of the month, but she suddenly had this overwhelming curiosity to discover what women used before the modern convenience of tampons, pads, and, apparently, underwear.

"N-no," Faith managed to choke out. "I just wondered . . . well, what do you use when it *is that* time?"

Asking her to wait a moment, Molly disappeared from the room. She returned minutes later holding a thin belt of soft leather. Faith gazed at it with disbelief as it dangled loosely from Molly's fingers. "Ye tie the rag here," the older woman said, pointing at an additional strip of leather that was connected to the front of the belt and looped around the back. " 'Tis quite comfortable, really. When 'tis time for your flux, ye may stay in bed till it passes."

"Stay in bed?"

"Oh, aye," Molly repeated. " 'Twould no' do to have a lady o' your stature up and about when bothered by the monthly affliction."

Faith stared at her speechless until Molly set the belt aside and took up the linen towel, rubbing Faith's hair vigorously. "Now enough o' that. Ye just tell me when ye have need o' it. Ye know, lass, 'tis an interesting exercise for me to talk wi' ye. The English manners are far different than ours, I fear."

"More different than you know," Faith murmured under her breath.

"Miles will be pleased with ye, tho'," Molly said, picking up the wooden comb and running it through Faith's still damp hair. " 'Tis clear he has some interest in ye. We must make ye look your very best."

"What for?" Faith protested. "His interest in me is strictly professional."

Molly gave her a puzzled look. "I'm no' certain what ye mean by that, but a lady should always look her best in the presence o' a gentleman, whatever his intentions."

Faith frowned. "Oh, for pity's sake, I'm not a lady. I'm a prisoner. Besides, I hardly think it prudent to try and impress Miles."

Molly pulled sharply on the comb and Faith yelped in pain. "I suppose it's too much to hope for a hair dryer," she muttered.

"A what?" Molly asked, bending over Faith's shoulder.

"Oh, never mind," Faith said wryly. "Just wishful thinking, I suppose."

With a sigh of resignation, Faith closed her eyes and gave herself up to the older woman's capable hands.

Chapter Seven

Shaun, the dwarf, escorted Faith to the library, leading her down a long staircase and along a drafty corridor. Faith's gown swished loudly as she walked, but she fought the urge to gather the material in her hands. When she first left the room she had clutched the sides of the skirts, lifting them up so they wouldn't hamper her movement. After several of the servants stared at her exposed ankles in apparent shock, Faith dropped the skirts, keeping her hands safely at her sides.

Still, she felt like a lumbering elephant with the numerous petticoats and skirts billowing around her. The corset, which she had unsuccessfully argued against wearing, kept her rather short of breath. A bone from the damned thing kept poking her right beneath the rib. Faith swore she would break the bloody thing in half when she finally got it off.

She nearly bumped into the back of Shaun as he stopped abruptly at an ornately carved wooden door. Without bothering to knock, he pushed open the door and then stepped aside so she could enter.

Moving across the threshold, Faith saw a cozy room with an open hearth and two chairs placed invitingly in front of it. A bookshelf with a handful of leather-bound volumes had been positioned against the wall, and in the center of the chamber stood a beautiful polished wooden desk and chair. Slightly behind the desk stood a striking antique liquor cabinet, containing several crystal glasses and bottles.

"Where's Miles?" Faith asked when she realized the library was empty.

"He will join ye in a moment," the dwarf answered. Inclining his head slightly, he took a step backward. "I'll be leaving ye alone now, but I'd advise ye not to try to escape. There'll be guards outside both the door and window."

"I appreciate the warning," she replied wryly. "By the

way, that's a splendid sword you have there. Is it a Welsh shortsword?''

The dwarf's mouth fell open in astonishment as he looked down at his sword. ''H-how did ye know?'' he stammered, placing his hand on the hilt.

''It's a passion of mine. It's in splendid condition.''

''Remarkable,'' Shaun breathed in awe. ''The fey folk have an interest in weapons? 'Tis most astonishing.'' Muttering to himself, he turned and left the room, leaving the door ajar behind him.

Feeling guilty for having played on the dwarf's superstitions, Faith walked over to the bookshelf, curiously examining the handful of titles available in Miles's collection. Most appeared to be written in Latin, one presumably in Gaelic and another in English. Pulling out the English volume, Faith opened to the first page, discovering that it was a book of Irish poetry, translated into English. Awed, she realized the book had been hand-bound and each page individually scribed. Intrigued, she read the first poem silently.

> Crystal and silver
> The branch that to ye I show:
> 'Tis from a wondrous isle—
> Distant seas close it;
> Glistening 'round it
> The sea-horses hie them;
> Emne o' many shapes,
> O' many shades, the island

The poem was beautiful and it reminded Faith of Ireland— an island of many shapes, of many shades.

''What do ye have there?''

Miles's voice was deep and rich. Nearly jumping from her skin, Faith gasped, whirling around quickly.

''My God, you nearly frightened me out of my wits,'' she said angrily. ''Do all Irishmen creep around so quietly?''

A slow smile curved across his mouth. ''Do all English keep their backs to their enemies?''

Faith tilted her chin up slightly. ''Are you my enemy?''

He shrugged, giving her a slow and thorough perusal from

head to foot. Faith felt her heart flutter at the warm glint in his eyes.

"I've never had an enemy quite so fetching," he commented.

Faith resisted the urge to shrink away from his disconcerting gaze. "I thought you said I was just skin and bones," she replied, clutching the book to her chest.

Miles lifted an eyebrow, clearly amused. "Och, but I'm finding there is much more to ye than that, lass. That gown is most agreeable on ye."

"It was your mother's."

"My mother's?"

She nodded. "Molly said I was nearly the same size as your mother, although perhaps a bit taller. I didn't have anything else to wear. She said you ordered my clothes burned."

Absently, Miles reached out to lightly finger the material of her sleeve. "Aye, your disguise was ruined beyond mending. But I must say that ye look a sight better in my mother's gown than ye did in those ridiculous breeches."

Faith's cheeks warmed, partly because his fingers brushed against her skin, sending waves of heat skittering across her nerves, and partly because she sensed his words were genuine. Dropping her gaze from his, she looked down at the book still held tightly against her chest.

"I hope you don't mind that I was browsing," she said, her voice shakier than she intended. Damn, his mere presence was making her jittery. Why in the world did he have to be so bloody handsome?

Miles reached out and took the book from her, looking down at the open page. "Were ye reading this?"

"Is that a crime?"

He looked at her with interest. "Nay, but 'tis most intriguing." He rested his muscular forearm on the shelf, leisurely leaning close. Faith could feel the heat of his breath on her cheek and was mortified when her traitorous pulse leapt in response.

"Read it to me," he ordered her softly.

She looked at him in surprise. "Read it yourself," she said, holding out the book.

He made no move to take the book from her. "I can't."

99

"You can't read English?"

"I can't read."

"You can't read?" Faith gasped, aghast at his confession. Even though she knew full well that in the seventeenth century most people could not read or write, the fact that this virile and powerful man was illiterate utterly shocked her. Quickly she glanced over at the desk, where several half-written parchments, a quill pen and an ink blotter stood.

"If you can't read, then who wrote those letters?" she demanded, still unable to believe his words.

"Father Michael."

"A priest?" she asked. When Miles nodded she looked over at the bookshelf. "Are those books for him?"

Miles frowned. "I said I didn't read. I didn't say I don't enjoy good literature."

He stood so close, she could see the faint rise and fall of his chest beneath his shirt. Wanting to move but afraid she might touch him, she instead flattened her damp palms against her skirts.

"I'm sorry. I didn't mean to imply otherwise."

Miles reached out, setting the book aside. Faith watched in fascination as the muscles in his shoulders shifted and bunched beneath the white shirt. She could feel the warmth emanating from his body and suddenly felt terribly hot herself.

"Then what did ye mean to imply?" he breathed softly, curving his fingers purposefully beneath her chin.

She shuddered as he caressed her skin. Even though Faith knew he waited for an answer, she found herself incapable of speaking or thinking beyond the spot where his fingers held her chin. Every nerve in her body seemed focused on that one point.

"Lass?" he murmured. "What do ye really want from me?"

As Faith watched in captive fascination, his gaze slid to her lips and lingered there. She drew in a sharp breath and held it. Her heart was fluttering like a trapped butterfly in her chest. With a sense of numbing shock, she realized she wanted him to kiss her. She knew that she should pull away, but she couldn't. She was rooted firmly to the spot, half-terrified, half-fascinated by the stirring range of sensations her body was experiencing.

With a low murmur, Miles leaned over, brushing his mouth across her ear. His lips felt softer than feathers. A delicious shiver raced up her spine.

"Please," she said, her voice coming out in a breathless rush. "I think . . . I think you shouldn't do that."

"I shouldn't?" he asked softly.

Faith swallowed hard. "No. I need to . . . to sit down," she said, her voice little more than a feeble whisper.

Miles pulled back, his eyes slightly mocking. "Of course," he said smoothly. "I've clearly forgotten my manners."

"No, it's all right," Faith replied, fighting for composure. Her entire body was tingling from their encounter.

Miles took her elbow, steering her toward a chair. "Your injury surely pains ye. Please sit down."

Faith sat, leaning back against the cushions. "Is it hot in here or is it just me?" she asked, fanning herself with her hand.

Miles smiled. "'Tis no' just ye," he commented as he strode to the wooden cabinet. "Would you care for a wee dram o' claret?" he offered, holding up the glass container.

Faith shook her head. "No, thanks." *I need to keep a clear head,* she thought.

Miles shrugged and then poured a glass for himself. Returning to the hearth, he sat in a chair opposite her, his long fingers playing absently with the stem of his glass. He sat for some time in silence before speaking.

"Ye know, Faith, I find ye to be very interesting. I've never before encountered a woman who could read. How were ye permitted to learn?"

Startled by his question, Faith searched for an explanation a man of his time could understand. "Well, it's not as strange as it sounds. My father and mother were both well educated. As I was their only child, I suppose they wanted me to be able to . . . well, manage for myself."

"Manage for yourself?" Miles repeated, confounded. "Is that why ye have never wed? Had your father no means to see ye joined?"

"Of course he had means. I . . . ah . . ." she trailed off

lamely. How in the world was she supposed to explain that in her time, women didn't have to get married to get by?

"I didn't have any . . . I mean, *many* . . . suitors," she blurted out, knowing her words must sound ridiculous to him. "Besides, I didn't want to get married."

Miles's eyes widened, clearly appalled by her explanation. "And your father didn't see it necessary to have ye wed? Christ's wounds, what kind o' man was he?"

Faith stiffened in defense. He was dredging up old hurts and they had no place here. "Just what is that supposed to mean?"

"It means that if ye were safely married, ye wouldn't be here in this awkward situation. I daresay that even your father would no' be pleased to discover his maiden daughter has been traversing Ireland without proper escort."

"My father is dead," she said flatly. "And even if he were alive, I don't think he would care."

"Have ye no' any other male kin to take care o' ye?"

Faith bristled. "I don't *need* any male kin, or anyone else for that matter, to take care of me. I'm perfectly capable of making decisions on my own, thank you."

Miles stared in fascination at the heightened color in her cheeks. "Ye are the oddest woman I've ever met. Imagine a woman who thinks she can manage her own affairs." He leaned back in his chair, pressing his fingers together thoughtfully. "Tell me, what does a lass like ye read?"

Thankful he no longer wanted to discuss her family or marital status, Faith felt the tension begin to drain from her body. In spite of herself, she was intrigued by his question.

"I read everything. Reading lets me escape my everyday life. It takes me to places where I don't have to deal with people."

"Ye don't like people much?"

Faith flushed. "I didn't mean it to sound so harsh. I just prefer being alone. I'm more comfortable that way."

"Well, it sounds a wee bit lonely to me," Miles commented, taking a sip of his wine. "But I think I understand what ye mean about traveling to different places, even if it is just in the mind. Father Michael has read me every book in this library at least twice, and that includes the Bible. Did ye know that I paced this room for a week when Father Michael went to Drogheda to conduct a wedding? He left me speculating as to whether Jonah would escape the sharp teeth o' the whale. I could hardly sleep nights for worrying. When Father Michael came back to the castle he didn't have time to change his traveling cloak before I dragged him into the library, demanding that he finish the story. He told me later the whole incident was part o' his teaching—ye know, 'patience is a virtue, my son' and all that.''

Faith laughed, imagining this large Irishman dragging the priest by the collar and ordering him to relate the rest of the story. "So why didn't you ever learn to read for yourself?"

He looked genuinely surprised at her question. "For what purpose?"

"I mean, so you could read anytime you wanted . . . without having to wait for Father Michael."

"But Father Michael likes to read to me."

Faith leaned forward in her chair, resting her chin on her hand. "I know, but you don't need a priest for that. You could learn to read for yourself."

"Och, I'm too old to learn."

"That's rubbish. You are never too old to learn to read. And it's really not that hard, not as long as you apply yourself."

"And who would teach me? Father Michael has enough to occupy his time saving the wretched souls o' this castle, mine included. I'm fortunate that he reads to me as oft as he does."

Faith fell silent for a moment. "Well, yes, I suppose that's a problem. No one else at the castle other than Father Michael can read?"

Miles lifted his booted foot and rested it on top of a basket of logs positioned near the hearth. "Nay, but 'tis o' little consequence. I have little time for such indulgences anyway."

His voice was oddly resigned, and Faith felt sad that this man who enjoyed literature so much would never learn to read. "I'm sorry," she said quietly.

Miles did not answer, but instead twirled the liquid slowly in his glass. "Ye know, Faith, I'll admit that ye are not the sort o' spy I expected. Everything about ye is odd. Your speech, hair, garments, manners . . . all beg questions. I even found ye on May Eve, the night o' great magic in Ireland.

Shaun warned me to beware o' your charms, lest ye cast a spell on me. He's convinced ye are a witch, or a rather tall offspring o' the fey folk.''

Faith's gaze was riveted on his glass and the way his long, sensual fingers caressed the stem of his wineglass. For a moment she imagined them touching her breasts. Taking an uneven breath, she dragged her eyes up to his face. ''I assure you that I am not a witch, nor am I here to spy on you. In fact, I'm not even supposed to be here at all. I urge you to release me. It would be in the best interest of all of us.''

Miles lifted the glass to his lips and took a sip of the claret. ''I'm afraid I can't do that, lass. I think ye know why.''

''I *think* you are wrong about me.''

He regarded her thoughtfully over his glass. ''Mayhap; mayhap no'. But your reluctance to answer my questions only raises my curiosity.''

''I've answered everything that I could.''

'' 'Tis no' enough.''

''Then what do you intend to do with me?''

Miles leaned forward in his chair, pressing his hands together. ''What would ye like me to do wi' ye?''

His tone was light but clearly suggestive. Faith felt a responding tingle in the pit of her stomach. ''I'd like to go to the Beaghmore Stone Circles,'' she said, firmly ignoring his gaze. ''You said we could discuss it.''

''I'm no' going to take ye to the stones today. But if ye are feeling well enough, I have another spot in mind.''

Faith crossed her arms against her chest, frowning. ''This is not a discussion if you've already made up your mind.''

'' 'Tis your choice. We can go where I want or ye can stay in your chambers.''

Faith blew out her breath in frustration. ''You know, we'd get along a whole lot better if you'd stop ordering me around.''

His mouth opened incredulously. ''Me ordering ye around? Why, I doubt ye'd take an order from the king himself. Now, do ye intend to ride wi' me or no'?''

She frowned, weighing the pros and cons of the offer. ''All right,'' she finally said. ''If it will get me outdoors, I accept.'' She determinedly pushed aside her misgivings about riding a horse with a sore leg and hampered by the voluminous skirts of her gown and the tight corset. After all, women had been riding for hundreds of years in such outfits. How hard could it possibly be?

Nodding, Miles stood. "Let me see to the arrangements and I'll return shortly." He disappeared into the corridor.

After several minutes he returned, offering his hand to help her out of the chair. "I've ordered mounts saddled for us. Shall we go?"

Faith nodded, starting as his warm, strong fingers firmly clasped hers. A jolt of heat shot through her. Flushing, she wondered if her pulse would continue to skyrocket every time he touched her.

For God's sake, get a grip on yourself, Worthington. This is not the time to behave like a sex-starved teenager.

He led her down a long corridor and out into the courtyard. Faith blinked for several moments in the bright sunshine, covering her eyes with the back of her hand.

"It looks like a beautiful day for a ride," she commented as her eyes adjusted to the light.

Miles smiled without comment and led her to the stables. Two horses had been saddled and were waiting out front. A young stable boy rushed about the horses, checking the reins. Faith cocked an eyebrow and looked up at Miles.

"Only two horses? No other guards will follow us?"

"I've yet to let a bonny lass out o' my sight, if I'm no' o' a mind to see her go."

"Aren't you afraid that I've planned some kind of ambush for you?"

"Have ye?" Miles asked, amused.

Faith sighed. "Unfortunately not. But I don't suppose you would take my word on it?"

To her astonishment, Miles lifted her hand from his elbow, taking her fingers between his strong hand and lifting it to his lips. Lightly, he brushed a feather-light kiss across the top of her knuckles, sending a warm shiver skittering down her back.

"To the contrary," he said softly. "An Irishman always takes the word o' a lady. Come now, let's take a ride."

Faith hesitated. "Ah . . . there's one problem. I've never ridden sidesaddle."

Miles looked at her curiously. "Ye've never ridden in a

saddle like this?'' When she nodded he shook his head in disbelief. '' 'Tis most unusual. Well, ye'll find 'tis much easier and safer for a lass to ride like this. I'll help ye up.''

Seizing her around the waist, he gave her a backward hoist into the sidesaddle. Faith quickly grabbed the reins, holding on for dear life.

''Well, this is interesting,'' she declared brightly, although she was certain she would slide out of the saddle at any moment. To top it off, her leg was throbbing, her knees were caught in her skirts and she couldn't figure out how in the world she would guide the horse from her current location. But she swallowed her doubts, thankful she was at least on a horse and ready to have a look around the area. She would gladly suffer a hundred indignities just to get home.

Yet her confidence quickly faded when she saw the strange expression on Miles's face. She thought he looked as if he had swallowed something that didn't quite fit down his throat.

''What happened?'' Faith asked quickly, looking around in alarm.

''Your skirts,'' he said in a rather strangled voice, pointing at her legs. ''Have ye no wish to arrange them?''

Looking down, Faith realized her ankles were exposed. Thinking Miles to be scandalized, she fussed with the gown unsuccessfully, trying to get the skirts to lay down correctly over her legs. Unfortunately, the gown was hopelessly tangled about her hips and legs. Finally she gave up, holding out her hand in resignation.

''I'm not going to be able to do this from here,'' she announced. ''Would you be so kind as to help me dismount, so that I may try again to arrange myself properly on the saddle?''

''Certainly,'' he said gallantly, offering her a hand.

Faith placed her hand in his and slid into his arms amid a flurry of petticoats and skirts. During this extremely awkward exercise Faith was certain she heard him snort with laughter. Realizing that he wasn't scandalized at all, but was actually enjoying her discomfort, she glared at him, pushing the hair out of her eyes. Her ire increased when she saw his expression was one of inscrutable politeness.

''You find this amusing, don't you?'' she accused him.

His lips twitched into a smile. ''Truthfully? Aye, but I do.''

"Well, I'd like to see you try to mount a horse sideways, dressed in an outfit like this. I daresay you wouldn't find it so amusing then."

He laughed. "Ye are probably right. Come on now, lass. Let's try that again."

This time she was ready when Miles lifted her into the saddle. With a little maneuvering, she managed to seat herself properly, ankles safely covered. "There," she said triumphantly. "I knew I would get it."

Grinning, Miles swung onto his own steed with ease. "Ye know, lass, ye are as refreshing as a breath o' air after a long rain. I've never met a woman who could read, curse and throw propriety to the wind. 'Tis most enjoyable."

Faith pursed her lips. "I'm glad you approve."

"Aye, but I do," he said, giving a soft cluck and urging his horse forward. Faith followed him.

"Ye may be a stranger to a lass's saddle," Miles commented over his shoulder, "but I'll no' ask ye if ye can ride, as I have already been witness to your skill. Will ye permit me to ask where ye learned to ride like that?"

Faith pulled alongside Miles. "There was a farm . . . ah, a village . . . not far from where I used to live as a child. Occasionally I was allowed to visit and ride the horses."

"Well, perhaps our ride today will permit ye to see your time at Castle Dun na Moor as something other than a terrible memory," he said quietly.

Surprised by the sincere tone of his voice, Faith slowly raised her eyes to meet his and then quickly looked away. He cut a dangerously attractive figure on the horse, his green eyes sparkling, his white linen shirt open at the throat, revealing a strong broad chest. She would have to guard herself well against the extraordinary charm of this Irishman.

They rode for some time without speaking. Faith took the opportunity to soak up the beauty of the day and the lush green surroundings. The breeze lifted her hair from her neck and the sun felt good against her skin. Although she still had a dull, aching pain in her thigh, it felt so wonderful to be outside that she could almost ignore it. Taking a deep breath of the clean air, she tried hard to forget her precarious situation and let the tension flow from her body.

Entering the forest, they rode single file until they reached a large clearing. Pulling back gently on the reins, Miles stopped and Faith guided her mount beside him.

"Lough Emy," Miles said proudly, gazing at a deep-blue, sparkling lake. The sun shone down brightly, causing golden sparks of light to dance cheerfully off the water. "I've spent many a happy hour at this lough. Even now, I sometimes come to her banks just to think."

When she said nothing Miles turned in the saddle to face her. Her face was drained of color and her fingers clutched the reins so tightly they were bloodless.

"Saints above, lass, are ye unwell?" he exclaimed in concern, reaching over to touch her shoulder. "Faith, what is it?"

She blinked, exhaling a deep breath. "It's nothing," she replied shakily. "You didn't tell me we were going to a lake."

"I didn't know 'twas important for ye to know."

She managed a tremulous smile. "It just took me by surprise, that's all. I wasn't expecting this."

Miles stared at her for a long moment, puzzled by her strange reaction to the lake. Frowning, he slid off his horse and took her reins in his hand. "Let's walk a bit," he said, reaching up to help her out of the saddle.

He tied the horses to a nearby tree before offering his arm. She took it and he purposefully led her away from the lake and to a nearby meadow that flourished with an assortment of colorful spring flowers and shrubs.

Relaxing, Faith expressed admiration for the beautiful array of tree ferns, spring holly and wavy purple heather. Reaching down, she plucked a bit of heather, absently tucking it in her hair. It had been years since she had wandered aimlessly about a meadow.

Idle hands lead to a lazy mind, her father had always said.

"What did ye say, lass?"

Faith looked up quickly, unaware that she had spoken aloud. Miles leaned against an old gnarled tree, a bright yellow flower dangling between his fingers. With the sunlight playing against his dark hair, he looked like an archangel from heaven. The hard lines along his jaw had softened, accentuating the sensual and sulky curves of his mouth and lips. Faith marveled at the handsome picture he made.

108

"It was nothing," she answered softly.

"Well, for a lass who says naught, ye have a particularly serious look on your face. Here, 'tis for ye," he said, holding out the flower and flashing her a heart-stopping grin. When she stared at it—he gave her hand a nudge. "Go on, lass, take it."

Touched by the gesture, Faith took the flower, lifting it to her nose. Her hair fell over her shoulders, partially hiding her face. "Thank you," she said softly. "I can't remember the last time someone gave me a flower."

"Och, a pretty lass like ye? 'Tis hard to believe."

She smiled, her eyes softening as she looked at him. "Remember what I said about flattery?"

"Aye, I do. Ye said that flattery 'twill get me nowhere wi' ye."

"Well, in this case, it worked."

His grin deepened. "Och, 'tis good to know, lass. I'll have to use it again sometime."

Still smiling, Faith let the flower dangle from her fingers. "Miles, may I ask you something?"

"What is it ye wish to know, lass?"

"What can you tell me about the stone circles where you found me?"

"The Druid circles?" he asked, surprised. "The stones have been there for ages. They're magic, or at least that's the legend."

"When you say magic, have you heard of any strange events taking place there?"

"Such as?"

"I mean, have people . . . well, disappeared there? Have you heard of strange lights or unusual humming sounds at the site?"

He shrugged. " 'Tis a great many things said about the site. But to tell ye the truth, no' many people venture to the stones. 'Tis a sacred site, and one that most o' us do no' wish to disturb."

"But it's on your land."

"Aye, but the stone circles do no' belong to me, lass. They belong to Ireland."

She mused over his words for a moment. "You called them

Druid circles. Do you think some kind of holy or religious ceremonies took place there?''

"Mayhap. If ye look closely, two rows o' the stones point directly at the sunrise and two others toward the moonrise. 'Tis almost as if they are trying to mark the passage o' the sun and moon. I suppose 'twould suggest that some kind o' rituals took place there.''

"It most certainly would," Faith breathed. "Miles, I really must get another look at the stones. Will you take me there now?''

He studied her face for a long moment before holding out a hand. "Come here, Faith. Let's sit down." They sat, and Faith carefully arranged her skirt as Miles rested his back against the trunk of the tree. "Now, why have ye such an urgent need to return to the circles?''

"I think I may have dropped something there. I would like to go back and see if I can find it.''

"Why don't ye just tell me what ye lost and I'll find it for ye later?''

"No," she replied quickly. "I want to go with you. I must.''

Miles plucked a long piece of grass and chewed on it thoughtfully. "Just what are ye plotting, Faith? Is someone waiting for ye at the site?''

"No . . . I don't think so.''

"Then what's so important there?''

Faith inhaled, trying to calm herself. "Look, I don't belong here, Miles.''

"Then where do ye belong?" he asked softly, reaching out and taking her fingers in an easy and familiar gesture.

Faith closed her fingers around his strong hand. Somehow, it seemed as if her hand belonged in his. It felt right and safe.

"I . . ." Faith faltered. "I belong in England.''

"Aye, and I'll see ye returned there, if that is what ye want.''

"You can't," Faith whispered. "You don't understand. It's not possible.''

Miles leaned over, his green eyes studying hers intently. "If there is one thing I've learned in my life, 'tis that all things are possible. Even between the English and the Irish. Even between us.''

110

She blinked in surprise. "What do you mean?"

He squeezed her hand. "I wish to bed ye, lass. Surely ye can feel the attraction 'tween us."

She gasped at the matter-of-fact way he stated his intentions. Yet at the same time, an undeniable warmth began to form in the pit of her stomach.

"You don't know anything about me," she protested.

"I know that I've never found myself so intrigued by a woman. I can't stop thinking about ye."

Her heart gave a traitorous leap. "Don't be ludicrous. I'm your enemy, remember?"

"I haven't forgotten. I only wish ye would trust me and tell me what ye are doing here."

"I'm not spying on you, Miles."

"Then why are ye here?"

"I told you, I came here by accident."

"Is what's between us an accident? Can ye feel it, too, lass?"

She swallowed hard. God help her but she could feel it— an intense physical attraction, yet something more. It was as if some greater force were drawing them together, heightening their senses and sharpening their emotions. Her tongue slipped out to moisten her bottom lip. Oh yes, she could feel it all right. And it was insane.

Utterly insane.

She quickly pulled her hand from his. "I think we should go now," she said shakily.

But Miles did not move, instead letting his gaze drift over the straight, high curves of her cheekbones, her adorable nose and the pink fold of her mouth. He wanted nothing more at that instant than to kiss her, to taste her lips and feel her body beneath his. But the time was not yet right and he knew it.

He rose, offering a hand and helping her to her feet. "All right, lass, we'll do it your way. But first, I want to show ye Lough Emy."

Faith looked up at him in horror. "The lake? I'd rather not. If you must go, I'll wait here."

In a curiously tender gesture, Miles reached out and took her hand. " 'Tis naught to be afraid o', Faith. I'll no' let anything happen to ye."

"I never said I was afraid," she said defensively.

He looked at her calmly and with an odd softness. "Then permit me to show ye the lough. She's a pretty lass, indeed."

When she hesitated Miles squeezed her hand gently. " 'Tis better to face your fears than run from them. 'Tis what my da always told me. Come with me, Faith?"

She would have rather jumped off a tall building than go near the lake, but she realized that showing him her utter terror of the water might expose a vulnerability that he might try to use against her.

"I told you that I'm not afraid," she repeated angrily, jerking her hand away from his and swallowing the awful dread that surfaced in her throat. Smoothing down her skirts, she determinedly marched past him. She stopped when she reached the edge of the lake, her stomach clenching so tightly, she feared she might retch.

"See, I'm here, aren't I?" she forced out between gritted teeth.

Miles brushed past her and knelt at the lake's edge. With a mischievous grin, he scooped some water into his hand and lightly spattered her with it.

Faith took a step back, blinking at the cold. "My God, it's freezing," she said in shock, the fear of standing so close to the edge momentarily forgotten.

Miles rolled up his sleeve and thrust his arm into the water, up to his elbow. "Och, 'tis warm enough for a swim." As if to prove his point, he shook the water off his arm and abruptly pulled his shirt over his head with one hand.

Faith's mouth fell open. Her first glimpse of him half naked showed her a man of raw power with broad shoulders and bulging biceps. His chest was massive, with hard slabs of muscle beneath tanned, taut skin. He had a few scars running from his shoulder down to his stomach, apparently made by a jagged knife or sword. At that moment Faith was certain she had never seen a man so dangerously handsome in all her life.

"What are you doing?" she asked.

"I've decided to take a dip in the lough," he answered calmly.

"Now?" she squeaked.

"Aye, now," he repeated, reaching down and pulling off

one of his boots. "How is it that an educated lass like ye never learned to swim?"

She took a protective step back as her heart began to beat erratically. "Who said I don't know how to swim?"

Miles grunted. "O' course ye don't know how to swim. I presume 'tis why ye are trembling so."

"I am not trembling," she countered fiercely, crossing her arms against her chest.

" 'Tis most odd. Ye seemed eager for a bath," Miles observed speculatively.

"That's different."

"No' really," Miles disagreed amenably, pulling off his other boot. "A man can drown in the bath as easily as in the lake."

"I didn't say anything about drowning," she retorted heatedly.

He studied her face intently. "Ye know, Faith, in Ireland we have this saying, 'a man isn't a man 'til he faces his worst fears.' I suppose ye could say the same o' a lass."

"Oh, please," Faith snapped. "Spare me your righteous Irish morality."

He paused, clearly puzzled by the sharp tone of her voice. "What are ye so afraid o'?" he asked, a lock of dark hair falling across his eyebrow. " 'Tis more than just a fear o' water here. I've never seen a lass turn so pale."

"I'm not pale, I'm fair-skinned. Now go ahead and take your bloody dip."

Ignoring the sharp tone of her voice, he slowly and deliberately removed his stockings. "Swimming is a luxury I don't oft afford myself, but today I plan to indulge. Ye may wait for me on the bank."

Horrified, Faith realized her breath had begun to come in short, terrified snatches. "Suit yourself," she snapped, jerking her head sideways, partly to keep him from discovering her terror, which was growing by leaps and bounds, and partly to keep her eyes averted from his gloriously naked chest. "If you wish to try and drown yourself, I'll not stop you."

"Well, I'm sorry to disappoint ye, lass," he said cheerfully, "but I won't be drowning today." He looked down at his breeches ruefully. "I'm afraid, though, I'll have to keep these

113

on. I wouldn't want it to be said that Miles O'Bruaidar had offended the delicate sensibilities o' one o' his female guests.''

"Prisoner," Faith corrected him distractedly, her eyes again drawn to the rippling muscles in his arms in spite of her efforts to look away. "In case you have forgotten, I'm a prisoner at your castle.''

He took a step toward her until they were standing inches apart. His bare chest was directly at eye level, and Faith was mortified to discover she could not look away.

"Forgetting is no' in my nature, lass," he said softly. " 'Tis best ye know that now."

The air hummed with a sexual tension Faith had never experienced. For a moment she was certain he was going to yank her into his arms and crush his mouth to hers. But instead he exhaled a deep breath and stepped back.

"Now, I'll be but a moment," he said gruffly. "Ye'll see that there is naught to be afraid o' here."

Before she could voice further protests he ran two steps to the water. She held her breath as he dived in and breathed in relief when, moments later, he bobbed to the surface, laughing and shaking the water from his hair.

" 'Tis truly refreshing," he shouted at her.

Faith thought he was mad, demented . . . and foolish. He had just given her the perfect opportunity to escape.

"Of course it's refreshing," she called out agreeably. As soon as he disappeared under the water a second time, Faith stumbled away from the bank and toward her mount with as much speed as she could manage.

When she reached her horse Faith desperately slipped her foot into the stirrup, grasping the saddle and pulling herself up sideways. Her breathing was erratic from the exertion and fear. Rearing the horse around, she stole a glance out at the water, fully expecting to see Miles racing toward her dripping wet. To her astonishment, she saw him calmly treading water, watching her every movement.

"Look here, Miles, I'm sorry about this," she called out, guilt pricking her conscience slightly. "Are you going to be able to swim your way out of there?"

"Climb off the horse, lass," Miles called back evenly. "Ye'll no' be going far."

114

Faith shook her head. "I'm afraid I can't do that. I have to be going now. Cheerio." Quickly, she slapped the horse with the reins and guided the mare into the forest.

A shrill whistle stopped her horse in its tracks. "What in the world?" Faith murmured, hitting reins against the horse's neck again. When the mare refused to move she felt a surge of panic.

"Come on, now," Faith urged, bending over the horse's neck. "Let's go."

Another whistle split the spring air. Immediately her horse turned around and trotted back in the direction of the lake.

"Stop," Faith shouted, pulling back hard on the reins. "Whoa."

The horse didn't respond to her commands and returned jauntily to where Miles's steed stood, snorting softly. Miles had already left the water and casually stood waiting for her, the sunlight gleaming off his wet back and shoulders.

"How delightful to see ye again so soon," he said, the corners of his mouth curving with amusement.

"You knew all along," Faith accused him angrily. "You knew I would try to escape. You didn't trust me."

Miles reached up and pulled her off the horse. "Aye, I knew," he replied calmly. "And nay, I didn't trust ye." He kept his strong hands on her waist, even after her feet touched the ground. "Given what ye just did, can ye blame me?"

"You arrogant bastard."

He frowned. "I'm afraid I'm far more insulted at being abandoned while in the midst o' instructing a lass on how to face her fears than by what ye just called me."

"I don't need your bloody instruction," she retorted hotly.

"I think ye do," he replied softly, his breath warm on her cheek.

Faith's heart skipped a beat when she realized just how close they stood. His wet, bare chest was just inches from her fingers. Panicked, she tried to squirm from his grasp, but it only caused him to pull her closer, until their bodies nearly touched.

He bent his dark head toward her, his green eyes flickering with an emotion she could not read. Frightened, she pressed her hands against his chest as if to hold him off, but he only shuddered as her hands touched his naked skin.

115

"I'll ask ye again," Miles whispered, his fingers tightening his hold on her arms. "What are ye doing here? What do ye really want from me?"

At that moment Faith knew exactly what she wanted. She wanted him to pull her into his arms and kiss her hard with his strong, sexy mouth. For a panicked moment she wondered if he could read her mind as his gaze slid to her mouth and lingered there. It was a shockingly seductive look and Faith held her breath, afraid that if she even breathed, her last shreds of reason and caution would desert her.

"I . . ." she faltered uneasily. "I don't know . . . what I want."

Miles locked his gaze on hers, and Faith felt her pulse leaping erratically beneath his fingers. Slowly, his fingers slid up her arms and into her hair. He cupped the back of her head, tilting her face up toward him.

"Och, lass," he murmured huskily against her cheek. "I surrender. Ye've clearly accomplished what ye set out to do, so let's no' waste any more time sparring."

Before she could reply his mouth settled on hers, burning, demanding and hungry. Shock waves reverberated through her, sending her senses reeling. She had never been kissed like this. It was long before she remembered to breathe, and even longer before her own arms left her sides and wound slowly around his neck and her fingers into his damp curly hair.

Miles drew her closer, his tongue expertly probing the sensitive parts of her mouth. His hands stroked her back, then curved round and under her breast. He groaned softly when she made a small noise in the back of her throat, shifting restlessly against him.

Pushing the sleeve of her gown off her shoulder, he began to kiss a hot trail to her neck. Faith threw back her head, closing her eyes and leaning into the curve of his body.

"God's wounds, ye are beautiful, lass," Miles murmured between kisses. "Come, let me lay ye down amid this bed o' flowers."

Somewhere in the deep recesses of Faith's mind a warning bell sounded. Her eyes flew open. With a small cry, she wrenched from his arms so violently that Miles could only gape at her in astonishment.

"What in saints' name . . ." he started, his bare chest rising and falling rapidly.

"Keep your hands off me," Faith warned between quick snatches of breath, trying to slow the fierce race of her heart. "Just what do you think you are doing?" Angrily, she yanked her gown up around her bare shoulder.

Miles's green eyes darkened like thunderclouds. "Losing interest in the game?" he asked coolly.

"Game?" Faith repeated, moving her hands protectively across her breasts. The tingling awareness she felt in them only heightened her anger. "Why, do the Irish always attempt to seduce their prisoners?"

A dark scowl crossed Miles's face as he thrust his fingers through his still damp hair. "Och, lass, ye are good. For a moment in the library and then again at the edge o' the lake, I thought I was mistaken about ye. But I can see I've been wrong. I know damn well why ye are here and what ye want from me. So, if ye wish to seduce me, then let's be done wi' it now. I warn ye that a man can only be pushed so far before he loses his patience and endurance for the game."

Faith was shocked into a stunned silence. "Seduce you?" she finally managed to choke out.

"Why else would ye agree to ride out alone wi' me in the forest, or fancy yourself up wi' perfume and my mother's gown? Oh, aye, I know what ye are trying to do. Ye know damn well that I want ye. But just remember that two can play this game."

Not knowing which outrageous statement to counter first, Faith's voice raised dangerously near a shout. "Of all the bloody idiocy . . . how *dare* you suggest that I've been plotting all along to seduce you! I'll have you know that this perfume was put into my bathwater without my prior knowledge, but I assure you it was not intended to attract your oversexed sense of smell. And it was Molly's idea to give me one of your mother's gowns, not some devious plot designed by me. Besides, *you* were the one who burned my clothes. Your mother just happened to be the only woman in the castle that even remotely came near my height."

Miles reddened slightly, but his eyes remained angry. "Aye, but 'twas ye who insisted on riding out wi' me alone, and ye

117

were enjoying my kisses. Ye can't deny that.''

Faith's cheeks flushed crimson. "All right, then, I won't deny it. But I assure you it won't happen again.''

A cool, unnerving expression settled on Miles's face. "Don't make promises ye can't keep," he warned softly. "And don't try to escape from me again.''

"I don't take orders from thick-headed Irishmen," Faith retorted, glaring at him.

His hand snaked out and fastened firmly around her wrist. "Ye will take them from me.''

Faith's pulse leaped wildly as he moved closer, wondering if he would kiss her again. As her body tingled from the contact, Faith realized with frightening clarity that she wanted him to do so. Mortified at her appalling weakness when it came to him, she deliberately turned her head away.

Seeing her turn away, Miles dropped her wrist as if it burned him. Cursing all women to the fires of hell, he reached down and yanked his shirt off the ground. After sliding it over his head he thrust his feet into his boots and swung onto his horse. With an impatient jerk of his head he motioned for her to remount.

Keeping her head high in defiance, Faith awkwardly pulled herself up into the sidesaddle. Her skirts were wound about her knees, exposing her ankles, but she pursed her lips defiantly and left them as they were.

Neither spoke for the duration of their ride back to Castle Dun na Moor. As they entered the courtyard, Furlong met them, taking the reins from Miles's hands.

" 'Twas it a pleasant ride, my lord?'' he asked innocently, although Miles's fierce scowl clearly indicated that it had not been.

" 'Twas as pleasant as a sword through the heart,'' Miles muttered darkly, dismounting in one fluid motion. Without another word he stalked off, not bothering to wait until Faith had slid from the saddle.

"Bloody rude Irishman," Faith hissed under her breath as she dismounted. Her leg was killing her, and she figured she'd probably have to ask Molly to change the binding.

Worse than that, she was appalled at herself for what had happened. She had permitted him to kiss her.

No, she had *wanted* him to kiss her.

Murmuring a curse under her breath, she lifted her skirts, not caring a bloody whit that her ankles were fully exposed, and followed him into the castle.

Furlong watched the two of them march off, their backs stiff. He shook his head for a moment in bewilderment before a crooked smile unexpectedly lit his weather-lined face.

Chapter Eight

"He's requested what?"

Molly wrung her hands nervously as she faced Faith's rising temper. "Miles has requested that ye join him tonight for supper," she repeated uneasily. "He's having a few guests and would like ye to be present."

"Well, he can bloody well forget it," Faith responded fiercely. "If he thinks I will docilely sup with him and his friends while he holds me a prisoner in this castle, he's out of his mind." She stalked to the window and yanked aside the drape, staring moodily out onto the courtyard below. If nothing else, what had happened on their ride to Lough Emy had convinced her that she had to get out of this place and fast, or she would lose her increasingly fragile grip on her sanity.

Molly scurried over to Faith's side, her voice softly pleading. "Please, lass, I don't know what happened 'tween the two o' ye on your ride today, but I've no wish to see ye brood alone in your chamber. 'Tis no' healthy for a young lass."

Faith released an exasperated breath. "For pity's sake, need I remind you that I am not a young lass to be groomed for your precious Miles? I'm a prisoner in this castle, being held against my will. I want it to be made clear to him that I have no intention of playing along with any more of his absurd attempts to glean information from me."

Molly's fingers fluttered to her breast in dismay. "I ask ye to reconsider, lass. Miles is a good lad. I know he can be a wee bit impertinent sometimes, but—"

"A *wee* bit impertinent?" Faith said incredulously. "Why, he's little more than an arrogant, reckless, insensitive . . . Irishman. I will not agree to eat in the same room with his likes, and that's final."

Molly sighed. "Och, indeed ye've seen a bit o' the rogue in our lad. 'Tis true that on occasion he can act a wee rashly.

120

But I promise ye, he has a heart o' gold.''

"Bloody doubtful," Faith muttered heatedly. Leaning her forehead against the cool stone wall, she looked below at the courtyard just as she heard someone shout. A tall woman with long, plaited chestnut hair and a flowing crimson cloak rode into the courtyard, escorted by a half dozen riders. Men scurried out of the castle to greet her, bowing effusively and offering their assistance. Faith watched in astonishment as the woman permitted no fewer than three men to help her down from the horse. Once on the ground, she began to command them to and fro, as if they were her personal foot soldiers.

"Who's that?" Faith asked in wonder.

Molly peered over Faith's shoulder. "Och, 'tis Arabella Dunbar. Her da shares a border wi' Miles."

Faith turned to look at Molly, wondering about the strange note of disapproval in her voice. "What is she—some kind of royalty?"

"Och, hardly," Molly snorted.

"Will she be at this dinner tonight?"

"I would say so."

Again Faith noticed the lines around Molly's mouth tighten with displeasure. Not wishing to pry further, Faith turned back to the window. "How many other people will be at this dinner?" she asked curiously.

Molly shrugged, turning and fussing with the covers on Faith's bed. "Och, Father Michael and Shaun for certain, and most likely Miles's friend Rory O'Shea and his wife, Corinne. I don't know who else, but there is certain to be more. Miles likes company."

Intrigued, Faith returned her attention to the regal Arabella Dunbar. Her long, beautiful hair gleamed in the sunlight as she headed for the castle, trailed by several men loaded down with various parcels and bundles. She herself carried nothing, but stopped to severely admonish one poor man who had dropped one of her parcels.

"Not a friendly sort, is she?" Faith murmured.

Molly hadn't heard her. "Well, if that will be all, lass, I'll be going," the older woman said quietly.

Faith turned abruptly from the window, her curiosity getting the better of her. "Wait, Molly. Perhaps you are right. It won't

121

serve me to sit alone in this room. If I still may, I think I'd like to take Miles up on his dinner invitation.''

Besides, she added silently, *maybe I'll be able to find someone sympathetic and willing to take me to the stone circles.*

Molly's face lit up with genuine delight. "Och, lass, ye don't know how much it pleases my heart to hear that. I even have the perfect gown for ye to wear." She bustled over to the wooden wardrobe that stood in the corner of the room and pulled out a gown of dark blue silk. The material swished as she eagerly held it out for Faith's inspection.

Faith drew in her breath sharply at the beautiful sight. Running her fingers lightly over the soft material, she shook her head. "I can't wear this, Molly. It's too lovely and expensive. Knowing me, I'll be certain to spill something on it.''

"Why o' course ye'll wear it," Molly responded firmly. "I had it altered especially for ye.''

Faith dropped her hand from the material. "No, it's more than that. I don't think Miles approves of me wearing his mother's gowns.''

" 'Tis nonsense, that is. Men don't bother themselves about such things.''

"Well, Miles does.''

Molly tapped her finger on her chin thoughtfully. "I've never seen the lad take notice o' a gown before. Will ye wear it if I promise to talk to Miles myself about this matter?''

Faith sighed in resignation. "It appears as if I don't have much of a choice. But I'm not wearing that bloody corset.''

Molly gave her a stern, motherly look. "Come now, lass, I know they are a bit uncomfortable, but 'tis unthinkable to go without one. Why, 'twould be indecent.''

Faith thought it absolutely absurd that she could walk around without underwear, but as soon as she balked at wearing a corset, everyone was scandalized.

"No," she repeated stubbornly. "I'm afraid I'm going to have to put my foot down on this one. It hurts.''

"Oh, but lass, ye must," Molly pleaded. "I want ye to look beautiful tonight. And it's been so long since I dressed a lady properly.''

Seeing the imploring look on Molly's face, Faith felt her

resolve crumble. "Oh, hell," she muttered. "I can't believe I'm saying this. All right, I'll wear the bloody thing, but don't pull it so tight. I can't breathe when I'm sitting down."

Molly beamed and reached over to pat Faith on the hand. "Ye'll be the most enchanting lass there. But I must warn ye that in Ireland 'tis no' fitting for a lady to employ the use o' profanity. I know ye English have different ways, but 'tis much frowned upon here."

Faith flushed guiltily, feeling like a naughty child who had just got caught with her hand in the cookie jar. "Sorry," she mumbled apologetically.

"Och, I know ye have a kind heart, lass. No matter what the others say about ye, I don't believe ye mean to bring harm to Miles."

"I don't wish him harm," Faith replied earnestly. "I just want to get back home."

Molly's eyes softened kindly. "Well, if that is what ye want, lass, then I'm certain Miles will see ye there."

"If only it were that easy."

Molly carefully laid the dress on the bed, smoothing out the skirts. "Ye must believe that Miles will take care o' everything."

"That," Faith murmured softly, "is exactly what I'm afraid of."

Miles stood at the bottom of the stairs, chafing restlessly and tugging on his stiff collar. Dressed in a tight-fitting velvet doublet of dark green and a pair of matching breeches, he wondered for the hundredth time what was keeping Faith from appearing. For a moment he wondered if she had changed her mind and refused his invitation. By God, he would go to her chamber and drag her out kicking and screaming, if he had to. Letting out a frustrated breath, he calmed himself, knowing full well that Molly would have informed him by now had the lass made such a reckless decision.

"Then what the devil is taking her so long?" he muttered, resuming his pacing.

He wondered if she were still angry at what had passed between them at the lake. Undoubtedly she had spent the rest of the day plotting his demise, her escape or both. Amused at the thought, a smile touched his lips. Saints preserve him, despite her stubbornness he had yet to meet a more spirited lass.

A rustle at the top of the stairs caught his attention. Quickly he whirled on one boot-clad leg, lifting his gaze. He blinked once, then twice.

Faith stood on the top stair, her hand resting lightly atop the wooden banister. She was clad in a simple gown of dark-blue silk with a high waist and fitted bodice. Her shoulders were bare, her décolletage edged with a delicate white brocade. Her pale hair was swept back off her neck in a simple style, but small ringlets cascaded about her cheeks, catching the light as if each strand were made of finely spun gold.

She was beautiful.

Saints above, Miles thought dimly, if Cromwell had wished for a spy lovely enough to coax secrets from the Irish Lion, he had certainly chosen well. Dazed, he watched as she descended the stairs.

"Ye came," he said softly.

"Of course I came," she replied lightly. "I'm hungry."

There was no hint of anger in her voice; in fact, she was slightly breathless. Miles wondered whether it was from the exertion of descending the stairs or simple excitement. Bowing slightly at the waist, he took her hand and lifted it to his lips.

"Hungry for me, sweet?" he whispered huskily, brushing his mouth across her fingertips. He heard the sharp intake of her breath and felt his own pulse quicken in response. God's blood, he had only to touch her and the blood pumped crazily through his veins.

"So what do ye think o' our lass, Miles?" Molly said excitedly, coming down the stairs behind Faith.

Realizing he had held on to Faith's hand a bit longer than was necessary or proper, Miles released it and took a step backward. He consciously reminded himself to beware this mysterious Englishwoman, lest he fall for what was certainly a Cromwell plot.

"She is enchanting," he said, never taking his gaze from Faith's face.

" 'Twas your mother's gown," Molly explained quickly. "She had some concern about wearing it, but I told her ye'd approve. Am I right?"

Miles let his gaze rest on Faith's creamy white neck and shoulders, feeling the kindling of a warm, familiar sensation within him. Christ, she was lovely—too damn lovely for her own good.

"Ye were right, Molly," he said softly. "I approve."

Faith lowered her eyes at the seductive note in his voice, remembering all too clearly what had passed between them in the meadow. There was some kind of magnetic attraction between them, something she seemed to have no control over. Inwardly she frowned, annoyed and dismayed that this man could so easily cause a physical reaction in her. One look from his remarkable green eyes and reason deserted her. One touch of his hands and logic fled.

She couldn't let this attraction distract her. She had to get back to the stone circles. As a result, tonight she planned to employ another approach to get Miles to do what she wanted—a more demure and agreeable one. Perhaps if she pretended to be more submissive, he might be convinced to return her to the stone circles.

But she would have to be careful with whatever game she decided to play. Miles was utterly a man of his time, strong and imperious, his towering physique intimidating and commanding. She suspected he would not suffer fools gladly, nor would he let a woman deter him from whatever goal he had set to achieve.

She stole a sidelong glance at him. He even wore his clothes like a cloak of power. The breeches, jacket and even the stockings looked right on him. Yet despite his wealth, he wore only one adornment, a heavy gold ring in the curious shape of a lion. Faith turned her head to study it closely as he lifted his hand to tug on his collar.

" 'Tis the family's crest," Miles said, observing her interest. "The ring has been in my family for centuries."

"The lion," she said softly. "How appropriate."

"Is that a compliment on my prowess?" he said with a teasing grin.

"Yes," she replied, a smile touching her lips. "I suppose it is."

Still smiling, he offered his arm and Faith took it, acutely aware of the way his muscles bunched and tightened beneath her touch. He felt warm to her touch, even through all the layers of his clothes.

"Are ye still angry about what happened this afternoon?" he asked as they began walking.

"I've put it completely out of my mind," she lied.

"And that's why ye are being so agreeable?"

"Why shouldn't we try to get along? There is no sense in arguing all the time."

To her astonishment he laughed. "What are ye plotting now, Faith? One minute ye are all fire and claws, and in the next ye are demure and submissive. Do ye think to play me for a fool?"

She flushed guiltily. "I don't know what you mean."

"O' course ye do," he said, lightly caressing her elbow. "What do ye have in mind for me now?"

His fingers sent a shiver from her scalp to her toes, leaving everything tingling. Annoyed, she yanked her elbow from his hold. "Don't do that," she snapped.

"Why? Afraid that ye might like it?"

"Don't be ridiculous."

"Then don't try to play me for a fool, Faith," he warned softly. "It won't work." He leaned his dark head toward her, lowering his voice. "But I will tell ye that I'm ready to continue what we started at the lake today."

Faith was taken aback at his boldness. "I told you that was a mistake."

" 'Twas no mistake, Faith, and ye know it. The sooner ye are ready to recognize that, the easier 'twill be. For both o' us."

Faith opened her mouth to retort when she realized they had reached the Great Hall. As they entered the chamber, she could not help but gasp in astonishment. The room was enormous, with a high, vaulted ceiling. Beautifully stitched tapestries hung on the rough stone walls and fresh rushes had been placed about the floor. A long wooden table stretched down the center of the room, lined with backless benches on either side. A dozen people were already seated at the candlelit table, drinking and laughing. Faith recognized Furlong and Shaun but knew none of the other people.

Upon seeing the pair pause in the entranceway, the men in

the room hastily stood, all eyes turning curiously to study Faith. Feeling horribly self-conscious, she forced herself to keep her head high and her chin steady. Calmly, she tried to meet the eyes of everyone in the room, instinctively searching for a sympathetic look that might translate into help.

"I should tell you right now that I'm not good at social events," she whispered to Miles. "I usually avoid them at all costs."

He shrugged. " 'Tis naught to concern yourself wi' here. Just a few close friends o' mine."

"A few close friends" seemed to consist of nearly 30 people. As Faith looked over the guests, her eyes alighted on the face of a middle-aged priest with ruddy cheeks, receding reddish blond hair and sparkling blue-gray eyes. Clearly a man of God, he was dressed in a black woolen robe with an exquisitely fashioned wooden cross around his neck. As their eyes met and held, Faith sensed a genuine warmth and friendliness in the priest's expression. She wondered if this was Father Michael, the priest Miles had mentioned earlier.

"Please allow me to present the Lady Faith," Miles announced to the guests, pausing as he pulled her forward.

For a moment Faith suffered the eyes of everyone in the room before she realized the silence was stretching on indefinitely.

Leaning over, Miles whispered in her ear. "I don't know your family name or proper title, lass."

"It isn't necessary for you to know," she whispered back, her nerves beginning to stretch to the breaking point. Her stomach churned and her hands were cold and clammy. Had she really thought she could pull this off? What had made her think that just because it was nearly 350 years in the past, her fears would be any different?

Miles gave her a discreet squeeze on her elbow. "Lady Faith is a visitor o' mine from across the sea," he finished smoothly. "I hope that ye will show her every courtesy." He guided her forward, indicating the end of his brief and unusual introduction.

As murmurs of welcome and interest sounded in the chamber, Miles led her to her seat. As Faith placed one foot across the bench preparing to sit, the woman already seated to her

127

right turned around and looked up.

Faith's mouth fell open in absolute admiration. Arabella Dunbar was utterly gorgeous at close view, with satiny white skin and enormous brown eyes. She wore a gown of deep crimson, complementing her long, thick chestnut hair. The neckline of her gown dipped dangerously low, revealing a very ample bosom. Small sparkling jewels were sewn along the neckline and in the cuffs of her sleeves, flashing every time she moved.

"This is the Lady Arabella Dunbar," Miles said, presenting the woman to Faith. Arabella gave Faith a charming smile, but as soon as Miles glanced away, her eyes narrowed into a subtle but contemptuous look from beneath her luxurious lashes.

Faith was taken aback at the woman's open hostility. Following Arabella's angry gaze, she realized that Miles still had a possessive grip on her elbow. Her cheeks flaming, Faith pulled her elbow from his grip and sat down on the bench with an unladylike thud. The hasty action caused a flash of heat to shoot up her injured leg, and a groan of pain slipped past her lips.

Concerned, Miles knelt beside her. "Is your leg still causing ye discomfort, lass?" he asked softly.

The look of genuine concern in his eyes warmed Faith's heart. She suddenly had the strangest urge to throw herself into his arms and blurt out her entire inconceivable story.

Stop it, she urged herself frantically. *For God's sake, get a grip on yourself. You are his prisoner. This attraction is insane.*

Scowling heatedly, she turned away from him. "I'm fine," she said shortly.

For a moment Miles stared at her in surprise. Then, shrugging, he seated himself on the bench next to Arabella. Once he was in place, the servants appeared carrying plates heaped with meat, bread and cheese and quickly began to distribute the food. As Miles became engaged in discussion with a man to his right, Arabella turned to Faith.

"Well," she said, deftly patting a stray hair into place, "Miles says that ye are from across the sea. Is that Scotland or Wales?"

Faith immediately noticed the casual yet possessive way Arabella said Miles's name. She felt irritated at the woman's tone, although she couldn't imagine why she should care.

"Neither. I'm English," Faith replied calmly, using her fingers to pick up what appeared to be a leg of some kind of fowl. She looked around curiously and then took a bite of it in the same manner as the others.

"English?" Arabella gasped in horror, clutching a hand to her breast. "English? Oh, my!"

Insulted by the woman's dramatic and rather horrified tone, Faith deliberately set down her food on her plate with a thud. "Oh, please, spare me the bloody theatrics."

Miles heard Arabella's gasp and turned slightly on the bench. "What ails ye, Arabella? Has the lass said something to offend ye?"

"Miles, ye didn't tell me the lass is a *Sassenach*," she moaned, fluttering her eyelashes. "How could you bring her here? And to place her at the table next to me! For the love o' God, have ye wish to see me swoon?"

"Och, did I forget to mention that the lass is from England?" Miles said, a twinkle in his eye. "How careless o' me."

"Miles, ye wicked man. Ye are teasing me."

"Aye, lass. Mayhap I am a wee bit."

Arabella leaned over in an intimate fashion to whisper something in Miles's ear. Miles roared with laughter and Arabella rewarded him with a dazzling smile.

Faith rolled her eyes in disgust at Arabella's antics, observing that the woman clearly had designs on Miles. Grumpily, Faith picked up her food again, tearing off another bite of the meat and chewing furiously. The worst part of the matter was that Miles happily played along, like a lamb being led to slaughter. Christ, how stupid did a man have to be to fall for such age-old feminine wiles as batting eyelashes, heaving bosoms and distressed sighs?

Her mouth still full, Faith stole another glance at Arabella. In spite of herself, she felt a flash of envy at Arabella's poise and elegance. The woman had perfect hair and a figure to die for. She wasn't skin and bones, nor was her hair chopped off at her shoulders and hanging over her eyes. Besides, it was obvious the woman knew how to handle herself around a man.

A slight touch of her fingers or a flash of her eyes and it was perfectly clear what she was after: seduction with ease. Christ, she made it look so simple.

Frowning, Faith swallowed the lump of meat in her mouth. Why should she care how Arabella Dunbar conducted herself? She didn't care one whit about these people and certainly wasn't going to get involved in their sordid affairs. They could act however they pleased for all she cared.

"Lass?"

Faith started guiltily, mortified that Miles had caught her staring at Arabella. "What?" she snapped.

"Would ye care for some wine?"

Releasing a breath, she held out her goblet. "Thank you. Actually, I rather think I could use a drink."

Miles poured, leaning across Arabella. Faith observed that the chestnut-haired woman took full advantage of his position by lightly brushing her breasts against his forearm, nearly causing him to spill the wine all over Faith's gown. Faith shot Arabella an angry glance.

After Miles had set the flask back on the table, Arabella smugly picked up her own goblet and took a delicate sip of wine. Ignoring Faith completely, she turned toward Miles.

"Pray tell, Miles, how in God's name did an English lass find her way to Castle Dun na Moor?" She put her hand lightly on top of Miles's arm, shifting ever so slightly on the bench.

Faith noticed that Arabella's new position gave Miles an excellent glimpse down the front of her gown. Frowning, she took another bite of her food, pretending disinterest in their conversation.

"Mmmm," Miles murmured, taking full advantage of his unobstructed view. "Well, 'tis a most curious situation, Arabella."

"Come now, Miles, tell me the truth," Arabella purred. "Is she a kept woman; ye know, a strumpet who travels with English patrols?"

Faith choked on the piece of meat she was chewing on, the leg sliding abruptly from her fingers and landing on her plate with a loud plop. Quickly, she looked around for a napkin but saw none. Glaring at Miles over Arabella's shoulder, she resisted the urge to wipe her hands on Arabella's gown and instead rubbed them together and put them in her lap.

Miles met Faith's glare with a smile before leaning closer to Arabella and speaking in a loud whisper. "She's a most unusual lass, Arabella. She won't say why she was wandering alone in my forest and she hasn't taken much o' a fancy to my hospitality."

"Hospitality, my foot," Faith hissed indignantly, interrupting the conversation. "Keeping me prisoner in your castle hardly constitutes acceptable hospitality."

"Prisoner?" Arabella interrupted with considerable surprise. "Ye're keeping her a prisoner?"

Miles grinned, a stray lock of his dark hair falling across his forehead. "Aye, but only until she agrees to answer some o' my questions."

Faith opened her mouth to retort when a sudden commotion near the entrance to the chamber sounded. She gasped in surprise as the room abruptly filled with the sound of swords being drawn from their sheaths. Looking around in wonder, Faith saw that every man in the room stood ready, sword in hand.

The door suddenly swung open and a large figure swept into the room. All eyes locked on the stranger.

"*O'Rourke!*" Faith heard someone shout.

As she heard the name, Faith slowly rose to her feet, her face draining of all color. A bear of a man stood in the doorway with light red hair and a beard. If she hadn't known better, she would have sworn he was Paddy O'Rourke, except somehow . . . somehow this man was different. His hair was longer and more unkempt, and he had a jagged scar running aslant the length of his lower lip and chin, stopping halfway down his neck. His eyes were also different, darker than those she had studied in the pages of Paddy O'Rourke's dossier. When this man smiled the scar twisted his mouth into a frightening grimace.

Shaking his head, Miles sheathed his sword. "Damnation, Donagh, ye nearly had a sword run through ye. Had ye no' the courtesy to send news o' your travel?"

Donagh stepped forward, throwing off his cloak. "Forgive me, Miles. I had an unexpected visit from one o' my kin. I came as soon as I got word o' your captive. Where is the English lass?'' he asked, looking about the chamber. His eyes lit up as they landed on Faith.

''There,'' he said confidently, striding across the room to bow gallantly in front of her. ''Madame, may I present myself?'' he murmured, taking her hand and pressing his lips to the back of her hand. ''Donagh O'Rourke at your service.''

Faith immediately felt a cold chill creep up her spine. She felt slightly ill and not a little disoriented. To be standing here, apparently shaking the hand of the ancestor of one of the most famous Irish assassins of the twentieth century was a little more than she could handle. Quickly, she snatched her hand away, pressing it protectively to her breast.

''So, we've caught ourselves an English spy,'' Donagh said softly, his dark eyes flickering with admiration. ''And a bonny one at that.''

Instinctively, Faith moved closer to Miles. Whether it was woman's intuition or just his uncanny resemblance to Paddy O'Rourke, Faith didn't trust this man for a moment. She was grateful to feel Miles's hand circle protectively around her waist.

''Let's retire to my private chambers,'' Miles said quietly to Donagh. The hall had fallen silent. Donagh nodded, keeping his eyes fixed on Faith.

''Ye'll come wi' us, too, lass,'' Miles added.

They began to move when Arabella suddenly stood, effectively blocking their way. ''Miles, ye have guests,'' she reminded him.

Miles's mouth curved into a displeased frown. ''I'll see to them later, Arabella. I've a matter that requires my immediate attention.''

For a moment Faith saw a flicker of anger in her eyes before her generous mouth slipped into a pretty smile. ''O' course, my lord. I'll see that your guests are well attended.''

Miles nodded briefly. ''I appreciate your help, lass.''

She curtseyed and Miles turned away. Faith moved to follow when she felt an iron hand grip her elbow. Surprised, Faith glanced over her shoulder to see Arabella shoot her a venomous look. The message was clear.

He's mine.

Before Faith had a chance to react, Miles pulled her along behind him. He steered her out of the Great Hall and down a long corridor in silence. When they reached the library Miles ushered her and Donagh in, closing the door firmly behind him. Faith immediately walked to safety behind the desk, resting her hands on the back of the chair.

A heavy silence descended on the chamber. From beyond the window Faith heard a clap of thunder. Moments later, rain began to fall, lightly at first and then in torrents. The sound of the rain slapping relentlessly against the stone walls echoed eerily throughout the chamber.

"Well, well," Donagh said, breaking the silence first. "What shall we do wi' the lass, Miles?"

Miles walked to the hearth and added several logs to the fire. Picking up the fire iron, he bent over to stir the embers until they sparked to life, licking at the dry wood. Satisfied, he stood, carefully putting the fire iron back against the hearth.

" 'Tis a most unusual situation," he said in a grave voice.

"Has she admitted to being a spy?"

"Nay, she still denies it."

"Look, there is no need to be rude, nor do you have to speak as if I'm not here," Faith interrupted. "I'm perfectly capable of speaking for myself."

Donagh grinned. "The lass has a sharp tongue. A fiery one, is she no'?"

"That she is, Donagh. Cromwell has chosen well."

Donagh lifted his head sharply. "Cromwell? Ye think Cromwell sent her?"

"I do."

"For Christ's sake," Faith spluttered angrily, "how many times do I have to tell you that Cromwell did not send me?" To her great annoyance, both men continued to ignore her.

"Shall we trade her?" Donagh asked softly.

Miles nodded in confirmation. "Aye. I'll be wanting the O'Flahertie brothers and Douglas O'Leary in exchange."

Faith shook her head in disbelief. "Why isn't anyone bothering to listen to me? You are wasting your time. There will be no exchange."

Miles turned his head sharply, his expression dark and serious. "Why do ye say that, lass?"

Because my superiors live in another time. No one in seventeenth-century Ireland has the faintest idea of who I am.

"You'll just have to trust me on this," she said firmly. "No one will trade for me."

Miles strode across the room and put his hands on her shoulders, the muscles in his face unyielding and hard. "Then tell me who sent ye. 'Tis all I want to know."

His expression was grim, a single muscle in his jaw twitching as if he was holding back his anger. For a fleeting moment Faith wondered if they tortured spies in the seventeenth century. If she had any luck at all, perhaps some code of chivalry would prevent them from harming a woman. Yet as she looked up into the grim green eyes of her captor, she wasn't so sure.

"N-no one sent me," she said, swallowing hard. "I came here by accident."

Miles exhaled the breath he had been holding, dropping his hands from her shoulders. "Ye see, Donagh, the lass is clearly hiding something. 'Twill be o' great interest to me to see just how much the English value her."

"You're still going to try to trade me?" Faith said, unable to believe her ears. "I just told you, they won't agree to it."

"Ye've told me naught, lass," Miles answered quietly.

A long silence followed. "Perhaps we should move the lass to my keep," Donagh suggested, breaking the quiet.

Faith drew in her breath sharply, drawing a curious glance from Miles. Slowly, he crossed his thick arms against his chest.

" 'Twill no' be necessary, Donagh, altho' I appreciate your offer," he said. "Ye know 'twill be safer to keep her here while ye make contact wi' the governor."

A flash of disappointment showed in Donagh's eyes, but he managed a tight smile. "As ye wish, Miles. I'll take the message to the governor. If all goes well, I should be back in two weeks' time."

Miles nodded. "Good, Donagh, because I'm most curious about the lass here. I think 'tis long past time that we found out just who she really is."

Chapter Nine

Faith declined the invitation to return to the Great Hall for the rest of her supper. Instead, she pleaded fatigue and was reluctantly permitted to return to her room, accompanied by an anxious Molly.

"Och, lass, are ye certain ye don't wish to have more to eat?" Molly fussed nervously. "Ye ate as little as a bird. I could have a tray sent up, if ye wish it."

Faith paced back and forth in her chamber, her mind whirling. "No, Molly, I'm not hungry. I just have to think, that's all. I need some time to sort things out."

"As ye wish."

Faith could feel Molly's worried gaze as she continued her pacing. "No one understands," she suddenly blurted out. "It is imperative that I be released at once."

Molly sighed. "Now don't fash yourself, lass. Everything will be all right. Miles will see to your welfare."

"I don't *need* Miles to see to my welfare," Faith snapped. "I *need* him to take me to the stone circles and put an end to this bizarre nightmare. For God's sake, I had a conversation with . . . with Donagh O'Rourke tonight. Do you know who he is?"

"Miles's neighbor," Molly offered helpfully.

"No," Faith exploded, resuming her furious pacing. "He's apparently the ancestor of . . . of . . . oh, Christ, forget it. I have to get a hold on myself."

Before Molly could comment there was an abrupt knock on the door. Molly called out permission to enter and the door swung open. Standing in the entrance was the middle-aged priest Faith had seen seated at dinner. He held a long wooden box under his arm.

"Good evening, ladies," he said politely. "I'm sorry to interrupt. I wondered whether I might have a word with the

Englishwoman.'' He directed his question to Molly, as if she were Faith's guardian.

"Well, what do ye say, lass?'' Molly asked, giving Faith an inquiring look. "Do ye feel well enough?''

"Why not?'' Faith said cynically, sweeping her hand across the room. "My prison is your prison.''

The priest showed no offense at her tone and instead calmly entered the chamber. Molly picked up the tray of untasted tea and carried it toward the door. "I'll be back later,'' she said to Faith over her shoulder. "Enjoy the father's company.''

Faith and the priest stood staring at each other until Faith realized he was waiting for her to speak. "Sit down,'' she said, motioning him to a chair near the fireplace and then seating herself. "Miles has spoken of you. Why are you here? Do you wish me to confess my numerous sins, or have you come to read me my last rites?''

The priest laughed, his friendly blue-gray eyes sparkling. "I can see that Miles did no' exaggerate in his description o' ye. Ye have a sharp wit and a bonny face. Nay, lass, I've no' come to read ye your last rites, nor to hear a confession. I simply wanted to meet ye.''

Faith looked suspiciously at the long wooden box he now held in his hands. "Then what do you have there? Some kind of torture device?''

The priest put the box on a nearby table and opened it. Carefully, he pulled out several intricately carved wooden chess pieces and set them to the side.

"Chess?'' Faith asked in surprise.

"Do ye know how to play, lass?''

Faith smiled in spite of herself. "I do. My mum taught me. I used to play quite often when I was young. That is before she . . . passed on.''

Father Michael paused for a moment at the trace of pain in her voice but did not comment. Instead he continued to remove the pieces until the box was empty. With a flick of his wrists he turned over the box, revealing a chessboard. Deftly he began arranging the pieces on it. Faith watched him thoughtfully.

"Come now, why are you really here, Father? Did Miles ask you to question me?''

"He did no','' he replied firmly.

"I don't believe you."

"A man o' the cloth is forbidden to lie."

"Then why wile away the hours with a despicable English prisoner?"

The priest folded his hands together, the sleeves of his long robe brushing gently against the table. "I fear ye are hardly despicable. 'Twas just a feeling I got when I saw ye in the great chamber tonight; that's all. Ye seemed rather alone and troubled. When ye didn't return to the hall I thought ye might be in need o' someone to talk to."

"I pleaded fatigue, Father. That's why I didn't return."

"Did ye no' enjoy the company?"

Faith laughed, thinking of Arabella Dunbar and Donagh O'Rourke. "Honestly? Not much."

"I'm sorry to hear that. Would ye like me to leave?"

Faith sighed. "No, it's all right. I can't see any harm in playing a game of chess. In fact, I might rather enjoy the distraction."

"Are ye certain?"

"Actually, I am."

The priest nodded. "Then the first move is yours."

Faith bent her head over the board, studying it before she moved a pawn forward. "Do you live here in the castle?" she asked.

"Aye," Father Michael replied, lifting one of his own pawns and setting it down directly in front of Faith's. "I've been at Castle Dun na Moor for nearly twenty years."

"How many other people live here?"

"About three hundred, including the servants and their families."

"Three hundred!" Faith exclaimed, lifting her head from the board. "My God, where does everyone sleep?"

Father Michael looked at her strangely. "There is sufficient room for all who require a place."

Faith stared studiously at the chessboard, embarrassed by her obvious lack of knowledge about castles. "Oh, I see. Does that include the Lady Arabella Dunbar?" She was mortified to feel her cheeks warm.

The priest's pale eyebrows rose slightly. "Nay. She is the daughter of Lord Thomas Dunbar of Castle Craigh. The Dunbars own land to the west o' Castle Dun na Moor. They and the O'Bruaidars have been allies for nearly one hundred years. Lady Arabella recently became Miles's betrothed. The two families saw need to strengthen their alliance in face o' increasing English presence in the area.''

Faith felt her stomach flip strangely at the news of Miles's engagement. Now she understood why the woman was so possessive of Miles. Quickly, Faith moved another of her pawns forward. "Tell me more about Miles."

"What do ye wish to know?"

"Is it true that he does not know how to read?"

Father Michael lifted his head at her question, clearly puzzled. "That surprises ye?"

"I suppose it shouldn't," she answered quietly. "Doesn't he wish to learn?"

"What would be the purpose?"

"Then he wouldn't need you to read to him. He could read for himself."

" 'Tis no burden for me to read to him, lass. I rather enjoy the responsibility."

"But he could do it himself with a little instruction," she commented softly. "You could help him."

"Ye disapprove o' our ways?" He looked genuinely baffled.

"It's really none of my business."

"Perhaps no', but your disapproval is intriguing."

"Then forget I ever said anything. I'm not interested in becoming involved in the affairs of this castle. Why should I care what happens to Miles? After all, he is the one who holds me in this castle against my will."

The priest lowered his head, studying the board. "Ye know very little about Miles. He is a just and fair man."

"Does he make it a practice to abduct whoever may stumble onto his land?"

"Only those who are English."

"I see. How fortunate for me."

Father Michael raised an eyebrow at Faith's sharp tone and looked at her steadily across the table. "Ye should not think ill o' him. He is a most honorable man. If ye are no' a spy for the English, ye have naught to fear from him."

Faith was silent for a long moment. "And if I am?" she finally asked quietly.

Father Michael lifted a pale eyebrow thoughtfully. "Then ye shall deserve his wrath. But have a care, my lady, for Miles O'Bruaidar is no' a man easily fooled."

Faith stood alone at the open window of her chamber, wrapped in a wool blanket from the bed to ward off the chill, and stared up into the night. The golden moon hung in the sky, bathing the countryside in a soft, soothing light. The sky was clear; the stars sparkled like jewels. As she stared at the familiar objects, she again wondered how it had come to pass that she was living in a different century . . . a prisoner to a fate that was not her own. Events were happening so quickly, she barely had time to sort them out, let alone reflect on how they affected her situation.

For instance, what had been the purpose of Father Michael's visit? Had he been trying to warn her . . . or had he been searching for information of his own? Strangely enough, he had seemed content to let her ask all the questions, not hesitating to tell her about people at the castle. If he had truly come to question her, he had done a miserable job of it. On the other hand, he had turned out to be rather engaging company. A strange lot, these people at Castle Dun na Moor.

In any case, Faith had no intention of waiting around for the return of Donagh O'Rourke. The priest's visit had only further convinced her to put a plan of escape into motion. After all, she was a trained professional, and she'd be damned if she'd sit around until Donagh returned to announce that no one had ever heard of the strange Englishwoman. Besides, she didn't have enough knowledge to determine whether or not her actions in this time were already affecting the outcome of events in the future. *Her future.* She couldn't permit herself to become involved in happenings that might inadvertently change history as she knew it. Nor could she afford to wait another day to make her escape. She would make an all-out effort this night.

Again her eyes scanned the courtyard for signs of activity. It was empty save for a lone guard, who paced about restlessly. Earlier Faith had seen two guests stroll out through the courtyard and into the gardens, apparently wishing to have a breath of fresh air. But that had been at least two hours ago, and they had long ago returned to the warmth and safety of the castle. As Faith had witnessed no mass exodus of guests, she assumed they would be staying the night at the castle. She hoped that would work to her advantage. The more people there were in the castle, the more confusing it would be to find her when they finally discovered she was missing.

Determinedly, she moved away from the window and tossed the blanket from her shoulders onto the bed. Dressed in the simple gown of yellow, minus the petticoats and corset, she felt almost human again. It was time to put her plan into action.

Recalling a trick from her younger days, she quickly stuffed plumped pillows on the bed beneath the covers to make it appear as if she was sleeping. Then she blew out all the candles and banked the fire until only a little light came from the hearth. Picking up a small but sturdy log, she wished herself good luck and moved behind the door.

Opening her mouth, she issued a pained groan. When she heard no response she frowned and then groaned again, this time louder and more theatrically.

"My lady," she finally heard the guard posted outside her door call out anxiously, "are ye all right in there?"

Encouraged by his interest, Faith moaned again. This time the guard opened the door a crack and looked in. Holding her breath, Faith waited. When he finally stepped across the threshold and headed for her bed she lifted the log and brought it down on the back of his skull. With a surprised grunt, the man slumped to the floor.

Quickly, Faith shut the door and bent down, rolling him over and feeling for a pulse. She felt a twinge of guilt when she saw how young he was; no more than sixteen, she thought. Silently, she said a prayer, hoping he would recover with nothing more than a splitting headache.

Telling herself there was no use fretting over what had already been done, Faith dragged his body out of view to the far side of the bed. Deftly, she tied his hands and feet with the linen strips Molly had provided for her bandage. She was almost finished when he began to come around, so with a sigh of regret she gagged him as well.

Finally she snatched the wool blanket and threw it around her shoulders. She had yet to be provided with a cloak and she feared the wind would be bitingly cool. Her heart racing, she took a deep breath and slipped out into the corridor, closing the door softly behind her.

Cautiously, Faith felt her way down the dark hallway, pausing at the top of the stairway. There were murmured voices coming from below as she crept down the stairs, hugging the shadows until she could see who was speaking. The doors to the great chamber were open and a faint light flickered deep within. Creeping along the wall, she paused near one of the open doors. She could hear Miles's voice and felt an unexpected stab of satisfaction that he was not cozily bedded somewhere with Arabella.

"Aye, Furlong," he was saying, "we'll need to send a messenger to Ian, urging him to bring the supplies as early in the spring as he can. Ormonde must be informed o' the new developments as well."

The voices dropped and Faith frowned. Ormonde? Could they be speaking of the Marquis de Ormonde, the famous general who fought against Cromwell? Before she could further contemplate what sort of relationship Miles and the famous marquis might have, she heard Furlong speak.

"What about the English lass?"

Faith stiffened, pressing herself tighter against the wall. She prayed silently that no one would choose that moment to step out into the corridor.

"Och, the English will trade for her; I'm certain," Miles answered. "I'm more convinced than ever that she belongs to Cromwell." Their voices fell to a low murmur until Faith could not hear them any more.

How wrong you are, Miles O'Bruaidar, Faith thought wryly. *Haven't even met the man.* She had a strange urge to laugh at the growing absurdity of her situation, but fear and prudence kept the sound locked in her throat.

Lifting her gown, she darted quickly past the open door, hoping that no one had seen her. When she didn't hear an alarm she headed for a side door she had seen the servants use. Slipping out into the cool night, she avoided the courtyard and raced swiftly across the grass, coming to a crouch behind

141

a few flowering shrubs. She knew the most dangerous part of her escape was yet to come, as she had to slip undetected past the guardhouse. The walls were far too formidable for her to scale, and besides, she had no rope. She had already determined her best chance for escape would be through the gatehouse and into the forest. She only needed a diversion, something that would momentarily take the guards' attention off the gate.

She quickly analyzed the possibilities, her eyes falling upon a small torch flickering outside the stables. A plan abruptly clicked into place. Stealthily, she crept closer to the stables, shrugging out of the blanket and lifting a corner of it to the flames. Once it had caught fire, she set it down in the grass and darted back into the shadows. In moments the smoke and fire had caught the attention of the guards. Shouting, they came running from the guardhouse. As a group of them ran past her location, Faith lifted her skirts and shot past the guardhouse and through the gate, running as fast as her leg would permit. Faintly, she heard someone shout from behind her and feared she had been spotted. Gasping for air, she finally reached the edge of the forest, stumbling into the welcoming darkness and taking a moment to catch her breath before plunging on.

She stopped only once more to tear her gown up the front, making it easier for her to run. She had already decided to head for the village, hoping she could persuade someone to take her to the Druid ruins. Fighting back panic, she pushed on, ignoring the painful ache in her leg and the dry taste of fear in her mouth.

She stumbled upon the village almost by accident, crashing through the bushes and into the village clearing. Several men jumped up from their pallets around the fire, drawing their swords. As their voices raised in alarm, women came running from the shacks, some carrying children, others peeking out from behind the doors of the huts.

"I need your help," Faith said quickly, her breath coming in short, quick gasps of fear. "Can someone take me to the stone circles? Haste is of the essence."

The villagers simply looked at her, their mouths agape. She was barefoot and without a cloak, her dress was torn scandalously up the front and she had no corset or petticoats. Faith also knew she looked desperate and afraid, both of which, she supposed, were not terribly inspiring.

"Please," she pleaded anxiously.

Scanning the crowd, she saw the young village boy, Kevin. A big, burly man, presumably his father, stood behind him, his hands placed lightly on the lad's shoulders. Concerned by her desperation, the man stepped forward. "Are ye in some kind o' distress, my lady?" he asked.

"Actually, I am," Faith replied, looking over her shoulder. "I'm being held against my will and it's all a mistake. I beg you to take me to the site at once."

Before he could answer, a horse abruptly crashed into the clearing. Panicked, Faith uttered a small cry and whirled around, instinctively searching her waist for a weapon. When she came up empty she clenched her hands at her side in frustration.

A large man sat astride the horse staring at her, his face hidden by the hood of a cloak. Without provocation, Faith felt the hairs on her arms rise.

The stranger dismounted, his booted legs hitting the ground with a heavy thud. As he strode purposefully toward her, a strange hush fell over the villagers. The night was so quiet that Faith could hear the faint hoot of an owl and a crackle from the fires.

"I'll assume responsibility for the lady now," the man spoke suddenly, causing Faith to jump in surprise. His accent was Irish and strangely familiar.

"She'll be coming wi' me." He gripped her hard around the soft flesh of her upper arm, his fingers digging into her skin.

"No," Faith cried, trying to pull away. As she struggled against his hold, his hood fell partially away from his head. The moonlight danced across bold, familiar features and thick red beard.

Faith immediately froze, her heart skipping a full beat. "My God," she whispered when she found her voice. "Paddy O'Rourke . . . you are here, *too*." For a split second she experienced two staggering emotions—an overwhelming relief to see someone from her own time and abject fear that he was a dangerous assassin.

143

Paddy twisted her arm behind her back with a hard jerk, shoving her back against him. "Aye, I'm here, and it looks like the tables have turned since we last met. Now, let me give ye a piece o' simple advice. Stop struggling or I'll shoot ye." Faith felt something cold and hard press into the small of her back.

Oh, Christ, he had a gun. A gun from the twentieth century.

"Let's take a little walk to my horse," Paddy instructed softly. "Smile for the country folk, will ye?"

When she didn't move he pressed the gun painfully against her spine. "I said, now," he growled. "Or I'll shoot them as well."

"You'd shoot your own countrymen?"

"If it gets me what I want. And right now I want ye on that horse."

"All right," Faith said softly. "There is no need for anyone to get hurt."

They moved slowly toward the horse, Paddy guiding her with a steel grip on her upper arm. When they reached the animal he indicated with a jerk of his head that she was to mount. Silently, Faith pulled herself up into the saddle, holding tightly to the horse's mane. Paddy mounted swiftly behind her. Faith saw the villagers were watching them with wide and curious eyes. She fell back against Paddy with a jolt, as he pulled hard on the reins, turning the horse around and guiding it into the forest.

"So, my little English spy," he said softly when they were out of sight of the villagers. "We meet again. It seems that fate keeps throwing us together."

Chapter Ten

"How did you find me?" Faith asked between gritted teeth as Paddy guided the horse through the dense undergrowth.

"I had rather hoped to see ye at dinner, but by the time I arrived ye had already retired for the evening."

Faith twisted around in the saddle. "Dinner? You mean to say that you've been at Miles's castle all along?"

He chuckled softly. "Oh, so it's Miles to ye, is it? No, I wasn't staying at O'Bruaidar's castle. However, I was an invited guest at his dinner tonight."

Faith stiffened. "I find that hard to believe. Where did you get the horse and the clothes? Ambush a nobleman?"

Paddy pulled hard on the reins, bringing the horse to an abrupt stop. "Well, lass . . . or should I say Faith, if that indeed is your real name? I think it's time we had a little talk."

Faith shivered, chilled by the cool wind and the underlying threat in his words. "About what?"

"Leave it to an Englishwoman to understate the obvious," he snorted. "For Christ's sake, we are living in the seventeenth century. That's worth a wee bit o' discussion, is it no'?"

"You tell me."

Paddy growled in annoyance. "Damn all women for their stubbornness. Get off the horse, but don't try anything adventurous."

Faith shook her head stubbornly. "Forget it, O'Rourke. Why should I cooperate until I know what you are going to do with me?"

He gave her an unexpected shove that sent her tumbling from the horse. She managed to grab the side of the saddle and keep herself upright, but the shock of her legs hitting the ground sent a fresh wave of pain searing across her bruised thigh. "Christ, was that really necessary?" she gasped in agony.

The burly Irishman grunted and then dismounted. "Ye expect me to show mercy to a woman who tried to kill me?"

"Oh, that's calling the kettle black."

"Shut up and sit down," he ordered, motioning to a rotten log. When she hesitated he pulled the gun out from beneath his cloak and pointed it at her.

Sighing, Faith dutifully sat. Paddy found a seat nearby and lowered his burly frame onto another log across from her. "So, how did we get here?" he asked.

"How am I supposed to know?" she snapped. "Do I look like a physicist?"

He frowned. "Well, the last thing I remember is trying to reach your gun. I heard ye call my name and then fire at me."

"Yes. Unfortunately, I bloody well missed."

He ignored her comment. "I felt a strange tingling sensation in my legs and arms. And then I was falling. The next thing I remember is waking up with a splitting headache. You were lying no' far from me on the ground, my gun right beside ye. 'Twas a fortunate stroke o' luck for me, I suppose."

Faith pursed her lips. "Then I presume it was you who rifled through my pockets."

"Och, had ye treasures in your pockets? Nay, lass, 'twasn't me."

"Then why didn't you kill me?"

"Would ye believe me if I told ye I had a change of heart?"

"No," she answered wryly.

"All right, then; I heard someone coming. I didn't have time to figure out what had happened to us, let alone look through your pockets. The fact o' the matter was that I barely had time to take my gun and melt into the shadows. Believe me, I had no desire to meet an English welcoming party."

"That's when you decided to head home to O'Rourke Castle?"

"Why shouldn't I? It's my home, after all. Only along the way the forest seemed denser than I remembered. But it wasn't until I saw O'Rourke Castle that I was struck by what had happened. Everything was the same, except it was different. When I discovered that Donagh O'Rourke was the owner o' the castle I realized that I had somehow traveled back in time. Christ almighty, I have a portrait o' the old bastard and the

146

twisted scar over his lip hanging above the mantel. 'Twas lucky for me that I possess the unmistakable features o' the O'Rourke clan. I simply passed myself off as a distant cousin who decided to visit my long-lost kin. A small fabrication about a band o' robbers that had set upon me during my journey was enough to earn me a new batch of clothing and a mount o' my own. What I was really buying was time until I could figure out what had happened to me.''

Faith pondered his story for a moment, seeing how he might have pulled it off. ''Very clever, O'Rourke. But how did you know I was at Miles's castle?''

''A messenger from Castle Dun na Moor brought word to Donagh that a strangely dressed English spy had been caught on O'Bruaidar land. I wasn't certain 'twas ye, but I thought it merited a closer look. I asked if I could accompany Donagh to the castle and he agreed. But he rode on ahead o' me and the others. As embarrassing as it was, I couldn't keep up. It's been some time since I'd been on a horse, ye see.''

''How did you manage to follow me now?''

''Oh, I'd been trying to think o' a way to get into your room all night long. I'd finally decided to physically remove the guard outside your door, but when I arrived at your room it was completely unguarded. I slipped into your room and found the guard bound and gagged. Curious, I went to the window and saw a small fire flare up near the stables. I figured 'twas ye, up to mischief, and that ye had probably started it as a way to distract the guards from the gate. Running out to the stables, I secured a mount and headed out just in time to see ye dart into the trees. From there ye left a trail so obvious, a child could have followed it.''

Faith recalled her hasty flight through the trees and figured he was probably right. ''Which means the others will soon be looking for me.''

Paddy grinned. ''Ah, but I found ye first. Now I have only to determine what to do with ye.''

''You sound suspiciously cheerful.''

''Well, the truth of the matter is, when I first discovered that by some freak o' nature I had traveled back in time, I damn near shot myself. That was, o' course, before I realized

147

that this might be the golden opportunity I had sought all my life.''

Faith lifted her head sharply. "What sort of opportunity?"

"Need ye ask? In seventeenth-century Ireland I possess a priceless commodity: the knowledge of events to come. Yet in our time I am little more than one man among many, looking for a way to rid Ireland o' her English oppressors. In our time my success will always be limited, dictated by the historical events o' the past, which have already shaped the future. But now, in this time, the history I know is not yet written."

His voice had dropped to a revered hush, and Faith felt a wave of apprehension sweep through her. "Careful, O'Rourke," she warned. "We don't have any idea what we're playing with here. Christ, we don't even know how we got here."

Paddy waved his hand dismissively. "I don't care how it happened, lass. Unlike ye, I have no wish to look a gift horse in the mouth. I want only to take charge of the destiny which has been given to me."

"This was an accident, O'Rourke. We don't know what might happen next. We might not even exist."

To her surprise, he leaned over and slapped her hard across the face. The metallic taste of blood filled her mouth. Dazed, Faith reached up to touch her bruised and swelling lip.

"Did ye feel that, lass?" he asked softly. "If we don't exist, then why can we feel pain?"

She dropped her hand and stared at him steadily. "You know I can't answer that. I only think it prudent to return to our own time before anything else happens here. For Christ's sake, something is bloody wrong with all of this. We don't belong here."

"Ah, but that is where we differ, lass. I believe I've been brought here for a reason. I'm not going back. Not now, when there's the chance to put things right—to remake the history o' Ireland."

"Jesus, O'Rourke, you're scaring me."

Her words seemed to please him for he smiled widely, his white teeth gleaming in the moonlight. ":Hmm, let's see who's running England now . . ." he mused. "Oh yes, King Charles. Odious man. But no need to kill him—his own Parliament will do away wi' his head soon enough.'' He laughed, amused with himself. ''Ah, but then we have Oliver Cromwell. Oh, what satisfaction it would be to rid the earth o' that pious bastard.''

''No,'' Faith exclaimed, her pulse leaping erratically. ''Listen to yourself. A political assassination in the seventeenth century? It's deranged. We have no idea what would be the consequences of changing history as we know it. As it is, every day we stay in this time increases the risk of involving us improperly. We have to figure out a way to get back to our own time.''

''Shut up,'' Paddy snarled, pointing the gun at her. ''Shut up or I'll shoot you.''

Faith clasped her hands in her lap, forcing herself to control the shivers that racked her body. She knew full well that he could effectively carry out an assassination. He was a professional with a handgun and a silencer in a time where such things had not yet been invented. He was also equipped with knowledge of the future and a fair understanding of Ireland's history. If he really wanted to assassinate Cromwell, he could bloody well pull it off.

''What are you going to do with me?'' she asked, her voice surprisingly calm.

He rose to his feet slowly. ''It's a pity, but I'm afraid I'll have to kill ye. Can't have you interfering wi' my plans. O' course I'll have to make it look like it was an accident. There's a lake just beyond the trees; I passed it on my way to O'Bruaidar's castle.''

''Lough Emy,'' Faith said, her mouth going dry. ''Look, don't be stupid, O'Rourke; you all but kidnapped me in front of the entire village.''

''Ah, yes,'' he conceded, ''but no one saw my face clearly and no one can identify me. Besides, most of them will have forgotten me by the time your body is found. These days it probably takes weeks, even months, before a body at the bottom of a lake is found. Perhaps they'll not even be able to identify you. I suppose it isn't so exact a science these days.''

Before he finished the sentence Faith leapt up and crashed into the bushes. She cursed as she tripped over a log, falling heavily to the ground. Before she could scramble to her feet she heard O'Rourke shout and fall on top of her, his body crushing the air out of her lungs.

Faith's fingers curled into the damp and pungent earth an instant before a crashing pain hit her on the back of the head and her world exploded into blackness.

"The lass has escaped," Furlong announced breathlessly, running to the front of the castle where Miles stood, watching his men putting out the small fire in the grass. "She knocked Dennis o'er the head and trussed him up as neatly as a cooked goose. 'Tis likely she who set the fire. One o' the mounts is missing, but the stable boy said it was taken by a guest. The lass has surely fled on foot."

Miles frowned angrily. "Send some of the men to search the castle and the grounds. Then have the rest o' the men saddle up and spread out. If she has left the castle grounds, she couldn't have gone far."

"Aye," Furlong agreed, moving off to do Miles's bidding.

Furiously, Miles strode to the stables, securing a mount for himself and galloping off toward the forest. Behind him, he heard the rest of his men scrambling to follow. When he reached the forest edge he slid off his horse and examined the bushes and broken limbs. From what he could determine there was a clear trail heading south toward the village. What bothered him more was the fresh set of hoofprints following her. Grimly, he remounted, slapping his reins on the horse to urge it forward.

When he reached the village a woman raced up to meet him. "Me lord," she said breathlessly, "a woman was here just moments ago. 'Twas the same woman yer lordship brought to our village when ye returned me lad, Kevin. She said she was in distress, being held against her will."

"Where is she now?" Miles asked briskly, looking around.

"Another man came and took her, yer lordship. But I don't think she wished to go wi' him."

"What man?"

"I don't know. I couldn't see his face."

Miles swore softly under his breath. "Which way did they go?"

The woman lifted her hand, pointing into the forest. Briskly nodding his thanks, Miles jerked on his reins, guiding his horse into the trees. He stopped only once to examine the trail. It was fresh and the hoofprints deep, indicating that there were, indeed, two riders on one horse.

Who had taken her? Miles wondered, remounting his horse. Was one of his guests responsible for spiriting her away? The mystery of the horse missing from his stables and the hoofprints pointing toward the village was suspicious enough. But why had the villagers thought she hadn't wanted to go with this rider? What in the devil was going on?

In minutes Miles realized the trail headed directly for Lough Emy. As he neared the lake, he dismounted within the shelter of the forest, giving his steed a quiet and reassuring pat on the nose. Stepping quietly into the shadows, Miles threaded the rest of the way through the trees, his hand resting ready on the hilt of his sword. As he crept closer to the clearing, he saw a hooded figure at the bank of the lake. The figure was dragging something heavy along the ground.

By the rod o' Christ, it looked like a body.

Before Miles could move, the figure lifted the load, swung mightily and dropped it out into the water. There was a muffled splash before the hooded figure turned, walking away from the edge of the lake.

"What the devil?" Miles roared, drawing his sword and racing from the forest edge. "Halt there, I say!"

Startled, the figure froze in his tracks. Then, giving a small cry, he whirled around and began to run, his dark cloak swirling around his booted legs.

For a moment Miles hesitated, debating whether to pursue the mysterious figure or go after whatever had been dropped into the lake. Glancing back at the water, Miles cursed once before dropping his sword, tearing off his cloak and charging directly into the lake.

Chapter Eleven

As the chilling shock of the water closed around him, Miles called himself a fool—a bloody idiotic fool. What in the devil was he doing? The water was freezing; cold enough to suck the air from his lungs and damn near cold enough to stop his heart. Besides, he had no idea what had been dropped into the water. For all he knew it could have been a peasant disposing of a dead animal. In the meantime the Englishwoman was escaping. Spluttering, Miles surfaced and took a deep breath.

"Is anyone there?" he shouted, his eyes scanning the surface. It was unlikely that even with the aid of the bright moon he would find what he was looking for. Lough Emy was notoriously deep and possessive of those things she claimed as her own.

When there was no answer he started to dive again when he heard a faint spluttering noise. "Miles?" came a weak answer.

Not far from him, Miles saw a small black shape floundering in the water. "Faith?" he shouted, his heart leaping to his throat. "By all the gods, are ye all right, lass?"

When she did not answer he began to swim furiously in her direction. "Hold on, I'm almost there," he called out reassuringly, his powerful arms cutting rapidly through the water.

Finally he touched her. She was gasping in short breaths, apparently struggling to stay above the water. In the reflection of the moonlight off the water, her eyes looked glazed and panicked. When he made contact with her hand she practically threw herself into his arms, clutching his neck and nearly taking them both under. Firmly, Miles slipped his left arm around her.

"Don't fight me, lass, or ye'll drown us both," he warned, spitting out a mouthful of water. She immediately stilled and Miles felt a stir of wonder that she trusted him so completely.

Holding them both up, he began to swim toward the bank. She wasn't terribly heavy, but after only a minute Miles felt as though he'd been swimming for an hour. The cold water was sapping his strength, and he wasn't used to swimming fully clothed and in heavy boots. Gritting his teeth, he continued his strokes until he felt the bottom of the lake beneath his feet. Pulling himself up and dragging Faith from the water, he collapsed on the bank, rolling to his side and pulling her into his arms.

"Ye are safe now, lass," he murmured, kissing the top of her head as she shivered in his embrace. "Ye've naught to fear. I'm here." Pressing her face against his chest, he held her close, trying to warm her body with his.

"He t-tied s-stones around m-my neck," she sobbed. "B-but the cold water m-must have r-revived me. I g-got them off, b-but I could have d-drowned. N-no one would h-have known."

Miles stroked her wet hair. "Hush now, 'tis all o'er. There'll be no drowning tonight."

A crack of a branch sounded near them and Miles lifted his head quickly, realizing too late that he was without his sword and too damn tired to lift it even if he had it.

"Ye found her, did ye, Miles?"

The voice was familiar and Miles breathed a sigh of relief. "Damnation, what took ye so long, Furlong?"

The hawk-nosed man stepped out of the shadows with Shaun Gogarty close on his heels. Both men had their swords drawn, but they sheathed them quickly when they saw their lord.

"By all the saints," the dwarf gasped, kneeling beside Miles and Faith. "What the devil happened here?"

Propping himself up on one elbow, Miles frowned grimly. "I'll explain it later. Just fetch a cloak for the lass and let's return to the castle at once. There's something very peculiar going on here."

Miles paced in front of the blazing hearth in the library, loosely holding a glass of whiskey in his hand. He had changed into a dry robe, but his dark hair still clung in damp curls to the back of his neck. Furlong and Shaun sat uneasily in their chairs, watching their lord walk back and forth in frustration.

Their heads turned as the door opened abruptly and Father Michael walked in. "How is she?" Miles asked. "Will she be all right?"

Father Michael nodded. "Aye, she'll survive. 'Tis lucky that ye were there, Miles. She had enough water in her lungs to fill a small barrel. But Molly has given her a draught and is staying wi' her."

"I'm telling ye, someone deliberately tossed her into the lake," Miles exploded, clenching the glass angrily in his fist. "He was cloaked and I couldn't see his face. But he threw her into the water and calmly walked away as if he had just disposed o' a rotten animal."

Furlong scratched his head in wonder. "But who would want to kill the lass?"

Miles lifted his hands impatiently. "I don't know. But she has taken more violence to her person than I care to imagine. Have we determined who secured the missing mount?"

Shaun nodded. "Aye, 'twas the kin o' Donagh O'Rourke. The stable boy said the man told him he had decided to return to O'Rourke Castle early to settle a matter o' a personal nature."

Miles frowned. "Furlong, send a man to O'Rourke Castle. I'd like to find out just what kind o' matter was so urgent it would send a man out in the middle o' the night."

Furlong nodded, rising to his feet and slipping out of the room. Miles took a long and thoughtful drink of his whiskey as a heavy silence descended on the room.

"How much longer before Donagh returns wi' his answer from the English governor?" Shaun spoke up, interrupting the pause. "Perhaps he'll bring the answers we seek."

Miles sighed, dropping heavily into the chair recently vacated by Furlong. "He shouldn't be but a week. God's wounds, I wish him haste, for I will no longer tolerate this kind o' activity on my land. No' only that, but the lass had better be ready to finally answer some o' my questions."

"I'd advise ye to be gentle wi' her," Father Michael cautioned, running his fingers through his wispy hair. "She's been terribly frightened. 'Tis likely that she'll no' be up to rigorous questioning.''

Miles exhaled deeply. "Aye, I know, Father. 'Tis only that I think o' her safety. If she'll no' tell me who she is and what she's doing here, how can I protect her?''

The men remained silent. Setting his glass on a nearby table, Miles stood and walked to the window. He jerked aside the drape and stared out at the rose-colored morning sky.

"Damnation, but I want answers," Miles murmured softly, "and 'tis long past time that I had them.''

Faith could smell the water; the damp, dark scent of swirling death. The foul wetness filled her nose and her mouth until she could no longer breathe; until her body welcomed the liquid into her lungs. It flowed inside her, replacing the blood in her veins, making her a part of the water forever. . . .

"No!" she gasped, sitting straight up in bed, her arms flailing. "Oh God, please, stop it.''

Strong, secure arms were around her in an instant. Faith immediately pressed into the embrace. From the reassuring scents of leather, smoke and oatmeal soap, she knew instantly it was Miles.

"Miles," she said, her voice muffled against his chest. "Thank God it's you.''

"Hush, lass," he replied. "Ye had a bad dream. 'Tis little wonder, seeing what ye have been through.''

"No, you don't understand. It isn't just that. My mum . . . she drowned. She was trying to save me and she drowned.'' She gave a soft, spluttering sound and clutched his shirt beneath her fingers.

Miles's arms tightened around her. "Hush, lass. I see now why ye have a fear o' the water. But ye survived and ye are safe.''

"I was so bloody frightened," she whispered. "If you hadn't been there . . .''

"But I was," he said quietly, nudging up her chin with his finger and thumb. His eyes were kind and compassionate. "Ye will be all right now.''

Tears filled her eyes, blurring her vision. "I'm so ashamed of my fear of water," she said softly. "For pity's sake, I'm an adult. I should be able to conquer this.''

"We all have fears, Faith. Ye have only to learn how to face them properly.''

"But I don't know how."

"Mayhap ye'll let me help ye sometime."

His words had a gentle emotional underpinning that went straight to Faith's heart and settled there. He seemed to know her inside and out, as if he could reach into her heart and heal the scars that had formed there. Now, as his strong arms settled around her, she felt buttressed from a world she did not understand and protected from those forces beyond her control. It was no longer just a physical attraction to him. As impossible as it was, she was falling in love, and falling hard.

Lowering her gaze, she saw the wrinkled mess she had made of his shirt. "I'm sorry about your shirt,'' she said, pulling away. "How long have you been here?''

He shrugged, rubbing his unshaven jaw with his hand. "Och, a wee bit, I suppose."

Looking over his shoulder, Faith saw an empty glass on the table and a discarded blanket in the chair by the hearth. The fire had burnt low in the grate, and from the state of his rumpled clothing she wondered if he had been sleeping in the chair.

"I'm surprised you even bothered to save me,'' she said. "You should have been angry enough to let me drown."

"Och, it crossed my mind,'' he jested, but his voice was rough and concerned. "Why did ye try to escape again?"

She sighed deeply, guilt, frustration and helplessness sweeping through her. "I think you know the answer. I was trying to return home."

"Do ye no' believe I'll see ye there?"

"You can't,'' Faith replied softly.

"Ye know little about me, lass."

"Yes, that's true. But I also know that you can't help me. Not with this.'' She pressed her hand to the back of her neck, where a nasty lump served as a reminder of how much trouble she was in. "Christ, I've made a royal screw-up of things.''

Miles reached out, taking her hand from her injury and curling his strong fingers over hers. "What happened?''

Her brow furrowed. "It's rather simple, really. I tried to

escape and I failed. I'm sorry about the guard. I hope he's all right.''

"Dennis is fine, altho' understandably embarrassed by what happened.''

"I didn't want anyone to get hurt.''

"Then who dared to harm ye?''

Faith hesitated, not wanting to name Paddy O'Rourke, knowing that accusing a man from a powerful Irish family would only raise more questions than she could afford to answer. Besides, if it came down to her word against Paddy's, who would Miles be more likely to believe? An Englishwoman who had already twice tried to escape his castle and whom he suspected of being a Cromwell spy, or an Irishman, kin to one of his neighbors? She wanted to trust him but knew it simply wasn't possible.

"I don't know who it was,'' she lied. "It was dark and I couldn't see him properly. He captured me at the village and then knocked me over the head and tried to drown me.''

She could see that he didn't believe her. The muscle in his jaw tightened and his mouth formed a hard, firm line. She could hardly blame him for not believing her, but what alternative did she have? Admit that she was an English agent from the twentieth century who had somehow traveled 348 years into the past? After such a confession she would most certainly be burned at the stake or stoned to death. Or perhaps even drowned . . . but this time with the whole castle looking on and cheering.

She shivered at the thought. What she really needed was time to think and determine what she would do now that she knew Paddy O'Rourke was on the loose in the seventeenth century with a gun and apparent intentions to kill Oliver Cromwell. God almighty, how in good conscience could she go back to her own time now, leaving this century at the mercy of a madman?

"Faith?''

She lifted her head quickly, wondering how long she had been lost in her thoughts. "I'm sorry; did you say something?''

"I asked why someone would want to kill ye.''

She ached to trust him—to tell him the truth. "I . . . I don't know," she finally said.

He swore fiercely under his breath before angrily rising to his feet. "Damnation, lass, why are ye lying to me?"

"I'm not—" she started, but Miles furiously cut her off.

"Why in God's name would ye want to protect the identity o' a man who tried to kill ye? Do ye understand what happened to ye last night, Faith? Ye could have died."

Faith closed her eyes to his anger. "I understand fully," she said softly. "Believe me, Miles, if there were more I could tell you, I would. I don't know how to make you understand."

"If ye don't talk to me lass, I can't protect ye."

"I know," she said miserably. The fragile emotional bond that had stretched between them seemed to have disappeared. Once again they were enemies, at odds with one another. A strange heaviness settled in her chest.

Miles crossed his arms and stared coolly at her. "Is this how ye wish to leave it, Faith? After all that has happened, ye still refuse to tell me who ye are and what ye are doing here?"

"I don't want to leave it this way, but I have no choice," Faith whispered, feeling the chill between them grow and thicken. "If there were any alternative, I would take it. But there isn't."

For a moment he studied her intently, his green eyes piercing hers. Then he turned sharply on his heel and headed for the door. He yanked it open with one hard pull.

"Miles, wait," she called out softly.

He paused in the doorway, his back still toward her. "Aye?"

"I want to thank you again for saving me. You didn't have to risk your life on my behalf."

He gave a short laugh, but there was no humor, only a harsh, uneven strain to his voice. "Aye, but I did," he said quietly.

"I don't understand."

"I know. 'Tis what makes it even more damnably hard." He crossed the threshold and pulled the door shut behind him with a loud bang.

After he left Faith pulled her legs to her chest and unhappily wrapped her arms around her knees.

"Damn you, Miles O'Bruaidar," she whispered softly. "Why do you do this to me? Just when I think I can manage without you, I realize I need you more than ever."

Chapter Twelve

Two more days passed and there was still no sign of Donagh O'Rourke. Faith thought them to be the most frustrating two days of her life. Confined to her room with extra guards posted outside, she paced the chamber like a caged animal. What was worse was knowing that while she sat locked in this godforsaken castle, Paddy O'Rourke was somewhere out roaming about Ireland or England, plotting the death of one of the most well-known political figures of the seventeenth century. She had to do something to get out of this castle, and soon.

She had been released from her room only once, for supper in the Great Hall last night, but Miles had been conspicuously absent. When Faith asked Shaun where he was, the dwarf told her that Miles often preferred to dine alone.

Yet she wondered just how alone Miles really was. Arabella Dunbar still remained as a guest at the castle and had also been absent from dinner last night. On two other occasions Faith had seen the woman prance about the courtyard on a white stallion, her crimson cloak and thick chestnut hair streaming out behind her. She both acted and looked like a queen, dressed in breathtaking gowns and giving orders with a haughty air. It bothered Faith to no end that every man in her presence seemed dutifully awed.

Including Miles.

So what? Faith thought angrily. Why did it matter how Arabella Dunbar acted? Lest she forget, Arabella was Miles's betrothed, and the inhabitants of Castle Dun na Moor would soon be hers to rule. She shouldn't give a damn what the two of them did. Besides, if things went her way, she'd be out of here soon, leaving Miles O'Bruaidar far behind. It would be better that way. She didn't belong here, and emotional entanglements would only be a nuisance when she finally determined how to return to her own time.

"They probably deserve each other," she muttered, plopping into a chair and picking up Molly's unfinished mending. She wasn't any great shakes at sewing, but anything was better than brooding about her feelings for Miles. Her stitches began to come in slow, concentrated strokes when she heard a knock on the door.

"Come in," Faith called out, not even bothering to lift her head from her mending.

"Am I intruding?" a deep voice asked.

Looking up from her cozy seat in front of the hearth, Faith saw Miles lounging casually in the doorway. He was dressed in a long-sleeved shirt of white linen, black breeches and boots, his muscular forearm resting against the wooden doorframe. His dark hair hung unhindered to his shoulders and his green eyes stared at her steadily without a trace of the anger she had last seen in them. Not having seen him for two days, Faith realized with a start that she had sorely missed his company. Carefully, she set aside the gown and rose to her feet.

"No, you are not intruding," she said quickly, her heart skipping a beat. "To tell you the truth, I'd rather welcome some company. I'm not much good at mending."

Dropping his arm from the doorframe, Miles entered the chamber. As he approached her, Faith noticed that he held a slim leather-bound volume in his hand.

"What's that?" Faith asked, pointing at the book.

He held up the book to her with a flick of his tanned wrist. " 'Tis the volume o' poetry ye were reading earlier. 'Tis my only book in English. Ye see, Father Michael is at the village tonight, conducting a wedding, and I thought that since ye hadn't been out o' your chamber much ye might wish for some company."

Faith smiled, the contours of her face softening. "Would you like me to read it to you?"

He lifted a dark eyebrow expressively. "Nay, I'd like ye to read it *with* me. I know most o' the poems by heart."

Touched by his quiet pride, Faith reached out and took the book from his hand. Their fingers brushed, and for a moment she simply stared at him, warmed by the contact. Faith dropped her gaze first, moving back a step and holding the book against her chest.

"We'll read the poems together then," she said, sitting down in the chair and waiting for him to do the same.

Yet instead of joining her, he bent down on one knee in front of the hearth, lifting the fire iron from against the hearth and gently stirring the logs.

"Ye may start when ye are ready, lass," he said, without turning to look at her.

Faith took the opportunity to stare at his handsome profile and the way the firelight shimmered off his dark hair. He had already become familiar to her; the straight line of his nose, the firm cast of his jaw and the thoughtful intelligence about his green eyes. It was odd, but in spite of Miles's imposing size, she had never been intimidated physically by him. She could only remember the heat of his mouth against hers and the way he held her tightly on the bank of the lake, whispering comforting endearments in her ear.

"Ye are safe now, lass. I'm here."

The truth was that she *did* feel safe when he was around. For most of her life she had been self-sufficient and independent. She had learned to rely on herself and no one else. But in seventeenth-century Ireland she felt adrift and lost . . . like the frightened and helpless child she had been in the days after her mother died. Now, much like then, she wished for someone to give her strength and advice. She needed Miles's friendship and companionship more than she cared to admit. But what did she really know about this man?

Looking down at the leather-bound book in her lap, Faith lightly ran her hand across the binding. Books in this century were very expensive and considered a rare treasure. That Miles had purchased or commissioned seven of them meant he held them in high regard—a man who could not read but loved literature just the same.

"Pull a chair over by me," she said to him quietly. "I'll point out the words as I read them. As you already know the words by heart, it'll help you learn to recognize them by sight."

Miles looked over his shoulder curiously, a dark lock of hair falling over one eye. He brushed it aside with his long fingers, staring at her intently. "Ye wish to teach me to read?"

"Why not? Care to give it a try?"

He gazed at her for a moment longer before nodding. Standing, he dragged a chair toward her, positioning it to her left. Then he hooked his finger in the curve of an ornate candleholder, bringing the candle closer. Seating himself in the chair, he leaned on one elbow in her direction until his shoulder lightly touched hers.

His closeness was intoxicating, Faith thought distractedly, feeling warmth actually radiate from his large frame. He was every inch a man—from his broad shoulders to the iron-hard muscles of his thighs beneath his breeches. She felt a catastrophic weakening of the heart she was trying to steel against him.

I'm falling for him. God help me, I'm falling for a man engaged to another woman who was born more than three centuries before me.

Shaking her head, Faith opened the book. She chose a poem from the center of the volume. Angling the page toward the light of the candle, she began to read the flowing script softly.

> *"Do ye remember that night*
> *That ye were at the window,*
> *With neither hat nor gloves,*
> *Nor coat to shelter ye;*
> *And ye ardently grasped it,*
> *And I remained in converse with ye*
> *Until the lark began to sing?"*

She lowered the book, looking into his green eyes. "Now it is your turn. Except this time, instead of simply reciting from memory, I want you to say the poem slowly. I will put your finger under each word as you speak it. This way, you will come to recognize the words by the way they look and sound."

He nodded in understanding and she took his large hand in hers. It was warm and callused, presumably from years of use of the sword. Gently, she unfolded his index finger and placed it under the first word.

"Do ye remember . . ." he started to say, but she shook her head firmly.

"No, that is too fast," she said. "Recite it slowly."

"Do . . . ye . . . remember . . . that . . . night," he repeated haltingly, watching intently as she moved his finger beneath the words.

"Yes," Faith encouraged. "That's it. See, the first word is *do*. It is spelled D-O. That's how it looks when it is written."

"Do," Miles repeated softly, this time moving his own finger under the word. "Do . . . ye . . . remember . . . that . . . night." He bent closer to the page. "There are spaces between the words," he observed.

Faith smiled. "That's right. Now what about the next line?"

"That . . . ye . . . were . . . at . . . the . . . window."

Faith again moved his finger along the page, and Miles stared at the words for a long moment. " 'Tis odd, but these words look alike," he finally said, tracing his finger from the first line to the second."

"Yes," Faith said, nodding vigorously. "Repeat the two lines aloud and see which of the words you say more than once."

"Do ye remember that night, that ye were at the window." His brow creased. "I said 'that' and 'ye.' Those are the words I repeated." Looking down at the page, he concentrated as Faith slid her finger between the words *ye* and *that* in both the first and second lines.

"Aye, I see what ye mean," he said excitedly. "These words look the same. They *are* the same words."

He looked up at her with such triumph in his voice that Faith felt a funny clutch in her chest. "Yes; now say the next lines." She positioned his finger beneath the first word.

"Wi' . . . neither . . . hat . . . nor . . . gloves, nor . . . coat . . . to . . . shelter . . . ye," he recited, observing carefully as she moved his finger beneath the words.

This time he murmured the lines without her prodding, moving his own finger beneath the words. The first time he said the word *nor* he paused, staring at it for a long moment. Seemingly satisfied, he read on, until he spoke it the second time.

"I found the words myself," he said, throwing Faith a grin so charming that it took her breath away. "These are the words I repeated twice," he said, holding the candle closer to the page and peering at the words. His finger searched eagerly until it fell on the words *that* and *ye* and *nor*.

"You are a quick learner," Faith said quietly.

He bent down, setting the candle on the floor near the chair. Straightening, he slid his booted leg beneath him and turned to face her sideways. "And ye are a good teacher," he said softly.

Faith smiled. "Remember that recognizing the words is just a start. It'll only work for the text that you know by heart. In order to really read, you'll have to learn the letters. That way you can sound out the words you don't recognize."

He nodded thoughtfully. "Aye, lass, 'tis no' an easy task, I'm certain. But tonight ye showed me a wee bit o' magic. Those words came alive for me on the page."

Faith felt an odd rush of pleasure at his compliment. She had to admit it was rather magic, sitting side by side with a handsome, virile man in the warm glow of the fire, reciting poetry. "I'll be happy to work with you—at least for the duration of my stay," she said softly.

He reached out and lightly touched the top of her hand. "Ye are the most remarkable woman I've ever met. Everything ye do intrigues me. Even after our argument, I couldn't stop thinking about ye. I couldn't stay away." He lifted her hand and held it to his lips.

Faith closed her eyes, concentrating on the delicious sensations coursing through her body. She had never been wanton or loose, but she suddenly had an overwhelming urge to rip off her clothes and permit this handsome Irishman to ravish her right in front of the blazing fire. What did it matter that he was from a time more than 350 years before she was born? Why not simply look at it as an opportunity for reckless and delicious abandon? An exciting adventure she could savor later in private when she finally returned to her own time? This felt so right.

"Lass?" he asked softly.

Faith's eyes snapped open. Hastily, she snatched her hand away, her cheeks flaming guiltily. Had she lost her senses?

"Yes?" she replied, certain that he had been able to read her thoughts.

His eyes swept across her flushed cheeks. "Why do ye pull away from me? For what purpose do ye wish to deny this attraction between us?"

Faith laughed shakily. "I just don't want you to do something you might regret later."

"Something I might regret?" he asked, raising a dark eyebrow.

"Well, you do have a reputation to worry about—you are engaged, after all. My reputation . . . well, let's just say there aren't many people here who would give my reputation a passing thought."

He looked at her incredulously. "Ye are worried about *my* reputation?" he repeated in a strangled voice.

She waved her hand dismissively. "Look, let's be honest with each other. Once I'm gone you won't even miss me. This attraction between us, well . . . it's just temporary. So I'd rather not complicate matters, if you know what I mean." She looked away, nervously plucking at a stray thread in her skirt. "Don't look at me like that. I'm just trying to do what is best for both of us."

Miles blinked and then expelled a harsh breath. "Do ye really think ye know what is best for us, Faith?"

"Believe me, I do."

"Have ye no idea o' the pleasure we could share?"

Faith swallowed, refusing to meet his eyes. "I know what happens between a man and a woman. More or less, I mean." Her voice cracked with embarrassment. She reached up to touch her bangs, but mostly to hide the look of pure mortification on her face.

I sound like a bloody idiot. Why can't I just follow my instincts on this one?

Because you risk too much of yourself. He's a man from a different world—a different time. You were not meant to be with him. Better you understand that now than regret it later.

"Let's read another poem," she suggested brightly, looking down at the book on her lap.

Miles reached over with a firm hand and closed the book. His fingers rested lightly on her wrist. "Nay, lass, the hour is late and I fear I have stayed longer than I should."

Faith swallowed the odd ache of disappointment in her throat. "Of course. I understand completely."

The pads of his fingers brushed across the top of her knuckles, sending a skittering of warmth up her arm. "I don't think ye understand at all, Faith."

Pulling her gaze away from his, she steeled herself against the fierce attraction she felt for him. "I'm sorry you feel that way. Don't forget the book," she said, holding up the volume.

Glancing at the book, he shrugged impatiently. "Ye may keep it until next time."

"If there is a next time," she said softly.

Standing, he placed one booted leg on a table and leaned over her. His breath was warm on her cheek. "Och, there will be a next time. Ye can be certain o' that."

He straightened and walked toward the door. Pushing down the latch, he opened the door. "By the way, I'd advise ye no' to concern yourself about my reputation. 'Tis long beyond repair anyway."

A faint smile rose to Faith's lips as he shut the door firmly behind him. "Somehow, Miles O'Bruaidar," she said softly, "that doesn't surprise me at all."

Chapter Thirteen

During the following days of her captivity, Faith spent most of her time alone or with Molly. Occasionally she was granted a visit by Father Michael or Shaun Gogarty. She particularly enjoyed the visits by the dwarf, finding him to be excellent company. He spun the most delightful tales of ancient Ireland and played an unorthodox game of chess. In fact, one afternoon while engaged in a particularly close match with him, she heard a commotion outside her window.

"Oh, God, not Arabella again," Faith groaned, slapping the flat of her hand against her forehead. Shaun looked up from the chessboard, grinning.

"Och, the lass is a bit o' a thorn, I agree. But the gossip is remarkable when she's around."

"Leave it to you to see the bright side of things," Faith said, grimacing. "Why does she come here? Doesn't Miles ever go to visit her castle?"

Shaun scratched his chin thoughtfully. "Aye, I suppose he does. But Lady Arabella would see little o' him if she were no' to visit her so oft. Miles is a man occupied wi' many important tasks."

"Hmph," Faith said grumpily, carelessly moving a pawn.

The dwarf gleefully swept it off the board with his knight. "Your thoughts are no' on the game, my lady."

Sighing, Faith stood and walked to the window. "I know. But how can anyone concentrate when *she* is in the castle, ordering everyone about as if they are her personal slaves?"

He looked up at her thoughtfully, his bearded chin resting in his hand. "If I didn't know any better, I think that a bit o' the green-eyed devil has got to ye."

"Green-eyed devil? Oh, please," Faith said, rolling her eyes.

He waved a stubby hand. "Miles is a handsome lad, indeed.

Ye wouldn't be the first lady to fall for his charms.''

"Don't be ridiculous," Faith snapped, mortified to feel her cheeks grow warm. "I haven't fallen for his charms." Ignoring the muffled laughter of the dwarf, she leaned out the window, expecting to see Arabella chastising some poor servant. Instead, she was astonished to see Donagh O'Rourke tossing his reins to a servant before sliding off his horse.

"My God," Faith exclaimed in a breathless rush, "it's Donagh O'Rourke."

"O'Rourke is back?" Shaun said, leaping from the table and hurrying over to join her at the window. "By the love o' God, ye are right," he said, eyes gleaming. "I'll go and see if I can find out what happened."

Faith nodded anxiously as Shaun left the room. Several minutes later Molly entered, her eyes alight with excitement.

"Miles just took Donagh into the library and Shaun is hovering about the door, trying to see through the keyhole. 'Tis terribly exciting. At last everything will be settled wi' ye, lass.''

"Yes, it will," Faith said quietly.

Molly sat in a chair, picking up her embroidery. "How do ye feel?''

"Nervous," Faith admitted honestly. In all actuality, she had no idea what would happen to her. She had no logical reason to assume the English would agree to trade three Irish prisoners for a woman they knew nothing about. She could only hope that Miles would cease to believe she was of any value and set her free. Once that happened, she would have to track down Paddy O'Rourke and figure out a way to bring him back to their own time or kill him before he could do any irreparable damage in this century.

Faith's brow furrowed into a deep frown. The thought of killing O'Rourke was not a comfortable one. In fact, in her two years as an operative she had never killed anyone. It wasn't that she didn't have the skills or training; she had been prepared both psychologically and technically for such an occasion. She had even fired at O'Rourke in the clearing when she thought he meant to kill her. But she only wanted to stop him—not take his life. She wondered, if it really came down to it, whether she could actually end the life of another human being.

Molly saw the worried expression on her face and reached over to pat her hand. "Don't fash yourself, lass. Everything will work out for the best."

"I hope so," Faith murmured under her breath as she began to pace back and forth in front of the fireplace. Her full skirts swished over the floor with every step.

Minutes ticked past endlessly.

"Sit down, lass," Molly ordered when Faith did not slow her step. "Ye are making me dizzy."

"Where could Shaun be?" Faith asked, wringing her hands together. "It's been nearly an hour. He should have been able to eavesdrop on something worthwhile by now."

"Patience," Molly said, clucking her tongue disapprovingly. "A lady always shows patience."

Sighing, Faith sat down in one of the chairs. Anxious to keep her mind off the matter at hand, Faith stared at Molly while the woman methodically drew small stitches. "Why don't you have a family of your own?" she suddenly blurted out.

Molly paused in midstitch. " 'Tis a curious question. Why do ye ask, lass?"

Faith exhaled deeply, rubbing her temples wearily. "I'm sorry, Molly; I don't mean to pry. It's just that you have such good mothering instincts, I wondered . . . well, whether you had any children of your own."

The question was far more personal than Faith had intended, but the truth of the matter was that she had grown rather fond of Molly. If ever she got out of this mess and back to her own century, she would do a little research of her own to discover what had happened to these people who had begun to mean something to her.

For a brief moment Faith saw a flicker of pain in Molly's eyes. Then she shrugged. "I once had a husband. He gave me the most beautiful bairn in the land; a wee girl with perfect little fingers and toes and a tuft o' hair as pale as yours. But she never opened her eyes, nor would she utter a sound. She just lay in my arms as still as a doll until they took her away from me. My husband died a few years later o' the fever. I

169

never had any more bairns, but I had Miles. The O'Bruaidar family never deserted me.''

"I'm sorry," Faith said softly. "You've made a fine mother to Miles. I can see how very fond he is of you."

"Thank ye," she said, her voice catching. " 'Tis kind o' ye to say so. Ye know, English or no', I think that ye are just how I would have pictured my little lass."

"I'm honored," Faith replied quietly.

Molly resumed her stitching, clearing her throat. "And ye'd honor me by trusting Miles. He is a very thorough man and a good judge o' character. He'll no' be jumping to any conclusions about ye, lass. His decisions are always based on the good o' Ireland."

"Like his decision to marry Arabella Dunbar?" Faith replied without thinking. As soon as the words left her mouth she regretted them. "Forgive me," she said, her cheeks flaming. "His affair with Lady Arabella is none of my business."

Molly looked up. "What do ye know o' the woman?"

"Very little," Faith answered, coming stiffly to her feet. "Other than the fact that she is very beautiful."

"A pretty face oft hides a cold heart," Molly murmured.

Faith lifted her head quickly. "It does?"

Molly absently rubbed her knuckles. "I shouldn't be saying this, as she'll soon be my new mistress, but the lass has a bit o' the reputation for fancy dressing and expensive jewels. 'Tisn't just any man who'll catch her fancy. She nearly married Tom Devlin, rich old goat he was, but he died o' the fever a few days 'fore the wedding. Most people say 'twas a blessing for him. Rumor had it that Arabella raged for three days and nights. When she recovered she set her sights on Miles and has been after him ever since."

"And Miles knows none of this?" Faith asked curiously.

"O' course Miles knows."

Faith looked at her in disbelief. "Then why on earth would Miles agree to marry her?"

Molly clucked her tongue. "Och, child, 'tis little ye know o' us. Arabella's da convinced Miles that the families' alliance needed to be strengthened in face o' the growing English threat to the area. As Miles is long o' marrying age and needs an heir, 'tis a convenient as well as a practical arrangement."

''Oh,'' she said, disappointment tinging her voice. ''Why didn't Miles ever marry before?''

Molly shrugged. ''Miles is a man wi' his own reasons for doing things. But if ye ask me, I believe 'twas simply because he hadn't met the right lass.''

Faith fell silent, contemplating Molly's words. The older woman set her embroidery aside and stood up, stretching.

''I'm growing a wee bit impatient myself. Perhaps I'll fetch us a cup o' tea and see if I can find out what is happening down there.''

Faith nodded gratefully as Molly left the room. She welcomed the momentary solitude to muse over what Molly had said. So, Miles wasn't marrying Arabella for love, but to strengthen the Dunbar–O'Bruaidar alliance. Faith couldn't help but be appalled at the very notion, even though she knew full well this was a common practice for the time. How could a man of Miles's stature and intelligence bind himself to a woman for life based on such a proposal?

Because he is honorable, Molly's words echoed in her mind. *And because he puts the good of Ireland before his own needs.*

Faith laughed aloud at her thoughts. Who was she kidding? Miles hadn't looked all that miserable when she had caught him staring down Arabella's dress at supper. He was most likely leaping in joy at the prospect of bedding someone as beautiful as Arabella; that is, if they hadn't been at it already.

Faith snorted, disgusted with herself. Why did she torture herself even thinking about it?

''Och, so ye're the *Sassenach* lass.''

Faith blinked once in surprise and then looked up directly into the face of a young boy. He stood near the partially open door, his hands resting squarely on his hips. His hair was nearly as fair as hers and he was dressed in a light tunic with breeches, stockings and buckled shoes. A lightweight sword hung around his waist on a leather belt.

''Ye shouldn't have come to spy on us,'' he said arrogantly. ''Miles will surely do away wi' ye.''

Faith managed to find her voice after the boy's surprise appearance. ''Who are you?'' she asked.

He puffed out his chest a bit and took a few steps toward her. ''I'm Patrick O'Farrell. Miles is my cousin and the best

171

swordsman in all o' Ireland. Ye should be quaking in your shoes in fear o' him.''

Faith nearly smiled at the boy's bravado. ''I see,'' she said gravely. ''Well, thank you for the warning. I'll be sure not to challenge him to a sword fight.''

The boy cocked his head at her, measuring her words. ''Ye are jesting wi' me.''

Faith's eyes twinkled. ''Perhaps a bit. Please have a seat.''

Patrick shook his head. ''I'll stand. Ye see, an Irishman never lets down his guard in the presence o' the English.''

Faith raised an eyebrow. ''Oh. Are you at least permitted to speak with me?''

He shrugged. '' 'Twould be o' no harm, I suppose. You're just a woman, after all.''

''Yes, of course,'' Faith said wryly. ''Why haven't I seen you around the castle?''

Patrick shifted his weight from one foot to the other, continuing to eye her warily. ''I was visiting my uncle in Armagh. There's a monastery there, founded by Saint Patrick. I'm named after him, ye know.''

''Really? How fascinating. Do you usually live here at the castle?''

The boy nodded. ''Miles took me in when my da was killed in the uprising o' forty-one. My mother died when I was just a wee babe.''

''I'm sorry to hear that,'' Faith said quietly, and she meant it. Tragedy seemed to follow the people of Castle Dun na Moor.

''But the English will pay for killing him,'' Patrick boasted. ''I'll see to it myself, when I get a bit older.''

Before Faith could reply a noise at the door caused them both to glance up. After a moment's hesitation a tall figure stepped into the room.

''Miles,'' Patrick said happily, his face lighting up at the sight of his cousin.

''Welcome back, Patrick,'' Miles said, leaning against the door. His hair hung loosely to his shoulders, his shirt opened casually at the throat. As he spoke, his lips parted in a dazzling display of straight white teeth. ''How is Uncle Thomas?''

''Och, he was ill-humored as usual, recovering from a bit

o' the gout. He gave me a letter for ye.''

Miles put a gentle hand on the boy's shoulder. "Thank ye, lad. Leave the letter in the library and see if ye can find Father Michael.''

"But I thought ye might need my help in questioning the lass," he protested. "I was watching her. She invited me to sit, but I refused.''

"Good lad," Miles said softly. "But it won't be necessary. I need to speak wi' her alone.''

"As ye wish, Miles," Patrick replied. He left the room, shutting the door quietly behind him.

Miles turned toward Faith. Her arms were crossed tightly against her chest, as if in defiance of what he was about to say. "How have ye fared, lass?" he asked when she said nothing.

"How have I fared?" she finally exploded. "Do you know how bloody long I've been waiting? What were you two plotting for so long? Did you plan to torture me to death with anticipation?''

His lips twitched suspiciously close to a smile. "What do ye think we were plotting?''

"I have no idea. What did the governor say?''

"What do ye think he said?''

"I think the English refused to trade for me.''

"I see. Why do ye say that?''

"I've told you the reason all along. No one knows who I am.''

Miles walked to the hearth, leaning his elbow back against the mantel. "All right, then, Faith, just who are ye?''

She exhaled a deep breath. "We've been over this before. I've told you everything I can. The truth of the matter is that I didn't come to Ireland to spy on you. I'm here by mistake.''

His long fingers drummed restlessly against the wooden mantel. "Why do ye keep evading the truth, lass?''

Because if I told you the whole truth, you would have locked me away in a seventeenth-century funny farm.

"I have told you what I can," she said, dropping her hands to her side.

Miles strode across the room until he towered above her. "I need more than that. Tell me who ye work for in England.''

Julie Moffett

Faith shook her head. "I'm not working for anyone. Just release me, Miles. Please."

His face darkened angrily. "Do ye understand how precarious your situation is, Faith? In a few days' time I may have to turn ye o'er to Donagh O'Rourke."

"O'Rourke?" Faith gasped in shock. "No, you mustn't do that."

Miles reached out and gripped her shoulders firmly. "Why are ye so afraid o' him?"

"I . . . I can't tell you. I just know that if you turn me over to O'Rourke, you'll never get the answers you seek."

Miles shook her, swearing fiercely under his breath. "Damn and be damned, woman. Ye've done nothing but fight me ever since I found ye at the stone circles. Talk to me, Faith."

She struggled to free herself from his hold, ineffectually hitting his chest with her fists. "I've told you the truth. I'm not here to spy on you. I can't give you an exact reason, but you mustn't turn me over to O'Rourke. There's more at stake here than you can possibly understand. For pity's sake, there is more at stake than *I* understand. In just a few weeks my entire life has been turned upside down. Now I'm alone in a place I know little about and I don't even know if I can get back home."

She stopped struggling and Miles relaxed his grip. In one angry jerk she pulled free, turning away from him. She pressed her hands over her face just as the last shred of her resolve crumbled. The tears came very much against her will, but she was unable to stop them.

"Christ, I'm pathetic," she sobbed. "What's wrong with me?"

Miles stared at her in stunned silence before resting a hand on her shoulder. "Faith," he whispered softly, pulling her back against his chest. "Don't weep, lass. I never wanted to bring ye tears."

"Get away from me," she choked, trying to shrug out of his embrace. "Don't touch me. I must be losing my grip on sanity. Christ, I didn't even cry when my father died."

He kept his hold on her gentle but firm. "Ye have a lot o' hurt bottled inside ye. What happened to your father, lass?"

Faith drew in a deep, shaky breath. "He died of a terrible

disease.'' She thought of the cancer that had slowly killed the man she had once thought of as impenetrable. "It was a rather abrupt end to a man many considered brilliant."

"Except when it came to his daughter," Miles commented softly. "What about your mum? How old were ye when she drowned?"

"Eight." Even after twenty years the memory was still achingly fresh and painful.

"Do ye wish to talk about it?"

"There isn't much to talk about. She died and it was my fault."

Miles lifted a dark eyebrow. "Ye drowned her?"

"It was my eighth birthday. I was playing near the lake after I had been expressly forbidden to do so. I got into water over my head and . . ." she paused, the memory causing her stomach to ache, ". . . and she jumped into save me. It was an accident."

"Och, so 'twas an accident?"

"If only I had listened to my father, none of it would have happened. My life might have been so different."

"Your father . . . he held ye responsible? A wee lass?"

"Yes . . . no," she said shifting uncomfortably. "It doesn't matter. He was right, in any case. But now he's dead and there is no one left to blame me."

"Except for yourself."

She stiffened. "I don't want to talk about this anymore."

"Ye should, ye know. I think 'twould help. Have ye any other family, Faith?"

She stared at her hands, willing the pain away. "I have a cousin named Fiona."

Loneliness swept through her as she pictured her pretty cousin's face. Was life in the twentieth century going on as normal? Was Fiona still dating Edward Hawthorne? What had MI5 told her about her cousin's abrupt disappearance? Was anyone still looking for her, or did they think her dead?

"My God," Faith whispered, realization suddenly dawning on her. "Things will never be the same, even if I do get back. No one will ever believe what I've been through."

"Lass?"

175

Faith shook her head. "It's nothing, Miles. You wouldn't understand."

"Can ye no' try to reach this cousin o' yours . . . Fiona? Won't she help ye?"

Faith shook her head. "No, it's not possible. Fiona is . . . well, she's not exactly living."

"No' exactly?"

"In a manner of speaking. The truth of the matter is that right here, right now, I have no one. But I'm strong enough on my own. I've handled plenty of regrets by myself."

"Must ye really face them all alone?" His voice was gently curious.

"I've always faced them alone. I don't need anyone else."

"Mayhap ye do, lass," he murmured, placing his hand under her chin and lifting her face toward him.

Faith felt her heart skip a beat as his lips brushed the curve of her cheek. His hand slid into her hair, his fingers gently caressing the smooth skin of her neck. Standing there in his embrace, Faith marveled at the warmth of his arms and how safe it felt to be held and comforted. How long had it been since she had leaned on someone else for support?

She pulled back slightly, gazing up into his face. There was an inherent strength in his features, certainly born of leadership, conviction and kindness. Now, as his calm green eyes met hers, they seemed to be asking her to trust him.

Hesitantly, Faith reached up and touched his jaw. It felt scratchy and rough, covered with the dark stubble of a day's beard. She felt the quick intake of his breath beneath her fingertips as she traced a line to his mouth.

Miles reached out and captured one hand with his own, holding it tightly against his chest. With the other he tenderly brushed the wetness from her lashes with his fingertips. She trembled as he bent his dark head toward her, pressing a gentle kiss on her mouth. His lips were warm and moist, his breath mingling with the salty wetness of her tears. He kissed her slowly at first, a gentle massage that sent currents of desire racing through her. As his tongue began to gently stroke the soft fullness of her mouth, Faith wound her arms about his neck, surrendering at last to the comfort he offered.

Miles's breathing was ragged as he rained a searing trail of kisses along the soft skin of her neck. Sighing with pleasure, Faith clutched at his shoulders, arching against him. She gasped as his hands skimmed across her breasts and shoulders, coming to a halt at the curve of her cheek.

She stiffened, and Miles instantly stilled his movement. "What is it, lass?" he asked softly.

She swallowed hard, her hands beginning to tremble. "I'm frightened of what is happening to me . . . to us."

Miles lifted a handful of her hair, letting the pale, silky strands fall lightly through his fingers. "Will ye trust me, Faith? Will ye tell me why ye are here? I'll take care o' ye, I give ye my word."

Every fiber in Faith's body wanted to blurt out the story. But he could not understand, and would not believe her in any case. As much as she needed him, in the end he would not be able to help her. As it had been for most of her life, she would have to stand alone.

"I'm sorry, Miles. I can't."

He stared at her for a long moment before releasing her. "I can see that I am no' going to change your mind. Well then, Faith, I give ye your wish. Ye're going home to England."

"I am?"

Miles nodded, striding to the window. For a moment he simply leaned against the windowsill, gazing out onto the courtyard. "Ye were wrong about your countrymen," he finally said.

Faith's blue eyes widened, her heart beginning to hammer uncomfortably in her chest. "What do you mean?" she whispered.

Miles turned to give her a long, penetrating look. "It appears as if ye are important to someone after all. Donagh brings word that the English have agreed to a trade for ye. We leave on the morrow."

Chapter Fourteen

Faith quietly observed the gray fingers of dusk as she rode through the hills of the Irish countryside. The warm evening breeze lifted her hair from her neck, soothing her with its gentle touch. She had been riding for hours and was exhausted both physically and mentally, having spent the entire journey worrying about the events unfolding around her.

Too many questions about this exchange still begged answers—why had the English governor agreed to trade three presumably valuable prisoners for a woman he had most certainly never met, and what was Donagh O'Rourke's role in all of this? She had seen the scarred Irishman staring intently at her on several occasions. What did he know, if anything, about her?

And where was Paddy O'Rourke? When she had discreetly inquired about him through Father Michael, the priest had shrugged, saying Donagh's kin had abruptly disappeared. Was he headed for London, making his preparations to assassinate Oliver Cromwell? Could she stop him in time?

Wearily, she pushed her bangs off her dusty forehead, looking ahead to where Miles rode. He seemed deeply preoccupied and she wondered what he was thinking. Most of the journey he had spent riding alongside an older gray-haired gentleman, talking quietly with him. Earlier, Shaun had pointed him out as Finn O'Flahertie, the father of two of the boys who would be swapped in the exchange for her. Faith assumed that the elder O'Flahertie sought Miles's reassurance that the exchange would not put his sons in greater danger.

Who could blame him? she thought. *If they were my kids, I'd be worried, too.*

"Have a care on the path," Miles suddenly shouted at her over his shoulder, jolting Faith from her thoughts. They were moving down into a valley on an increasingly rocky path. Faith

178

slowed her horse, waiting for the other riders to merge into single file. Miles nodded curtly at her as she passed, guiding his mount in behind her. His eyes betrayed nothing.

As soon as everyone had safely entered the valley, Miles called a halt. The area was well-protected, surrounded by several large trees and thick, dense brush. A small stream gurgled nearby, and Faith swallowed with difficulty, wishing for a drink of cool water to ease her parched throat.

Seemingly satisfied with the location, Miles gave his men instructions. "Rory, keep an eye to the north, and Daniel, ye take the south. Dennis and Gerald, ye watch the east and west, respectively. Keep your heads up, lads, and eyes sharp." The men nodded and rode off in their specified directions.

Donagh O'Rourke wheeled his horse around, pulling up alongside Miles. "Are ye daft, man? We're nearly at the rendezvous point."

"We stop here," Miles repeated firmly. "I'll arrive at the rendezvous point when I am good and ready. Perhaps 'tis simply no' in my nature to be as trusting o' the English as ye are, Donagh. I know they agreed to this trade on our terms, but it won't hurt to show a little prudence."

Donagh's eyes narrowed, but he offered no further protest. "As ye say, Miles." Sliding out of the saddle, he led his horse to the water.

Faith climbed down from the horse, rubbing her lower back to get the kinks out and watching the rest of the men dismount. Several of them milled about, talking and brushing the horses, while others left to gather dry brush for a fire. Stiffly, she walked to the edge of the stream, kneeling at the bank and cupping the cool water to her mouth. When her thirst was quenched she headed for a large, sheltering tree and collapsed on the soft grass beneath it, resting her back against the trunk.

After a moment Shaun joined her, lowering his small body to the ground with a heartfelt sigh. Closing his eyes, he put one stubby hand under his head and the other across his eyes.

" 'Tis a good thing Miles called a halt," he said. "My arse was losing all feeling."

Faith smiled in spite of herself, tiredly rubbing a hand across her brow. "Why are we stopping here?"

" 'Tis a safe place to camp till nightfall."

179

"Nightfall?" she asked in surprise. "The exchange of prisoners is to take place in the dark?"

"Aye, that it is, lass."

"But why? Doesn't that make it more dangerous?"

"For the English, perhaps."

Faith shook her head in disbelief. "Why in God's name would the English agree to such conditions?"

Shaun lifted his arm from his eyes and turned to look at her. " 'Tis obvious that they think ye worth it, lass. 'Twas a bit o' a gamble for Miles to set such a term, but they accepted it without argument."

"They did?" she whispered in wonder.

Shaun pushed himself into a sitting position. "Aye, 'tis odd, indeed. Especially since I happen to believe that ye are speaking the truth about no one among the English knowing who ye are."

"You do?"

The dwarf nodded. " 'Tis something about ye that speaks o' magic and mystery. Ye are no' a common woman nor a simple spy. Ye have an aura that cloaks your true purpose here, but that purpose exists, nonetheless. 'Tis a gift o' mine, ye see. I can spot those wi' the powers and wiles o' the fey folk. The ability has been wi' me since birth." He looked at her speculatively, as if he expected her to wave a magic wand and whisk them away to wherever the fairies lived.

Faith sighed, shaking her head. "I'm sorry to disappoint you, Shaun, but I'm not a member of the fey folk. I'm afraid that this time your gift is wrong."

The dwarf shook his head. "Nay, the gift is never wrong. Ye shall see, lass. Ye shall see."

Bemused, Faith turned her attention to the men as they brought a fire to life and placed a small kettle above it. Talking softly, they crouched about the flickering light, occasionally stirring something in the kettle. Soon the air was filled with the delicious smell of cooking food. Faith's stomach grumbled hungrily.

Trying to ignore the sound, she scanned the small camp for Miles. He walked restlessly about the campsite, occasionally bending over to speak softly with one of his men. The flickering glow of the fire cast shadows on his face, emphasizing

180

the chiseled strength of his jaw and heavy, dark brows. With the others, his manner implied decisiveness, but Faith thought she could detect a trace of uneasiness and strain about him.

He must have sensed her staring, for he abruptly lifted his eyes and met her gaze. The meeting of their eyes was like a physical jolt, and Faith caught her breath at the look in his eyes.

My God, he still wants me, and God forbid, I want him, too. Why can't we shake this attraction?

Her gaze was interrupted by Patrick, who appeared, holding out a wooden bowl of what appeared to be a thick, savory stew. Faith gratefully accepted the bowl, wondering how to eat it. Looking over at Shaun, she saw the dwarf cheerfully lift the bowl to his mouth and slurp. Shrugging, she did the same, savoring the taste of the spicy stew.

When she finished she set the bowl aside, certain she had never eaten a more delicious meal. A languorous warmth spread over her and she had an uncontrollable urge to slip into the folds of sleep. The low murmur of voices and the now familiar crackle of an open fire lulled her to close her eyes. Suddenly, her fate didn't seem to matter all that much as long as she could have a few blessed moments of uninterrupted sleep to forget about her precarious situation. . . .

"Faith?"

Her eyes sprung open to see Miles bent over her, gently shaking her shoulder. The fire had burned low and two men were preparing to douse the ashes.

"How long did I sleep?" she asked, rubbing her hand across her eyes.

"An hour, mayhap two."

"Is it time to go?" she asked, the familiar jittery feeling returning to her stomach.

Miles nodded, his dark brows knitting together in concern. " 'Tis no' too late, Faith," he said softly. "If ye tell me the truth about your situation, there may still be a way to help ye."

"I . . ." she faltered and then fell silent. "I just wish things were different. But I'm glad that you will be getting a few of your men back."

Miles stared at her for a long moment without speaking.

181

"For a lass who is going home ye don't look all that happy. 'Tis what ye wanted, is it no'?"

"I suppose it will be better than being a prisoner."

Miles sighed, dragging his fingers through his hair. " 'Twas hard on ye, I know. But I had little choice."

Faith put her hand lightly on his forearm. "You conducted yourself as a gentleman. For that I thank you."

He reached out to lightly touch her cheek. "Ye are an intriguing woman, Faith. Altho' ye are English, I'm finding turning ye o'er to them harder than I expected. But your silence has given me no other choice. I only hope that ye know what ye are doing."

She looked into his eyes for a long moment before turning away. "So do I," she whispered fervently. "So do I."

Faith cursed softly as she stumbled over another rock in the darkness. She heartily wished that Miles hadn't insisted they leave their mounts a ways back, with Patrick and a few other men, and continue to the rendezvous point on foot. She not only stumbled over every little stone, branch and bush, but she kept tripping on the hem of her own cumbersome gown.

Exasperated, Faith hiked her skirts to her knees and bit back another curse as she nearly twisted her ankle on a sharp, jutting rock. As far as she could see, her situation was fast approaching the realm of the absurd.

If a few weeks ago someone had told me that I would be hiking through a forest in the middle of the night with a bunch of Irishmen from the seventeenth century, all the while dressed in an old-fashioned gown, I would have sent them directly to the psychiatric ward of the nearest hospital for a permanent check-in. Geez, I should send myself there.

A sharp branch scraped across the top of her scalp, painfully jolting her from her thoughts. She screeched, stopping to rub the top of her head ruefully.

Miles called a halt, muttering something about her making enough noise to alert the entire English army of their arrival. In a low voice, he ordered Furlong to guide her through the forest.

The going seemed easier after that. Faith was grateful for Furlong's steady hand on her elbow, and he helpfully pulled treacherous branches out of her way that might have otherwise torn her clothes or skin.

She had no idea how far they had walked when a whispered order came filtering back to them. Much to Faith's astonishment, Furlong abruptly grabbed her around the waist, putting a firm hand over her mouth.

Before she could squirm in outrage Faith heard the faint noise of a horse's whinny. Her heart started hammering in her chest as she realized with some trepidation that they had arrived at the rendezvous point.

"Sorry, lass," Furlong whispered apologetically. "We couldn't have ye announcing our arrival just yet."

Miles and several other men disappeared into the darkness and came back minutes later. Miles quickly whispered something to Donagh, and he and two other men slipped off into the shadows. Moments later Faith heard the sound of swords being drawn, and then Donagh's voice calling out clearly.

"It is I, Donagh O'Rourke. I am here to make an exchange o' prisoners, agreed upon by the governor."

Furlong leaned over and pressed his mouth to her ear. "Don't fash yourself, lass. 'Tis just the sentry we spotted. He'll take Donagh to the officer in charge o' the exchange."

She nodded the best she could, given the fact that his hand was still clamped firmly over her mouth. Her pulse was racing with uncertainty and fear and she pressed her damp palms against the sides of her dress.

Time seemed to crawl. Furlong had pulled her deeper into the shadows, where she could see nothing. She knew Miles was probably only a few steps from her, but she could neither see nor hear him. Only the sounds of Furlong's steady breathing and her own frantic heartbeat seemed to break the night's stillness.

After what seemed like hours Faith heard footsteps approaching their position. The sound of steel blades being drawn from their scabbards abruptly filled the air. In one quick movement Furlong dragged her sideways, out of the way of the footsteps.

"Lower your weapons," came a hushed voice from the darkness. " 'Tis I, Kevin O'Flahertie."

"By the wounds o' Christ, 'tis ye," Faith heard Miles reply quickly. "Where is your brother, lad?"

"Here," said another voice from the darkness. Faith heard a small cry of joy and assumed Finn O'Flahertie was becoming reacquainted with his sons.

"They've kept Douglas O'Leary until ye return with the English lass," Kevin added quickly. "Who is she, Miles?"

" 'Tis a story for another day, lad," Miles said shortly. "For now, be glad ye are among friends."

Donagh O'Rourke suddenly materialized beside Faith, putting a hand on her arm. Faith nearly jumped out of her skin at his touch.

"Come, Miles, let's take her to the English," he said eagerly.

Miles strode over, nodding briefly at Furlong. The stocky man immediately dropped his hand from her mouth. With a sigh of relief, Faith reached up to rub her mouth with her fingers.

"First, I want Furlong to take all o' the men, except two, and head back for the castle," Miles instructed softly. "We'll meet up wi' ye later."

Upon Miles's order, the men melted into the darkness, with the exception of two shadowy figures. Miles walked over and spoke to them softly before returning to where Faith and Donagh stood.

" 'Tis time, lass," he said, taking Faith firmly by the hand. "Let's go."

Donagh led the way through the trees. Faith gripped Miles's hand, her stomach knotting in fear.

"Miles?" she whispered quietly as he helped her over a rotting log.

"Aye, lass?" he asked, slowing his step.

"Don't you think it is just a bit strange that the English agreed to the trade without even seeing me?"

"Perhaps," he said mildly.

"But what if it isn't me they want?" she asked, stumbling forward. "Perhaps it's you."

Miles caught her easily around the waist, bringing her up against the hard length of his body. "Could it be that ye are actually worried about me?'' he asked softly, pressing his mouth against her ear.

Faith tingled as the heat of his breath fanned across the side of her cheek and neck. ''I just think the whole thing is rather odd, that's all.''

Although she couldn't see his face clearly, she could hear the smile in his voice. ''What I think is strange is an English lass implying that her countrymen may no' be all that honorable.''

Faith stiffened in his arms. ''I'm just trying to point out something you might have overlooked in your hurry to get rid of me. Why I should even care an iota about a thick-headed Irishman like you is beyond me.''

''Then ye do care,'' Miles said gravely.

She pulled herself from his embrace, moving forward on her own. ''I can't see how that matters now.''

''Everything matters, Faith,'' he replied softly. ''Everything.''

''What in God's name is taking ye two so long?'' Donagh hissed over his shoulder.

''I've a lass wi' me, Donagh,'' Miles answered calmly. ''Or have ye forgotten?''

Donagh snorted. ''Well, make haste. We're almost there.''

They came quite unexpectedly upon the small English armed camp. Faith blinked at the sudden light from the fires, shielding her eyes with the back of one hand. She felt Miles squeeze her hand in reassurance and, after a moment, they moved into the clearing.

''Here is the English lass, as promised,'' Donagh announced loudly.

A tall blond man with a finely trimmed mustache stepped forward. He was impeccably dressed in a flowing white shirt of linen, a pair of breeches that ended just above his knees and dark stockings that disappeared into a pair of sleek black boots. A light cloak of black was fastened around his shoulders, in spite of the fact that it was a warm night. As a gentle wind blew past, it lifted the cloak from his shoulders, billowing about him like wings. Shuddering, Faith thought it made him appear to be some sort of evil apparition from hell.

She felt Miles stiffen beside her. ''Well, if it isn't Nicholas

185

Bradford,'' he called out. "I shouldn't be surprised that the governor would put ye in charge o' this exchange.''

"You know him?'' Faith whispered in surprise.

"Aye, I do,'' Miles replied softly. "Last year he invited me and several other Irish noblemen to a meeting, presumably to discuss peace. Instead, 'twas a ruse. Bradford killed two and the rest o' us barely escaped wi' our lives. He is a man without honor.''

Faith frowned, turning her attention back to the Englishman. He was looking at Miles with a cold, angry expression on his face.

"Well, well, if it isn't Miles O'Bruaidar,'' he replied in a clipped English accent. "What a pleasant surprise to see you again. I wasn't sure that I'd ever have that opportunity, as you left rather hastily after our last encounter.''

"Sorry to see me go, were ye, Bradford?'' Miles asked, cocking an eyebrow with amusement. "Have ye jabbed any other unsuspecting lads in the back since our last encounter?''

Faith watched as a tight smile settled on Bradford's face. "Let it suffice to say that I was surprised you managed to get away. Shall we get on with this?''

He gave a sharp wave of his hand, and one of his men brought forward a young man with his hands tied behind his back. His face was dirty and his clothes ragged. As soon as the young man saw Miles, his eyes lit up and he raised his head proudly.

"Miles, 'tis good to see ye again.''

"Aye, 'tis good to see ye, too, Douglas. Are ye ready to come home, lad?''

"Aye, that I am, Miles. That I am.''

"All right,'' Bradford said coldly. "You've seen the final prisoner. Now bring forth the woman.''

"Untie him first,'' Miles said firmly.

Bradford stared at Miles for a long moment before nodding. "All right, untie the boy,'' he instructed one of his officers. The man walked over to Douglas and removed the rope from his hands. The young man rubbed his arms frantically to get the feeling back in them.

"Now bring me the woman,'' Bradford ordered.

Miles looked down at Faith and their eyes locked. He

seemed to be asking her once more whether she wished to stay. For a fleeting moment Faith entertained the idea of returning to Castle Dun na Moor but then shook her head resolutely. No matter how strong her attraction to Miles, she did not belong in this century and she knew it. As an Englishwoman in the Irish countryside, she would be watched and perhaps even guarded once again if she returned to his castle. Back with the English, she would no longer be a prisoner. She would be free to hunt down Paddy O'Rourke and put a stop to his mad plans. Once that was accomplished, she would go home where she belonged—if it were possible.

Surprised that she would feel such regret, Faith turned slightly toward Miles to say her final good-bye. As she did, she saw a small flash of light out of the corner of her eye. Startled, she realized it was the reflection of light off metal. It came from a tree, directly above the small campfire. Her brow furrowed slightly as she wondered why metal would be in trees.

The answer hit her like a fist in the stomach. The Irishmen hadn't left for the castle as Miles had instructed. Instead, they had doubled back to make sure the English didn't try to renege on their agreement or attempt to capture their leader.

And Miles had known all along. That was why he was giving her one last chance to come with them.

Frightened, she glanced up at Miles, her eyes widening. His eyes met hers calmly, never once wavering. In an instant, she realized he was ready to risk his own life as well as those of his men, if she should signal her readiness to leave with him.

Her breath caught in her throat. "N-no, Miles," she whispered hastily. "I'll go with them peacefully."

"I said bring the woman forward, O'Bruaidar," Bradford repeated, a note of impatience creeping into his voice.

Tearing his eyes away from her, Miles stepped forward, bringing Faith along with him. Bradford stared at her openly, his eyes sliding appreciatively down her body.

"You are the Englishwoman named Faith?"

She nodded, still gripping Miles's hand. "I am from London."

"These barbarians have held you prisoner?"

"I have not been harmed."

"Then you have been most fortunate, my lady. From this

187

moment on you may consider yourself fully under the protection of His Majesty's Third Regiment.''

"Thank you," she said softly.

"Now please, my lady, step away from him," Nicholas ordered, his eyes no longer on her but on Miles.

Faith turned to face Miles for the last time. "Thank you for treating me so kindly," she said softly, feeling ridiculously close to tears. "I just wish things could have been different."

Miles smiled at her. "It's all right. Let go o' my hand, lass," he said gently.

She dropped his hand quickly, unaware that it was she who had held it in such a death grip. "I'm sorry if I . . ." she started to say when, over Miles's shoulder, she caught the sudden movement of Bradford's hand. In an instant she realized that Bradford was reaching for his sword.

"No," she screamed as Miles suddenly grabbed her, thrusting her behind him. She fell to the earth with a bone-crunching thud as Miles drew his sword, barely in time to prevent Bradford's steel blade from slicing into his shoulder.

"Aaaaattack!"

The primal sound of the voices struck terror in Faith's heart. Awkwardly, she rolled to her knees amid a tangle of skirts as Irishmen came from everywhere, dropping from trees and materializing from the shadows of the forest. Screams of rage and clashing steel filled the night air.

Panicked, Faith began to crawl toward the relative safety of the forest when she felt someone grab her shoulder from behind. Uttering a frightened gasp, she looked up to see one of Miles's men standing above her.

"Come on, lass," he said urgently, holding out a hand. "I'll see ye to safety."

Faith put her hand in his, expecting to be pulled up, when a look of surprise abruptly crossed his face. Before she could move he toppled forward, landing directly on top of her.

Horrified, she pushed at his weight, struggling to get out from under his body. As she managed to roll him sideways, Faith felt the warm stickiness of blood on her hands. Sitting up, she noticed for the first time the sword that was deeply embedded in his back.

"Oh my God," she whispered in shock. Lifting her stunned

gaze, Faith saw Donagh O'Rourke looming above her. While she watched in stark terror, he calmly pulled the steel from the man's back in one swift movement, holding the bloody point toward her chest.

"Get up," he ordered sharply.

"Look," Faith said, her voice shaking unevenly, "I don't know what is going on here."

Muttering a curse, Donagh sheathed his bloody sword before leaning over and pulling her roughly to her feet. "Ye stupid English wench," he growled at her. "Ye've ruined everything. If no' for ye, O'Bruaidar would be dead by now. By the Rod o' Christ, I hope ye are made to pay for your stupidity."

He hit her forcefully across the mouth with the back of his hand. Dazed, Faith staggered backward, lifting her hand to touch the tender swelling of a bruise starting to form. She felt sick, not only from the senseless death of the man at her feet, but also from the unexpected violence against her own person.

"You are mad," she whispered, taking a wobbly step backward. "Why did you kill that boy? Just whose side are you on?"

"I could ask the same o' ye," Donagh snarled as he reached out and seized her around the waist. Before Faith could protest he threw her roughly over his shoulder. Her stomach hit the bone in his shoulder with such force that it knocked the breath out of her. As she gasped to bring air to her lungs, Donagh quietly slipped into the forest and away from the fighting.

Weakly, Faith raised her head and took a last look at the clearing. Miles was still engaged in a furious swordfight with Nicholas Bradford. Furlong fought valiantly at his side, and even Shaun was deftly wielding a sword against an opponent twice his size. There were blood and bodies everywhere, and what seemed to Faith like a lot more Irishmen than had originally traveled with them to the rendezvous. Had Miles been expecting treachery all along?

Donagh stumbled, causing Faith's stomach to lurch crazily. "P-please," she whispered hoarsely, feeling the bile rise in her throat. "Where are you taking me?"

"Ye'll learn soon enough."

"Put me down."

"Ye are in no position to ask for anything," Donagh hissed, his breathing becoming labored, apparently with the exertion of carrying her. "No' another word from ye. Do ye hear me?"

Faith made a choking noise and Donagh stopped in his tracks. "What is it now?" When she didn't answer he swore angrily. "Damnation, woman. Tell me what ails ye."

"I think I'm going to be sick," she whispered.

"Oh, Christ, nay," he growled just as she threw up all over his back and shoulders.

Chapter Fifteen

Faith had little strength or will left to fight Donagh as he half carried, half dragged her through the forest. Some time later he set her down, sighing with relief to be rid of the burden of her weight. He grunted as she slipped from his back and then with a groan stretched his arms over his head.

As soon as Faith's feet touched the ground, she made a clumsy run for it. She got only a few steps before Donagh fell on her from behind, throwing her to the ground. He jammed his knee uncomfortably in the small of her back.

"Ye try that again and ye'll be sorry," he said, pressing Faith's head into the dirt, the smell of earth and grass filling her nose. Small rocks dug into the soft skin of her cheeks.

"Do ye understand me, lass?"

"Yes," Faith whispered.

He released the pressure on her head and then stood, pulling her roughly to her feet.

"Why are you doing this?" she asked softly. "Why did you kill that innocent boy and where are you taking me?"

"I have my orders," Donagh said shortly.

"Orders?" Faith replied as understanding dawned on her face. "My God, you are working for the English . . . for Bradford."

"A most insightful observation."

"Then this whole thing was a trap. You intended all along to betray Miles. But why risk so much to kidnap me? I would have gone peacefully with the English."

"That is none o' your concern. Now, I'd advise ye to keep your mouth shut and stay close to my side. We've still a way to go until I can secure mounts for us." He grabbed her by the hand, jerking her behind him.

They made their way through the forest, Donagh pulling Faith along unmercifully. After some time the way became easier as the morning sun rose in the sky, lighting their path. Still, Faith barely managed to keep up with Donagh. She had long since begun to feel the effects of no sleep, jangled nerves and an upset stomach. When she was certain she would not be able to take another step Donagh abruptly came to a halt.

"We should be nearly there," he said, squinting up at the sky and then checking their direction.

As exhausted as she was, Faith didn't even hear the footstep behind her. Her mouth simply gaped open in surprise as a sword came from behind her and pressed lightly against Donagh's neck.

"Turn around, nice and slow."

Faith took a step sideways as Donagh turned around, his hands raised. Faith's heart skipped a beat as she prayed with all her might that one of Miles's men had followed them. Her hopes plummeted when she saw a look of relief cross Donagh's face.

"Corporal Cunningham," he said. " 'Tis good to see ye, man."

Turning herself, Faith saw a short, balding man with a few missing teeth. His skin was wrinkled and tan, and a bulging stomach hung obscenely over the waistband of his tight breeches.

The pudgy soldier lowered his sword, putting it back in its sheath. "O'Rourke," he said in a Cockney accent. "Why have you come without the others? What happened?"

Donagh jerked his head toward Faith. "The lass here prevented Bradford from taking O'Bruaidar cleanly. Also, unbeknownst to me, Miles had instructed his men to double back. He must have suspected something."

"Wise man," Faith murmured softly.

Donagh's eyes narrowed at her words, but he continued. "A skirmish broke out. As instructed, I brought the woman to safety."

Corporal Cunningham nodded, his two chins jiggling. Faith felt an odd urge to laugh at the ridiculous sight but thought better of it.

"So, this is the mysterious Englishwoman," he observed, taking a step forward. Before Faith could move he shot out a dirty hand and grabbed her jaw. Curiously, he turned her head from side to side, as if examining a horse for sale. As soon as he dropped his hand, Faith reached out and slapped him resoundingly across the face.

"Keep your filthy hands off me, you idiot," she said between clenched teeth.

Howling in a mixture of anger and astonishment, the corporal raised his hand to strike her when Donagh smoothly stepped between them.

" 'Tis no' worth your while to damage the goods, Corporal, altho' I've been tempted to do so myself. Just have a care wi' her, for she has a tongue as sharp as a shrew and the wits o' a fox."

Faith glared at both the corporal and Donagh. In response, the corporal's meaty fists opened and closed at his side. "So what do we do now?" he asked Donagh sullenly.

"There's a chance that O'Bruaidar may try to come after the girl," Donagh said. "I need two mounts and an armed escort to Drogheda. We should leave at once."

"Drogheda?" Faith whispered in wonder. The Irish port city of Drogheda was one step closer to England, but in the seventeenth century it was also the home of an enormous English garrison. What were they going to do with her there?

"Dear God," she murmured under her breath.

Donagh turned to face her, his scar making his smile seem like a sneer. "Weary o' my company already, lass?"

Faith frowned. "I make it a point to never enjoy the company of murderers."

Donagh's face reddened with anger. "Ye insolent wench. Have a care how ye speak to me. I'll have the proper respect if I have to beat it out o' ye."

Faith glowered back at him. "Oh, go ahead, O'Rourke. Show your manliness by beating up on me."

Donagh took one step toward her before Corporal Cunningham stepped between them, chuckling. "She's a feisty bit of goods, indeed. I suppose, O'Rourke, that now would be a good time to remind you of your advice on not damaging the goods."

Donagh took a deep breath, letting his hands drop to his sides and unclench. After a moment he turned away from her.

193

"Damn wench is more trouble than she is worth," he muttered under his breath.

"As are most women," the corporal agreed, nodding sympathetically. Turning to Faith, he swept out his arm, his chubby face gleaming with oil and perspiration.

"Shall we be on our way, my lady? My comrades are camped not far away. Once properly furnished with a horse and some food, perhaps you will enjoy seeing Ireland through the eyes of a proper Englishman."

"I bloody doubt it," Faith muttered, but the corporal only laughed.

Miles wiped the sweat from his forehead with his sleeve and looked around the clearing. The fighting had ended a quarter of an hour earlier, but it had taken him this long to round up all his men and assess the damage. Three men lost and six wounded, two of them rather seriously.

The English had suffered far worse casualties. Sixteen dead, including the three sentries his men had taken out before the exchange. Bradford, damn his black soul, had managed to escape, ordering three of his men to engage Miles while he fled on horseback.

"Damned English coward," Miles swore angrily.

He was furious for letting Bradford slip through his fingers. Yet he was even more incensed by the actions of Donagh O'Rourke. It was one thing for an Englishman to kill an Irishman, but Miles had seen O'Rourke thrust his sword into Gerald McKinney's unprotected back. Donagh had committed the ultimate treason—the murder of a fellow Irishman. Miles would see Donagh to the grave for it.

It didn't matter that Donagh's treachery came as no surprise. He had long suspected Donagh of collaboration with the English and believed the Irishman had plotted this trap from the beginning. When the opportunity had presented itself Miles had used the capture of Faith, certainly an English spy, to try to expose O'Rourke and put an end to his crooked dealings. He had involved Donagh in the exchange specifically to see what would happen.

At first the situation had seemed clear. Faith's obvious fear of O'Rourke had indicated to Miles that the two were tied together in some plot, most likely designed to put an end to his life. Faith was probably an unwilling participant, obviously being coerced in some manner. Donagh served to remind her of that coercion every time he saw her, thus inspiring her fear. As Miles had expected all along, Donagh returned to Castle Dun na Moor miraculously having convinced the English governor to accept all of his demands, some of them purposely outrageous. The exchange was arranged, and to Miles, everything seemed perfectly predictable.

Except that there were too many things about Faith that begged questions. 'Twas true that she was beautiful and intriguing, and he was incredibly attracted to her. But her dress and manner were extremely odd, and she spoke English in a way that was so foreign, Miles often had difficulty following her. Why would the English send a spy so unfamiliar with Irish customs and life that she became an oddity herself? It didn't make any sense.

And who was trying to kill her? If he suspected the mysterious kin of Donagh's who just happened to appear at a most opportune time, why had the man disappeared so abruptly? And why hadn't Donagh himself killed the girl in the clearing? Instead he had seen fit to kill an Irishman in full view of the others and make off with her over his shoulder. What the devil did it all mean?

Miles exhaled a harsh breath. All he knew was that he had to discover what had happened to Faith. If she had been harmed, there would be hell to pay. He would see to it personally.

He swore again, his mind wrestling with the conflicting emotions she aroused in him. The truth of the matter was that he had become fiercely attracted to her. She sparked a desire within him that seemed insatiable. He could not explain his longing for her, but when he held her in his arms he felt a sweep of certainty that this woman was going to be someone of importance in his life.

God's blood, who was she?

All she wanted was to be returned to the stone circles. He had originally denied her request because he assumed it was part of her and Donagh's plan. But later he had ridden to the spot, his curiosity piqued. He found nothing unusual there, no sign that anyone had been there since he had found her.

So who was she really? And why was she so valuable that Donagh O'Rourke would risk everything by openly killing a fellow Irishman in order to slip away with her?

"My lord?"

Miles jerked his head up. "What is it, Furlong?"

"We're ready to travel. And we'd best make haste or I fear we may lose Dennis along the way."

Miles nodded briskly. "Aye, let's be gone from this place." In three long strides he reached his stallion and swung himself up into the saddle. As he took one last look at the clearing where he had seen Faith being carried off by Donagh, he felt a tightening in his gut. He would find her. He would not rest until he knew that she was safe.

"I mean to find out just why ye are so important to everyone, including myself," he promised grimly under his breath.

Then, in one quick movement, he brought the flat of his hand down on the horse's muscular hindquarters.

"To Castle Dun na Moor," he shouted.

Chapter Sixteen

The journey to Drogheda took two full days. By the time they arrived Faith was dazed with exhaustion and covered from head to foot with dirt, dust and grime. Thankfully, no sidesaddle had been available, so she had ridden in the way with which she was accustomed, straddling the horse. As a result of having no undergarments, however, her thighs burned painfully from the incessant rubbing against the leather, and her fair skin blistered from the bright summer sun. When at last the walls of Drogheda came into view she was actually thankful that they had reached some kind of civilization.

As they passed through the gate and into the city, Faith looked around in wonder. Hundreds of people milled about, bartering and selling goods. She could hear a mixture of Gaelic and English being spoken and realized with surprise that these people lived in peace with one another. English soldiers holding lances and pikes stood flirting with pretty Irish women in long gowns. Children threw balls back and forth, racing about the courtyard amid a cloud of dust.

They crossed a beautiful stone bridge under which, Corporal Cunningham informed her, flowed the River Boyne. Strangely, the Irish had built one city on two sides of the river—dividing Drogheda into two parts, the North and the South Town.

"Who is the governor here?" Faith asked him as they passed a rather fancy house.

"Sir Arthur Aston. A fine man he is."

"Arthur Aston?" The name sounded familiar, and Faith racked her brain trying to remember his place in history.

"Aye, he's a real character. He commanded a dragoon regiment for the king a few years back. Lost his leg for it, but 'tis said that he single-handedly saved six of his own men. The king rewarded him by giving him the governorship here."

Faith straightened in the saddle. Oh God, his leg; that was

what she remembered about him. Sir Arthur Aston, governor of Drogheda, was fiercely loyal to Charles I. If she remembered correctly, approximately one year from now he would refuse to surrender to Cromwell's troops, holding Cromwell responsible for the brutal execution of the king. Cromwell would eventually storm the walls of the city, killing everyone inside, including Aston, who would reportedly be beaten to death with his own wooden leg. . . .

"We've arrived," the corporal announced, jolting Faith from her grim thoughts.

He dismounted and then helped her from the saddle. When her legs touched the ground she groaned with excruciating pain. Every muscle in her body ached.

"What building is this?" she asked, rubbing her back and looking up at the square structure in front of them.

"Garrison headquarters," Donagh answered shortly as he came to stand beside her. It was the first time he had spoken to her since their journey begun, having left Corporal Cunningham and the other men with what he clearly considered to be the odious task of guarding her. Now, however, he had apparently decided to take charge of her again, grabbing her elbow and dragging her toward the entrance.

"Do what I tell ye and keep your mouth shut," he snapped at her.

"It's always so pleasant conversing with you," Faith said derisively. "Such a lovely man, you are."

Donagh didn't bother to answer as he pulled her up the stone steps and into the building. They walked down a corridor lined with several rooms. English soldiers lounged around talking, but they stared at them curiously as they passed. Donagh stopped to talk briefly with one of the men before leading her to a room at the end of the corridor.

The door was open and Donagh pushed her across the threshold first, his hand never leaving her arm. A young soldier sitting behind a desk scattered with several parchments looked up as they entered.

"May I help you?" he asked politely.

"My name is Donagh O'Rourke. I have the Englishwoman Bradford wanted."

The young man gave Faith a thorough inspection. From the

expression on his face Faith could see that he was not terribly impressed with what he saw. Two days of traveling had left her absolutely filthy. Her gown was torn in several places and one of her sleeves hung in tatters near her elbow. Her hair was a complete disaster, with pieces of branches, grass and dirt sticking out in every direction.

"Where are the others?" he asked Donagh sharply.

"A skirmish broke out. I assume they'll be along shortly."

Nodding at Donagh, the soldier stood. "Well, we've been expecting her. Arrangements have already been prepared." Turning toward the door, he called out sharply. A young boy raced into the room and stood stiffly at attention.

"Fix Mr. O'Rourke a glass of claret. I'll escort our guest to her quarters." The boy nodded and retrieved a bottle and glass from a nearby wooden cupboard. Donagh sank into a chair, accepting his drink with obvious pleasure.

The soldier turned back to Faith and offered her his arm. After a moment of hesitation she took it, glad to be rid of Donagh. The two of them walked down the long corridor and back outside. Faith walked stiffly, her muscles crying out with every step she took.

Noticing her discomfort, he smiled sympathetically. "You must have had a most difficult time of it, my lady."

"Oh, it really wasn't that bad," she said lightly. "After all, I came out of it in one piece."

"But to be left at the mercy of those Irish barbarians," he remarked, shuddering. "I cannot even imagine how difficult it must have been for a gentle lady such as yourself."

Faith felt mildly annoyed at his dramatic statement. "It is kind of you to worry about me," she said firmly, "but I'm perfectly fine."

"Of course you are," he answered graciously as they approached a small house. He lifted his hand, knocking twice on the wooden door. It was opened by a petite woman with curly brown hair. She took one look at Faith, her eyes widening in surprise.

"Good heavens, George," she gasped. "What happened to the poor girl?"

George stepped forward. "She is unharmed, Lady Catherine. She just arrived from a long journey."

"Then by all means, come in at once," she said, taking Faith by the hand and ushering her into the house. The inside was small, but a pretty carpet had been thrown across the wooden floor and a few paintings hung on the walls. Catherine led them to a tiny sitting room with a hearth and several chairs placed conveniently about the room.

"Sit down, my dear," Catherine said, a concerned expression on her face. "You must be exhausted. What is your name?"

"Faith," she said, gratefully sinking into a chair. "Faith Worthington." It now seemed ridiculous that she had stubbornly withheld her last name from Miles. At the thought of him she felt a piercing stab of worry and concern.

Dear Lord, I hope you are all right, Miles.

Catherine gently shooed George from the room. "You can leave her in my hands. I'll attend to her now."

"As you wish," George said politely, bowing slightly before turning and leaving the room.

With a sigh, Catherine returned her attention to Faith. "You look simply famished. Would you care for a cup of tea and something to eat?"

Faith nodded wearily, pushing a stray strand of hair from her face. "That would be most kind of you."

"Lucinda," Catherine called out sharply. A young girl of about fifteen came rushing into the room.

"Aye, milady?" she said, dropping a small curtsey.

"Please bring tea and scones for our guest. And see that a room is readied for her." The young girl nodded rapidly as Catherine continued to give instructions in a soft voice.

Leaning back in the chair, Faith closed her eyes, attempting to ignore the painful aches of her body and heart. She had never thought that leaving Miles would hurt so much. Of all the men in the universe—both in her time and beyond—why did this man have to be the one to capture her heart? Caring for him was illogical and foolish, and doing so was behavior very unlike the sensible, intelligent woman she had always been. But she was no longer the same person she had once been. Miles had changed her. And now, sitting here without him, she realized just how much he meant to her.

"I hope to God you are safe," she whispered. "I never

knew how much I'd miss you."

"Did you say something?"

Faith's eyes flew open abruptly. Catherine was standing over her, a steaming cup of tea in her hand. "It was nothing," Faith replied, sitting up and pushing her bangs from her forehead.

"I really think you should drink some of this," Catherine continued, placing the cup and saucer on a nearby table. "It should help ease the ache of a long journey."

"I'm sorry. I'm afraid I've been pitiful company, and I'm sure I look a sight."

Catherine shook her head. "You look like a young woman who has had a long and frightfully tiring journey. What you need is a fresh gown, a bite to eat and a good night's sleep."

"And a bath," Faith added emphatically before taking a sip of tea.

"A bath?" Catherine gasped, a horrified expression on her face. "Why, don't you know that water breeds sickness? In fact, it's only twice a year that I'll permit a bath to be drawn in this house."

Faith sighed inwardly. People's aversion to bathing was one aspect of life in the seventeenth century she would never get used to. At that moment she would have gotten down on her knees and begged for just five minutes in a hot tub.

"I suppose a bowl of water and a cloth will do just fine," Faith said with a sigh, setting her cup down on the saucer.

"Certainly. But please, eat something first," Catherine said, holding out a silver tray with several scones piled on it.

Faith reached out to take one, her mouth watering. The bread practically melted in her mouth. "It's delicious," she exclaimed.

Catherine blushed, clearly pleased at Faith's words. "Why, thank you . . . Faith." She looked up quickly. "May I call you that?"

"Of course," Faith said, her mouth full of scone.

"Then you must call me Catherine," she said shyly.

Faith nodded, swallowing the last bit of scone and settling back in her chair. "It feels wonderful to sit on something other than a horse's saddle."

Catherine nodded sympathetically. "You've had a long journey?"

"You can't imagine."

"You're from London, yes?" When Faith nodded she leaned forward in her chair. "However did you find yourself so far from home?"

Faith hesitated. "It's a long story and quite dull. I wouldn't dream of boring you by re-telling it."

Catherine's eyes were wide, clearly impressed. "Oh, but it must have been terribly dangerous. How could you bear being around the Irish? I try not to associate with many of them here in Drogheda. They are . . . well, you know, uncivilized."

Faith winced inwardly at the condescending note in Catherine's voice, wondering if her own voice had ever held the same traces of prejudice. "The Irish are not as uncivilized as we are led to believe," she replied quietly. She thought with no little amount of irony that for as much as she had studied and read about the Irish, she had been remarkably ignorant.

Catherine looked at her doubtfully. "Perhaps it is as you say. But I still feel better avoiding them."

Wishing to change the subject, Faith picked up another scone. "May I ask you, Catherine, what has brought you to Ireland?"

Catherine took a dainty sip of her tea. "Oh, my husband is one of the commanders of the garrison here in Drogheda. It's been rather difficult, but we've managed so far. I'm lucky, you see. Very few wives are allowed to accompany their husbands to Ireland. Nicholas was one of the few exceptions."

Faith paused in mid-chew. "Did you say Nicholas?" she asked with her mouth full.

The petite woman nodded in surprise. "Yes, of course. Do you know of my husband, Nicholas Bradford?"

Faith paced anxiously across the width of the small chamber that was to serve as her bedroom. She fought down the urge to climb out the window and disappear into the crowd of the garrison, knowing it would be counterproductive. As far as she could tell, she was not being held prisoner. But if she ran away, her behavior would immediately become suspect. Besides, where would she go without money? As it stood now,

Faith sensed that she was in no immediate danger. In fact, she told herself firmly, she should finally feel safe and protected—an Englishwoman back among her own people.

Faith smoothed down the skirts of the gown Catherine had lent her and stared out the window. "Except that I don't feel safe at all," she murmured aloud. "Instead, I have the strangest feeling that something terrible is about to happen."

Exhaling a deep breath, Faith clasped her hands in front of her and continued pacing. Her wariness concerning the whole situation was justifiable, she told herself. After all, she had been forcibly abducted from the scene of the exchange by a man who had turned out to be a traitor. And she was currently housed in the home of Nicholas Bradford, a man who had tried to kill Miles and had shown deplorable behavior for an officer of the Crown. She could certainly see why Miles had spoken so passionately about his mistrust of the English. In this particular case, he had been right.

Faith suddenly shuddered at the thought of what might have happened to Miles had she not noticed Nicholas drawing his sword. Her stomach clenched in protest. The thought of Miles lying dead or wounded on the forest floor was more than she could bear. She put a hand on the windowsill to brace her suddenly unsteady legs.

Would she ever see him again? She had tried so hard not to think of him—his heat, his passion, the way he held her when she told him she was afraid. But she had failed miserably.

"Perhaps I should have stayed with you, Miles," she said softly. "And let history be damned."

She shook her head as soon as the words were out of her mouth. Her conscience would never permit her to stand by and allow a known terrorist to roam the country, shaping history to suit his whim. And she herself could not stay in this time. She had to determine a way to get both of them back. It was far too dangerous to stay.

How much of history had she already changed? She could indirectly hold herself responsible for the deaths that had occurred during the exchange, including that of the young man who had tried to help her up before he was viciously cut down by Donagh O'Rourke. Presumably the exchange might have never taken place had she not been offered for a trade. And what about Miles? Was he even alive?

Faith began to pace again, her mind racing. She had to put Miles out of her mind. Worrying herself sick about him would not solve anything. She had to relax and think logically. Finding Paddy O'Rourke and putting a stop to his plans of violence was of paramount importance now. She couldn't change what had already happened, but she *could* stop O'Rourke.

A soft knock startled Faith from her thoughts. Walking over to the door, she opened it. The young serving girl, Lucinda, curtseyed shyly.

"I'm sorry to bother you, my lady, but your presence is requested in the library."

Nodding, Faith followed the girl down a narrow corridor. After a moment Lucinda stopped in front of a closed door.

"Here, my lady," Lucinda motioned before disappearing down the hallway. Taking a deep breath, Faith raised her hand and knocked.

"Enter."

Faith pushed the latch and the door swung open. After a moment's hesitation she stepped into the room. She had a fleeting impression of thick, colorful carpets, large, ornate portraits and several shelves lined with leather-bound books before her eyes fell on the person who had summoned her. He was lounging in a chair behind a huge desk of dark mahogany, his boots resting casually on top of the desk, a crystal goblet in his hand.

"So, we meet again," he said, lifting the goblet to her in a mock toast.

"Nicholas Bradford," Faith said softly.

"Surprised to see me, or had you hoped that O'Bruaidar might have finished me off?"

"I wished for no one to be harmed."

Nicholas laughed and motioned for Faith to be seated. "Most diplomatically said, madam. However, I'm afraid you have me at a disadvantage. We did not have the time to be properly introduced. May I inquire as to your full name?"

"Faith Worthington."

Nicholas swung his legs down from the desk and stood slowly. "Worthington is your husband's name?"

"No," Faith said shortly.

"Then you have no husband?"

Faith frowned. "I can hardly see how my marital status could be of any interest to you."

Nicholas smiled. "Ah, madam, everything about you interests me."

Faith exhaled a deep breath. "If you must know, I am unmarried."

Nicholas walked over to a wooden cabinet and opened the glass doors. "How utterly fascinating. An unmarried Englishwoman wandering about the Irish countryside. I can hardly wait to hear more." He took a decanter from the cabinet and removed the glass lid.

"May I offer you some claret?" he asked, holding up a glass.

"Thank you, but no."

Nicholas poured some liquid into his glass and replaced the decanter. "All right then, I suppose there is no need to engage in further pleasantries. Now that we are afforded a bit of privacy, perhaps you would be willing to tell me what you were doing on O'Bruaidar land."

"I'm afraid I'm not at liberty to discuss that with anyone."

A look of incredulity flashed in Nicholas's eyes. "You are not at liberty to discuss it? Have you any idea who I am?"

"An officer in the Third Regiment of His Majesty's army?" she offered helpfully.

He leaned over the desk, his eyes flashing angrily. "I am the Crown's Representative Officer in Ireland. I am to be informed of all activities conducted here. Now, as I have no knowledge of anyone with your name or description being permitted to undertake any activities in Ireland, I demand an explanation from you."

Faith leaned forward in her chair, placing her hands firmly on the arm rests. "If you have no idea who I am, then why did you agree to trade three Irish prisoners for me? Or was it all just an attempt to trap Miles O'Bruaidar and kill him?"

Nicholas set down his glass on the table with a thump. "And if it was, why did you interfere with the exchange?"

"I objected to the fact that you were going to kill a man who came to you in good faith," she said, looking him directly in the eye. "I don't believe this is behavior fitting for a sworn officer of the Crown."

Nicholas leaned forward angrily, astounded by her impertinence. A lock of his blond hair fell across his forehead, shadowing his furious eyes. "And when did it become fitting for a woman to judge the actions of one of His Majesty's most honored officers?"

Faith bit back an angry retort, knowing that she had already stepped beyond the boundaries of propriety. What in the world was she doing? She needed to stay on the good side of this man. Baiting him would not serve her interests. Taking a deep breath, she looked down at her hands.

"May I suggest a truce? I'm afraid this whole affair has been rather unsettling for me."

Nicholas stared at her for a long moment, the anger fading from his face. Lifting his glass to his lips, he took a long drink.

"Meekness suits you," he said after a few moments had passed. "I suggest you employ it more often."

Faith clenched her teeth angrily, swallowing the urge to tell Nicholas exactly where he could stick his observation.

"What happened to Miles?" she asked, her heart squeezing into a tight ball. "Is he still alive?"

Nicholas sat back in his chair, pressing the tips of his fingers together thoughtfully. "I certainly hope not."

"But you yourself did not harm him?" she inquired hopefully.

"His welfare concerns you?" Nicholas asked sharply.

More than you could ever imagine.

"I'm just curious, that's all," Faith said, mortified when her hands began to shake. She clasped them tightly in her lap.

"And I rather think that you, mistress, are a most curious woman."

"Am I to be flattered?"

He laughed, delighted by the spark of defiance in her eyes. "Indeed, you should. You see, I'm finding it increasingly difficult to imagine you as an Irish spy."

"Me, an Irish spy?" Faith said, her mouth gaping in astonishment.

Nicholas nodded, his face suddenly serious. "Do you know the penalty for treason, my lady?"

"Treason? Don't be ridiculous."

"The penalty for treason is death," Nicholas continued calmly. "And I have good reason to suspect your activities. Do you know who Miles O'Bruaidar is?"

"An Irish nobleman, I presume."

Nicholas laughed dryly. "I *presume* that is what he would like most people to believe. We, however, suspect him of being the Irish Lion, a rebel leader who has consistently been attacking our soldiers and threatening English settlers."

Faith's heart skipped a beat. Miles's heavy gold ring had been in the shape of a lion. " *'Tis the family's crest,*" he had said. *"The ring has been in my family for centuries."*

There had been several occasions on which she had heard the soft whinny of horses being saddled well past midnight. And there was the case of the strange black hood he had been wearing the night he had found her in the forest.

Maybe Bradford was right.

"How can you be certain that Miles O'Bruaidar is this Irish Lion?" she asked quietly.

Nicholas clasped his hands behind his back and walked over to stand in front of her. "I cannot be absolutely certain. However, my sources inform me that he could be the rebel leader we seek."

"Sources like Donagh O'Rourke?" Faith asked, a slight trace of anger flaring in her voice.

Nicholas smiled. "Donagh O'Rourke is a very shrewd man. He realizes the advantages of helping us."

"Such as?"

"Let me put it this way, Mistress Worthington. Ireland is a land in need of conquering. Those who stand in the way of England doing so will be removed. Those who assist us will reap the benefits. You may rest assured that Donagh O'Rourke's holdings in Ireland will remain secure . . . as long as he continues to serve us well."

Fleetingly, Faith recalled the stately O'Rourke Castle, preserved well into the twentieth century. Apparently, Bradford and the English would be true to their word. Yet, wouldn't Paddy O'Rourke cringe to know that his famous ancestor was actually a traitor to his own country?

"Well, I don't see what good Donagh will do you now,"

Faith said slowly. "He'll not be able to return to O'Rourke Castle. He murdered a fellow Irishman in plain sight of everyone."

Nicholas's eyes gleamed. "I fear, my dear, that you are overly concerned with the fate of Donagh O'Rourke. He'll return to his castle sooner than you think. And he'll be well rewarded, as are all men who follow my orders properly. He was instructed to bring you here at all costs, and he did."

"But why?" Faith asked in stunned amazement.

Nicholas gazed at her speculatively. "There are those who are most curious about you, my lady. And I am as well. Perhaps you will now tell me why you interfered when I attempted to put an end to Miles O'Bruaidar's questionable activities."

Faith exhaled a shaky breath. "I told you I could not bear to see a man cut down in cold blood."

"Is that the only reason?"

Faith stood angrily, crossing her arms tightly against her chest. "Just what are you trying to imply? If you suspect Miles O'Bruaidar is this Irish Lion, why not just storm his castle and arrest him? Why all this trickery?"

Nicholas pushed himself up from his chair. "You understand surprisingly little, my dear. Miles O'Bruaidar is a very popular man in Ireland. To kill him in battle is one matter. But to storm his castle and drag him out is something else entirely. I have no wish to make a martyr of this man."

"So you used me to trick him?"

"It seemed a most logical step. Unfortunately, I never suspected an Englishwoman would be moved to help him."

"I reacted out of instinct," she snapped.

Nicholas raised his eyebrows a notch. "Perhaps. Or perhaps my assumption that you are an Irish spy is correct after all."

Faith laughed. "This is a most absurd conversation. If I were an Irish spy, why would O'Bruaidar be willing to trade me?"

"Why, indeed?" Nicholas murmured, stroking his chin thoughtfully. "Well, I suppose I'll have my answer soon enough."

Faith blinked in surprise. "You will?"

"There is a ship leaving for London tomorrow. On it will

208

be a letter from me to His Grace, Oliver Cromwell, requesting information on the activities of a certain Englishwoman by the name of Faith Worthington. If neither he nor anyone else, for that matter, has any knowledge of you, I'm afraid I'll be forced to assume my suspicions about you are correct."

Faith clenched her teeth in anger. "Are you saying that you plan to keep me, an English citizen, here in Drogheda against my will?"

Nicholas nodded mildly. "Though I might be convinced to reconsider my decision if you'll tell me who you are working for and what you were really doing on O'Bruaidar land."

Faith exhaled a deep breath. God help her, her plan had gone terribly awry. Somehow she had gone from being an Irish prisoner to an English one. Now, no matter what she told Bradford, he would undoubtedly send a letter to London asking for confirmation of her story. Then it was only a matter of weeks—or months, if she were lucky—before another ship returned with the information that no one had ever heard of Faith Worthington.

Frantically, she twisted her hands together in front of her. She had to play for time, to make Bradford think that she was a valuable English spy. If she could convince him of this, then she was certain he would not harm her until he had word back from London. By then she hoped to have devised a plan that would get her out of Drogheda.

"Why not send me to London with that letter?" she suggested quickly.

Nicholas thought for a moment, staring at her with interest. "No," he said finally.

"Why not?" she demanded.

"Because you wish it."

Faith dropped her hands to her sides. "Then go ahead and send your bloody letter," she said angrily. "You'll soon find that you've made a grave mistake in your dealings with me. There are people who will be livid at the way I've been treated."

Nicholas gave her a charming smile, but Faith sensed a chilling coldness behind the gesture. "You should be warned, my lady, that my instincts have never served me wrong."

"There is a first time for everything," Faith muttered under her breath.

Nicholas laughed coolly. "Ah, but we shall see, my lady. We shall see."

Chapter Seventeen

Weeks passed before Faith formulated a plan of escape. During that time she remained confined largely to the house with Catherine Bradford. Nicholas was rarely at home, and Faith saw him on only two brief occasions. He did not speak to her, barely acknowledging her existence with a curt nod of his head.

He had, however, taken the precaution of assigning a guard to her. Faith saw his presence as utterly unnecessary. Without money to get to London, she was as good as stuck in Drogheda anyway.

Oddly, Catherine seemed unconcerned about Faith's semi-prisoner status. Faith thought that Catherine's desperate need for companionship caused her to ignore the rather bizarre arrangement and instead act as if she were on some kind of extended holiday.

In some ways her attitude was useful. Faith used her daily chats with Catherine to learn all she could about the garrison. She also determined where Catherine stored the money for marketing. Once a day Faith smuggled a coin or two out of the jar and stored it under her bed. Although she felt shame at being forced to steal, she reminded herself that desperate times required desperate measures.

Stealing was only one of the things she had begun to do in a state of blind automation. She was unable to come up with anything else to penetrate the disbelief and doubt inside her. Too much had happened too fast. Traveling back in time, meeting Paddy O'Rourke, falling for an Irish rebel . . . it was madness. Her emotions and feelings had gone haywire and then finally short-circuited.

In some ways she welcomed the numbness. It kept her feelings at bay, at least most of the time. But she couldn't stop the emotions that came to her at night when she lay in bed thinking about Miles.

Somewhere along the line he had changed her. Once, when Catherine had given her a small looking glass, Faith had stared at herself, wondering if she could see what was different. She looked like the same sensible woman who had come from the twentieth century, but she wasn't. She had changed. And it was for the better.

For the first time in her life someone had chipped a small hole in the wall around her heart. He had shown her a tenderness and a kindness she never knew could come from a man. He had given her hope that maybe one day there would be a chance for love in her life. It was something she had never hoped for before.

And I don't even know if you are alive.

She kept thinking about how she had last seen him, standing in the clearing amid the flickering firelight, wielding a sword against Nicholas Bradford. He had looked so strong, so powerful. Then she remembered the startled face of the young boy in the clearing as he had attempted to take her to safety. It took only one unguarded moment—one traitor—and a life could be lost.

She squeezed her eyes shut. "It didn't happen to you, Miles," she whispered fiercely. "I'm certain of it."

She shouldn't care so much. Miles O'Bruaidar was trouble. Big trouble. If indeed he was the nefarious Irish Lion, he apparently made a practice of hunting down and harassing Englishmen. He wasn't exactly someone to bring home to the family. The fact that he had a body like Adonis and a kiss that could melt Medusa was simply not important. She never should have gotten involved with him.

Faith kept telling herself that until she almost believed it. Then she remembered how gently he had held her after she had nearly drowned, whispering sweet words in Gaelic and chasing away her fears.

"Damn you, Miles O'Bruaidar," she whispered fiercely. "I can't stop thinking about you. I've got to get out of this place."

But it took two more weeks before the opportunity for escape presented itself. It came one warm August afternoon when Catherine mentioned that she was feeling a bit faint and was not up to their weekly trip to the market.

"Just tell me what you need," Faith offered helpfully, barely able to contain her excitement at the chance to put her plan into motion.

Catherine weakly pressed her hand to her brow. "I'm not sure. Perhaps we should just go tomorrow."

"Don't be silly, Catherine. I'll be able to manage just fine."

Catherine nodded. "All right. But let me get you some coins." She pushed herself up, disappearing from the room and returning with the money. "Shall I fetch Lucinda to accompany you?" she asked, dropping the coins into Faith's hand.

Faith shook her head. "That won't be necessary. Besides, I'll have plenty of company." She glanced out the window at her guard, who was leaning against a tree, arms folded across his stomach.

"Yes, of course," Catherine said absently.

"I'll fetch my basket and be right back," Faith said, darting into her room and reaching under the bed for the wrapped bundle of coins. She unrolled the linen strip and slipped several of the coins into the small pouch strapped around her waist. Then, rolling up the remaining coins, she returned them to their hiding place. Hastily, she arranged a kerchief on her head and slid the basket over her arm. Calling out a farewell to Catherine, she hurried out the door before the woman could change her mind.

The afternoon was bright and sunny. Faith shielded her eyes from the sun, wistfully wishing sunglasses had already been invented. Her guard rose from his shaded position under the tree and bowed slightly.

"Where is Lady Catherine?" he asked, squinting his eyes.

"I'm afraid she is not feeling well today. Just the two of us will be going to market."

He grunted acknowledgment of her words and pushed his cap back on top his head. Faith walked past him, happily swinging the basket on her arm.

The market square was teeming with people, many of whom were shouting loudly to advertise their wares. Women carrying large woven baskets filled with fruits and vegetables hurried

213

past, jostling Faith in their haste, while vendors in every direction called out, inviting her to try their goods. Faith shook her head, pushing deeper into the crowd.

Finally she stopped at a stall and bought a half-dozen shiny red apples. She took a bite of the crisp fruit while talking with a man selling pears from a three-wheeled cart.

After some time Faith checked to make sure her purchases were secure in the basket before looking around to see where her guard was. She spied him a few steps away, chatting eagerly with a buxom brunette who was flirting outrageously with him.

It's going to be now or never, Faith thought.

Reaching into the pouch, she drew out a handful of coins. With a furtive flick of her hand she scattered them about the ground.

"Oh, help me," Faith wailed in a loud, dramatic voice. "I've dropped my coins."

Complete pandemonium broke loose as people shouted and scrambled to retrieve the coins. Faith was swallowed up by the crowd, giving her exactly what she had hoped for—anonymity and distance from her guard.

Pushing her way through the people, she ducked into an alley and darted through it to the other side. Once on the street, she took a moment to assess her location. If she remembered correctly from her conversations with Catherine, the docks were located just north of the market. Setting her mouth in a hard line of determination, Faith lifted her skirts and hurried in that direction.

She soon realized from the air's salty tang that she was on the right track. She quickly came upon several majestic wooden ships with billowing white sails. One vessel in particular caught her eye—it looked heavily laden and ready to sail. A few sailors were hauling a large barrel onto the deck with the aid of several ropes. An older man with silver hair and a beard appeared to be directing the sailors' activities. From the way he was ordering them about, Faith decided he was a man with some kind of authority.

Summoning her courage, she strode forward, stopping directly in front of the man. "Good day, sir," she said, pulling herself up to her full height. "May I ask how one goes about securing passage on this vessel?''

The old sailor stared at her in surprise, his piercing blue eyes sweeping down the length of her clearly expensive gown and back up to her face. ''Shouldn't ye first ask where we are headed, my lady?'' he asked in a thick Irish brogue.

Faith met his gaze evenly. ''Where are you headed?''

The old man chuckled at her impertinence. ''London,'' he said with a toothless smile. ''But ye're a bit old to be running away from home. Having trouble wi' the lad now, are ye?''

Faith drew herself up to her full height. ''I am not having trouble with my lad, as you put it. What I need is safe passage. Can you help me?''

''Mebbe I can, mebbe I can't,'' the old man said, assessing her from under his bushy gray eyebrows. ''Ye are English, are ye no'? What are your reasons for needing such passage?''

''My reasons are my own,'' Faith said firmly.

The old man stroked his beard thoughtfully. ''Do ye have money?''

Faith pulled out the few remaining coins and dropped them into his outstretched hand. ''This is just to show you that I am serious. I'll bring you twice as much if you secure me passage.''

The man looked down at the coins and then lifted his eyes to meet Faith's unwavering gaze. She saw genuine astonishment reflected in his eyes and wondered with growing nervousness if she had overpaid him. Good God, she had no idea of the actual value of the coins. She had just given him what she had, praying it would be enough.

''How soon would ye be willing to leave?'' he asked softly.

''Tonight,'' Faith answered without hesitation.

Surprise flashed in his eyes, but he pressed his lips together tightly, as if to quiet the question forming there. Gingerly, he pocketed the coins.

''I'll be waiting for ye here come nightfall. The ship leaves on the morn. Don't be late.''

Faith slipped stealthily from her window as night fell upon Drogheda. Once on the ground beneath her window, she paused a moment to look around in the dim moonlight. Her nerves were stretched thin, her stomach jittery. It had been an eventful day. After her discussion with the old sailor at the docks she had hurried back to the house. Her guard was already there, clearly relieved to see her. Breathlessly, Faith explained to Catherine how she had dropped the coins and then been swallowed up by the crowd. Much to Faith's relief, Catherine dismissed the guard and seemed content to let the whole matter drop.

Pulling her cloak tighter around her shoulders, Faith took a deep breath to calm herself. Feeling a twinge of guilt, she wished she could have left a note behind for Catherine, apologizing for taking the money and disappearing so abruptly. In her own way, the woman had been kind. Besides, Faith could hardly blame her for the actions of her husband. But in this century paper and parchment were not easy to come by; nor did she have access to a writing utensil. Unwilling to risk searching for them, she had regretfully decided not to jeopardize what might be her only chance at escape.

Stepping out into the light, she quietly threaded her way along the darkened streets. She was careful to remain as concealed as possible in the shadows—she had no wish to be either accosted or stopped by anyone. She breathed a sigh of relief when the docks finally came into sight. Swiftly, she headed for the ship she had seen earlier. There was no one on the dock, but a small rope ladder dangled from the side.

Swallowing the lump of fear that lodged in her throat at the sight of the water, she reached out for the ladder.

"It's just water," she whispered firmly to herself. "And this ship is the only way to London. Now get on with it."

Her heart pounding nervously, she hiked up her skirts and began climbing the shaky ladder. "Is anyone here?" she whispered loudly when she reached the deck. "I've returned as promised."

There was no immediate answer; then suddenly she heard the sound of a flint hitting stone. A moment later an eerie light spilled across the deck. A shadowy figure stepped forward.

"I'm here."

Faith sighed with relief. "Thank God. I wondered whether . . ." She stopped in midsentence when the light flickered over his face.

"Bradford," she whispered.

Nicholas took a step toward her as the old sailor moved out of the shadows and into the light.

"You told him," she hissed at the old man accusingly.

"He only did as he was instructed," Bradford said calmly. "No one procures passage from this garrison without my knowledge. Most fortunate for me, you were unaware of this little regulation."

"You bloody tyrant," Faith said through clenched teeth.

Nicholas laughed. "I must admit that this was quite an ambitious plan, my dear. London, indeed? I rather envisioned you rushing back into the arms of Miles O'Bruaidar."

"Is he alive?" Faith asked, her heart skipping a beat. "Were your men unable to harm him?"

Bradford frowned, striding toward her. "I assure you, I'll have the head of your Irish rebel if it is the last thing I do."

She gave an audible sigh of relief. "He's not my Irish rebel," she corrected absently, but a smile rose to her lips anyway.

Miles was alive! Thank God, he was alive.

Her emotions soared and then plummeted. Despite her enormous relief that Miles was all right, she realized with growing trepidation that her carefully laid plans had just fallen apart. Now Nicholas would certainly confine her to quarters, if not throw her directly into the garrison prison. Even worse, he would soon discover—if he did not know already—that she had stolen money from Catherine. This made her a thief as well as a suspected Irish spy. She had no idea what the punishment was for stealing in the seventeenth century. For all she knew, they executed people for such crimes.

Yet despite her precarious situation, exhaustion, nerves and frustration sent a giggle bubbling from her lips. Here she was, stuck in the year 1648, a woman with a college education as well as a priceless knowledge of events to come. But at this very moment, standing on the deck of the ship, her whole situation was absurd. It was so Kafka-esque that Faith suddenly burst out laughing.

Bradford's eyes narrowed suspiciously. "You find this amusing?"

Faith nodded, wiping her eyes with a corner of her sleeve. "Frankly, yes. I find this entire situation exceptionally amusing. To think that I am in Drogheda in the year 1648 on the deck of an antique vessel in the middle of the night, arguing with a stiff-necked English garrison officer who believes I'm a dangerous threat to king and country. Yes, I'd say this is sufficiently absurd to merit amusement." Another burst of laughter sprang from her. "God," she gasped, "not only is it absurd, it's absolutely farcical."

Nicholas and the old deckhand exchanged disgusted glances. With a disapproving frown, Nicholas strode across the deck and grabbed her by the arm, shaking her firmly.

"You face very serious charges," he said angrily. "What do you have to say for yourself?"

Faith ceased her laughter and looked at him, a glint of anger flashing in her blue eyes. "I have nothing to say for myself. But I do have something to say to you."

Nicholas stopped in his tracks, gripping her arm so tightly she winced in pain. "And what might that be?"

Faith drew herself up to her full height. For the first time she realized the advantage her height gave her in this century. She actually stood an inch taller than this Englishman.

A completely serious expression on her face, she looked him directly in the eye. "You, Mr. Bradford, are a pompous idiot and an embarrassment to the Crown. God save us from Englishmen like you."

She had only a moment to see the rage in Nicholas's eyes before he raised a fist and stars exploded behind her eyes.

Chapter Eighteen

Faith wasn't exactly thrown into prison, but it was not the comfort of Bradford's home either. After her escape attempt had been foiled, Nicholas confined her to a sterile room in the same ugly building she had first been brought to upon her arrival in Drogheda. She had little more than a cot, a threadbare blanket and a chamber pot. She was constantly under lock and guard and rarely permitted to leave the room. Days passed in isolation and Faith waited, alternating between fits of extreme frustration and moments of deep fear.

The isolation was what frightened her the most. She had no one to talk to and her room was without a window of any kind. One morning, when she could bear it no longer, she begged her guard to permit her to visit the church. Although she had never been terribly religious, she believed this to be her best chance of getting out of her prison room. Besides, she reminded herself, praying could hardly make things worse.

Although at first her guard denied her request, he promised to bring it up with one of his commanding officers. Three days after her original request, the bolt was drawn from her door and she was led outside into the hazy, hot summer air. She barely had time to let her eyes adjust to the bright light when she was forced to move along a dirt road toward the church. As they reached the massive stone structure, he hastily ushered her up the steps. Once at the top, he gripped her elbow painfully, warning her in no uncertain terms that he would be watching her every move. With those harshly whispered words, he thrust her forward into the gloomy stillness of the church.

Sunlight filtered in through the magnificent stained-glass windows as Faith walked slowly down the center aisle, marveling at the beauty of the old Catholic cathedral. A few people sat or knelt in the pews, mouthing prayers and reciting their

219

rosaries. After a moment Faith slipped into one of the pews and settled on the hard wooden bench.

Bowing her head, Faith let her thoughts turn to her family—her mother, her father and Fiona. Painful regrets swept through her. If she were to die tomorrow, who would miss her? Only Fiona, dear, sweet Fiona, would shed a tear for her. And Fiona would never know what really had happened.

"I've no' seen ye here before, child," a voice said in a deep Irish burr.

Startled, Faith raised her head to see a gray-haired priest with kind eyes. "I'm not from Drogheda, Father," she replied.

"It doesn't matter. Have ye need to confess?"

"I'm not Catholic either."

"Ah, so ye are English. Well, 'tis a formidable affliction to overcome, but one that can still be absolved if the proper humility is shown."

A small smile rose to Faith's lips. "Why, if I didn't know any better, Father, I'd say you were teasing me."

The priest nodded cheerfully. "Aye, but that I am, child. Truly now, have ye need to talk to someone?"

Faith's smile faded. "I don't know. Perhaps I do."

He put a gentle hand on her shoulder. "Then what ails ye? Surely God will hear all and forgive, if ye are truly repentant."

Faith fell silent for a long moment before speaking. "It is hard for me to say, Father. I am guilty of a terrible sin." She swallowed hard, fighting down an overwhelming urge to stand up and leave. The priest squeezed her shoulder lightly.

"Speak with your heart, lass. Do no' be afraid."

Faith exhaled a deep and painful breath. "It's . . . about my father."

She wasn't sure why she suddenly had the urge to blurt out her painful past with her father. Perhaps the anonymity of the priest and his kind blue eyes finally offered her the chance to ease her pain.

"What about your father?"

Her throat tightened and she struggled to push the words out. "He . . . he . . ."

"Harmed ye?"

She exhaled a heavy breath. "Yes . . . in a way, I suppose he did. You see, he loved my mother very much. When she died he made me feel that it was my fault—that I was responsible. After that, he would have nothing to do with me. I felt so hurt and abandoned that he didn't love me that I . . .'' she choked on a lump in her throat, feeling the tears well in her eyes, ''. . . I told him that I would hate him forever.''

''I see,'' the priest said gravely.

Faith pressed a trembling hand to her fair brow. ''Things didn't change even after I became an adult. We rarely spoke, except to argue. Even when he lay dying I didn't go to him. I thought he deserved to suffer as I did.'' A tear slid down her cheek. ''But it wasn't true, Father; it was all a lie. I loved him so terribly much. The truth is that all my life, no matter what I did and no matter how often I told myself that I hated him, I always aspired to win his love. But he never knew. I couldn't bring myself to tell him while he was alive. And now it's too late.''

The priest reached over, placing a comforting arm around her shoulder. ''Hush, lass. 'Tis never too late. I never knew your da, but 'twould no' surprise me to know that he knew o' your love all along. And perhaps in his own way he loved ye too, although mayhap his guilt and shame would no' allow him to show ye. 'Tis sometimes difficult for men to express their feelings, especially if there has been much hurt and pain.''

She brushed at the tears with her fingertips. ''I'm so ashamed of what I did. I'm more like him than I ever thought possible.''

''I sincerely doubt that. Ye must be strong and find it within yourself to end the pain. But ye don't have to do it alone, nor should ye keep your pain inside. 'Twill only cause ye more suffering.''

She lifted her head to look at him. ''Your advice sounds remarkably familiar. There's a man . . . an Irishman . . . who told me the same thing. What is it with you people that you have such remarkable insight?''

He smiled. ''Och, there's a saying that the Irish have a way with words.''

She smiled a little. ''I thought the saying was that the Irish have a way with horses and women.''

The priest laughed. ''This Irishman, he told ye that too?''

"He did."

"Well, I suggest that ye take the advice, but question the version o' the saying. This man—is he someone ye love?"

"Love?" Faith exclaimed. "Of course not. I mean, even if I did, it would be impossible."

"All things are possible in the eyes o' the Lord."

"Yes, well, I'm afraid this is not. I'm sorry, Father."

He patted her hand comfortingly. "Don't be sorry. Just remember that God made us all for a purpose, lass, to love and be loved in His sight. Don't let this experience wi' your father stop ye from daring to love again."

He stood, moving farther down the pews. After a moment Faith rose to her feet and made her way to a small alcove lit with dozens of prayer candles. She picked up a votive candle and lit it from another. Bending to her knees on a small velvet-lined bench, she closed her eyes in a silent prayer.

Dear Lord, I ask for guidance and help. Why have I been brought back to this time? What do you wish for me to do?

Her eyes opened when she felt someone kneel on the bench beside her. Looking sideways, she saw that another priest clad in a hooded black robe had joined her. Not wishing to disturb him, Faith quickly averted her eyes, turning back to her prayers.

"Is your soul at peace, my child?" the priest asked softly.

Faith's head jerked up at the sound of the familiar voice. Slowly, the priest pulled back his hood. Faith looked directly into the dancing green eyes of Miles O'Bruaidar.

Faith's mouth gaped open in astonishment. "My God," she whispered. "It is true. You are alive."

He smiled. "Glad to see me?"

She suppressed the urge to fling herself into his arms and instead stole a furtive glance over her shoulder to see if her guard was paying any undue attention. When she saw he was not she took a deep breath and turned back around, staring straight ahead.

"Of course I'm glad to see you," she said in a low voice. "What are you doing here?"

"Looking for ye, and, may I say, having a most interesting time." He lightly fingered the sleeve of his black robe. "Father Michael lent it to me. Do ye think it suits me?"

She frowned. "This is hardly a time to jest. Can't you see that I'm being held prisoner? It is dangerous to associate with me."

"Ah, so I've heard. An Irish spy now, are ye? 'Tis most fascinating."

"You know I'm not an Irish spy."

"Aye, 'tis what makes this a rather curious development." He looked carefully at her face, noticing the redness and puffiness around her eyes. "Ye've been weeping," he observed, his jaw tightening. "Have they harmed ye, Faith?"

She shook her head, warmed by the protective note in his voice. "No, I haven't been harmed . . . yet. I tried to escape, and that's why they are keeping me under lock and key. How did you know I was in Drogheda?"

Miles softly blew out a breath. "Have ye forgotten the exceptional skills o' Shaun Gogarty? It took him only a week to discover ye had been taken here. Believe me, 'tis little in Ireland that can be hidden from Shaun once he puts his mind to it."

Faith couldn't help the brief smile that rose to her lips. "I should have known. But you must leave at once. English soldiers are looking for you. They suspect you of being a rebel they call the Irish Lion. If they capture you away from Castle Dun na Moor, they will kill you for certain."

Miles smiled dryly. " 'Tis odd how ye worry about me when 'tis ye who is a prisoner. I've come to offer ye safe passage out o' this garrison."

The hand holding the candle suddenly trembled. "You have?"

"Unless ye prefer your accommodations here."

"Not hardly. Can you really free me?"

He snorted. "If anyone else had asked that, I'd be offended enough to draw steel. O' course I can get ye out o' here. Just tell me if ye want my help."

"Is there a price for such passage?"

Miles's green eyes met hers steadily. "Truthful answers to my questions. All o' them."

She shook her head. "You don't want to know any more about me, Miles. Trust me on this one."

Miles raised an eyebrow. "It doesn't matter what ye tell

me, Faith. It won't change how I feel about ye."

Her heart leapt in her chest. "I wish I could believe you," she whispered.

"Ye can. Now do ye want out o' here or no'?"

Faith closed her eyes for a long moment. "All right," she finally said. "What's the plan?"

He hesitated. "I don't have one yet."

She looked at him incredulously. "You don't have one yet?"

"I'm figuring this out as I go along."

"Splendid," she breathed.

"Will they let ye attend church next Sunday?"

"I don't know."

"Well, if they do, be ready. If they don't, I'll have to think o' something else. Just remember, Faith Worthington, that I'll be true to my word, if ye'll be true to yours."

A flicker of surprise flashed in her eyes. "How did you know my full name?" she asked. "No wait, don't tell me— Shaun, presumably. Send him my greetings, will you?"

Miles laughed softly. "Aye, I will."

"I've missed you, Miles," she said softly. "I can't believe how much."

"I missed ye too, lass."

His expression darkened momentarily. "I'll see that Donagh pays for his treachery."

"I think he is still here in Drogheda. Be careful, Miles, please."

"I will," he whispered, leaning toward her, appearing to be nothing more than a priest murmuring comforting words to a woman in need. His face came so near that Faith could feel the light warmth of his breath on her cheek. His hand slid momentarily across hers, entwining his fingers with hers.

"Do no' be afraid, Faith. I'll no' let anything happen to ye. I give ye my word."

They looked at each other for a long, meaningful moment before a sudden movement caught Faith's eye. Turning slightly, Faith saw her guard walking toward them.

"My guard is coming this way," she murmured quickly. "You'd better go. I'll be ready on Sunday."

"Be careful, Faith. Don't trust the English."

"That's easy for you to say," she whispered back. "You're Irish."

He muffled a laugh before setting down the candle and pulling the hood back over his head. Standing stiffly, he crossed himself before turning and walking to the entrance. He passed her guard in the process and Faith held her breath, fearing the guard would see through Miles's disguise and detain him. When she heard no ensuing commotion she sighed with relief.

"Come on; you've had enough time here," her guard said gruffly, coming to stand beside her.

Nodding, Faith placed her candle down in the alcove and stood. Her face was tranquil and serene, as if soothed by her time spent in prayer. No one would have suspected that her insides churned madly with a mixture of excitement and consternation.

Sunday, she thought to herself. *Please Lord, let me last until Sunday.*

The days passed with agonizing slowness. Faith constantly paced her room, shooting anxious glances at the door. Each morning she made a small notch in the leg of her table with a sharp piece of wood to count the passing days. Her mind kept reliving those few minutes alone with Miles in the church. She hardly dared to believe that he was in Drogheda and had promised to rescue her.

On Saturday Faith sought and received permission to attend church the next day. By the time Sunday morning arrived she thought she would burst with anticipation.

She woke at the crack of dawn and quickly donned her gown. Forcing herself to sit quietly on her cot, she folded her hands serenely in her lap and waited for the hours to pass. Her mind played with a hundred scenarios for escape until she was exhausted, yet none seemed plausible.

Finally a knock sounded on the door. "Enter," she called out, trying to keep the eagerness from her voice.

There was a long pause before the bolt scraped against the wood and the door swung open. Her guard stepped cautiously into the room.

"Good morning, my lady," he said stiffly.

"Good morning," she replied politely. "When can we leave for the church?"

The man shrugged. "Someone wishes to see you first. I'll allow you a moment of privacy to ready yourself while I go and see if your audience is ready." With that announcement he turned on his heel and left the room, shutting the door and bolting it firmly behind him.

Faith took a deep breath, tucking her fair hair behind her ears. Coming slowly to her feet, she walked over to a small table that held a basin of water. She splashed some of it on her face, patting it dry with a linen cloth. Who could wish to see her? Was this part of Miles's plan?

Faith felt increasingly uneasy. What if it wasn't Miles at all? Perhaps the escape plan had been discovered. She shook her head, forcing herself to quell an overactive imagination. Speculation would serve no purpose other than to stretch her already taut nerves.

She managed to calm herself sufficiently by the time the guard returned to fetch her. He led her down a long, empty corridor before he stopped in front of a closed door. Lifting his hand, he knocked sharply, and Faith heard someone call out permission to enter. The guard opened the door, motioning that she was to go in alone. Exhaling a nervous breath, Faith crossed into the room.

An older gentleman with gray sideburns sat in a chair by the hearth, an ornately carved cane propped beside him. His legs were stretched out in front of him, but his eyes of startling blue stared at her with undisguised curiosity. A strapping youth Faith judged to be no more than sixteen stood behind the seated man, apparently ready to assist the older gentleman if he were called upon.

"Ah, Mistress Worthington," the gentleman said, waving a jeweled hand at her. "Forgive me if I do not stand, but I have an injury that makes it difficult for me to do so." He tapped on his leg and Faith heard a hollow echo.

Horrified, she stared at the leg for a long moment before dragging her eyes to his face. "Sir Arthur Aston," she whispered. "Governor of Drogheda."

He smiled, seemingly unembarrassed by the horrified expression on her face. "Yes. I presume you have heard about my wooden leg. I hope it does not offend the delicate sensibilities of a young woman such as yourself.''

Faith shook her head, realizing that he misunderstood her morbid fascination with his leg. ''No, of course it doesn't offend me. I apologize if I was staring.''

He shrugged, resting his hands lightly in his lap. ''I'm afraid it does seem to unsettle some people. However, I have found myself getting quite accustomed to it.''

Faith nodded, wondering how he could bear the discomfort of a wooden leg. It seemed so barbaric and primitive when compared with the lifelike and flexible prosthetics of the twentieth century.

''Please, sit down,'' he said, motioning her to an empty chair across from him. ''May I offer you some tea?''

''That would be most kind of you,'' she said, perching on the edge of the chair.

''Roland, see that tea is brought at once,'' Sir Arthur said with a barely discernible flick of his hand. The young man bowed slightly and left the room, shutting the door behind him. Sir Arthur leaned back in his chair and stared at Faith for some time before speaking. ''You, mistress, have caused a bit of excitement since your arrival here eight weeks ago.''

Eight weeks? Faith thought with astonishment. *Has it been that long?*

''May I ask what day it is?'' she inquired curiously.

''It is the twelfth day of August.''

The twelfth of August? She had traveled back in time on her birthday, the first of May. That meant she had already been living in this century for three and a half months.

''I'm afraid my presence here in Drogheda is far from exciting,'' Faith said, quickly composing herself. ''There has been quite a bit of misunderstanding.''

''Has there now? Well, I've only recently returned from a trip to Dublin, and I've heard little other than talk of a most mysterious Englishwoman. You can well imagine how anxious I was to meet you.''

She spread out her hands. ''I'm afraid there is not much mystery. As you can see, I am just a simple woman.''

''According to Nicholas Bradford, you are quite a woman, indeed.''

Faith smiled lightly. "He flatters me."

"Something he is not often accused of doing. You have, Mistress Worthington, most certainly piqued my curiosity. What has brought you to Ireland?"

"Well," Faith said, sitting back in her chair, "as I've already explained to Mr. Bradford, I was sent here on a mission of great secrecy. Unfortunately, I'm afraid I'm not permitted to reveal its true nature to anyone, even to someone as distinguished as you, sir."

Aston studied her for a long moment, stroking his chin thoughtfully. "Charles would never send an agent here without my knowledge. However, this does, of course, leave open the possibility that you are an agent for someone in the Parliament. May I be so bold as to suggest Lord Oliver Cromwell, perhaps?"

Faith quickly considered an appropriate response. Aston was loyal to King Charles and would certainly see Cromwell as a threat.

"I assure you, sir, that my mission here in no way seeks to undermine or harm His Majesty King Charles in any way. You may consider me a most loyal subject."

She was interrupted as Roland returned, carrying a tray with a teapot and two cups. He set the tray carefully on the table and stepped back as Sir Arthur reached over and poured tea into Faith's cup before filling his own.

"Forgive me, madam, if I say that I am not overly reassured by your words," he remarked, setting the teapot back on the tray. "Even to me, it seems most unlikely that King Charles would send an unmarried woman alone on a dangerous mission to Ireland."

Faith picked up her cup and saucer, balancing it carefully on her lap. "However unlikely, may it not also be said that unusual circumstances often require unusual measures?"

Sir Arthur leaned forward in his chair, eyeing Faith speculatively. "Why did you try to escape from us?"

Faith kept her face carefully composed. "My mission is of great urgency. Keeping me prisoner in Drogheda only delays me from my task."

"And what of Bradford's suspicions that you are an Irish spy?"

"His claims are unfounded and ridiculous. I'm as much an Irish spy as you are."

Her answer took Aston by surprise. After a moment he burst out laughing. "Touché, my dear. You do most pleasantly surprise me with your quick wit. However, you may rest assured that I harbor no such suspicions of you."

Faith exhaled a deep breath. "Thank you."

Aston picked up his cup and took a small sip of the tea. "You see, I received instructions about you just last night. A messenger has returned with an answer to Bradford's letter. It seems that his inquiry created quite a stir in London."

"It did?" Faith said, feigning surprise as the palms of her hands suddenly became damp.

"Yes, it did. And quite frankly, madam, no one has ever heard of you or your supposed mission to Ireland."

"Oh," she said rather weakly. "Perhaps the people involved are simply not at liberty to speak up."

Aston smiled. "That is rather doubtful. I'm afraid you have left me with no other recourse than to side with Mr. Bradford. You see, had you been sent by the king or any of his closest advisers, I certainly would have been informed of it, albeit in a most discreet manner. As I have not, the most logical conclusion to be drawn is that you are an agent of the English Parliament, or more likely Oliver Cromwell himself. That vile man has long been posturing to undermine the king. What he plans for Ireland, I do not know. But I will not sit idly by while he moves his agents here and waits for an opportune time to call them to action."

Faith's mouth dropped open in horrified astonishment. "You are mistaken, sir. I told you I do not work for Oliver Cromwell."

Aston's blue eyes grew steel cold. "Publicly I will agree with you. You see, it will much better suit my purpose to see you branded as an Irish agent, participating in a variety of nefarious activities that threaten both King and country. So unless, my dear, you tell me post haste who you really are and what you are doing in Ireland, your fate will be most dire, indeed."

Icy fingers of dread wrapped around Faith's heart, squeezing until she could barely draw a breath of air. If she told him the truth, he would never believe her. And she certainly couldn't fault him—she could hardly believe it herself.

"I have told you everything I can," Faith said slowly. "But I cannot emphasize enough that I do not in any way work for Mr. Cromwell or for anyone in the English Parliament."

Sir Arthur watched her silently, drumming his fingers lightly on the top of his cane. After a moment he struggled to his feet, brushing off the hand of the young man, who reached out to help him. "Well then, it appears that things are quite settled. The execution shall proceed as planned."

Faith's heart stopped beating altogether as she looked up at Aston with an expression of mingled horror and disbelief. "Did you say execution?" she squeaked.

He nodded. "Yes, my dear, execution. Your execution, to be exact. It seems that upon the morn, the English Crown shall thankfully rid itself of another one of its odious traitors. Good day, mistress."

With those words, Sir Arthur turned to leave, his cane tapping rhythmically as he and the young man exited the room. Faith watched them go, her mouth incredulously agape.

"Execution?" she murmured in stunned amazement. After a moment, she leapt to her feet.

"*My execution?*" she shouted at the top of her lungs.

Chapter Nineteen

Faith wasn't allowed to attend church that morning, nor was she returned to her room. Instead she was taken directly to a dark, cold holding cell in the basement of the garrison building. There was no water, no food and little light in the cell. The only furniture was a small rickety cot with a moldy straw mattress and a wooden bucket which she assumed was for relieving herself.

Faith walked to the mattress but refused to sit on it when she saw that it was crawling with bugs. Trembling, she backed up against the cold stone wall, unable to believe this was happening to her.

She leaned against the wall for support, fighting to keep herself from spiraling into despair. What had happened to Miles? Had he and the others waited long for her to appear in church? Was her fate really to die here in Drogheda?

She hugged herself tightly as her teeth began to chatter from the cold. Several times she asked for a blanket, but her cries were ignored. Pacing back and forth in her tiny cell, she attempted to stay warm by rubbing her chilled extremities to keep the blood flowing though her veins.

The hours ticked past while Faith paced the small cell, knowing that with each passing minute her chances for escape were growing dim indeed. When the little light there was in the cell faded into complete blackness Faith experienced a frightening panic. Nervous sweat broke out on her forehead as she fought to hold on to the last vestiges of sanity. Murmuring encouragement to herself, she stayed rigid against the cold wall for the entire night, her nerves jumping each time she heard the rustling sounds of what she imagined were large rats and other crawly night creatures. Their small whining cries and the scrape of tiny claws as they moved across the stone floor filled her mind with images upon which she did not care to dwell.

When Faith finally spied a sliver of light creeping beneath the door she did not know whether to be frightened or relieved. Closing her eyes, she hoped that she would somehow wake up in her own bed and have a good laugh at her rather imaginative dream.

"Please let this all be a dream," she murmured to herself, squeezing her eyes shut as tightly as she could. "Please let it be a dream."

She was still standing against the wall, her eyes tightly closed, when her cell door was flung open. Letting out a small cry, Faith's eyes flew open in surprise. Sir Arthur Aston and a tall priest she did not recognize stepped into the cell. Aston immediately wrinkled his nose at the dank, musty smell. Shaking a kerchief from his pocket, he held it daintily to his nose.

"I trust you had a comfortable night," he said, his voice muffled by the kerchief.

"Forgive me if I find your sense of humor to be rather lacking," Faith replied wryly.

Sir Arthur snorted into his handkerchief. "Ah, but how delightful to find that your spirit is not." He waved the priest forward. "Permit me to introduce Father McLeary. He is here to offer you spiritual counseling."

Faith took a firm step forward. "This is ludicrous. You just don't go about executing innocent people without trial or due process of law. Come, we are still English subjects, are we not?"

Sir Arthur lowered the kerchief, his eyes cold. "Lest you forget, madam, Drogheda is my jurisdiction, granted in full to me by His Majesty King Charles. It is I—the Governor of Drogheda—and no one else, who determines what constitutes treason under the laws of England. You may rest assured that you have been fully afforded due process of law."

Faith laughed hoarsely, shaking her head. "God, is this what England has come to? What is it you want me to confess, Aston? What must I say to put a stop to this insanity?"

Sir Aston lifted his cane, pretending to examine the tip with extraordinary curiosity. "I wish only to know who sent you."

Faith closed her eyes for a moment before opening them. "King Charles," she said softly.

The side of his cane hit her face so quickly that she stumbled sideways, clutching her cheek. "Have care to speak such blasphemy in my presence," he warned, his face black with anger.

Faith gingerly touched the side of her face, already able to feel the tender swelling of a bruise. "Then what do you wish me to say? Would you stop this execution if I told you Cromwell sent me?"

Aston stepped forward, dragging his wooden leg behind him. "Did Cromwell send you?"

"Will such a confession put a stop to this purported execution?"

Aston's eyes gleamed. "Yes."

Faith raised her eyes to meet his. "All right. Then Cromwell sent me."

A slow smile crossed Aston's face. "So I suspected. You cannot imagine the delight I will find in hanging an agent of Cromwell's."

Faith's mouth dropped open in outrage. "You said such a confession would cease all talk of execution."

Aston waved a hand to dismiss her anger. "Tsk, tsk. You should not be so naive as to believe all the promises you are told."

"Damn it, Aston," Faith shouted, "I said only what you wanted to hear. You know it's not the truth."

Aston looked shocked at her language. "Please restrain yourself, madam. Have you forgotten we are in the presence of a man of the cloth? Now, because I am a generous man, I grant you five minutes to clear your soul and conscience. Farewell, madam."

Faith lunged for Aston but was intercepted by the tall priest, who pulled her arms tightly behind her back.

"You lying bastard," she shouted as the cell door slammed shut, leaving the sound of Aston's laughter ringing in her ears.

She was living in a nightmare. Faith begged the priest to listen to her, to help her escape, but he only touched her forehead, murmuring nonsensical words, absolving her of guilt and sins. Realizing he would not listen to her pleas, Faith stalked to a corner of the cell and stayed there until the priest left her alone.

She wanted to scream and yell, to force herself out of this

nightmare, but she did neither. It would be too easy, too cowardly to slip into the safety of madness. Besides, she had been a fighter her entire life and wouldn't allow herself to crumble now. If she were to die, she would do it with the dignity befitting a Worthington.

When two men came to take her away Faith stood calmly. She stumbled only momentarily as she walked from the cell, the muscles in her legs weak from the cold. One of the men put a sturdy hand on her elbow, keeping her upright. The light was bright after her dark confinement, and she narrowed her eyes to slits, proudly shrugging her arm out of the grip of the guard.

She blinked rapidly as she was led outdoors. After her eyes adjusted to the brightness her gaze fell on a harnessed wagon that stood empty and waiting. Several guards lined the path to the wagon, many of them leering and staring openly at her. Faith swallowed hard, feeling her courage falter.

"N-no," she whispered.

She was pushed forward as someone grabbed her hands, tying them roughly behind her back. "Let's go, mistress," someone said, dragging her toward the wagon.

She gasped in anger as one of the guards grabbed her and lifted her into the wagon, letting his hands rest longer than necessary on her derrière. Furious, Faith kicked out at the soldier angrily, meeting only with air. The soldiers howled in laughter before one of them knocked her to the floor of the wagon with a heavy backhand.

"Get the wench out of here," one of them shouted at the driver. After a small jolt the horse plodded forward, the wagon creaking loudly. Faith bounced about the wagon without the luxury of her hands to brace her from the jarring bumps and holes the wagon hit with increasing frequency.

Soldiers rode beside and behind the wagon, some of them shouting insulting jeers, calling her everything from a traitor to a doxy. She kept her gaze straight ahead, refusing to give them the satisfaction of seeing her humiliation. Even as she summoned what little resolve she had left, a jolting bump threw her against the side of the wagon. A rough piece of the wood tore her gown somewhere beneath her left breast. When she felt the cool breeze on bare skin, Faith realized she was partially exposed. Whistles and taunts confirmed her worst fears as her cheeks burned with the shame of it.

She angrily jerked away from a soldier who reached down into the wagon to fondle her, clenching her teeth shut to stop from weeping with the hopelessness of her situation.

Oh God, if only I could lose consciousness and never wake up. Never in my worst dreams did I imagine a fate such as this one.

Her jaw unclenched slightly as she felt the wagon come to an abrupt halt. Slowly, she struggled to her knees and then lurched to her feet. What she saw caused her mouth to go dry with fear. A huge scaffold stood in the center of the square, surrounded by a throng of people jostling and laughing as if they had come out for a picnic. As their eyes fell on the prisoner to be hung standing stiffly in the wagon, they hushed momentarily before shouting and surging forward to see her.

Faith hardly noticed them. Her gaze was locked morbidly on the oversized scaffold and the noose that hung from the crossbeam, swaying gently in the breeze.

I am going to die.

The knowledge hit her with such force, she felt as though she had been punched in the stomach.

Oh God, this is how I am going to die.

A guard grabbed her roughly, pulling her from the wagon. He dragged her forward as a group of soldiers cleared the way through the noisy throng. Struggling in vain to free herself from his grip, Faith anxiously scanned the crowd for Miles. Did he know what was happening to her? Even if he did, how could he save her? She was surrounded by dozens of guards and would soon be out of reach on the scaffold.

Someone in the crowd reached out and tore the sleeve of her gown, holding up the material as if it were a souvenir. Hands reached for her, touching and grabbing wildly for pieces of her clothing. Every time someone pulled another strip of cloth from her, the crowd roared in approval. Faith kept her gaze focused straight ahead even as she felt her stomach lurch sickly at the leering faces around her.

As they reached the stairs of the scaffold, her guard prodded her in the back until she took the first step up. He continued to poke and pinch her to his great amusement until she finally turned around and kicked him hard in the balls. He coughed once in astonishment and then dropped to his knees on the stairs, moaning loudly while the crowd cheered bawdily and shouted with laughter. Turning, Faith marched up the remaining stairs alone, feeling oddly proud of herself. Although it had been only a brief moment of control over her situation, it made her feel better than she had in days. At least her dignity might survive, even if she didn't.

Then the executioner stepped forward.

Faith's mouth dropped open in mingled disbelief and horror as the giant man moved toward her. He wore no shirt, and the rippling muscles of his bare arms and the ugly scar on his thick neck looked as threatening as the noose that swung in the breeze above her. He rubbed his hands together in what looked suspiciously like glee as he stepped toward her, clad only in a pair of dark breeches held up by thick leather suspenders. Fighting back the hysteria bubbling in her throat, Faith presumed the absence of a shirt was to prevent bloodstains if the prisoner did not die easily and had to be beheaded. She shivered, certain he was smiling behind the tiny slits in his black hood.

The crowd cheered with excitement. Shouts for the hanging to begin rang in her ears until she felt dizzy. Christ, had these people nothing better to do than to attend a hanging as if it were some kind of sport?

Come one, come all. Faith Worthington takes on the black-hooded executioner from hell. Let the game begin!

It was all she could do to keep from dissolving into complete hysteria when the executioner took her by the hand and led her to a stool. After inhaling several deep gulps of air to keep herself from fainting, Faith managed to step onto the stool while the executioner steadied her trembling legs. Then, climbing up onto an adjoining stool, he reached over and slid the noose around her neck, tightening it until it fit snugly. Stepping off his stool, he pulled it back out of the way.

Her fate thus determined, Faith lifted her face to the warm summer breeze, sorrow engulfing her. Never again would she breathe clean, fresh air or walk through the forest and marvel at the beauty of nature. Never again would she feel the sun on her shoulders or smell the salty tang of the sea. But those things paled against her regret that she would die before putting an end to the treachery and chaos Paddy O'Rourke planned in this century. Without her to stop him, he would likely commit a series of assassinations in an attempt to create a future of his own choosing. She had not done one thing to stop him, nor had she told anyone of the danger. She had in a word . . . failed.

The crowd fell silent in hushed anticipation. Murmurs of impatience and excitement rippled through the crowd.

"Have you any last words you wish to say, madam?" someone called out from the front of the crowd. Faith recognized the voice of Sir Arthur Aston.

Startled, she looked down at him, realizing that these would be the last words she would ever utter. "Only that you, sir, are hanging an innocent woman. May God forgive your soul . . . and mine," she whispered as an afterthought.

Shouts erupted from the crowd as a drumroll began. Faith took one last look around the crowd before a movement in the front row caught her eye. A hooded man had drawn his cloak aside, and the sun glinted brightly off an object at his waist. Intrigued, Faith raised her eyes to his face. As she watched, the man threw back his hood, revealing the grim face of Miles O'Bruaidar.

Their eyes met for an endless moment, the loud shouts of the crowd fading into nothingness as the sound of her own heartbeat filled her ears. Her eyes were dry, but she felt her throat choke with emotion.

"Prepare to meet your death," she heard the executioner say, jolting her from her thoughts. She looked again at Miles and gave him a tremulous smile that she hoped made her appear brave. His eyes remained trained calmly on her face, as if he was willing her to stay alive. She took a deep breath and held her head high, looking straight ahead.

I will not be afraid. I will not be afraid.

The roar of the crowd reached deafening proportions before falling abruptly to an eerie silence. Faith heard the single wail of a baby and a melancholy cry from a bird flying above before the drumroll started again, softly at first before building to a furious crescendo.

Good-bye, Miles, Faith thought, closing her eyes.

Her hands clenched into fists as the executioner drew back his leg to kick the stool out from beneath her feet.

Oh God, I hope this is quick, was her last coherent thought.

Chapter Twenty

The crowd's cheering and the frenzied sound of the drumroll easily hid the movement of the small dwarf who deftly stepped away from the crowd and into the shadows of a nearby building. After several attempts at scraping flint against stone, he was rewarded with a small spark, which he touched to some tinder. Nursing the tiny flame, he carefully held it to the tip of an oil-soaked cloth attached to an arrow he pulled from a small quiver at his belt.

The dwarf's timing was perfect. So intent was the crowd on the dramatic event unfolding on the scaffold that no one noticed him. As soon as the arrow was lit, Shaun saw the executioner move forward to kick the stool from beneath Faith's feet. Stepping out of the shadows, the dwarf lifted a bow concealed beneath his cloak and fitted the flaming arrow tightly into it. Taking careful aim, he shot it directly at a barrel that had been placed at the south edge of the scaffold. Moments after impact, the south part of the scaffold exploded in a blazing mass of fire and wood, collapsing the crossbeam and dropping the prisoner amid the ruins.

After a horrified moment of shock, people began screaming and running about in terror. Thick black smoke billowed up into the sky, filling the air with an acrid smell and causing tears to stream down the faces of all those near it. Soldiers shouted orders and ran about wildly, not knowing where or whom to strike.

Amid the shrieking panic of the crowd, one man leaped easily to the broken and burning scaffold. Swiftly, he whipped out his sword and slashed the rope that still remained around Faith's neck as she lay facedown on the splintered wood, gasping for air.

"Miles," she said weakly, lifting her head. "Is that you or have I died and gone to heaven?"

Miles knelt down beside Faith, brushing her hair gently back from her face. "You're going to be all right, lass," he said before untying the rest of the rope from her neck and lifting her over his shoulder.

"Watch your back, Miles," he heard Furlong shout from below as the dreaded executioner rose from the debris and staggered toward him, an ugly-looking ax in his hand. Miles stepped slightly to the side, easing Faith off his shoulder and safely behind him.

"There ain't a man alive who can keep me from me job," the burly executioner said, tearing the hood off his head as he advanced on Miles.

Holding his sword before him, Miles stepped boldly forward. The flames were rapidly approaching their position, but Miles held steady. With a bellow of rage, the executioner rushed toward him, waving the ax. Miles ducked beneath his blade, circling around so that he still stood between the man and Faith.

The executioner screamed in anger, his face black from the smoke, his eyes wild. Again he charged forward, the heavy ax swinging in a deadly arc. Miles lifted his sword to meet the ax, and a clang of metal vibrated through the air.

"Death to ye," the executioner screamed as flames rose up behind him.

Realizing the entire scaffold was about to go, Miles feinted sideways as the man swung again. Lunging forward, Miles thrust his sword into the executioner's unprotected side. As the man fell heavily to the wreckage, a flash of orange engulfed him. Miles heard him scream in terror as the flames began to consume him.

Quickly resheathing his sword, Miles bent down and swept Faith into his arms. She was coughing, groggy and faint from the smoke. Swiftly, Miles made the short jump to the ground, still carrying her, moments before another small explosion rocked the scaffold. As he ran for the safety of the forest, the entire structure collapsed.

Glancing back over his shoulder, Miles saw that his men were melting into the crowd, slowly heading for their mounts. If all went according to plan, they would meet later at a predetermined location. Nodding with satisfaction at the way his plan had unfolded, Miles turned and plunged into the forest, still carrying Faith.

Nicholas Bradford paced back and forth across the room, his face black with rage. "How could this happen?" he spat out furiously. "How could you let Cromwell's agent escape?"

Sir Arthur Aston sat in a plush chair, watching Bradford stalk angrily about the room. He lifted a crystal goblet to his lips and drank deeply from it before setting it down on a small table near him.

"She was officially accused of being an Irish spy," Aston commented mildly.

"You know what I mean," Bradford said, glaring. "It doesn't change the fact that you let her escape."

"I would hardly say that I *let* her escape. Her departure ◦was, might I say, rather unexpected."

"This situation is intolerable," Bradford said, slamming his fist against the wooden door. "I'll not stand for having Cromwell's agent running loose about Ireland."

Sir Arthur leaned forward in his chair, his blue eyes remarkably cold. "Cease your dramatics about Cromwell, Nicholas. I know full well where your sympathies lie."

Bradford halted in his tracks. "I don't know what you mean."

"I think you do," Aston said dryly. "Your support for King Charles holds firm for as long as he is in a position to aid you with your ambitions in Ireland. If that position were ever to weaken, there is little doubt in my mind that your sympathies would quite easily shift."

Bradford's face turned red from the affront. "How *dare* you accuse me of such treachery against the king."

Sir Arthur leaned back in his chair and picked up the goblet again. "I accuse you of nothing, Bradford. Your actions speak for themselves."

Nicholas strode across the room and stood directly in front of Aston. "Damn you, Aston. Are you suggesting I had something to do with the woman's escape?"

Sir Aston shook his head. "No; not even you would be so foolish. However, I must admit to being baffled as to who staged the rescue."

Donagh O'Rourke, who had been sitting silently in the corner of the room, suddenly stood up. "I think I know who might have wanted her free. I can't be certain, but I believe I saw Miles O'Bruaidar jump from the scaffold carrying the lass in his arms. The smoke was thick and 'twas difficult to see, but it could have been him."

Bradford swore softly while Aston thoughtfully took a drink from his goblet. "Why?" murmured Aston, resting the glass on his knee. "What interest could O'Bruaidar have in the woman?"

"What interest?" Bradford snapped furiously. "Damn it all to hell, Aston, she must have been working for the Irish all along."

O'Rourke shook his head doubtfully. "Nay, I don't think so. I thought at one time the lass might have been part o' a plan O'Bruaidar devised to test me. But my spies at Castle Dun na Moor told me the lass tried several times to escape O'Bruaidar and she never once approached me in any manner, altho' I provided her plenty o' opportunity to do so. Instead, the talk among the servants was that she was a mystery; a fairy lass with some kind o' magic."

"Christ," Bradford snorted. "The Irish are so obsessed with superstitions, it turns my stomach."

"Have a care to speak o' my people in such a way, Bradford," Donagh growled, coming to stand in front of Bradford. "There is usually good reason for such talk."

Nicholas's face purpled with anger. "You're a fine one to talk about your people, O'Rourke, when all you care about is filling your pocket."

O'Rourke's hand shot out and grabbed Bradford around the neck. "And ye are falling over yourself to fill it, Bradford. Ye need me and ye know it, bastard."

Aston frowned, waving his hand impatiently. "Gentlemen, gentlemen, please. Insulting each other will not solve our problems. Let us at least be civilized about our situation. What we need now is action, not affronts. I shall immediately dispatch a detail to O'Bruaidar land to see if, indeed, he has the girl. Legally, he cannot hold her; she is an English subject and accused of a crime. But I must say that this daring rescue does make for a most interesting development. Yes, gentlemen, a most interesting development indeed.''

Faith's eyes fluttered open and for a moment she lay where she was, flat on her back on the cool earth, looking up at a canopy of leaves and branches. Sunlight filtered in through the cracks, warming the side of her cheek. The scene was so peaceful and soothing that Faith simply marveled at it until the memories abruptly came flooding back.

She bolted upright, her hand circling around her neck for the rope. "Miles?" she croaked hoarsely, realizing her voice had all but left her. "Miles?" she whispered again, her entire body beginning to shake.

He was beside her before she could open her mouth again. With a strangled cry, she threw herself in his arms.

"Hush, Faith," he said, wrapping a heavy blanket about her shoulders. "Ye're alive and everything is going to be all right."

Faith clutched him tightly, afraid that if she let go he would disappear. He held her close, stroking her hair and arms, murmuring to her in Gaelic. Although she understood nothing, the words were soft and comforting, his voice a gentle caress.

She had no idea how long she clung to him, only that when she pulled away, his shirt was soaked with her tears. "My God, what happened?" she whispered. "One minute I have a rope around my neck, the next I'm in the middle of a raging inferno."

"Och, there was a wee bit o' an explosion. But it appears the English have lost their valuable prisoner."

"Lost me?" Faith repeated incredulously. "Christ, they tried to hang me. Some valuable commodity I turned out to be."

"Well, ye are a bit o' a mystery to all o' us, lass. If ye aren't working for the English and ye aren't working for the Irish, who are ye spying for? The French? The Scots? Or did Cromwell throw ye to the hounds?"

"Cromwell has nothing to do with this," she insisted. "But I'll be damned if anyone believes me. Look, the truth is I'm not working for the English or the French or the Scots. I came here by accident."

Miles sighed. "Back to that now, are we?"

She rested her head against his shoulder. "Give me time, Miles. I've just been through a rather ghastly experience. And so have you. You risked a lot to save me. There is a chance someone will have recognized you. Why did you do it?"

He reached up to sweep a strand of her pale hair off her cheek. "Because I promised ye I would."

She shook her head in disbelief. "But I wasn't worth risking your life over. I've caused you nothing but trouble from the moment you set eyes on me."

He laughed. " 'Tis said that there are women worth dying for. Are ye one o' them, lass?"

She looked at him, frowning. "I'm serious. Can't you see how becoming involved with me has made matters worse? You could be punished severely for what you have done."

"Och, I fear ye worry far too much about me. I've yet to be intimidated by the English, and I'm no' about to start now."

"You're the most exasperating man I've ever met. Don't you fear anything?"

His fingertips traced the curve of her cheek. "Aye, there are things that cause me concern. But ye are safe now."

She leaned into him, craving the warmth and safety of his arms. "I know. It's the craziest thing, but I feel so safe around you. I've been shot, chased, drowned, abducted and even hung—yet through it all you are always there smiling at me, telling me it is going to be all right."

Miles chuckled softly. "Christ's mercy, but I was so proud o' ye, standing on that scaffold, looking death square in the eye. I've seen men ten times your size break down and weep, yet ye held your head high and refused to give in, even to the end. How did ye do it, Faith? What magic do ye possess that gives ye such remarkable courage?"

She shook her head. "No magic, Miles. Believe me, had there been magic I would never have been on that scaffold. I was utterly terrified. It took everything I had not to dissolve into hysterics or drop to my knees and beg for mercy. But I can be bloody stubborn too. When I saw you standing in the front row it helped. I thought that at least there was someone out there who cared for me and might feel sad at my death."

Miles turned her head toward him so that she would look directly into his eyes. "I do care for ye, Faith," he said softly.

She lowered her gaze. "I know. Thank you, Miles. You saved my life . . . again."

Chapter Twenty-one

"We can't stay here," Miles said, rising to his feet and pulling her up with him. "They'll be looking for us. We must go."

"Where?" Faith asked as he untethered the horse.

"Back to Castle Dun na Moor," he said, turning around. "Unless ye have an objection to that."

She hesitated. "This may surprise you, but I do . . . sort of."

Miles frowned, anger flitting across his face in a dark shadow. "Ye care to explain that?"

Faith held up a hand in a truce. "I promised you answers and you will have them, as strange as they may sound. But for now, the truth of the matter is that I really must go to England. London, to be exact."

"London?" he exclaimed in shock. "Have ye gone mad? Need I remind ye that the English just tried to hang ye?"

"I know it sounds insane, but I do have my reasons."

Exhaling a frustrated breath, Miles narrowed his eyes. "What in the devil are ye plotting, Faith?"

She ran a hand wearily through her tangled and sooty locks. "It is a long story, Miles, and we haven't the time to go into it now."

"Nay, we don't." His frown deepened as he mounted the horse, offering a hand to help her up. "I'm no' taking ye to London, Faith, at least no' now. We'll proceed to the rendezvous where the others are waiting for us. We must make haste; we have a long ride ahead o' us."

Seeing that she had little choice, Faith reluctantly nodded in agreement. She climbed up on the horse with him and he lightly slapped the reins, guiding the stallion forward. They were silent by tacit agreement, with Miles concentrating on the trail, often leaving it to make certain they were not being followed.

"We'll have to stop here for the night," he finally said,

pulling gently on the reins. "We're still several hours from the rendezvous and dusk is falling. 'Twould be too dangerous to ride farther in the dark."

Nodding, Faith slid off the horse, groaning as her aching muscles protested the movement. Miles dismounted after her and opened a leather pack tied to the saddle.

"There is a burn no' far from here. I'll water and brush the horse. Ye'll find a bedroll and another wrap inside," he said, handing her the pack. "Settle yourself on it and when I return I'll start the fire."

Faith nodded as he led the horse away. Stiffly, she pulled out the bedroll and a blanket. Spreading them on the ground, she began searching the area for sticks and branches that would serve as kindling for the fire. She had stacked up a small pile when Miles returned from the burn with the horse. As he looked at her, a frown crossed his face.

"Ye are supposed to be sitting on the bedroll, warming yourself beneath the wrap."

Faith dropped a bundle of sticks and turned to face him. "I'm not an invalid, Miles. And there is no sense in you doing all the work when there are two of us."

He shook his head in disbelief. "If any other woman had said that, I'd have thought she was no' quite right in the head. But no' ye, Faith. Nay, ye can hang from the gibbet, fall to a burning scaffold, ride several hours through the forest and still have enough strength to gather wood for the fire. I've yet to meet such a hearty lass."

Faith wiped the dirt from her hands. "I'm actually flattered by that comment, coming from you. I may be a woman, Miles, but I'm not helpless. It may take a few centuries, but men will finally figure that out about women."

Miles approached her, raising a dark eyebrow speculatively. "Telling fortunes now, are ye?"

Faith looked up quickly, realizing how foolish her words must sound to him. "I suppose you could say that I am. Silly of me, isn't it?"

Miles shook his head slowly. "Nay, no' silly. Just unusual. 'Tis one o' the things I find most intriguing about ye, lass."

Looking into his smiling green eyes, Faith felt an urge to slip her arms around his neck and press her lips to his. But she did nothing, realizing such behavior would only complicate, not help, their relationship. Lowering her eyes, she took a slight step back.

"Do you have anything in that pouch to eat?" she asked, pulling the cloak tightly around her shoulders.

Miles nodded, staring at her for a long moment as if he was going to say something. But he seemed to change his mind, for he turned and pulled a flask and a cloth packet out of the pouch.

"Here," he said, handing them to her. "I'll set a spark to the kindling."

Faith took the items and set them on the bedroll as she pulled one of the thick blankets around her. Once seated and safely snuggled beneath the wrap, she pulled the top off the flask and sniffed the contents suspiciously.

"Is this some kind of alcohol?" she asked, wrinkling her nose at the powerful smell.

Miles walked around their small camp, gathering larger pieces of wood and dropping them near the kindling. "If ye're asking me whether that flask holds spirits, the answer is aye."

She sniffed again and then closed the bottle. "Ugh. I think I'd prefer water."

Miles shook his head. " 'Tis too dark to go down to the burn now. Ye'll have to manage wi' what we have in the flask. I promise ye, lass, 'twill go down so smoothly, ye will hardly notice."

Faith shuddered. "It will probably burn my insides. It smells like gasoline."

"Gasoline?" Miles asked, bending over the kindling and striking flint to stone. "What's that?"

Faith looked up quickly, realizing her mistake. "Ah . . . it's a foul-smelling liquid we have in England. It's . . . ah . . . not for consumption by people. It's poisonous."

She waited expectantly for further questions but he simply grunted, seemingly satisfied with her explanation. Faith let out a small breath of relief, reminding herself that she would have to be more careful with her choice of words. Setting the flask aside, she unwrapped the small cloth packet and found a chunk of dried meat. It looked about as appetizing as a house shingle.

"I suppose you consider this dinner," Faith said wryly,

holding up the meat with two fingers. "Do we cook it or just chew on it?"

Miles looked up at her and grinned. "Chew it. And to show ye how gallant I am, I insist ye have the first bite."

"Gallant, my foot," Faith muttered, examining the meat with distrust.

Miles grinned again as he continued to strike the stone against the flint. Finally he was rewarded with a small spark, which ignited some dried grass. Carefully, he held it to the kindling, blowing gently until the flames began to lick at the dry wood. A few larger pieces were added, and soon the fire began to blaze. He motioned for Faith to come closer and she wasted no time scooting the bedroll nearer to the warmth. As she settled down, her stomach growled loudly, causing her to flush with embarrassment.

"Ye'd better try a bite o' that meat, lass," Miles said, his lips twitching with a smile. " 'Twill be little else until we meet up wi' the others tomorrow."

She sighed. "Oh, all right, but if I get food poisoning, I'm holding you responsible." Closing her eyes, she gingerly took a small bite. Surprisingly, it didn't taste as bad as she had expected. The meat had a smoky, tangy taste but was extremely difficult to chew.

"Your turn," she said, handing the meat to Miles.

He smiled at her before leaning back on his elbows and tearing off a piece with his teeth. Faith watched him in wonder as he chewed enthusiastically and then washed it down with a large swallow from the flask.

"You actually like the taste of it?" she asked in amazement.

Miles shrugged, the firelight flickering off his square jaw and boldly chiseled mouth. " 'Tis nourishment. And there have been many times when I have gone without." Offering no other explanation, he tilted the flask and took another drink. With a sigh of contentment, he wiped his mouth with the back of his hand.

"You must have had a difficult life," Faith said, forcing herself to swallow the food she had in her mouth. "I mean, with the English coming over to Ireland by the boatloads."

Miles raised his head to look at her directly. " 'Tis true that my life hasn't always been easy. And ye, lass?"

"Well, I never went hungry. But there were ... other things."

"What other things?"

She looked down at her hands. "Oh, things I'm not that anxious to dredge up right now."

"Your relationship wi' your da, mayhap?"

She nodded. "Yes, and relationships in general. I'm dreadful company and a disaster on a date."

"I don't know what a date is, but I don't think ye are dreadful company."

She smiled. "That's the nicest thing you've ever said to me."

"Tell me more about yourself, Faith."

She shook her head. "Not yet, Miles. I'm not quite ready."

"Don't ye trust me?"

She managed a shaky laugh. "As ridiculous as it sounds, I think I've trusted you from the start, but I just didn't want to trust my instincts. I can't explain why."

Miles leaned over to brush a soft kiss on her cheek and Faith looked at him in surprise. "Some things do no' need explaining, lass," he said softly. "They just are."

An unexpected current of understanding and need leapt between them. Faith felt her pulse bounce erratically in her veins at the touch of his warm lips against her skin. She thought Miles to be affected too, for he stared at her intently before clearing his throat and dragging his eyes away from her face.

"Well, we'd better get some sleep," he said, his voice a bit unsteady.

Faith watched as he stood and then settled himself with a blanket on the other side of the fire. "Why are you moving over there?" she asked curiously.

"I'm going to sleep."

"Don't you want to share the bedroll? There is room enough for two."

Miles propped himself up on one elbow, his dark eyebrows rising a notch. "Is that an invitation?"

Faith's cheeks flushed red with embarrassment when she realized what he thought she was proposing. "No, I . . . I . . ." she stammered. "I just thought you would be more comfortable here."

Miles grunted, leaning back on the ground and crossing his arms behind his head. "Mayhap I would. But 'twill be safer for ye and your reputation if I keep myself at a distance."

Faith settled down on the bedroll, mortified at her words. Miles was right. Lest she forget, in the seventeenth century there was only one kind of woman who made such propositions to a man.

She flung her arm across her brow, closing her eyes. Perhaps she *was* propositioning Miles in her own way. She couldn't help it. He was the first man to whom she had ever been so fiercely attracted and who also made her feel physically desirable in return. Yet he was the exact opposite of everyone she had ever thought herself attracted to. He was an Irishman, poorly educated and had the rather inflexible and unenlightened opinions of . . . well, a seventeenth-century male.

She laughed softly. It was madness. Yet she was falling for him, in spite of herself. Despite his rather headstrong tendencies, he had shown remarkable warmth, tenderness and loyalty. He had risked his life for a woman he hardly knew, kept his promises, acted with honor and protected those around him. What more could a woman ask for?

Faith shook her head. It was ridiculous for a person her age to fantasize like a young schoolgirl, but he brought out such unusual feelings in her that she couldn't help herself. Besides, seeing how she had almost died today, she could permit herself a small, harmless fantasy. As long as she kept it that way.

She touched her cheek, remembering the way his warm lips had brushed her skin. Every touch of his hand electrified her, sending sparks racing across her nerve endings. He was in a word—incredible.

A small noise from the other side of the fire caused Faith to lift her head curiously. Miles was tossing about restlessly in his blanket, muttering a few choice phrases. A small smile of satisfaction crossed her lips as she put her head back down on the bedroll. Apparently sleep was not coming easy to him either.

Drawing the cover up over her head, Faith closed her eyes, hoping that sleep would drown the thrumming need pulsing through her body. Rolling over, she snuggled deeper within the bedroll and let herself drift off to sleep, dreaming of a handsome Irishman with dark hair and green eyes.

She was drowning; swirling water filled her nostrils, taking her under, pulling her down. Frantically, she clawed at the surface, fighting to stay above, screaming, screaming, screaming. . . .

"Faith, wake up."

Water everywhere. Dark, sucking, greedy.

"Wake up, lass. Ye're having a bad dream."

Faith bolted upright in a panic, looking about wildly before her eyes fell on Miles. "Oh my God," she choked, collapsing in his arms. "Oh my God."

"Hush, lass," he murmured soothingly in his thick Irish brogue. " 'Twas naught but a bad dream. And 'tis no wonder, given all ye have been through in the past few days. But ye are all right now."

Faith clutched his shoulders until the thundering of her heart subsided. "I was drowning, Miles, and this time there was no one to save me."

His arms tightened about her. " 'Twas just a dream." He gently stroked her back. " 'Tis many fears ye have in your life, Faith Worthington. Do ye ever permit yourself to just *be?*"

"I . . . I try. But it's not so easy."

"Aye, 'tisn't easy to face your fears. Especially when ye won't let anyone help ye."

"But my dreams . . . they seem so real sometimes."

Miles grasped her hands and pressed them firmly to his heart. "This time, Faith, 'twasn't real."

She inhaled an unsteady breath, the aftermath of the nightmare still haunting her. "I suppose you're right. I feel so foolish."

Miles stroked her back gently, whispering softly against her hair. " 'Tis no need. I'll hold ye for a bit."

She buried her head in his chest as his fingers lightly kneaded the corded muscles in her neck and shoulders. Beneath the magic of his fingers Faith felt the tension slowly drain from her being. A small sigh of pleasure escaped her lips as she wound her own arms around his waist, listening to the steady thump of his heart.

The hands on her shoulders abruptly ceased their magic. Puzzled, Faith lifted her head. His face looked strained, his green eyes dark with an emotion she could not read.

"Ye'll be all right now," he said stiffly, pulling back abruptly as if she had burned him. " 'Tis sleep ye need. We've a long day ahead o' us tomorrow."

Faith put her hand lightly on top of his, stopping him. "Please, don't go over there just yet. Sit beside me for a while longer."

Miles laughed hoarsely, but the sound came out as a tortured grate. "Christ's mercy, Faith, I am but a man. Do ye realize how hard it is for me to keep from touching ye, from wanting ye?"

"Me?" she whispered in surprise. "You really do want me?"

His hand slid to her chin, holding it firmly. "Because ye have a wit and a spirit like no lass I've ever known. And ye are so very lovely. 'Tis a damnable mixture, and one that even a saint couldn't resist."

She felt her cheeks warm at his praise. "I thought you said I was little more than skin and bones. And my hair . . . you don't like my hair."

He laughed softly. "How can a beautiful lass like ye be remarkably unaware o' your allure? Your body and hair—'tis true they are different. But 'tis exactly what I like about ye, Faith. Ye are unique. And to tell ye the truth, I even overheard a few o' the servant girls saying how they wished they were bold enough to try such a short style wi' their hair."

"You did?"

"I did."

She reached up to touch her hair in wonder. "Imagine that. Faith Worthington—trendsetter."

"I want ye, Faith."

Faith felt her heart take a perilous leap. "I want you too," she whispered. Slowly, she reached out, touching her fingertips to his lips.

Miles grasped her wrist, turning it over. One by one he kissed her fingers, lingering and savoring over each one as if

253

they were a precious treasure. A delicious shudder swept through her body as his lips moved to trace the veins in her wrist before drawing a stirring path to the bend of her elbow.

"Miles," she murmured softly as he bent toward her.

His mouth sought hers, his warm tongue gliding languorously across her lips. Her lips parted and she tasted the inside of his mouth with tenuous excitement.

The kiss was slow, hot and incredibly sensual. A warm heat seeped through her limbs. Her hands slid down to his shoulders, feeling the shifting, solid play of muscles beneath her fingers. In response, he eased her down on the bedroll beneath him, his lips never leaving hers. As she held firm to him, he pressed the full length of his hard body against her.

"Hell's fire," he whispered fiercely, releasing her passion-swollen lips. "What have ye done to me, woman? I haven't been able to stop thinking about ye."

Faith's breath caught in her throat as she stared up at him. He gazed at her openly and hungrily, his desire unabashedly evident. "Oh, Miles," she whispered softly. "You don't know anything about me or what I'm doing here."

He laughed unsteadily. "I don't care . . . I really don't. How could I no' want ye? Ye are magic to me—a woman made o' mist and mystery. Ye are willful and strong-minded, yet ye can be as soft and fragile as a single drop o' water on my fingertip. One moment I want to burn in the fire I see in your eyes, and in the next I'm afraid of touching ye, wondering if ye'll crumble beneath me."

Faith felt a warm glow flow through her, moved beyond words by his declaration. "I've never known a man like you," she finally whispered softly. "You have touched me here." She slipped her hand beneath his shirt and placed it directly over his thudding heart. "It both frightens and quiets me."

His hands cupped her face, gentle and strong. "I don't want ye to be afraid o' me, Faith."

"I'm not. Just kiss me," she murmured, pulling him closer. "Just kiss me, Miles."

Leaning over, his tongue slid across her lips. Faith moaned softly, splaying her fingers against his chest. Miles shuddered in pleasure as she skimmed her hands along his hot skin, marveling at the rock-hard muscles beneath her fingertips. His mouth moved feather light across her body as he rained kisses on her neck, cheeks and eyelids. Faith arched up against him, slipping his shirt from his shoulders.

He tasted like whiskey and smelled like green meadows, leather and smoke. His body was firm against hers, hard and throbbing with need. Throwing back her head, she pressed against him, allowing herself to spiral headfirst into a dark, forbidden tunnel of pleasurable sensations. The fall was deliriously fast and frightening but held a promise of glorious light at its end.

He touched her everywhere, first with gentleness and then with an urgency that had her aching all over. His breath was heated and seemed able to penetrate the very material of her gown, which still separated her skin from his. Impatiently, Faith reached up to slide the gown off her shoulders, but Miles grasped her hand firmly, stopping it in its place.

Surprised, Faith opened her eyes and looked up at him. "Miles?"

He did not answer but simply placed her hand down gently on the bedroll. As she watched, he glided his fingers up to her wrist and arms, halting at the satin ribbon that held her gown together at her breast.

"Faith," he said softly, "I need to know if ye really want to do this. 'Tis no' too late for me to stop if ye have no wish to continue."

"I wish to continue," she said, her blue eyes hazy with desire. "Please, I couldn't bear it if you stopped."

A lock of his dark hair fell across his forehead. "I don't want ye to think wi' your body." With his fingertip he traced a light circle at the tear in her gown beneath her left breast. "I want more than just your body, lass. 'Tis your heart I'm asking for. And I'll no' take ye now if ye cannot offer it to me."

Faith froze at his words, frightened at the reckless emotions coursing through her veins. "My h-heart?" she stammered.

Her brain screamed reason, beckoning her back to the safety of the walls she had spent so many years building around her heart. Although pain and loneliness existed in that fortress, at least it held none of the breathtaking fears she was beginning to have being held so tightly in the arms of this Irishman.

Run. Slip from his arms. If you let him touch your heart, you will shatter into a million pieces when you leave. You can't risk it. Not with him, not with anyone.

But to never know love? If only she dared to experience it for just this night, she could hold the memory in her heart forever. Fear clogged her throat, making it difficult to breathe. Oh God, she was terrified of opening her heart further, fearful that at the journey's end she would find only heartache and sadness.

"Faith?" he asked gently.

She bit her lower lip, lulled by the gentle concern in his rich, deep voice. Her body began to tremble so violently that her teeth chattered in her head.

"My sweet Faith," Miles said softly, smoothing back a strand of her hair. "Why are ye so afraid?"

Because you seem able to see through me to my heart. Because since my mother died the only thing that kept me strong was closing myself off to other people. Oh God, I never knew I needed anything more until I met you.

Panic crowded the edges of her mind, causing her breathing to come fast and fearful. She grasped his hand tightly, tense and scared.

Miles sighed, smoothing her hair back from her face. "Ye've naught to fear wi' me, Faith. Cease your inner struggles. I'll no' harm ye, ever."

Her hand gripped his so tightly, her knuckles turned white. "Why?" she whispered. "Why won't you just take my body? Is it not enough?"

"Nay, 'tis no' enough for me or for ye, and I think ye know it."

"But I'm frightened," she managed to choke out. "I'm frightened of the way I feel about you. And I know you'll be disappointed with me. I can be so cold, so unlovable. But that's not how I really feel inside. It is just a way to hide the hurt and loneliness . . . to protect myself."

"Sweet Jesu," Miles murmured, his fingers tracing the curve of her face and the line of her cheekbone. "How long have ye carried about such fears?"

"All my life," she whispered ashamedly, looking down.

Miles curved a finger beneath her chin and nudged it up

until she looked directly at him. "Ye are such a beautiful woman, Faith, both inside and out, that it makes me ache. I never felt this way for a woman before. 'Tis like all the other women I've known before ye were just shadows, shifting images o' something I've been searching for all my life. Then ye came along and hit me in the head, literally. 'Twas no' what I expected, falling for a *Sassenach,* but ye made me so daft, I could think o' nothing else. I need ye and want ye, Faith. But I'll come to ye only if ye can offer me your heart."

Faith swallowed the raw emotion that surged into her throat, fearful of the foolish things it might cause her to say. Biting her lower lip, she battled the urge to throw it all away, to retreat to the safety of her walls. Instead, she reached out and took his hand, pressing his long, slim fingers to the ribbon of her gown.

"I need you, Miles," she said, a tremor in her voice. "I need you to show me how to be happy."

"Faith, my sweet Faith," he murmured before grasping the ribbon and pulling once. The material parted easily. Gently, Miles slid the fabric aside, drawing in his breath as her warm and waiting breasts slipped into his waiting hands. Moaning, Faith arched her spine as he lightly brushed his fingers against the swollen tips. Slowly, reverently, he stroked and caressed her skin. He took his time with her, intensifying the pressure, then easing off slightly. Desire uncoiled deep within her body, awakened after years of slumber. Heat and pressure shot through her veins with such force that she gasped.

He worked miracles with his tongue. Raw pleasure pumped through her blood as he drew the tip of her breast into his mouth, his swirling caress setting her on fire. Patiently and tenderly, his mouth touched, tasted and teased her burning, tingling flesh.

"My God," she whispered. "What are you doing to me?"

"I'm showing ye what it can be like between a man and a woman who share no' only their bodies but their hearts."

He pressed his lips tenderly to hers, their mouths meeting and melding as if they had been made for each other. His tongue stroked the inner recesses of her mouth in a gentle, sensual rhythm that made Faith clench her fingers around his thick arms. She was on fire, burning, aching to feel every masculine inch of him.

"Miles, please," she gasped, as he reached for the fastenings on the front of his breeches and drew them down over his hips.

"We've time, lass," he said softly. "Tonight we have all the time we need."

His dark head bent toward her neck, nibbling a fiery path to her breasts. The edges of his teeth teased and tortured her rosy peaks until she was delirious with desire. A heavy, dreamlike pressure began to build between the apex of her thighs until she was nearly weeping.

"Please, Miles, it hurts. I need you . . . to . . . to . . ."

His own passion was running as hot and mindless as hers. Forcing himself to go slowly, he languorously slid his hand up her thigh and beneath her skirts. He let out a sudden breath of air as his seeking fingers found the soft curls at the font of her womanhood. She felt so soft, so warm, so ready for him. Murmuring sweet words in her ear, he began to stroke her intimately. A glow spread up her legs and thighs, leading her to a precipice of pleasure.

"No," she gasped, squirming beneath him. "I'm afraid . . . I'm f-falling."

"I'll be there for ye, Faith," he murmured. "Just let go, lass. Leave your fears behind and trust me."

Her fingers slowly unclenched from his arms and she leaned back against the bedroll. "I trust you. Oh God, I do trust you."

She fell headfirst into an abyss of pleasure, surrendering to the masterful hands that held her captive. Time seemed meaningless; all that mattered was the touch of his skin against hers, exploring. When the aching pressure finally burst she felt shudder after shudder go through her, shaking her to her very toes.

"Oh, Miles," she whispered, "I never knew it could be like that."

He smiled. "And there's still more to come, lass."

Gently, he pulled the rest of her gown and undergarments from her body until she lay naked beneath him. With one hand, he shed the remnants of his clothes and lowered his body to hers.

A Double-Edged Blade

Faith stared at him unabashedly. His body was magnificent. His skin was tanned gold and glowed in the flickering firelight. A thin line of dark hair started at his stomach and spiraled down, cushioning his manhood before thinning to a light coat over his thick, muscular legs.

He was so beautiful that she could hardly believe he was real. Tentatively, she reached out and touched his chest, tracing a line down the curve of his hip before resting her hand at the top of his thigh.

"I want to touch you too," she said softly.

He guided her hand to his chest and pressed it tightly against his skin. "Aye, and I ache for your touch, lass."

Slowly, she slid her hands down the muscles in his chest, stopping to stroke the hard, flat plane of his belly. His skin was hot to her light, cool touch, and she marveled at how still he lay beneath her gentle ministrations.

For a fleeting moment she reveled in the fact that she would not have to explain her virginity to him. Seeing how she had never been married, a man of his time would expect it of her. All her life she had dreaded the awkward moment of explaining that she had never slept with a man. But with Miles, she had none of those fears.

Bending over his chest, her mouth lightly brushed across the tips of his male nipples. She was rewarded with a groan and became bolder, nibbling a trail of small, hot kisses down to his stomach. Her hair fell over her shoulders, puddling in a silky pool of softness on his chest.

"Christ's mercy," Miles gasped after she moved lower, her tongue finding something more interesting with which to toy. "Come to me, lass, for I fear I can withstand your torture no longer."

With a growl, he rolled over on top of her, lifting her legs until they were wrapped tight around him. He pressed his shaft forward until it was poised at the entrance of the cleft between her legs and then stopped. Faith whimpered in surprise, clutching his shoulders, drawing him nearer.

"Nay," Miles said, his breath coming in ragged gasps. "Open your eyes and look at me, Faith."

Her eyes fluttered open and Miles drew in his breath at the look of utter trust and belief in them. His gaze never leaving her face, Miles grasped her hips between his hands and in one fluid motion thrust forward. As his shaft buried deep within her, she gasped and arched her back.

She fit him perfectly, like a hand in a glove. Gasping, he felt her squeeze him tightly, welcoming him to her body. Exhaling a shuddering breath, he began to rock in the age-old motion, setting their rhythm at a slow, sensual and utterly pleasurable pace. As they moved together, Miles cupped Faith's cheek gently with his hand, his eyes searching hers, as if gazing into her very soul.

Faith was captured by his gaze, as if pinned to a board like a butterfly. Her heart, her mind, her soul were drowning in the depths of his green eyes. His gaze was filled with fire, passion and possessiveness. In one night this man had given her everything she had ever dreamed of—safety, love and a sense of belonging. She had never felt so close to another human being—never felt so loved and cherished. She owed him everything for bringing her back to life again.

"Miles," she murmured. "You are magic."

He smiled, covering her face with warm kisses, winding his fingers through her hair. With each touch of his lips and fingertips, with his heated whispers, Miles softly described the pleasures she brought him. His breath on her neck, his words of passion were as hot and thrilling as the raging fire roaring through her body.

"Please," Faith whispered, "take me with you."

His thrusts became more powerful, more urgent, until she felt as if she would shatter into a thousand pieces. When her release came she buried her scream in his shoulder only moments before a violent shudder ripped through his body. As he collapsed on top of her, whispering her name, Faith drew her arms tightly around him, holding him close to her beating heart. Time was suspended in a glowing ecstasy.

After a time Miles rolled to his side, pulling her with him. Lifting her chin, he frowned when he saw tears shimmering in her eyes.

"Did I hurt ye?" he asked worriedly.

She shook her head. "Oh no, you didn't hurt me."

He caught a tear with the pad of his thumb and wiped it away from her cheek. "Have ye regrets?"

She shook her head. "No regrets."

"Then why are ye crying?"

Her smile was shy and tender. "I'm crying because it was so beautiful," she answered softly. "It was the most beautiful thing that has ever happened to me."

His face broke into a grin before he gently kissed the bridge of her nose. "Give me a few minutes, lass, and I'll make it the second most beautiful thing that ever happened to ye."

Laughing, Faith hugged him tightly. "A few minutes? I'll give you all night, Miles O'Bruaidar. Heaven help my soul but I'll give you all night."

Chapter Twenty-two

When Faith awoke Miles was already up and dressed, holding his hands out to a blazing fire. "How did ye sleep?" he asked her with a crooked grin.

Faith pushed herself upright, rubbing her eyes groggily. "Sleep? Did we sleep yet?"

Smiling, Miles sat down on the bedroll, pressing a warm, gentle kiss on her mouth. "Ye know, ye look inviting enough for me to join ya again under that blanket."

Faith groaned, feeling the soreness between her legs. "Oh God, I've created a monster."

Laughing, Miles reached behind her and held out her chemise, gown and skirts. "Would ye care to get dressed then?"

She nodded, taking her clothes from him. "Do we have any water? I'm dying of thirst."

Miles stood, picking up the flask. "I'll go fill it at the burn for ye."

"Thanks," she said, slipping out from beneath the blanket and pulling on her clothes. She was just putting on her shoes when Miles returned with the water.

"Here ye are, lass," he said, holding out the flask.

Faith took it, drinking greedily. "I never thought water could taste so good," she said, setting it aside. "What are we to do next?"

Miles shrugged, sitting back beside her on the bedroll. "We'll leave for the rendezvous point when ye are ready."

She exhaled deeply, twining her fingers together in her lap. "If we have some time, there is something that needs to be settled between us first. You've yet to ask me to hold up my end of the bargain. You risked your life to free me, and in return all you have asked for are answers. Are there no questions you have to ask me?"

Miles stared at her thoughtfully. "I won't lie to ye; I have

262

many. But ye nearly took your secrets to the grave wi' ye. Are they really that important?"

She nodded. "Yes, Miles, I suppose they are. But, truthfully, I need to tell someone what has happened to me, no matter how strange it will sound. Because if something happens to me, someone would need to know the truth."

"Then if 'twill give ye peace, lass, tell me."

"The problem is that I don't know how to start," she replied, briskly rubbing her bare arms with her hands. "And I'm afraid. Afraid you might change the way you think about me."

Miles frowned, draping his cloak lightly across her shoulders. "I've given ye my word I'll no' harm ye, Faith. No matter what ye may say."

"Yes, I know. It's not physical harm I'm worried about. It's about what's inside—it's how we feel about each other."

"Ease your mind, lass, and say what ye must."

She rubbed her temples with her fingertips. "Well then, how to begin? I suppose there is no simple way to ease into this." She summoned her courage and plunged on.

"I was born Faith Amanda Worthington in London, England, on the first of May, in the year 1968. I am presently a special agent in an English government organization known as MI5. It's a branch of the intelligence service primarily concerned with internal security, meaning within England. A few years ago it also took on responsibility for monitoring the situation in Northern Ireland. In my time Northern Ireland belongs to the English, you see. Well, on the last day of April in the year 1996, I was sent to the Republic of Ireland—that's the part that belongs to the Irish—on a mission to capture a known Irish assassin. We discovered each other by accident and had a confrontation at the Beaghmore Stone Circles. While we were struggling, he suddenly disappeared and I lost consciousness. When I awoke I was being carried through the forest by you. At first I simply thought you to be a bit odd; then I discovered that somehow I had become displaced three hundred and forty-eight years into the past."

She stole a sidelong glance at him and saw that he was staring at her in disbelief, his mouth hanging open as if unhinged. Her heart sinking, she reached out to touch his arm.

"I told you that you didn't really want to know. But it's the truth."

He jerked his arm away as if she had burned him. "Miles," Faith said worriedly, "please don't look at me like that. Say something. Anything."

"God's wounds," he finally rasped, his teeth chattering unnaturally. "Have ye gone mad or are ye admitting that ye have some kind o' witching powers?"

Faith lifted her hands helplessly. "I'm not mad, although I'll admit that possibility has crossed my mind more than once. And I'm certainly no witch. The truth of the matter is, I don't know how I came to be here, Miles. Even in my time such travel is not possible."

"Who . . . what . . . are ye, really?"

She noticed that the hairs on his arms seemed to be standing straight up, as if he had seen a ghost. "I told you who I am, Miles. I've wanted to tell you the truth all along, but I feared you wouldn't believe me or, worse yet, you'd burn me at the stake or whatever they do to people suspected of possessing magic. Look at you now—you think I've gone half cocked. If you must know, I can hardly believe it myself. It's been quite a shock."

"A shock for *ye?*"

"The expression on your face is exactly why I didn't want to tell you any of this in the first place. You can hardly blame me for being hesitant to blurt out the truth before."

"Then ye are an English agent."

"Yes, but my superiors live in another time, where the monarchy is a figurehead and the people actually run the country."

Miles looked at her incredulously. "The people run the country? The king a figurehead? Ye really expect me to believe that?"

"I know it sounds impossible to you, but it's true."

Miles was quiet for a long moment. " 'Tis a fact that there are many things about ye that puzzle me," he said finally. "Your speech, mannerisms and unfamiliarity wi' our ways is most odd. But this . . . 'tis too much to believe."

"I swear it, Miles," she said emphatically. "I can't explain how or why it happened to me—not yet, anyway—but it's the truth." She sought his eyes for reassurance, but his expression was doubtful, disbelief etched into every line on his face.

"Look," she pleaded softly, "this is why I can read and write and have a decent grasp of politics. All boys and girls in my time are provided with a good education. And that's why I already know what is going to happen. Don't you see now why I couldn't tell you who I'm working for? The English in this time don't have any idea who I am, nor do the Irish. For Christ's sake, the truth of the matter is that I don't even exist yet."

"But ye have special powers?"

"No, I don't have any special powers. I'm flesh and blood, just like you. I don't know how I came through time at the stone circles. I think it was some kind of accident, a bizarre occurrence."

"The stone circles. 'Tis why ye wanted me to take ye there."

She nodded her head vigorously. "Yes. I believe that somewhere among those stones, a portal . . . an opening to time exists. I only hope that it works both ways and I can get home."

Something akin to suspicion flickered deep in Miles's eyes. "Then if ye think that the stone circles will get ye home, why do ye wish to go to London now?"

Faith let out a deep breath. "Remember I told you that I was chasing an Irish assassin in my time? Well, he came through time too."

Miles gasped in astonishment. " 'Tis another like ye . . . here . . . now?"

"Yes. In fact, if you hadn't come along when you did that first night in the forest, he probably would have killed me."

"The other set o' footsteps," Miles murmured softly.

"He has a gun, Miles. It is a special weapon made in my time that's very small and very deadly. And now he believes he is on a special mission. He has decided to try and change the future we know by assassinating a major political figure of this time. An Englishman in London. I must stop him."

Miles blinked in surprise. "How do ye know this?"

"He told me. You see, it was he who tried to drown me at Lough Emy. He knows I will try to stop him. His name is Padriac O'Rourke. He is the kin of Donagh O'Rourke, but many generations later, of course.''

"The kin that was visiting Donagh?'' Miles asked, raising a dark eyebrow. When she nodded he rose to his feet, swearing. "Christ's mercy, lass. Donagh's kin an assassin? Ye a woman from the future? 'Tis too much ye ask me to believe. Ye and Donagh have plotted against me.''

Faith quickly scrambled up to face him. "That's not true. Listen to me. Donagh is working for the English; for Bradford, to be exact. Bradford has promised that his titles, land and Castle O'Rourke will be safe from English expansion if Donagh agrees to spy on you. And Bradford is true to his word, Miles. Castle O'Rourke is a stately landmark in my time. Generations of O'Rourkes have lived there, including Paddy O'Rourke, the man I am after.''

"I've long suspected Donagh o' collaboration wi' the English. But tell me the truth, lass. The part about your past was concocted by Donagh, was it no'?''

"No,'' she insisted fiercely. "I never worked for O'Rourke.''

"Then why are ye so afraid o' Donagh?''

"I've already explained,'' Faith shot back. "He is the ancestor of the man I am trying to hunt down. Later, when I found out that Paddy was actually living at Donagh's castle, it is understandable why I protested your threat to turn me over to them. Paddy O'Rourke would have killed me at the first opportunity. He damn near succeeded the first time. But I had no idea that Donagh himself was a traitor until he put the sword into the back of that young man during the exchange. Don't you see, the whole thing was just a plot to kill you. They never even knew who I was. Bradford believes you are the rebel leader, the Irish Lion. Everyone assumed that Bradford would take you cleanly except that I unexpectedly prevented it from happening. Donagh came after me then. Bradford had instructed his men that I was to be taken to Drogheda.''

"Why?'' Miles asked, frowning.

"I presume because I had so easily managed to get close to the man they had long sought—you. They were curious, and as they had no prior knowledge of me, they suspected I might be working secretly for Cromwell. They also wanted to find out what I knew about you.''

"And what do ye know about me?''

"Nothing for certain. I didn't voice my suspicions.''

"Which are?''

She exhaled a deep breath. "Are you the Irish Lion, Miles? It would make sense—the black hood, the midnight rides, the antique ring with your family crest.''

"And if I am? Will that change things between us, lass?''

She thought for a moment. "No, I don't think it would.''

Miles raked a hand through his dark hair. "I think ye already know the answer to your question.''

She nodded. "Yes, I suppose I do.''

"So why did ye protect me?''

"Because you protected me.''

"Is that the only reason?''

She paused. "No, it's much more than that. I care about you, Miles. You know that.''

He studied her thoughtfully. "And the English? For what purpose did they wish to hang ye?''

"In the end I really didn't know much about you, and Cromwell denied all knowledge of me, naturally. Still, Aston suspected I was working for Cromwell anyway. As Aston is loyal to King Charles, he ordered my execution, although he made it known publicly that I was to be hung as an Irish spy. He could ill afford to publicly call Cromwell a liar. You see, he thinks Cromwell is plotting against the king.''

"Is Cromwell plotting against the king?''

"He is.''

"How do you know that?''

"For God's sake, Miles, like thousands of other English children I learned my history in school. You'll just have to trust me on this one.''

"There are many other ways ye could have learned that information.''

"Yes, I suppose there are. But I've told you the truth. Look, I don't blame you for not believing me. In fact, I don't know what I would think if our positions were reversed. Probably that you had cracked completely and belonged in an institution. Not that I still won't end up there myself, if I ever get back to my own time.''

Miles stared at her for a long moment before walking over to the horse and removing a small bundle from the pouch. Carefully cradling the bundle in his hands, he walked back over to her, unwinding the white linen strip and emptying the contents into his hands. Curious, Faith stepped forward.

''Are these yours?'' he asked, thrusting out his hand toward her.

Gasping in surprise, Faith reached out, her fingers closing around a thin oblong object. ''My flashlight,'' she whispered, lifting it from his hand. Bending over, she inspected the rest of the contents in his hand. ''My compass, my map . . . breath mints and even tissues. Only my watch is missing.'' Making a small noise in her throat, she held up the soft tissue to her cheek. For a moment the past and the present seemed to collide in a strange surge of emotions.

''It was you who took them from me,'' she said in wonder. ''You had them all along.''

Miles nodded. ''These objects, Faith . . . I've never seen anything like them. I want ye to tell me the truth: Are ye a witch o' some kind? If ye are, I promise no' to harm ye. I just want to know.'' He pointed at her flashlight. ''Is that . . . object . . . a magical talisman?''

Faith leaned over and picked up the blanket from the bedroll. ''No. Come here beneath the blanket and I'll show you how it works.''

He looked at her suspiciously. ''Nay.''

''Miles, it's not magic,'' she pleaded. ''It won't hurt you; I promise. If you'll come here, I'll show you how it works. Please. Last night I trusted you. Now I ask that you trust me.''

He frowned but walked toward her. Faith drew the blanket over their heads until they were in relative darkness. ''Now watch this,'' she said, flicking on the flashlight and pointing it at him. Miles blinked in surprise and fear, stepping back hastily.

''It's just light,'' she explained quickly. ''This device is called a flashlight. In my time it helps us to see in the dark. Look on it as . . . well, a future version of the torch. Come here and hold it. It won't bite.''

After a moment of hesitation he held out his hand. Faith turned off the flashlight and handed it to him. "Press here," she said, guiding his thumb to the black button. "Push up on it and that will turn it on. Push down, and that turns it off."

Curiosity overtaking his fear, Miles pushed up with his thumb and the flashlight flicked on, sending a beam of light streaking across Faith's face. Gasping in horror, Miles dropped the flashlight, and the light abruptly went out.

Faith bent over to retrieve it. "Don't worry, it's a tough little thing. It runs on something called batteries." She pulled the blanket off their heads and unscrewed the bottom of the flashlight. Two AA batteries fell into her hand. "However, the flashlight will work only as long as the batteries. Unfortunately, I can't see how we'll replace them once they run out of juice." Curiously, she rolled them over in her hand.

"My God," she said excitedly. "Come read this, Miles. It says 'Best used before 9/98.' I've proof now. It means the year 1998. Now you know I'm telling the truth."

Miles peered over her shoulder at the batteries. "It could say anything ye want it to, lass. Ye know I can't read."

Frustrated, Faith ran her hand through her tangled hair. "Oh, rot. Well, if we meet up with Father Michael, perhaps he can confirm what I say."

Miles raised a dark eyebrow. "Do ye think it wise to repeat to others the story that ye have told me?"

She sighed deeply. "I suppose not, unless I want to take a long drink in the lake, courtesy of an angry mob of unbelieving villagers." She slid the batteries back into the flashlight and held it out to him. "Better keep them together."

Miles nodded, stepping forward and taking the flashlight from her. He returned it to the linen strip with the other objects. Rolling it up into a tight bundle, he returned it to its safe spot within the pouch.

"Now do you believe me when I tell you that I'm not working for Donagh?"

"Donagh is a crafty man. Mayhap he devised this story for ye."

"And then tried to have me killed?"

"Perhaps ye outlived your usefulness."

"That simply isn't true," Faith exclaimed in exasperation.

"I'm not in league with Donagh. I don't even know the first thing about him."

"Then ye don't know that he left his family behind? He has a wife, Eileen, and a young son. The bairn is but two summers I think."

Faith gasped in surprise. "He boldly committed treason in front of everyone and then left his family at your mercy?"

"The Irish take care o' their own. Neither she nor the bairn will be harmed for his actions."

Faith put a hand on his arm and was startled when he abruptly pulled away. "Let's go," he said, striding to the horse, his voice tense and distant. "We've still a bit o' a distance to ride today."

She realized with a heavy heart that the closeness they had shared last night seemed to have evaporated completely. Part of her couldn't blame him; probably she'd have felt the same way. But the tang of disappointment was especially sharp and painful in light of the tender lovemaking they had shared.

"All right, I'm ready," she replied, bending over to roll up the blanket and the bedroll.

Miles doused the fire and packed their remaining belongings onto the horse before giving her a boost into the saddle.

"Miles," Faith said, looking down at him from her perch, "I've told you the truth no matter what you may think."

He exhaled a deep breath between his teeth. "I don't know what to think. 'Tis true that we Irish are a superstitious lot, wi' a healthy belief in spirits and the fey folk. But 'twould have been a lot easier for me to believe ye were just a witch."

"Are you afraid of me?"

"Should I be?"

"No," she answered simply.

He frowned as he pulled himself up into the saddle. "Well, if what ye say about traveling from another century is true, by all the wounds o' Christ, I should be afraid."

"Then you do believe me."

He slapped the reins gently against the horse's neck. "I need time to think o'er what ye've said, Faith. Ye can't ask more o' me."

Sighing, she settled back against his chest as they began to move. "I know," she said softly. "But you can't blame me for trying."

Chapter Twenty-three

"How are ye faring?" Miles asked when they stopped to rest the horses. They had ridden for hours and were now sheltered in the curve of a hillside from which he could watch all approaches without being seen.

He had not spoken about what she had revealed, and Faith thought it better that way. She could hardly add anything to her story that would help matters, and anyway, what he really needed was time to think. What he would finally decide to do with her, she had no idea. But it had been such a relief to tell the truth that in spite of his disbelieving silence, she felt as if a weight had been lifted from her shoulders.

"I'm doing just fine," she answered brightly, ignoring the shooting pain in her shoulder blades, back and thighs. "It's not so difficult."

But by the time they had ridden another few hours Faith's bravado had changed into a gritty determination not to give up. Miles's resolute silence was beginning to wear on her nerves, and she could feel the tension rolling off him in waves. Her muscles were shrieking in protest and the constant effort of staying upright was making the pain nearly unbearable. Sheer pride kept her from tumbling out of the saddle, but the farther they rode, the wearier she became.

She was just about to beg Miles for another break when a man unexpectedly leapt from the bushes, brandishing a sword. Faith screamed in surprise, nearly falling from the saddle.

"Hush, lass," Miles said, holding her tightly around the waist. " 'Tis only Furlong."

Furlong sheathed his sword, looking up at her. "She's a bit skittish today," he observed.

"Of course I'm skittish," Faith replied angrily. "You just leapt wildly from the bushes, waving a sword. It's a wonder you didn't skew us first and ask questions later."

271

Miles grinned. "Och, I don't think Furlong ever skewed anyone by accident. Have ye, man?"

Furlong pushed his greasy cap back on his head and thoughtfully massaged his long nose between the thumb and forefinger of his left hand. "Now let me see . . . 'twas a time once after a wee nip o' the poteen when I thought Finn O'Flahertie meant to steal my horse. I suppose I may have given him a poke or two o' iron in the arse, but it didn't harm much other than his pride."

Miles chortled and Faith pressed her lips together wryly. "Very amusing, Furlong."

"Och, he's just having a spot o' fun wi' ye," Miles said, tossing the reins down to the stout man. "Don't hold it against the poor man."

"Don't you have a first name?" Faith grumbled irritably.

Furlong grinned, sweeping the grimy cap off his head and bowing at the waist. "Eoin Clarence Furlong, at your service, my lady."

"Eoin Clarence? My God, I can certainly see why they call you Furlong."

The stout man cocked his head at her good-naturedly. "Aye, 'tis so. And 'tis good to see ye again, my lady."

"Oh, it's good to see you too, Furlong," Faith replied with feeling. "It really is. I must say, though, you certainly have a way with entrances."

Furlong grinned widely, as if she had paid him a great compliment. Shaking her head, she watched as he took the reins of the horse and led them to where the others were waiting. Seated around the fire were Shaun Gogarty, Father Michael, the young lad, Patrick, and a few other men she did not recognize. Jumping up happily, Shaun let out a whoop when he saw Faith sliding off the horse.

"By the grace o' the gods," the dwarf said gleefully, clapping his hands together, "she's alive. The lass has the luck o' the saints."

Father Michael shook his head, coming over to greet her. "Don't listen to him, my lady. He's an expert shot with the arrow. 'Twas Shaun's excellent aim that brought the gibbet down."

"Then I'm indebted to you," Faith said softly, leaning over

to press a chaste kiss on the dwarf's cheek. "And I've always wanted to learn how to shoot using a bow." She thought fleetingly of the antique bow and quiver of arrows that hung over the mantel in her townhouse in London. "I used to own one. Perhaps you'll show me sometime how it works."

Shaun turned pink to the tips of his ears while the men laughed and ribbed him. Miles took a long draught of water from a leather flask and then turned to face the men.

"We still have several hours o' daylight left," he said. "We should make Castle Dun na Moor by nightfall."

"Castle Dun na Moor?" Faith protested, whirling around in surprise. "But I told you I need to go to—"

"Enough," Miles commanded, interrupting her sharply. "There's a reason for what I do. Ye must trust me."

"Can't we at least have a rest?" she protested.

"I'm sorry, lass, but we won't be safe until we are home. We have to ride on."

Faith swallowed the rest of her complaints as the men began gathering up their things. She wanted to get Miles alone to ask him about his decision to return to the castle without consulting her, but he turned from her and pulled Father Michael aside to talk. Biting back her frustration, Faith reluctantly returned to Miles's horse when the young boy, Patrick, stopped her.

"Nay, my lady, ye're to have your own mount now," he said, pointing at a horse tethered to a nearby tree. " 'Twill make the journey go faster."

An unexpected wave of disappointment swept through Faith. She hadn't realized how much she enjoyed the comfort and coziness of sharing the saddle with Miles. Now that he apparently had withdrawn from her physically as well as mentally, she felt more alone than ever. Sighing, she let the boy lead her to the roan mare, quickly making the acquaintance of the gentle beast.

In minutes the entire party was packed and ready to ride, including Faith, who sat stiffly astride her new mount. With a small shout, Furlong led them forward.

They made a few stops along the way, all of which Faith knew were for her benefit. On one occasion Shaun made an exaggerated excuse about his horse having a rock in his foot; another time Father Michael insisted that the flasks needed to be refilled with fresh water. Each time Miles reluctantly called a halt, clearly impatient to get back to the castle. Faith was grateful for the men's support but nearly wept in relief when the castle finally came into view.

Castle Dun na Moor was a magnificent sight, sitting proudly on the rise, its magnificent towers jutting up toward the heavens. Behind the castle the brilliant colors of the sunset were painted across the sky. Miles threw her an unexpected glance over his shoulder and Faith locked eyes with him, wondering what he was thinking. His expression was thoughtful but weary, and he turned away before she could study him further. Calling out something in Gaelic, he led the men toward the castle gate.

Soldiers and men spilled out into the courtyard, raising their voices in greeting. Miles pulled his horse to a halt in the center of the courtyard and swung down out of the saddle.

" 'Tis fine to be home," he said, tossing the reins to one of the men. "We have need to feast, though. We are as ravenous as wolves."

"I'll tell the kitchen, my lord," one of the young men said, breathlessly rushing off to relay Miles's request.

Faith grimaced as she dragged herself from her horse, thinking the romanticism of galloping into the sunset was far overrated. Groaning, she rubbed her lower back and buttocks. No matter what anyone said, riding a horse was bloody hard work.

As she staggered toward the castle, Molly came flying toward them, throwing her arms around Faith. "By the love o' the saints, ye are back safely," she exclaimed happily.

Faith was strangely touched by the warm welcome and impulsively gave Molly an enthusiastic hug in return. Molly beamed with pride and then drew away. Her round face dipped into a frown when she saw the grimy and ripped state of Faith's gown.

"What in God's name happened to ye?" she asked quietly, her question asking far more than just the condition of Faith's gown. "Are ye all right, lass?"

Swallowing hard, Faith nodded. "I'm fine . . . thanks to these men here." She turned and looked meaningfully at Miles, Shaun, Furlong and the others who stood quietly in the entryway.

274

Then Miles strode past her and into the castle without another glance. Faith felt her heart sink to her toes.

Molly saw the look on Faith's face and put a protective arm around her shoulder. "Don't worry, lass. I'll get ye cleaned up and put a smile back on your face. If I know anything o' Irishmen—and believe me, I do—there is going to be a big celebration here tonight."

Chapter Twenty-four

Miles sat moodily at the table in the Great Hall, making a minor adjustment to the sapphire brooch at his throat and flicking an imaginary speck of dust from the dark blue velvet of his jacket. The chamber was alive with light and merriment. Hundreds of candles had been placed throughout the room, illuminating the surroundings and casting flickering shadows across the walls. Molly had ordered a fresh coating of rushes placed on the floor, and an additional table had been added to accommodate all those who wished to celebrate with them. His men already sat, drinking and talking with one another.

Impatiently, Miles turned his gaze to the entryway. Faith still had not appeared. Hell and damnation, he thought silently, why in the devil did it take forever for women to be dressed? He was famished.

Tapping his fingers irritably on the table, he held out his goblet to be filled. He had been thinking a lot about what she had told him in the forest. Time travel? A woman from the future? It was certainly a falsehood, but what a tale she had told. The strange objects that she said belonged to her seemed so real and magical. And she had sounded absolutely certain when she spoke of the future, as if she really could foretell what would happen. Was such a thing as time travel truly possible?

A young serving girl hastened to his side and poured wine into his goblet, spilling a drop on his sleeve. She gasped in horror, but he waved her aside impatiently, still watching the doorway. He lifted the goblet to his lips as a sudden silence fell over the room. Faith stood shyly in the entrance, uncertain as to whether she should enter. For a moment he could only stare at her, his hand tightening around the stem of the goblet.

He had never seen her look so beautiful. Her gown was made of a shimmering gold material intertwined with red threads. The bodice was stiffened and the skirt opened in the front to show a richly embroidered kirtle. Her shoulders were partially bare, but her sleeves were long and tapering. She wore no jewels about her neck or fingers, but the simplicity of the look only enhanced her beauty. She stood as magnificent and regal as a queen.

"God's wounds, I have to talk to Molly," Miles muttered under his breath, realizing that every masculine eye in the room was focused on the lovely sight in the entryway. Fighting the surge of jealousy that swept through him, he pushed himself to his feet, striding to the entrance.

He offered his arm and she took it, trembling slightly. He recognized at once her painful insecurity at being the center of attention. Miles felt his heart lurch crazily in his chest. Hell and damnation, just when he was steeling his resolve against her, she showed a vulnerability and fragility that tugged at his heartstrings.

Why couldn't he put her out of his mind? He had never had a shortage of women at his disposal; why did he have this unending fascination with her? She was willful, reckless and utterly outrageous. And to top it all off, she was an English-woman. And this strange tale of traveling through time—why, it was the most outlandish thing he had ever heard. Why wouldn't she just trust him with the truth?

Swallowing his unsettling emotions, he led her to a seat directly to his left. Shaun had been given the place of honor to her right, and the dwarf puffed out his chest proudly when she smiled at him. Once she was seated, servants entered the chamber, heaping the table with fresh salmon, venison, pork and a variety of breads and cheeses. The low murmur of sub-dued conversation and clinking plates began to fill the room.

"Eat," he ordered Faith when he saw how little she put on her plate. "I know ye must be famished."

"Actually," she replied softly, "I'm not very hungry."

He noticed she avoided his gaze. Undoubtedly she was an-gry at him. God's blood, what did she expect of him? To calmly accept the most eccentric tale he had ever heard?

Frowning, he took a large swallow of his wine, his own appetite fading. Deciding to ignore her, he let Shaun engage

Julie Moffett

her in light conversation, his temper growing for a reason he could not fathom.

After he had drunk his way through dinner Miles summoned a musician. The man sat down on a stool near the fire and began to strum softly on a small, hand-held harp.

For the first time that evening Faith turned toward him. "What kind of instrument is that?" she asked.

Her question startled him from his thoughts. Turning slightly on the bench, he looked down at her. Her face had paled considerably, and dark circles were beginning to emerge beneath her eyes.

He felt a stab of guilt for pressing her so hard. He should have insisted that she rest, not dress herself and attend a celebration. By the Rod o' Christ, couldn't he do anything right with her?

"Miles?" she repeated questioningly.

Angrily, he grabbed his goblet, lifting it up to be filled again. " 'Tis a *clarsach*," he answered gruffly. " 'Tis said that on May Eve the fairies play the *clarsach* to lure handsome lads and bonny young lassies from their homes. Those who are captured by the enchanted notes are forced to live their days in the servitude o' the fey folk."

"Sounds remarkably like the Piped Piper," Faith mused softly.

"Who?"

"Never mind," she said wearily. "It's just an old fairy tale. Or a new one, from your point of view, perhaps."

She turned away, and again Miles wondered about her tale of time travel. Could she be telling the truth? Could her tale of coming from another century be the source of all her oddities? Christ's blood, it was too much to ask him to believe such a thing.

Scowling, he took another swallow from his goblet. He was slowly beginning to feel the effects of the wine. He was getting drunk, but he welcomed the numbness. It gave him a chance to ease the ceaseless torture of thinking about her.

She shifted restlessly on the bench and he caught the faint scent of roses. He felt the blood run warm in his veins. Christ's blood, even now he still wanted her.

Unexpectedly he reached out and touched the hair at her

temple. She turned to look at him in surprise and he quickly withdrew his hand.

"Do ye like the music?" he asked stiffly.

"Yes," she said softly. "I like it very much."

Miles lifted his goblet toward the musician and rose to his feet. "Ye honor Ireland with your music," he said, handing the man several coins. The man beamed with pride as he bowed and accepted Miles's payment.

Miles lowered his goblet and gazed down the length of the table. "Men, ye have traveled far o'er the past few days, and I can only say that I am proud o' ye. So tonight I grant ye all the ale and poteen ye can drink. *Slainte,* to your health!"

The men roared with approval and began noisily slamming their mugs and goblets on the table as the servants rushed hastily to fill them. Politely, Miles held out his arm to Faith.

"The hour is late, my lady. Shall I escort ye to your chamber?"

Faith stood, taking his arm. "I would be honored," she said simply.

They walked silently up the stairs and down a long corridor before stopping outside Faith's door.

"I'm sorry I had to ask ye to leave, but I'm afraid the hall will soon be no place for a lady," Miles said.

Faith crossed her arms against her chest, keeping her face expressionless. She didn't want him to know how much his cool behavior hurt her.

"To tell you the truth, I'm glad we're finally alone," she said calmly. "We need to talk. Why have you brought me back to Castle Dun na Moor, when you know I must get to London with due haste?"

Miles's jaw tightened. "Your story . . . ye intend to hold firm to what ye told me?"

"It's the truth, Miles. I can't expect you to believe me, but I do hope you won't try to stop me."

He leaned against the wall, his jacket pulling tight across his broad shoulders. "So, as ye told me before, ye truly believe that this man—O'Rourke's kin—is headed for London?"

"I do. How he will get there I don't know. But he has a number of advantages over me. He can travel alone without raising anyone's suspicions. It is also reasonable to assume he'll be able to steal or earn his passage across the sea without much difficulty.''

"Ye're certain that following him is what ye want to do?''

"I must do it. But I don't want to drag you into this. I ask only that you help me secure safe passage to London. The rest I must do on my own.''

He laughed hoarsely, looking at her in disbelief. "Have ye any idea o' what ye are proposing? That ye, an unmarried lass, travel to London without escort or coin. Once there, ye will attempt, by yourself, to hunt down a man who has a mysterious weapon and prevent him from killing one o' the most powerful men in all o' England.''

Faith leaned back against the door. "I know it sounds absurd, but I have little choice. I've got to stop him.''

Frowning, he put a hand on either side of her, trapping her between his muscular body and the door. His thighs pressed flat against hers. "Damn ye, Faith Worthington. Are ye scheming to get me to London?''

She bristled in anger. "Why would I scheme to get you to London?''

"So ye can deliver me personally into the hands o'Cromwell.''

"I told you I'm not working for Cromwell.''

"Aye; instead ye want me to believe some half-cocked story about ye coming from another century.''

She clenched her fists at her sides, frustration, exhaustion and fear finally catching up with her. "I knew it. I knew I shouldn't have told you.''

"Tell me the truth, Faith. 'Tis all I ask.''

"I have told you the truth, you hardheaded, obstinate . . . Irishman. I don't care anymore whether you believe me or not. For your information, I wouldn't take you to London if you got down on your knees and begged me.''

"I don't beg,'' Miles growled, his voice strident. "For anyone or anything. Ever.''

"Oh, a bloody tough bloke, are you?'' Faith cried furiously. "Well, take this.'' She balled her fist and aimed it at his chin with all her might.

Miles caught her wrist in an iron grip just before it made

contact with his jaw. "Ye little vixen," he growled. "So ye won't change your story?"

"Go to hell."

Leaning forward, he pressed his hard thighs against her, lowering his mouth until it was just a breath away from hers. "Ye first," he murmured, his eyes darkening.

Faith pummeled her fists against his chest to no avail. He yanked her into his arms roughly, his mouth settling on hers, hard and demanding.

Faith felt a flash of heat streak through her, leaving her breathless. He tasted like wine and his kiss was heady, hot and thoroughly sensual.

After a moment he dragged his mouth from hers, breathing heavily. "Do ye feel the passion 'tween us?" he murmured. " 'Tis so good."

"Let go of me,". Faith whispered, her own breath coming in short gasps. Damn him, but she *had* felt the passion.

"I know ye feel it, Faith."

"Stop it," she said fiercely.

His face darkened into a scowl. "Don't toy wi' me, lass. I don't like it."

"Then don't think with your hormones and expect me to do the same," she retorted. "Kissing me like that won't change my mind. I'll secure passage to London without your help, if I must."

A muscle tightened in his jaw. "Always wanting to do things on your own. What will ye do if I refuse to release ye?"

"Threats don't work with me. You'll soon tire of guarding me, and then I'll make my escape."

"Then what does work wi' ye?" he asked, drawing her near. The satin of her gown was crushed against the rough linen of his shirt. "Will this work, mayhap?" He lowered his mouth to hers. This time his kiss was soft and unbearably tender.

Faith closed her eyes, feeling herself weaken. God, how she wanted his kiss and the feel of his hands on her body. She didn't want to think about Paddy O'Rourke, getting to London and how she would return to her own time: She wanted to forget everything and simply lose herself in the heat and passion of this man.

"Was that better?" Miles murmured, lifting his lips from her mouth and nuzzling the soft skin behind her ear.

"No," she lied shakily, turning her head to the side.

He studied her face closely. "Look at me, Faith, and tell me honestly that ye don't wish for this."

"You miserable cheat," she whispered. "How can you expect me to think when you do this to me?"

"I don't want ye to think," he murmured. "For once I want ye just to feel. To understand what we have between us."

Slowly she lifted her hands and put them on his shoulders. She could feel the hard swell of muscle beneath his shirt. Her temperature was rising, sexual desire igniting and then burning like a fever in her blood. Without another thought she flung her arms around his neck, fiercely drawing his mouth down to hers. He crushed her to his muscular chest, his tongue plundering the inside of her mouth with breathtaking skill.

She heard him groan and reach behind her to fumble with the door latch. The door swung open and he half-dragged her into the candlelit room, never lifting his mouth from hers. He kicked the door shut with his booted foot and then propelled her backwards to the bed.

"No, wait," Faith gasped, pulling away. She could hardly breathe, her heart was pounding so hard in her chest. "I can't do this," she said, panting.

Miles looked at her in disbelief. "Ye can't?"

She crossed her arms against her chest, fighting for control. "I've got to start thinking with my head. I mean, we aren't even using any protection. What if I got . . . you know, pregnant?" Mortified, she realized she was blushing profusely.

Miles took a step back, raking his fingers through his dark hair. "Is that what worries ye, lass? That I will get ye wi' child?"

"It has crossed my mind," she admitted.

"I would take care o' both ye and the babe."

"That's comforting, but I don't think I'd play the role of mistress very well. Anyway, that's not the point. The point is that except when I'm around you I'm a rational, sensible person. I mustn't lose sight of what I must do here. I've got to get to London as soon as I possibly can. I've got to stop Paddy O'Rourke and get us both back to our own time.''

He was silent for a long moment. "Do ye believe in fate, Faith?'' he finally asked.

She shook her head. "No,'' she replied. "I believe we are responsible for our own destinies.''

"Then ye haven't once considered that there is something greater than us guiding our lives and bringing us together?''

"If you are implying some kind of magic, the answer is no. It's just fantasy. I don't believe in magic and fairy tales. There is no scientific evidence for such a phenomenon.''

"Was there scientific evidence for this time travel o' yours?''

"No . . . but that's different. I'm here, aren't I?''

Miles frowned. "Ye know, Faith, for all your knowledge and all that has happened to ye, ye are remarkably skeptical o' the unknown. Sit down, lass. I want to talk to ye seriously.''

Reluctantly, she perched on the edge of the bed with her back straight and her fingers curled around the edge of the quilt. She watched him open his mouth as if to say something and then snap it shut with a frown. Clasping his hands behind his back, he began pacing about the small confines of her chamber. His stride was so long that two steps took him nearly the width of the room. As Faith saw him struggle with what he wanted to say, her uneasiness grew.

"What is it, Miles?'' she asked worriedly. "You are making me nervous.''

He stopped his pacing, turning to face her. "First o' all, I want to know what ye meant by the word *hormones*. Ye said I think with it.''

Faith looked at him in astonishment. "Hormones? Oh yes, I suppose I did say that. Well, a hormone is . . . ah . . . a substance that is formed in the body and has a special effect on certain organs.''

When he looked at her blankly she sighed. "No, I suppose that won't do. What I was referring to in baser terms is the fact that men often think with their . . . uh . . . urges instead of their brains.'' She stopped abruptly, realizing how foolish her explanation sounded. "Oh, blast it, Miles,'' she finished crossly. "Forget the whole bloody thing. I won't say it again.''

" 'Twas it an insult?"

She exhaled a deep breath. "Yes. I'm sorry."

He drummed his fingers against his chin. "Well, in the future, if ye mean to insult me, I ask ye to extend me the courtesy o' doing it wi' words I know."

"All right, Miles. I promise."

He paused, his dark brows drawing together in thought. "Now, Faith, let's discuss what is really at issue here. The bare truth o' the matter is that I may have saved ye from the hangman's noose, but 'tis only a matter o' time before the English discover that ye are here. When they come—and have no doubt they will—they'll have every right to take ye from me."

"Then why did you bring me back here? I told you I needed to go to London."

"I needed time to think and plan. The problem simply put is that I have no hold, no claim, on ye to stop the English. But if . . ." he hesitated a moment, ". . . if ye were to be my wife, a lawful member o' the O'Bruaidar clan, 'twould be a different matter altogether."

Faith's mouth dropped open in utter shock. Whatever else she had thought he might say, a marriage proposal had not even been in the realm of possibility.

"Marriage?" she managed to croak. "To me? Are you mad?"

He firmly folded his arms across his chest. "I'm no'."

"B-but it's impossible," she stuttered. "What about the O'Bruaidar-Dunbar alliance? Have you forgotten that you're already betrothed to Arabella Dunbar?"

Miles shrugged. "I can handle Arabella's da. He'll take no offense as long as I sufficiently line his pockets to soothe the embarrassment."

"But what of Arabella?"

"What o' her, lass? She has no love for me and is comely enough to find another husband with a rich coffer."

Fleetingly, Faith wondered how Arabella would take the news. Not well, if she remembered the jealous look the woman had flashed at her. Inhaling a deep breath, she tried to make sense of the dizzy thoughts in her head, thankful that she was seated.

A Double-Edged Blade

"Look, Miles, I appreciate what you are trying to do for me, but it's not necessary. If you are worried about the English finding me, then let me leave the castle immediately. I won't lie to you; I do need your help in finding passage to England. I have no money and I'm not familiar with your customs. But that is as far as it goes. Lest you forget, you are a wanted man by the English and couldn't possibly accompany me to London. Besides, I'd never ask that of you. You're safe only as long as you reside at Castle Dun na Moor."

"I'm touched by your concern for my safety, lass, but I've made my decision."

"Your proposition is laudable, even honorable, but completely deranged. For Christ's sake, I've not even been born yet. How can I marry you?"

"Because ye want to."

"What I *want* has nothing to do with this. Look, I didn't *ask* to be thrust back to this time. I didn't *expect* to live my life in another century. And I certainly didn't *plan* on sleeping with you. It's all terribly wrong, can't you see? I don't belong here—with or without you—and I never will."

"Nothing ye've done wi' me has been wrong," he said firmly.

He made the statement with such certainty that Faith felt shaken. God, how she wanted to believe him. But she couldn't . . . *wouldn't* . . . permit herself to do so.

"You'd be marrying a woman who couldn't stay with you," she continued heatedly. "Don't you see? I have to go back eventually. You'd be taking an unnecessary risk with me."

" 'Tis little I've done in my life that hasn't been a risk."

"But I'm . . . English," she said, grasping at an explanation—any explanation—to get him to see how foolish his proposal was. "You can't marry me. I'm Protestant."

He frowned. "As long as the kirkman is Catholic, it matters little what religion ye are. Ye'll become Catholic like me."

"I will not," she protested.

He growled in frustration. "What good will it do ye, lass, if ye are Protestant and dead?"

Faith threw up her hands. "This is all beside the point. Have you thought about what your friends and family will think if you marry me? They'll think you've gone completely mad.

And have you considered that your activities as the Irish Lion might be compromised? They will think I'm influencing you, or worse yet, spying on you."

Miles calmly crossed his thick arms against his chest. "Since when have ye started worrying about what other people think? Ye're just being willfully stubborn."

"I'm being sensible. Thank God one of us is."

"If 'twill put your mind at rest, the fact that ye were nearly hung by the English raises your esteem in the eyes o' the Irish, my people included."

"Oh, bloody lovely."

"Ye let me worry about the rest, Faith. That includes my activities as the Irish Lion. I've always lived my life as I damn well pleased. And right now I know that wedding ye is the right thing to do."

"It's impossible."

"We are talking about your life, Faith."

"There has to be another way," she said fiercely. "I won't enter a marriage under false pretenses."

"We both know 'twill no' be an unpleasant experience."

"I just can't."

Because I love you.

The realization left her stunned and more than a little frightened. Her vow not to become involved with anyone in this time had been shattered. Although she had always been fully aware of the risks, she had never planned on the staggering cost of her moments of stolen happiness. She would have to put an end to this now or she'd never have the strength to leave him.

Faith's eyes slowly rose to meet his, dreading what she had to say. "I'm sorry, Miles. Your offer is generous, but I can't marry you. That's my final say on the matter."

"Hell and damnation, ye are the most stubborn, hardheaded woman I've ever met. Ye must marry me or face certain death at the hands o' the English. Is such a proposal so loathsome to ye, Faith?"

She shook her head, looking miserably away from him. "N-no," she whispered. "It's far from loathsome. But I'm not going to marry you, Miles. It's simply not an option for us."

Her resolution wavering, she walked to the window. "I need

your help to get to London," she continued. "I don't know how I'll be able to repay you, but if I have any coin left, I'll be certain to see that you get it. Can we at least agree to that?"

When she heard no answer she turned around to see the door ajar and Miles gone. For a moment she simply stared at the empty doorway with a deep, aching loneliness, feeling as if she had lost a part of herself she had never really known.

Stumbling to a chair, she collapsed in a heap and did the one thing she did really well lately—cried as if she were a bloody faucet.

Chapter Twenty-five

Miles tore off his boots and cast them to the floor of his bedchamber before striding over to a small table and grabbing a decanter of whiskey in his fist. Muttering an oath, he pulled off the glass top and angrily poured the contents into an empty goblet. He threw back the entire glass in a moment's time before setting it down and filling it again.

Scowling, he stripped off his blue jacket and removed the sapphire brooch, loosening his collar. Without bothering to replace the glass cap, Miles took the open decanter and the goblet to a chair near the fire and sat down. He took another large swallow of the whiskey, welcoming the burning sensation it created in his stomach. Moodily, he leaned back in the chair, stretching out his muscular legs in front of him.

His bedchamber was pitch black except for the red glowing embers in the fireplace. For now he preferred it that way—it suited his dark mood. He was angry and troubled by all that had happened. Swirling the liquid in his glass, Miles tried unsuccessfully to sort out his complex mixture of feelings given the scene that had just transpired in Faith's bedchamber.

She had refused his offer of marriage in spite of the fact that her life was in danger and had then told him that what had happened between them had been wrong.

Christ's wounds, but she was a rotten liar.

He rubbed the back of his neck where his muscles had knotted together so tightly they were like taut, twisted cords. She was still a mystery to him, a woman he couldn't understand and didn't want to trust. Yet he was bound to her in a way he couldn't fathom. He had always had a deep respect for science; still, he knew there were some phenomena in life that could not easily be explained. But even for him the idea of traveling between centuries was far more than he was ready—or able—to believe.

"God's teeth," he swore in frustration. Jumping to his feet, he seized the iron poker and jabbed viciously at the logs. Sparks flew everywhere until the blaze caught and the fire roared into life.

Why was this happening to him? His life had been carefully planned until now. Fighting against the English and his activities as the Irish Lion had been the basis of his existence. He was damn good at it . . . so good that he had even attracted the attention of King Charles himself. His marriage to Arabella Dunbar had also been strategic planning, a move designed to strengthen his northern border and make his position at Castle Dun na Moor more secure. In fact, his entire life had been a series of calculated moves. So how could he throw it all away for a woman who claimed to be from another century and handled magic objects with the ease of a witch or sorcerer?

Because, damn it all to hell, he was in love with her.

He let out a fierce stream of breath between his teeth. Christ, it must be madness or else magic. Perhaps she had cast a spell over him. Whatever the cause, he only knew the prospect of living the rest of his life without her was too grim to contemplate, even given the risk that she might leave him.

He wouldn't let the English take her. He had not saved her from death only to let her slip through his fingers again. She had to agree to marry him. It was the only way.

Still, he knew that his men would be shocked, and his neighbors and family would think him daft. Marriage to an Englishwoman who was hunted by her own countrymen and had nearly been hanged from the gallows? In many ways Faith was right. It would be perceived as utter madness. Had he somehow lost his reason?

Scowling, Miles leaned the poker against the hearth. Too many pieces of information were coming at him from too many different directions. One piece seemed to contradict the next, while some pieces had aspects of truth that even he could not deny. And damn it all to hell and back, the truth of the matter was that he *was* beginning to believe her. Whether it was because he so desperately wanted to, or whether it seemed to be making some kind of sense, he did not know.

Leaning down, Miles picked up the decanter from the table and took a long swig directly from the bottle. He held the neck of the bottle lightly in his hand, lifting it to the light and watching the play of shadows against the glass. He needed to make a decision at once and take control of the situation. He knew that it was only a matter of days, perhaps even hours, before the English discovered she was at Castle Dun na Moor. Then he would have to turn her over to them and to certain death. He had to convince her to marry him. He would take the risk and face the consequences, if only she would.

By all the saints, he'd force her to marry him if she made him.

Miles swore fiercely under his breath. By God, she was the most stubborn, insufferable, infuriating woman he had ever met. Why wouldn't she listen to reason?

The emotions rose higher and hotter inside him, tormenting him. "If this is some kind o' plot to lure me into trouble," he growled darkly, "by the rod o' Christ, I'll wring her neck wi' my own two hands."

His mouth tight with anger, Miles walked to the door and flung it open. Several determined strides took him down the long corridor to Faith's door. Furlong stood at guard, leaning against the wall, his arms crossed loosely over his chest. His face showed no surprise when he saw Miles come into view.

"Open the door, Furlong," Miles ordered sharply.

"I think the lass is finally asleep, Miles. She's been weeping for some time."

"I don't care if she wept enough to fill Lough Emy wi' her tears," Miles snapped harshly. "Open the damned door or I'll break it down."

Shrugging, Furlong drew the latch. The door swung open slightly, but no noise could be heard from inside. Setting his mouth in a determined line, Miles entered the chamber, shutting the door resolutely behind him.

For a moment he simply stood in the doorway, unnoticed. Faith wasn't in bed asleep, as Furlong had suspected, but instead sat huddled in a chair in front of the window. The fire had all but died out and a draft made the room chilly. A few flickering candles provided the only light in the room. Her face was hidden in her hands, though he did not hear her weeping. Steeling himself against the flood of emotions that suddenly surfaced, he took another step forward, clearing his throat to alert her to his presence.

When she did not turn her head nor acknowledge his presence, Miles walked to the window and calmly stood in front of her. Finally she raised her red-rimmed eyes to look at him.

"What do you want of me now?" she asked simply, her lips nearly blue from the cold.

Swearing softly, he strode to the hearth and began stacking several logs in the fireplace. Patiently, he stirred the dying embers until flames leapt and began to lick hungrily at the wood. When a warm blaze sprang from the hearth he stood, shaking the dirt from his hands.

"Come warm yourself by the fire," he ordered her firmly.

After a slight hesitation she obeyed him and came to stand at the hearth, holding out her hands to the heat of the fire. For several minutes they stood side by side without talking, staring somberly into the flames.

"I want to know everything, Faith," Miles said at last, turning to face her. "I want ye to start from the beginning and tell me who ye are and how ye came to be here. No matter how strange it may sound, I ask ye for nothing more than the truth."

Faith lifted her eyes slowly to meet his. "I've already told you."

He nodded curtly. "Then tell me again. All o' it. I want to know everything, including why ye believe ye must stop this man and who he is trying to kill in London." He reached out, cupping her cold cheek with his hand. "I need to know," he added softly.

Closing her eyes, she nodded. Miles picked up her chair from in front of the window and placed it in front of the fire. She sat down as he dragged a second chair parallel to hers and seated himself. He waited patiently as she adjusted her skirts, angling her feet closer to the warmth. Finally Faith leaned forward, her pale hair spilling across her shoulders.

"Before I start I want you to know that some of this may be painful for you to hear. The Irish will suffer greatly in the years to come. But I did not invent this—it is simply the history I know."

Miles nodded. "Go on, lass. I'm listening."

She spoke quietly and without emotion, relating the history of Ireland up to her time. Miles listened without comment, though he alternated between moments of anger and frustration. When she finished he came to his feet abruptly and walked to the hearth. For a long time he stood staring at the fire, his back to her. Finally he turned around, his brows drawn, his face grim.

"Answer me truthfully, Faith: Are ye really from the future or have ye just seen into it? I've heard o' people wi' the Sight who know things before they happen. Mayhap ye only think ye are from the twentieth century because ye have seen it and believed yourself to have lived it."

Faith sighed wearily. "No, Miles. If I was really from this time, wouldn't I be more familiar with your customs? No; I stepped, fell or stumbled through some kind of portal in time." Impulsively, she reached forward and took his hand. "I'm as human as you are."

He flinched in surprise at her touch but did not pull away. He had to hear the rest of the story, no matter how strange.

"Tell me the rest, Faith. Who does this assassin . . . Padriac O'Rourke . . . wish to kill?"

She paused a long moment before answering. "He plans to assassinate Oliver Cromwell," she finally said.

Miles looked at her in incredulous surprise. "Oliver Cromwell? *The* Oliver Cromwell?"

"Yes."

He snapped his mouth shut with a firm snap. "After everything ye just told me about the black-hearted bastard ye want to try and save his life?"

"It's what is supposed to happen, Miles. We can't interfere with history."

Miles raised his hand sharply in disagreement. "As far as I am concerned, my history hasn't yet been written. Have ye lost your senses, Faith? Killing Cromwell is exactly what needs to be done. I'd do it myself if I could."

"Then what will be next?" she retorted sharply. "Are you asking me to permit Paddy O'Rourke to play God with history? Cromwell is not supposed to die by his hand. I know that and so does he. I cannot permit it to happen."

Miles knelt down on one knee, grasping her hand between

his. "But the suffering ye say Ireland goes through—we can stop it, Faith. If ye let him kill Cromwell, it could save hundreds and thousands o' lives."

"What happened to Ireland was as history willed it," Faith responded softly. "Who knows, Miles? Perhaps the pain and suffering the Irish went through made them cling all the more fiercely to their traditions. Or it may have prevented the Irish from being quietly assimilated into an English way of life. We just don't know. We can't second-guess history; it is a game far too dangerous for us to play. Paddy O'Rourke and I were never supposed to be here. As a result, I have to stop him from carrying out his personal agenda. History must remain as it is. I'll do it with or without your help."

Miles searched her eyes for a hint of deception but found only a quiet determination. "Your predictions . . . are they really what comes to pass?"

She wearily brushed a strand of pale hair from her forehead. "Yes. It's the history I know."

Without a word, Miles abruptly rose to his feet. Faith watched him pace the room, his hands clasped behind his back, his face drawn in quiet contemplation. She knew he was struggling with what she had told him. To believe or not to believe. She could hardly expect a man of his time to believe such a thing. Yet she so desperately wanted him to believe, to understand just how much she had risked by telling him the truth.

She started in surprise when Miles suddenly stopped pacing and turned to face her. Planting his feet apart, he crossed his arms against his chest and frowned determinedly.

" 'Tis done. My decision has been made. I am going to marry ye tomorrow evening, with or without your consent. 'Twill serve two purposes. First, 'twill protect ye temporarily from the English soldiers who will undoubtedly appear at my castle gates at any moment. Second, 'twill protect me from ye, if what ye have said is just an English plan to draw me into illegal activities. As my wife, any actions ye may undertake become my responsibility, as in turn, my actions will speak for the O'Bruaidar clan, including ye. Ye'll be bound to me, Faith, and as a result 'twill be little opportunity for dishonesty or betrayal if your story proves to be false."

A flash of anger sparked in her eyes. "Damn you, Miles

O'Bruaidar. It doesn't matter what I told you; you still don't believe me. Do you really think I made this all up?''

"What I believe and don't believe is no' the issue. I'm giving ye protection, Faith. Tomorrow ye will become my wife and thus my property. 'Twill be most difficult for the English to take a piece o' my property from Castle Dun na Moor without my permission.''

"Property?'' Faith shrieked in outrage. "I can't bloody believe this. I trusted you and now you expect me to agree to become a piece of property?''

Miles shrugged. "Ye may agree or disagree; it matters little to me. Ye will marry me, Faith. 'Tis what is o' importance here.''

Incredulity swept over her face. "You barbarian. You can't order me into the vows of marriage. I don't give a bloody whit what century this is. I won't do it, Miles.''

He swore in Gaelic before grabbing her by the arm and hauling her to her feet. "Now ye listen to me,'' he bellowed. "I do know what's best for ye, altho' I'm cursed why I bother to explain. From the start ye have shown no respect for my wishes. Instead ye got yourself shot, drowned, imprisoned and sent to the gallows, leading me on a merry chase all o'er Ireland after ye. I don't know how women act in your time, and by the Holy Rod o' Christ, at this moment I don't care. We are in *my* time now. If ye want to stay alive in order to fulfill whatever task ye believe ye have before ye, ye had damn well better start listening to me.'' There was fire in Miles's eyes, and his hands gripped Faith's shoulders so tightly, she gritted her teeth to keep from crying out.

Defiantly, she raised her eyes to meet his furious gaze. "I'll not be threatened into marrying you, Miles. You can't make me do something I don't want to do.''

Miles laughed harshly. "Och, but I can, Faith. Ye know full well that I may do whatever I please. I'll drag ye to Father Michael, bound and gagged, if I must. And right now I find that course o' action exceptionally appealing.''

"How dare you!'' Faith gasped, raising her hand to slap him. He easily caught it, pinning it hard against his chest.

"I do dare,'' he replied, his breath hot on her cheeks. "And

I dare ye to find the courage to agree to my proposal. Ye will marry me and that is final.''

Furious, Faith flung back her head to retort when Miles's mouth abruptly crashed down on hers, stifling her protest. Frantically, she pounded her fists on his chest, but he only dragged her closer, sliding his grip tight around her waist.

Miles did not know what possessed him to act in such a manner with her. One moment he was calmly explaining what was to be done, and in the next moment he was all fire and fury, dragging her into his arms. Frustration mixed with desire inflamed his senses until he felt his blood surging hot and powerful through his veins. He couldn't understand his reaction; it was only that no woman had ever caused him to lose possession of discipline and reason as she did.

Breathing heavily, Miles pulled his lips away from her, sliding them slowly down her throat. Held tight in his iron embrace, Faith tried to remain stiff and unresponsive, but her skin tingled where his lips touched her skin. Closing her eyes, she tried to ignore the pleasurable sensations created in her body as his big hands glided across her back in exploration, gentle and strong.

"Tell me that ye don't feel this bond 'tween us, Faith. That ye don't feel it coursing in your blood," he murmured softly. "We were made to be together."

A tremor of desire swept through her body as he nibbled on her earlobe in a delicate caress. "Stop it," she said, the breathless tone of her voice betraying her attempt at an indifferent stance.

He abruptly released her. Surprised, Faith's eyes flew open and she took a hasty step backward. Smoothing down her disordered skirts, she willed her racing heart to be calm.

"I told you why I cannot marry you, Miles. Even if I wanted to . . . I can't stay in this time."

"And I've already told ye that I'm ready to take that risk." The firelight flickered over his strong face. His expression was steady and calm.

"How can you agree to such a thing?" she whispered. "You aren't even certain of who I am."

He deliberately claimed her hand, lifting it to his lips. "Aye, that much is true, but I'm certain that ye have come into my life for a purpose. 'Tis something 'tween us, Faith; a bond that keeps drawing us together.''

"Miles, please,'' she pleaded softly, "don't ask me to do this.''

He brushed aside her bangs with the tips of his fingers. "Ye know what I think, Faith? I think the real reason ye won't wed me has naught to do wi' chasing Paddy O'Rourke to London. I think your fears are keeping ye from taking risks wi' your heart. I am no' so timid, lass.''

His words, so close to the truth, were like a crowbar, prying open the bricks in the wall around her heart. Frightened, she wanted nothing more than to run from his penetrating gaze. Yet she did nothing, remaining perfectly still for an endless moment, every nerve in her body humming.

"You are right,'' she finally admitted, exhaling a deep and painful breath. "I'm not strong enough to marry you. I'm afraid.''

Miles released her hand, but only to draw her to her feet. "Afraid o' what, lass? That ye might come to care for me?''

"Yes,'' she said softly.

"Do ye think this is your only choice, Faith? That ye must harden your heart? That ye dare no' hold happiness to your breast, if only for a moment?''

"I don't expect you to understand,'' she retorted bitterly.

"Aye, but I do,'' he replied calmly. "I think I'm beginning to understand ye very well.''

"No,'' she exploded harshly. "No, damn it, you don't understand. Can't you see? I don't want to care for someone so much that I lose my heart and reason. It scares me . . . no, it terrifies me. I don't need those kinds of emotions in my life, Miles; I don't *want* them. I saw what happened to my father when my mother died. In essence, he ceased to live himself.''

"Then 'twas his mistake. He had a lot to live for,'' Miles said quietly. "He had a wee lassie who depended on him.''

"I think he never loved me. His love for my mum was so strong, so great, that it blinded him to all else, even his own child. It could happen to me.''

"So because o' your father, ye dare no' care for anyone again?''

"Yes,'' she cried with wrenching emotion. "I need to protect myself. But God help me, I'm afraid it's already too late for that.''

He was suddenly still. ''What do ye mean?''

Faith clenched her fists at her side. ''Damn you for forcing this from me, Miles O'Bruaidar. I don't just care about you; I'm in love with you.''

She paused for a horrified moment, shocked that she had actually said the words aloud. A hot crimson stain spread across her cheeks. Mortified, she wished with all her heart that the earth would open up and swallow her.

''Faith . . .'' Miles said softly, putting a hand on her shoulder.

She jerked away from him. ''Don't touch me. Please, just don't touch me. I shouldn't have said it, but I did. Now you know why I can't marry you.''

He stood close but did not touch her. ''What I know is that ye should marry me, now more than ever.''

''No,'' she cried, throwing up her hands in frustration. ''Don't you see? This kind of love frightens me. Sometimes, Miles, I feel so strongly about you that I can see myself turning into my father. I won't permit it.''

''Now ye listen to me, Faith,'' Miles said, firmly gripping her by the shoulders, ''ye are no' your father. Do ye hear me?''

''You're wrong,'' she countered fiercely through her tears. ''I'm just like him, Miles, in so many ways.''

''That kind o' love is destructive,'' he insisted firmly. ''It won't happen to ye, nor will it happen to us. I've seen the tenderness ye have inside. Ye've learned well the lessons o' your da. But ye must begin to live your own life and take yourself from the shadow o' your father. Otherwise, your life will be filled wi' naught more than bitterness, fear and unhappiness.''

''I don't know what to do,'' she said, leaning her forehead against his chest. ''Where do I start?''

''Let me help ye.''

''How can you help me? You don't even believe me about being from another time.''

He sighed. ''I think *ye* believe what ye are saying, and for now 'tis enough for me. Perhaps in time I'll come to accept it. But despite all o' this, ye must marry me or face certain death." He placed a finger on her lip to stifle the protest he saw forming there. "As my wife, no one will be able to take ye from the castle without a special edict o' the king. Besides, if what ye predict does come true, soon the king will have a lot more to worry about than a mere wisp o' a lass deep in the Irish countryside."

She lifted her head to look at him. "You won't stop me from leaving if I want or must return to my own time?"

"I'll no' hold ye back, Faith, even if it means returning from whence ye came."

"Why would you do this for me?"

"Because from the first moment I saw ye lying in the stone circle I thought ye to be a gift delivered to a weary soul. Ye've changed me, Faith, made me long to live for something other than battle wi' the English. Somehow I'm certain that ye are a part o' my destiny, just as I am a part o' yours. Whether 'tis only for a short time I do no' know. But 'tis something I truly believe. I ask ye to believe it wi' me."

Slowly, she wrapped her arms around his waist, leaning her head against his chest. For the first time in her life someone offered her a quiet respite from her past. Even though she knew that their relationship was temporary and tenuous at best, it offered her the first chance she had ever had at love and a family of her own.

"You have no idea what it's like to be alone," she said softly. "If you could know how many nights I spent lying in bed, hoping for a knight in shining armor to come and whisk me away from all the pain and loneliness. Now you are here and the bitter irony is that I can't have you—at least not forever."

"Will ye no' take what I can offer, lass?"

Faith looked up at him. The expression on his handsome face was calm and steady. She brushed her fingers over the curve of his strong jaw and felt him shudder with desire. It was a miracle that he still wanted her after everything she had told him—after everything she had done.

Her resolve weakened further. All of her life she had considered herself to be a strong, competent woman able to handle anything that came her way. But this she couldn't handle.

Miles O'Bruaidar had reached into her heart and pulled it out for display. To examine her old hurts was hard and painful, but it had started a healing process as well.

She knew it had been a mistake to become involved with him, but it was far too late to change that now. The truth was that she couldn't change what was in her heart, even if it was futile.

Surrendering her demons at last, she lifted her mouth to Miles. His lips claimed hers, hungry and seeking. Need and desire crashed over her, shattering the last vestiges of the wall she had so carefully built around her heart. Blood pounded in her brain, making her knees tremble. Grasping his shoulders, she closed her eyes and let herself drift in wonder at the heady feelings of trust and love.

Sweeping her off her feet, Miles carried her to the bed. Brushing the hair gently off her shoulders, he kissed her forehead.

"Faith?" he asked softly. "Will ye wed me, lass?"

She stared at him for an endless moment before touching the hair at his temple. "Are you certain you want to do this, Miles? You have everything to lose and nothing to gain."

He gave her a crooked smile. "On the contrary, lass, I'll have gained myself the most beautiful wife in all o' Ireland—even if she is a *Sassenach.* 'Tis odd, but ever since meeting ye I've realized that I want to marry a lass who matches me in wit and spirit. A woman I can talk to and who will listen to what I say. That's really why I wish to wed ye, all the other reasons aside."

Her heart surged with tenderness and something else, an emotion Faith thought long dead and buried. "Yes," she whispered with a smile. "I'll marry you, Miles."

Miles shed his clothes quickly and gently undressed her before Faith eagerly drew him down, cherishing the tenderness of his hands and the brush of his lips against her skin. She hugged him tightly to her breast, fearful that he might somehow escape. Threading her fingers through his thick, dark hair, she closed her eyes and let him sweep her away to a place where time no longer mattered.

Chapter Twenty-six

The dawn came bright and cold. A brisk wind beat against the stone walls of the castle, its lonely howling the only sound in the library, other than the snapping and crackling from the flames in the fireplace. Miles sat at his desk, looking at a stack of letters. For the first time in his life he wished he could read them himself, instead of having to wait for Father Michael. He rubbed his beard-roughened jaw against the back of his hand in frustration.

It was all because of Faith. She had become his tutor, giving him a glimpse of a new world by teaching him to read. Hell and damnation, she had done more than just teach him to read—she had changed the very core of him. And as much as he didn't want to admit it, she had changed him for the better.

It was strange, he thought, but never before had he felt so convinced that marrying her was the correct course of action. This morning, when he awoke with her cuddled in his arms, her pale hair splayed across his chest, he knew that marrying this woman was his fate. As she had sighed and snuggled closer, an unexpected contentment filled him. He'd found a peace in her arms he'd never expected.

Impatiently, he drummed his fingers against the desktop. He was restless for the early morning hours to pass so he could ride to the Dunbar estate to announce his betrothal to Faith. He did not relish the task but was certain that he could soothe any hurt feelings on the part of either Arabella or her da.

A ghost of a smile played across his lips. In spite of everything, he would still have some explaining to do when he announced that he wished to take an Englishwoman as his bride. He well imagined that the elder Dunbar would be in a fine rage. It would cost Miles a fortune to soothe the man's bruised ego and his daughter's reputation, but it would be well worth it. Dragging a hand through his hair, he considered the consequences. An insistent knock on the door brought his head up sharply.

"Enter," he called out.

The door opened and Patrick O'Farrell stepped into the room. "I heard ye were awake, Miles. I've wish to have speech wi' ye."

"Come in, lad. What is on your mind?"

Patrick walked in and stood before Miles's desk. "I've just been to the kitchen. The servants are saying ye told them that . . . well, that ye are planning to marry the Englishwoman tonight," he blurted out. "It can't be true. I mean, ye wouldn't do such a foolish thing, would ye?"

Miles leaned back in his chair, studying the pale-haired boy impassively. Patrick stood nervously, shifting his weight from one foot to another. "What ye may consider foolish, lad, some might consider wise," Miles said slowly.

Patrick's eyes flashed angrily. "But she is English. She is the enemy, and ye wish to draw her into the folds o' our family. Ye have no right."

"I've every right," Miles said coldly, leaning forward in his chair. "Lest ye forget, lad, this family is headed by me."

Patrick's fists clenched tightly at his sides. "By the rod o' Christ, Miles, I never thought I'd see ye turn your back on your family simply because ye were besotted by a pretty face."

Miles stood abruptly, the sudden motion sweeping the papers from the desk in a white flurry. He leaned forward, his eyes cold and hard. "Is that why ye think I'm marrying Faith? Because she is a comely lass?"

Patrick nodded vigorously. "Aye, I do. What other reason could there be? I think the English planned all along to send the lass here, hoping ye would be charmed enough to bring her into your confidence. Now that ye have asked her to marry ye, she'll be here permanently, spying on us for the English. How can ye be so blind, Miles?"

Miles strode around the desk in two steps, towering above his cousin. "If ye were a man, Patrick, ye would be facing a length o' steel now."

Patrick swallowed hard but kept his head bravely high. "I know, Miles. But someone had to tell ye."

Julie Moffett

There was a long moment of uncomfortable silence. Patrick jumped when Miles's hand fell heavily to his shoulder. None too gently, Miles propelled Patrick to a chair and forced him to sit in it.

"Faith is no' just any Englishwoman, Patrick. I have no cause to question her loyalty to me."

"It could be an English plan to trap ye, Miles."

"Aye, it could, but my instinct tells me 'tis no'. There is a lot about the lass ye do no' know, Patrick. Ye must trust my judgment of her."

"B-but . . ." Patrick began to protest when Miles raised a hand sharply, stopping his words.

"I've explained more than ye deserve to know. Frankly, my reasons for asking Faith to marry me are none o' your concern. As a member o' my family, I ask ye only to respect my wishes and follow them without question. Is that clear, Patrick?"

The boy nodded his head silently and Miles grunted in satisfaction. "Then be off wi' ye, lad, as I have much to do today. 'Tis my wedding day, after all."

Faith was alone when she awoke. Rolling over sleepily, she put out her hand and felt Miles's side of the bed. It was cold; he had been gone for some time.

Smiling at the memory of their tender lovemaking, she slipped from the bed and wrapped a linen robe around her body. Walking to the window, she lifted the edge of the drape and peered out at the morning sky. The sun was shining brightly and the sky was clear. A good omen, she thought.

A noise at the door startled her from her musing. She turned just as Molly came bustling in with a breakfast tray.

"Och, ye're finally awake," she said cheerfully. "Miles said to see that ye were awakened if ye hadn't roused yourself by midmorning."

Faith absently touched her tousled hair, a faint blush coloring her cheeks. The bed was rumpled, the sheets and coverlet in complete disarray. She wondered just what Miles had told Molly about the previous night.

"What else did he say?" Faith asked slowly.

Molly smiled broadly. "Why, he told us the news—that tonight ye shall become his wife. So rouse yourself, lass;

302

we've a lot to do. 'Tisn't every day that ye are wed.''

Faith reached out to brace herself against the wall, her legs suddenly rubbery. In the harsh light of day the decision suddenly seemed hasty and reckless. "Miles decided to go through with it, did he?'' she said weakly.

Molly deftly placed a piece of cheese on a slice of bread and handed the plate to Faith. "O' course he's decided. He's been up since before the crack o' dawn, ordering people about and making preparations for the grand feast here tonight. Father Michael brought me his robe to mend, and Miles commanded me to make certain ye had a suitable dress for tonight. He has the entire kitchen in an uproar—'tis hotter than the devil's lair down there. People are running about, screeching at the top o' their lungs. Miles himself rode off an hour ago to the Dunbar estate.''

"Oh,'' Faith said quietly. "I suppose you must think this is all rather sudden.''

Molly shook her head firmly. " 'Tisn't a soul in this castle who couldn't see what ye and Miles have 'tween ye. I only feared that the two o' ye wouldn't face up to it until 'twas too late.''

"You knew?'' Faith asked in wonder.

Molly's eyes twinkled. "O' course I knew. I've known that lad for all o' his life and I promise ye, I've never seen him so besotted wi' a lass. Ye have a quick wit and a spirit that matches his own, yet there is a tenderness about ye that is most enchanting. Miles needs someone like ye, lass, and 'tis my opinion that ye will do well wi' a man like Miles.''

Faith looked at Molly shyly. "He is a good man.''

Molly beamed happily. "Aye, 'tis what I've been telling ye all along. Ye'll be a fine mistress o' this castle and a good mother to his bairns. 'Twill be a day o' great celebration here at Castle Dun na Moor. Now, have a wee dram o' tea and some bread. Then we'll see ye fitted into the prettiest wedding gown in all o' Ireland.''

Faith groaned in relief as the heavy ivory-colored satin gown was lifted over her head and laid carefully on the bed. For four long hours she had stood patiently while six women cut, snipped and sewed on the gown that would be her wedding dress. It was the most beautiful gown she had ever seen, of satin and gold threads that looked as though it had been made for a queen. Everything was sheer perfection—from the sleeves edged with the finest lace to the bodice, which dipped so low it barely covered her breasts. Embarrassed, Faith tried to talk the women into sewing a piece of lace across the plunging neckline, but Molly adamantly refused.

"Ye are a natural beauty, lass. The gown fits like 'twas made for ye. We shan't change a thing other than to suit your height."

So the women had done their work, only now releasing her from the torture of standing still. While Faith drew a robe over her shoulders, Molly ushered the women from the room and then left herself, giving Faith a few moments of much-needed solitude.

Rubbing her arms to increase the circulation, Faith wandered over to where the wedding dress lay on the bed. This gown, like all the others Faith had worn, had belonged to Miles's mother, Moireen O'Bruaidar. Gently fingering the material, Faith wondered what Moireen had been thinking hours before she became the mistress of Castle Dun na Moor.

"I'll bet you weren't half as nervous as I am," Faith murmured as she pulled the robe tighter around her waist.

Sinking into a chair, Faith closed her eyes. So much had happened to her in the past few days that she didn't think she would ever be able to sort it all out. In some ways she was afraid to analyze what was taking place, fearful she would discover that she was making a horrible mistake.

"Don't think, Faith," she commanded herself aloud, pressing her fingers to her temples. Slowly, she rubbed the skin in a circular motion, ignoring the uneasy flutter in her stomach. Thankfully, a knock on the door jolted her from her thoughts.

"Come in," she called out, straightening in the chair.

The door opened slowly and the young lad, Patrick, stepped into the room. He flushed red to the roots of his pale hair when he saw Faith was clad only in a dressing gown.

"I b-beg your pardon, my lady," he stammered, careful not to look directly at her. "But Miles has just returned from the Dunbar estate, and he wants to know if ye wish to join him on a ride about the grounds."

Faith's eyes lit up at the thought of being able to see Miles and get some fresh air. "Oh, how thoughtful of him. Yes, tell him I'll meet him at the stables shortly. And thank you, Patrick."

The boy blushed again before nodding and hastily leaving the room. Quickly surveying her closet, Faith pulled out a blue and white gown of muslin and stepped into it, forgoing the corset. Cursing the numerous hooks and ties, she finally managed to dress herself.

"What I wouldn't do for a pair of jeans and a cotton blouse," she muttered as she grabbed her cloak and headed out the door.

A few of the servants curtseyed and bowed politely to her as she headed out to the stables. Faith realized with growing wonder that she would soon be their mistress. The thought filled her with an unexpected sense of pride, as well as a slight twinge of fear that she might not be able to live up to the beloved memory of the last mistress of the castle.

Faith pulled open the door to the stables and stepped inside. The moist smell of hay and the strong scent of horses greeted her. "Miles?" she called out, moving deeper into the stables and peering in the dim light. "I'm here."

"Aye, I can see ye are."

The voice came from behind her. Turning around quickly, Faith saw Arabella Dunbar, dressed in a black cloak with a hood, standing in the doorway.

"Arabella," Faith exclaimed in genuine astonishment. "What are you doing here?"

"Need you ask?" she replied coldly, carefully closing the door behind her. The stables darkened considerably, the only light coming through the thin slats of wood on the roof.

"Miles has been to see you," Faith said slowly.

Arabella nodded. "Aye, he has. Did ye think I would so easily allow an English whore to become the mistress of Castle Dun na Moor?"

Her words were as cold and biting as a sharp slap to the face. Keeping her expression emotionless, Faith met Arabella's cool gaze evenly. "I *think* you have little to say in the matter."

Arabella pushed the hood off her head with one graceful motion and shook out the locks of her thick brown hair. "Och, but I'm afraid ye are wrong, lass. 'Tis me he wishes to marry. A man of Miles's virility and strength needs a strong woman to match him. An Irishwoman.''

Faith stiffened, uneasiness creeping up her spine. Had Miles changed his mind once he had arrived at the Dunbar estate?

Her fear gave way to relief after a moment of rational thought. If he had, Arabella would not be here now.

"He appears to prefer an Englishwoman," Faith said calmly. "It is I who will exchange the vows of marriage with him tonight, not you."

"I'd no' be so certain, if I were ye," Arabella said confidently, sweeping her cloak open and placing her hands on her hips. "Even as we speak, my da and others are convincing Miles o' the error o' his ways."

Faith laughed, but her insides tightened uncomfortably. "I see. And I suppose you are here to persuade me otherwise, just in case they fail."

"There will be no failure in this matter," Arabella said throatily. "I've made certain o' that."

With her words, a dark figure stepped out of the shadows of the stables and came to stand beside her. Faith gasped in shock when she saw it was Donagh O'Rourke.

"My God," Faith breathed. "How did you get here?"

Donagh shrugged. "Ye underestimate my abilities, lass. Ye may be surprised to know that I still have friends at Castle Dun na Moor."

"After what you've done?" Faith exclaimed angrily. "You killed an innocent boy."

Donagh's mouth curved into a scowl, the scar on his lip and chin twisting horribly. "It was an unfortunate and unexpected turn o' events ye caused, lass. Ye have been nothing but trouble ever since I laid eyes on ye. I should have done away wi' ye myself, and would have, had I no' thought ye to be a genuine English spy. But ye turned out to be something quite different. Ye played us all for the fool, including O'Bruaidar."

Faith clutched her cloak tighter about her shoulders, trying to ward off a chill that did not come from the cool air. "Donagh is the traitor," she told Arabella quickly. "He's working for the English."

Arabella laughed lightly. "Do ye hear that, Donagh? The lass dares to call ye a traitor."

"Bradford told me how you cut a deal in order to protect your property in Ireland," Faith continued evenly, keeping her gaze steady on O'Rourke. "You knew the English had plans to expand in this area. So in order to save your own skin, you agreed to betray your people. You've been spying on Miles, and you killed a boy in cold blood."

Donagh's dark eyes flashed angrily. "Have care to call me a traitor, lass. I am required to serve no one other than myself. And I'll no' let a shrew-tongued *Sassenach* prevent me from getting what is due to me."

"Due to you?"

Donagh nodded his head slowly. "Aye, lass, 'tis true the English plan to come to Ireland with troops. And I'm no fool to know that Ireland is too weak to prevent them from taking what they want. It means little to me who wishes to be my king, and I see no harm in welcoming those soon to be our rulers. Long after all the other Irish noblemen are gone, 'twill be me left here."

Faith glanced at Arabella. "Are you listening to him? He is willing to turn over Ireland to the English without a fight."

Arabella linked arms with Donagh. "Did ye expect me to be shocked? How naive ye are, lass. I've known all along o'Donagh's plans. In fact, ye could even say that I am a large part o' them."

Faith stepped backward in surprise, understanding dawning in her eyes. "My God," she whispered, "you mean to betray Miles. Both of you."

Donagh grinned. "Miles's attempts at resistance against the English are weak and pathetic. Yes, we know he is the legendary Irish Lion. But there comes a time when a man must change masters or perish needlessly."

Faith faced Donagh, bristling. "So the two of you planned this together; I understand now. When your plan with Bradford failed to eliminate Miles during my exchange you convinced Arabella to work for you. Once she married Miles, you would have a highly placed spy at Castle Dun na Moor, able to effectively monitor his activities. Of course, you would then sell this information for a price to the English, until it suited you to get rid of Miles altogether, conveniently leaving his widow, Arabella, with his entire fortune."

A horse whinnied softly in the background. Donagh smiled at her, slowly cracking his knuckles one by one. "Ye have rather remarkable wits . . . for a lass, that is."

"I suppose it doesn't even matter that you have a wife and a young son," Faith spat at Donagh contemptuously. "After all you have done I'm certain it wouldn't bother your conscience to rid yourself of a wife."

Donagh wrapped his arm around Arabella's shoulder, pulling her closer. "Aye, 'twill be a grave misfortune when my wife passes away. An unfortunate riding accident, perhaps. The bereaved O'Bruaidar widow and I will look to each other for comfort and solace. And who would deny us these small pleasures after all o' the tragedy we have been through? Eventually we will marry and unite the O'Bruaidar and O'Rourke lands, along with Arabella's da's estate, as well."

Arabella flushed triumphantly. "Donagh will become one o' the wealthiest men in all o' Ireland. The English will no' touch us, and in fact will protect our holdings—all in exchange for a wee bit o' knee-bending to their king. 'Twill cost us nothing but gain us everything. 'Tis a magnificent plan."

Faith looked at Arabella in disgust. "And you called me a whore," she said quietly.

With a cry of rage, Arabella unexpectedly lunged forward, striking Faith across the face. After an initial moment of surprise Faith curled her fist and launched it directly into Arabella's stomach. It was a powerful punch, and a whoosh of air fled from Arabella's lungs as she sank to the floor of the stables, gasping and clutching her middle.

Donagh looked at the two women in astonishment. "Ladies, please," he said. "Let's be civilized about this."

"There is nothing civilized about either of your behavior," Faith said angrily, gingerly touching the bruise that was forming on her upper lip. "You'll never get away with your twisted plan of murder and deception."

"But I assure ye that we will, lass," Donagh said confidently. "And the first step is removing ye permanently from Miles's presence."

A cold chill crept up Faith's spine. "You are going to kill me?"

Donagh nodded. " 'Twould have been much simpler if ye had died on the gallows. I'm afraid your death this time will be much more painful."

Arabella lurched to her feet, glaring at Faith. "Ye'll rue the day ye ever set eyes on Miles O'Bruaidar. How dare ye touch me."

"How dare I, indeed," Faith said dryly. "I broke a nail."

"Enough, ye two," Donagh barked sharply.

"Oh, this is really pretty, O'Rourke," Faith said, shaking her head in disgust. "First you kill a boy by thrusting a sword in his back and then you turn out to be a traitor to your own people. Now you aim to murder a woman. Quite a manly performance."

Donagh's eyes narrowed angrily. "None o' this would have been necessary if ye hadn't forced me to play my hand wi' Miles earlier than I had planned. Now I have to wait out my time in Drogheda until the English move into this area. But still, 'twas no' enough for ye. Ye had to bat those pretty eyes o' yours, seducing Miles and filling his head wi' foolish notions of marriage. Ye are a comely and clever lass, but even I never suspected O'Bruaidar would choose a *Sassenach* o'er Arabella."

"He simply has good taste in women," Faith said softly. "Unlike some men, apparently."

"Donagh," Arabella hissed furiously, "cease this discussion at once. Let's finish the task at hand."

Nodding sharply, Donagh moved toward Faith. She backed away quickly, realizing with a sinking heart that the exit was effectively blocked by both Donagh and Arabella. When she came up against the wall of the stables a noise from above caught her attention. A slight form tumbled from the hayloft, falling directly at Faith's feet. Faith gasped in astonished horror as Patrick O'Farrell rolled to his feet and awkwardly drew his sword.

"Stand away from her, sir," he declared bravely, putting himself between Faith and Donagh, "or I will have to fight ye."

"Patrick," Faith said in stunned amazement. "What are you doing here?"

The boy ignored her question, keeping his eyes trained on Donagh. "Ye are both liars and blackguards. Ye told me she was the traitor—that she meant to bring harm to Miles. 'Twas why I agreed to help ye and bring her to ye in the first place. But ye lied."

"Ye made a grave mistake to eavesdrop, lad," Donagh said coldly. "Now 'twill cost ye your life."

Faith's heart leaped uncomfortably in her chest. "For Christ's sake, don't be ridiculous, O'Rourke. He's just a child. Let him go."

" 'Tis no' true," Patrick countered bravely, brandishing his sword. "I'm no' a child anymore. I'm a man. And I'll let no harm come to ye, my lady."

Faith might have laughed had the situation not been so dire. "Patrick, I command you to leave at once," she said in her sternest tone.

To her dismay, Patrick refused to move, and Donagh slowly drew his sword. She saw Patrick's arm falter momentarily, but he stoically pressed his lips together in a stubborn line and stood firm.

"For pity's sake, stop this charade, Donagh," Faith said desperately. "It's me you want. Well, you can have me. I'll not struggle if you'll just let him go."

Donagh shook his head. "Lads grow into men. He's heard what has been said here and will expect vengeance in time. 'Twill be better for me to take care o' him now than worry about facing him later."

"Then be done wi' it and make haste," Arabella ordered. "Someone might find us here any moment."

Donagh circled the boy, his sword pointing downward. When Faith moved up behind Patrick the boy gave her a surprisingly firm push backward. "Stay back, my lady," he ordered her.

"Damn you, O'Rourke," Faith cried in desperation. "If you hurt him, I swear I'll . . ."

Her words were lost as Donagh brought the blade up against Patrick's with a clang. Shaken by the blow, Patrick darted out of the way with surprising speed and warily circled O'Rourke.

A Double-Edged Blade

Faith's heart sank when she saw that Donagh was toying with the boy. His sword flashed everywhere at once, dipping, teasing and slicing Patrick on the arm, face and chest. Then, with a determined grunt, Donagh finally finished the game. With one swift thrust, he knocked the blade out of Patrick's hand and swiftly held his bloodied sword to Patrick's chest. Faith leapt to the boy's side.

"Please, Donagh," Faith implored, "I beg you to spare his life."

Donagh shook his head. "I'm sorry that it has to be this way, lad," he said to Patrick. "At least ye go to your death knowing ye did yourself proud."

"N-no," Faith choked as Patrick stood stiffly, looking straight ahead as Donagh lifted his sword.

Suddenly a sharp noise sounded at the door to the stables. Donagh hesitated a split second and then brought his sword down. Faith seized his moment of indecision to throw her entire weight against Patrick. The boy stumbled sideways as the blade meant for his head glanced off her shoulder. Faith crumpled to the ground in stunned pain, hearing a frightful bellow of rage reverberate through the stables.

"Damn ye to hell, Donagh O'Rourke!"

Weakly, Faith lifted her head and saw Miles standing in the doorway. He was clad in a dark cloak and knee-high riding boots. He was nearly unrecognizable, his face black with fury, his eyes frigid as a winter day. His furious glance swept over her and Patrick before it settled on Donagh.

"By the rod o' Christ, O'Rourke," he thundered, "ye'll answer to me for what ye've done."

Donagh faced Miles squarely, wiping the blood from his blade. "'Twould be foolish to challenge me," he said calmly, but Faith saw his hand shake slightly. "The English are but a day's ride from the castle. If ye harm me, they'll set upon ye with little more than a moment's notice. 'Twill be a costly blunder, Miles, and one ye can ill afford."

"Ye're a traitor, Donagh, a blackguard o' the worst kind, because ye've betrayed those who trusted ye. And now ye've dared to touch the woman who will be my wife. Draw steel," he ordered, pulling his sword from its scabbard. In one quick motion he unfastened his cloak and cast it to the floor.

311

Donagh reluctantly obliged, lifting his sword in salute. "Ye are acting foolishly, Miles. The lass is naught more than an English whore."

Miles growled with anger, ferociously charging Donagh. The big Irishman feinted forward, barely sidestepping the arc of Miles's sword. He brought up his sword just as Miles's blade slammed into his with such force, it caused sparks to fly. Warily, the two men circled each other.

As the men began their furious exchange, Patrick slipped quietly to Faith's side and cradled her head in his hands. Tears coursed down his young face. Pressing the flat of her hand against the warm wound in her shoulder, Faith tried to reassure the boy, and then realized that the tears were streaming down her own face.

She could hardly see between the blur of tears and the rapid pace of the swordplay. It became little more than a flurry of jabs, thrusts and slashes. Heavy breathing and muttered curses could be heard amid the fierce clashing of the swords. Faith pressed her lips together, feeling the warm stickiness of blood coating her fingers. She could hardly bear to watch the furious exchange. The men seemed evenly matched in size, but Miles swung his sword relentlessly and with cold precision, refusing to relinquish even a small step backward to Donagh. It was clear that O'Rourke was tiring.

Suddenly, Miles lunged forward with vicious speed, crashing into Donagh. The traitorous Irishman's sword went flying through the air, colliding with a wall and clattering to the floor. The two large bodies slammed into each other, sending both impacting heavily on the haystrewn floor, each grappling for control.

Pushing himself upright, Miles forced a knee into Donagh's stomach. Donagh slammed his fist into Miles's jaw, knocking him off balance. Panting, Donagh rolled to his feet, grabbing his sword and lunging at Miles with a rabid grunt.

Faith screamed in warning as Miles staggered to his feet, raising his blade. But in his haste Donagh tripped over his own feet, lurching directly onto Miles's protruding blade.

"Nay," he screamed in horror as the steel sliced into his skin. Miles quickly withdrew his blade, but the damage was done. Donagh fell to the earthen floor, writhing in pain and clutching his bloody middle.

Faith squeezed her eyes shut at the gruesome sight. When she finally opened her eyes again she saw Miles kneeling on the floor next to Donagh.

"Why did ye do it, man?" he asked Donagh quietly. "Why did ye betray Ireland?"

Donagh grimaced in pain and then managed a ghastly smile. "Riches," he said hoarsely. "The riches . . . o' Ireland . . . were to be . . . mine."

"Ye did it for riches?" Miles repeated in disbelief. "Ye turned traitor for riches?"

"Nay," Donagh said, coughing weakly. " 'Twas . . . no' only . . . riches. 'Twas . . . the power."

Miles swore softly. "Damn ye, O'Rourke, for playing into the hands o' the English. They promised ye everything, but it cost ye your soul."

With surprising strength, Donagh reached up with one bloodied hand, clutching the folds of Miles's shirt. "I'll . . . see ye . . . in . . . hell . . . O'Bruaidar," he whispered.

"No' if I can help it," Miles answered grimly as Donagh's hand fell limply to the floor. The wounded Irishman took a gurgling, gasping breath and then fell silent.

"Is he dead?" Faith asked shakily.

Miles stood abruptly and in two long strides was at Faith's side. "He won't harm ye again," he said, cradling her in his arms. "Are ye all right?" he asked, his gaze sweeping over her wounded shoulder. " 'Tis a fair amount o' blood ye have lost, but the wound looks shallow."

"I'm just a bit shaken," she replied, leaning against the solid safety of his chest. "Where is Arabella? What about the English?"

"I'll take care o' everything. I only feared . . ." his voice shook, "I feared I had lost ye."

Faith reached up and gently touched his cheek. "Patrick saved me. He put himself between me and O'Rourke."

Miles threw a glance over his shoulder at Patrick, who stood in the middle of the stables, his shirt torn and his face and hands bloodied and streaked with tears. " 'Tis time I call ye a man, cousin," Miles said quietly. "I could no' be more

313

proud o' ye than I am at this moment. Come wi' me and I'll see that your wounds are bound. Then ye are to tell me exactly what happened here today.''

Quiet pride touched the boy's face as he followed his cousin out of the stables. Faith slumped against Miles's broad chest in relief, her tears mingling with the blood and dirt on her cheeks. As they approached the castle, she looked up at him.

"Miles," she whispered softly.

Worriedly, he gazed down at her. "Aye, what is it, lass?"

"What if we've just changed history by killing Donagh O'Rourke?"

Miles stopped in his tracks, letting the weight of her question sink in. For a long moment he stared at her before he swiftly strode on.

" 'Tis little that can be done about it now," he said grimly. " 'Tis out o' our hands."

Faith was quiet for a moment before speaking up. "Are you going to help me stop the other O'Rourke?"

He didn't answer at first, only looked down at her thoughtfully. Then his arms tightened around her. "Aye, lass. I may have completely lost my senses, but I believe I am."

Chapter Twenty-seven

Miles insisted that the wedding take place as planned.

Although Faith still felt weak from the harrowing experience in the stables, Miles had been right—the wound on her shoulder was relatively shallow.

In a flurry of activity, Faith's shoulder had been cleaned and bandaged, and the lovely wedding gown altered to fit over the cumbersome binding. When she was finally dressed and her hair brushed and swept up off her neck, Faith stood in the middle of the room and curtseyed for Molly and the serving girls. She was rewarded by a murmur of awe from the women.

"It's the loveliest dress I've ever seen," Faith breathed, the heavy satin material swishing gracefully around her legs.

Molly beamed. "And ye are a stunning bride," she said, making a last-minute adjustment to Faith's sleeve. "It suits ye perfectly."

Faith smiled shyly, actually feeling beautiful for the first time in her life. She only wished that Fiona were here to share in this wondrous moment.

Molly observed the moment of sadness that passed across Faith's face. "What's troubling ye, lass?"

Faith looked up quickly. "It's nothing, really. It's just that I always imagined my cousin would stand beside me on my wedding day. I miss her."

"Well, she'd certainly be proud o' ye. I've no' seen two people so in love since . . . well, since Miles's parents were wed here." She took Faith's hand. "Come now, lass. He waits for ye."

"How can you be certain that Miles still wants to go through with this?" Faith whispered worriedly as Molly led her downstairs. "Perhaps he's having second thoughts."

"Don't be so nervous, lass," Molly whispered back. "See, he's already there waiting for ye."

She pointed through the open doorway of the Great Hall. Miles stood next to young Patrick and in front of a beaming Father Michael.

He looked as handsome as Faith had ever seen him, dressed in a splendid jacket of deep burgundy, a crisp white shirt and dark breeches, white stockings and a pair of polished black shoes. His thick hair had been combed until it gleamed and was tied back at the nape of his neck.

"He's utterly gorgeous," Faith breathed. "How can he want to marry me?"

"Cease your fears and go to him, lass," Molly instructed, giving her a firm push.

Taking a deep, nervous breath, Faith walked into the room. Fresh rushes had been strewn across the floor and the chamber had been scrubbed from top to bottom. The trestle tables had been pushed to the walls and the benches stacked like cordwood. Men and women were dressed in their finest garments and parted down the middle, giving her a clear path to where Miles stood. Taking small steps so she would not trip on the heavy gown, she made the seemingly endless journey to meet Miles.

When she finally arrived he took her elbow, indicating that she was to kneel beside him on a pair of pillows covered with heavy velvet. She obeyed, and Father Michael began to speak.

The ceremony was conducted in Latin and Gaelic, and Faith understood little of it. Yet as the full weight of what she was doing begin to sink in, she started to tremble, certain that she would either faint or retch.

Miles must have sensed her nervousness, for he took her hand, giving her a reassuring squeeze. Stealing a sideways glance at him, Faith was comforted by the fact that he appeared absolutely calm about what they were doing.

Eventually they came to what Faith presumed were the vows. Miles helped her to her feet and they stood facing each other, holding hands. Father Michael asked her to repeat after him in Gaelic and she stumbled her way through the sounds, half whispering, half choking as the priest prodded her on. When it was Miles's turn to speak his words echoed clearly and firmly through the hall.

When he was finished Patrick stepped forward, handing

Miles a ring of heavy silver. Taking her cold hand in his, Miles slid the ring onto her finger, squeezing her hand reassuringly. Looking down in wonder, Faith saw it was the traditional Irish *claddagh* ring, with two hands circling to meet in the front, jointly holding a heart above which was a crown.

Father Michael then led them to a table where the wedding papers had been laid out. Handing Faith an ink-dipped pen, he indicated where she was to sign her name. Wondering whether she should exhibit her writing skills, she flashed Miles a questioning look, but he only nodded at her. Bending over the parchment, she scrawled her name and handed the pen to Miles. He signed the paper with a flourishing X.

"We'll have to work on that," Faith whispered to him, managing a nervous smile as he returned the pen to Father Michael. The priest then held a candle over the right edge of the paper, letting the wax drip and harden slightly before pressing an official seal into it.

The formalities thus completed, Miles immediately drew Faith into his arms for a long and passionate kiss. A loud cheer rose from the spectators. Faith blushed to the roots of her hair at the very public display of affection, but her reaction seemed only to please the guests. Laughingly, Furlong and the others started the words to a rousing song in Gaelic, which Miles later told her was filled with ribald jests and comments about virgin lassies.

Amid the shouts and surging of the crowd, Miles swept Faith off her feet and into his arms. "Given the fact that we may soon have English visitors," he announced loudly, "I'm afraid the feasting will have to begin without us. As ye may have guessed, I have a pressing duty to instruct my bride on her first duty as the new mistress o' Castle Dun na Moor." A rowdy shout started up, and Faith's blush deepened.

"Wait," she protested as he shifted her weight in his arms. "I'm starving. Don't we even get to eat something first?"

"Ye'd rather eat than engage in pleasantries wi' your husband?" Miles asked, amused.

"I can't help it," she replied. "We haven't eaten for hours."

"Well, 'twill be plenty o' time to eat later. Ye are no' officially my wife until I've bedded ye."

317

"Oh God," Faith hissed. "Did you have to make an announcement of it?"

"Aye, but I did, lass," he said, chuckling. "It should be known to all what we are doing in my bedchamber. As if there could be any doubt," he added under his breath, grinning.

"For pity's sake," Faith retorted under her breath. "Hasn't anyone in this century heard of privacy?" She frowned as the bawdy laughter followed them up the stairs. "Why are those men following us to the bedroom?" she asked, peeking over his shoulder.

"Chin up, lass," Miles said firmly. "Don't let them know they've got ye flustered, or we'll never have a moment's peace."

"Flustered? You're not going to let them . . . ah . . . witness this, are you? I've read about such things in your time." When he didn't answer she poked a finger at his chest. "Miles O'Bruaidar, if you permit them to set one foot inside our bedroom, you can forget about this bloody bedding exercise."

Miles looked down at her, grinning. "I'll no' ask ye to do something that makes ye uncomfortable. Pluck up, lass, and trust me."

"Famous last words," she muttered, but dutifully raised her chin.

The men continued to trail them until they reached the bedchamber. Kicking the door open with his foot, Miles set Faith carefully down inside the room.

Faith quickly scrambled to the welcome anonymity of the dark chamber. Although dusk had just set, the windows had been heavily covered by the drapes, shutting out the light. Several wax candles ringed the room and a bottle of wine and two glasses had been placed on a small table next to the hearth. A fire blazed cheerfully in the fireplace.

"All right, lads," Miles called out from the doorway. "Ye've seen me bring the lass to my bed. Now be off wi' ye so I can begin my instruction in peace." More boisterous jibes and rowdy laughter ensued before Miles firmly shut the door on them, drawing the bolt across it. The men continued to pound on the door, offering Miles advice through the wood.

Faith drew in a deep breath, making her way to the edge of the bed and sitting on it. "Good God, I don't think I've ever been so mortified in all my life. Will they simply wait out there until we are finished?''

Miles spread his hands, the candlelight emphasizing the strong bones in his fingers. "Aye, they will, lass, for I have ordered them to do so. I'll have as many witnesses as possible to the consummation o' our vows. I'm no' taking any chances that the English will try to have our marriage annulled.''

A note of hysteria edged into Faith's voice. "You can't be serious. Do you mean those men are going to sit out there with their ears pressed against the door and listen?''

Miles laughed as he moved forward to stand in front of her. "Would ye rather have them watch?''

Faith's mouth dropped open in shock. "You wouldn't dare," she hissed. When he shrugged she narrowed her eyes. "You . . . you . . .''

"Unprincipled rogue?'' Miles offered helpfully as he maneuvered his way behind her, his deft hands unfastening the wooden pins that held up her hair. As the pale strands spilled into his hands, his mouth began a slow and caressing journey down her neck and shoulders. "Och, ye had naught to worry about," he murmured against her skin. "I couldn't bear to let anyone else look upon ye, lass. Ye are for me alone.''

His warm kisses fired the stirrings of Faith's desire. His hands seemed to know every sensitive part of her anatomy. "Are you always going to employ this method to win an argument?'' she asked wryly.

He murmured, nibbling on her earlobe. "Is it working?''

Unable to suppress a laugh, Faith turned into his embrace, her arms circling about his neck. "A bit, I suppose.''

A look of mock hurt on his face, Miles pulled away. "Only a wee bit?''

Faith nodded, her eyes sparkling in the flickering light of the candles. "Well, you could improve your performance by helping me remove this very cumbersome gown.''

Murmuring something inaudible, Miles turned her around, unfastening the hooks one by one. He had done half a dozen and still had a dozen more to go when a curse erupted from his lips.

"By the rod o' Christ, wi' gowns like these, 'tis a wonder Ireland has any bairns at all.''

Faith bit back the laughter that rose to her lips. When Miles finished with the last hook he lifted the gown from her head with a triumphant grunt and carelessly tossed it to the floor.

"Miles," Faith protested, "that gown probably cost a fortune."

"I'll buy ye a new one," he murmured, sweeping her off her feet and depositing her gently on the bed, where he made quick work of her shift and petticoats.

Faith lay back on the bed and watched as Miles quickly shed his clothes and cast them to the floor, joining the puddle of finery. "You're hopeless," she said, shaking her head.

He sank down on the bed beside her. "Hopelessly in love wi' ye, *madlise*," he said quietly.

Faith looked up at him. *"Madlise?"*

"My love," he said softly.

Faith's breath caught in her throat, her heart skipping a beat. "Love?"

He smiled. "Did ye think I wed ye only because ye are a comely lass?"

"I thought you were just being noble, trying to save my life and all."

He laughed softly. "Ye've a lot to learn about me, Faith. Do ye think I go chasing across Ireland after every bonny lass who catches my eye?"

She smiled tremulously. "I wasn't certain."

"Then let me make ye certain. This is what I pledged to ye during the ceremony." Taking her hand, he pressed it firmly against his heart.

> *"Ye are mine,*
> *Blood o' my blood,*
> *Flesh o' my flesh,*
> *All o' my love,*
> *For all o' my life.*
> *Ye are mine*
> *Forever my wife."*

Faith reached up and traced the curve of his cheek with her fingertips. "I've never been so happy and so terrified because of it. But even if this is just a dream and it all ends tomorrow, I wouldn't change a thing.''

"I mean every word o' it, Faith. I'd give my life for yours. Ye should know that I'll protect ye and care for ye.''

She lifted her mouth to meet his, and he gathered her close, kissing her tenderly and whispering sweet words as their bodies met and joined for the first time as husband and wife.

Running her fingers across the knotted muscles of Miles's bare shoulders, she forgot her concerns and let the wondrous wave of love sweep her doubts away.

Miles was roused from their bed around midnight with the news that the English had arrived. He dressed calmly in the dark with only a few candles to give him light. Faith watched anxiously, clutching the blankets to her chest.

"Oh, Miles,'' she whispered, "what if this was all a mistake? I've been so selfish. I never fully considered what the English might do to you.''

Walking to the bed, he grasped her chin firmly in his hand. "Twas no mistake, lass, and ye know it, so don't fash yourself. Nothing will happen to me now, except perhaps the English will watch me a wee bit more. As I've told ye before, I've never been afraid o' them and I'm certainly no' about to start now.''

"But I'm afraid for you. What about Donagh O'Rourke? He said the English would punish you for killing him.''

Miles's expression darkened for a moment. "Donagh O'Rourke is another matter. Let me take care o' it, Faith. Ye've no cause to worry.''

Quieted by his confidence, Faith came to her knees on the bed and pressed a warm kiss on his mouth. "I love you, Miles; that's why I'm so concerned. Please, whatever happens, just be careful.''

Miles's expression softened. "Ye know, lass, I think I rather like it when ye worry about me.''

Faith put her hands on her hips saucily. "Well, don't push it.''

He flashed her a grin and cheerfully tucked the remaining part of his shirt into his breeches. Giving her a quick peck on the cheek, he turned and left the room.

Sighing, Faith walked naked to the basin and splashed cold water on her face. The binding on her shoulder had loosened, and it felt hot and uncomfortable. She suddenly had a great desire for some fresh air and a chance to walk off her anxieties. Although a walk about the grounds with the English detail present was out of the question, she thought it would be safe enough to take a stroll along the top battlement of the castle towers.

Thankfully, Molly had already moved her gowns and undergarments to Miles's chamber. Faith quickly pulled on her shift, stockings and shoes, then took a gown of dark blue from the wooden wardrobe and stepped into it. The tight sleeve did not fit properly over her binding so she simply threw a cloak on top of it and opened the door to the chamber. Furlong straightened from his slouch against the wall and looked at her in surprise.

"My lady," he said, sweeping out his hand, "what do ye require?"

"Am I still a prisoner here?" she asked quietly.

Furlong leaned back against the wall, his face impassive. "Nay, my lady. Miles asked me to keep an eye on ye while the English are here. Ye will be free to move about the castle once they are gone."

Faith nodded, clutching the cloak tighter around her shoulders. "I just felt like some fresh air. I thought perhaps a turn on the tower walkway would do me some good."

Furlong scratched his long nose doubtfully. "I don't think 'tis wise, milady. Miles indicated that ye were to stay in the chamber and out o' sight o' the English. I can send Molly wi' some tea and food, if ye would like."

Faith sighed. "No, Furlong, it won't be necessary. I'll just pour myself another glass of wine."

She walked back into the room, shutting the door behind her. Removing her cloak, she draped it over a chair and poured herself a goblet of wine. Carrying the goblet, she walked over to the window and gingerly pulled aside the drape. It was dark and quiet, but she could distinguish a few torches bobbing in the courtyard. Worriedly, she sat down in one of the velvet-cushioned chairs, sipping the wine. As she sank back into the cushions, she looked down at the heavy silver ring on her finger. It felt odd against her skin, a constant reminder that she had bound herself to a man from a century more than three hundred and fifty years before she was born. A man with whom she had fallen desperately in love. How would she ever be able to leave him?

Her heart heavy, she sat there staring into the fire until the door finally opened and Miles walked into the room. Quickly, Faith rose to her feet, clasping her hands together.

"What took so long?" she questioned anxiously.

Miles closed the distance between them, taking her hands into his. "The English were in a small rage about our marriage, but I showed them our wedding papers, proving all was legal. 'Twas something they had no' expected, I can tell ye that."

"Did they suspect you of rescuing me in Drogheda?"

"Aye, they did, but couldn't prove it. I told them I'd been to my uncle's in Armagh."

"Will your uncle confirm your story?"

"He's kin, lass. He'll confirm it."

"But what will they do now? Certainly Aston and Bradford won't give up that easily."

Miles shook his head. "Nay, I don't suppose they will. They may try to get a special edict from the king to annul the marriage or take ye away from me, but it won't happen."

Faith was startled by the note of confidence in his voice. "How can you be so certain?"

"Because King Charles has asked me for help. He won't very well sign an edict that will endanger the wife o' a man whose assistance he needs."

Faith's mouth dropped open in astonishment. "You are working for King Charles?" she exclaimed in shock. "You? The Irish Lion?"

"Aye, and for his son, the prince, as well. They've suspected Cromwell all along o' posturing for the throne."

"My God," she said, staggered by his revelation. "That's why you thought I was working for Cromwell. You believed that somehow I had discovered or suspected your connection with the king."

" 'Tis so."

Faith looked at him incredulously. "Yet you've still agreed

to help me save the life of the man you consider to be your enemy.''

Miles exhaled deeply. '' 'Tis a most difficult situation ye've put me in, lass. But I thought a lot about what ye said, especially about playing God wi' the forces o' nature. If things are to be as ye described, then we should accept our fate. I may no' be a man o' great knowledge, but sometimes there are things that are better left alone.''

Faith launched herself into his arms, throwing her arms around his neck. ''Then you do believe me,'' she whispered into his cheek.

He squeezed her tight, lifting her off the ground. ''What choice do I have? Ye are my wife and I love ye. From this moment on we'll face whatever comes our way together.''

''Agreed,'' Faith promised, feeling strangely lighthearted. She had never before shared the burdens of her heart, but now she discovered she rather liked it.

''What else did the English say?'' she asked.

''Och, the soldiers demanded to see ye, but I told them ye were still fast asleep, weary from the recent hours spent 'tween the covers wi' your new husband.''

''Miles,'' Faith gasped, her cheeks flushing pink.

He grinned at her, clearly enjoying the moment. ''Don't worry, lass, I also told them that now, since ye are my wife, I plan to keep ye under a firm hand.''

''Not bloody likely,'' she muttered. ''Did they ask about the whereabouts of Donagh O'Rourke?''

Miles shook his head. ''Nay. 'Tis strange, but they seem to have had no idea that he was here. Whatever Donagh had planned, it appears to have been without the English's knowledge.''

Faith thoughtfully pushed her hair from her shoulders. ''I presume he didn't inform Bradford of his plan to take over both your and Dunbar's land,'' she mused. ''Have you told Donagh's wife about his demise? She had no part in his treachery, Miles. He planned to kill her and marry Arabella.''

''I sent Father Michael to tell her the news. I'll no' punish Eileen O'Rourke or her son. The secret o' Donagh's deceit will remain wi' us at Castle Dun na Moor.''

''What about Arabella?''

Miles sighed heavily. "Arabella is another story. I have little to hold against her, other than an oral accounting from ye and Patrick o' her treachery. 'Tis a most delicate matter, since her da and I share borders. To accuse Arabella outright o' such deception would serve me little and most likely bring me to arms wi' the elder Dunbar. Besides, I believe she has already been served her punishment. Donagh is dead and I'm a married man. But I'll no' forget what she did to ye and Patrick."

"Then the English have left, satisfied with your story?"

"They left, altho' I doubt they were satisfied wi' my story. They warned me that they would be back."

A distressed look crossed Faith's face. "Oh, Miles, I was afraid of this. Will it hinder your activities as the Irish Lion?"

Miles pulled her into his arms. "Nay," he whispered. "Anyway, we'll no' be at Castle Dun na Moor for much longer. We'll leave for London on the morn."

Faith looked up at him, her blue eyes worried. "Just the two of us?"

Miles shook his head. "Nay, 'twould be too dangerous for the two o' us to travel alone. We'll bring Furlong, Shaun and Father Michael wi' us. The father will be a deterrent to many thieves and knaves—most would no' dare to bring harm to a priest. Furlong has skills at tracking and traveling that we'll need, and Shaun is an expert wi' the bow and has a nose for gossip. If your Padriac O'Rourke is in London, Shaun will find him."

"But it's too dangerous," Faith protested. "I don't want to put any more lives in jeopardy. You and the others can help me obtain passage, but you shouldn't travel any farther."

He touched her cheek. "What about your life, lass?"

"I *must* go to London. I have no choice. You don't have the same responsibility."

Miles frowned fiercely, shaking his dark head. "Ye think protecting my wife is no' my responsibility?"

"I think it would be unwise for the Irish Lion to stroll boldly into London."

"Christ's wounds, lass, will ye ever cease insulting me?" he exploded. "Are all women as stubborn as ye in the twentieth century?"

"We aren't stubborn," she countered. "We are strong, independent and can take care of ourselves.''

"Then what in God's name do ye need men for?"

Faith tapped her finger lightly on her chin. "Hmm . . . intriguing question."

"Faith . . ." Miles growled warningly, gripping her around the waist.

"All right, all right," Faith said, laughing. "I was only teasing. Of course we need men. It's just that women are considered equal to men in my time. We can discuss the feminist movement later at greater length, if you want."

"We'll discuss it now. I am your husband, Faith. I intend to take care o' ye."

Her expression softened. "I know you do, Miles. Thank you."

"And I'm going to London wi' ye."

She sighed. "If you won't listen to reason, what can I do?"

"Ye can start behaving like my wife and begin obeying my instructions."

"Obeying your instructions? Miles, in my time marriage is a partnership. Women have equal say."

"Well in *my* time," Miles countered, "a woman listens to her husband." When Faith started to protest he held up a hand. "However, given our unusual circumstances, I do agree to listen to ye. But for now, ye must trust me to know what is best for ye. That is, until ye become more familiar wi' our ways. Agreed?"

Faith opened her mouth to protest and then shut it. "Agreed. I suppose that is only fair. But consider it temporary, and I want my concerns to be taken seriously."

Miles nodded. "Done. Now, there is something I want to give ye." He pulled out an object wrapped in a thick linen cloth from a pouch attached to his leather belt. " 'Tis a wedding present."

Touched, Faith took the present and began to unwind the linen strip. When the object fell into her hand Faith gasped in stunned amazement.

"Do ye like it, lass?" Miles asked worriedly. "I thought since ye were so fascinated by my sword, a present like this would please ye."

"My God," she whispered. In the flat of her hand lay the

long, slender dagger with a double-edged blade that she had purchased in her own time. She closed her fingers around the hilt, her hand shaking as she pulled the dagger from its leather sheath.

"This dagger," she said in wonder. "I bought it in my own time about one week before I came through time."

"This dagger has been in my family for a century," Miles replied, looking at her in wonder. "It has always belonged to the O'Bruaidar women. When my mother died—it came back to me until I took a wife."

She turned it over, studying the hilt. "In my time the emeralds in the handle are missing and there is an unreadable inscription on the blade. The dagger is also bent at a strange angle, as if it hit against something hard. But there is an identical flaw on the blade near the hilt. I'm certain this dagger is the same one I purchased three hundred and forty-eight years in the future."

"What does it mean, lass?"

She shook her head. "I don't know."

"Do ye wish to keep it, because it rightfully belongs to ye now."

Faith nodded, setting aside the dagger. She'd think about the strange coincidence at greater length later.

"I'd be honored. But I have nothing to give to you in return. No ring, no present."

Miles leaned forward, capturing her mouth in a warm kiss. "Well, there is one thing ye could give me," he murmured, nuzzling her ear, his hand stealing up beneath her skirts.

Faith affectionately tangled her fingers in his hair. "You are insatiable, Miles O'Bruaidar. Again?"

He nodded, his fingers already fumbling at the front of his breeches. "Aye, again, lass. For as long as ye will have me."

"For now and a whole lot longer." She laughed as they tumbled to the floor. "For always and forever, husband."

Chapter Twenty-eight

"What did you tell the others?" Faith asked Miles in a low voice as they stood in the courtyard, tying the supplies to the horses. The early morning mist was still visible, but the sun was just beginning to rise. Brilliant shades of yellow and pink streaked across the sky.

"I told them the truth," he answered. "We have an important task to complete in London—to find the kin o' Donagh O'Rourke."

"And they agreed, just like that?"

Miles turned to her, raising an eyebrow. "They are my men. They trust me wi' their lives."

Faith swallowed. "I know, but I just can't help but be worried. I've grown rather fond of them. Do you think they understand the risks?"

Miles touched her shoulder gently. "Ye are family to them now, lass. They'll give their lives to protect ye, just as I will."

Faith nodded, overwhelmed by what it meant to be part of a real family. She thought of Molly and Patrick, to whom she had just given a near tearful good-bye. "I can't tell you what it means to be part of a family again."

Miles leaned over, giving her a quick kiss on the forehead. "Ye're no' alone anymore, Faith. Don't forget that."

She smiled. "I know. It just takes some getting used to." Wrapping her cloak around her shoulders, she turned as Father Michael came out of the castle, carrying a small bundle. He raised his hand in a cheerful greeting to her.

"At which port city will we secure passage to London?" she asked Miles quietly.

"Dublin," he answered. " 'Tis an extra two days' ride, but we can't risk being seen in Drogheda again."

"No, I suppose not," Faith agreed. "Have you decided how

328

we'll go about getting to London? I presume it's not as simple as just purchasing a ticket."

"Nay, 'tis no'. 'Twould be far too many questions asked, and us with no' enough answers. So instead we offer them something else." He jerked his head toward the bulging pouches on his mount that contained three of Faith's gowns, a corset, petticoats and shoes. She had been surprised when he insisted she pack them but told her there was a purpose for it.

"My gowns?" she said in surprise. "We are to offer gowns in exchange for passage?"

Miles chuckled. "Nay, we create the disguise of the Lady Margaret Woodsworth, wealthy widow o' an honorable English officer stricken while on duty in Ireland. Brokenhearted and grieving, his young widow is returning home to London and will pay handsomely to do so in comfort. Your traveling companions consist o' three manservants—that's me, Furlong and Shaun—and a priest, Father Michael, who will serve as your chaperone, as well as your spiritual adviser. Both ye and the father will purchase cabins for the voyage, while the rest o' us will sleep where we are afforded a place."

"Good God, Miles, is that really necessary?"

"Do ye wish to create enough suspicions that Bradford and the others may follow us to London?"

Faith sighed. "No."

"Then ye must do as I say."

Her face brightened. "I suppose there is a good side to all of this. You'll be my manservant, will you not? Does this mean you must do as I bid?"

Miles growled. " 'Twill be only temporary."

"And a pity for that."

Miles playfully swatted her bottom. "I'm wed to a vixen. Ye will be on your best behavior, do ye hear me?"

She laughed, but before she could answer, Shaun and Furlong walked into the courtyard, the dwarf looking suspiciously as if he had a wicked hangover.

"Have a wee nip too much o' the spirits, did ye, Shaun?" Miles called out with a grin.

Shaun groaned, covering his ears. "By all the saints, Miles, do ye have to shout? 'Twas your wedding, man. Why do ye look so clearheaded?"

"Och, I just indulged in other pleasantries," he replied nonchalantly, pulling himself up into the saddle. Faith blushed at the inference, but none of the men, including Father Michael, seemed bothered. "Well, rouse yourself, man," Miles continued. "We've a full day o' traveling ahead o' us."

As they rode out of the courtyard, Faith took one last look over her shoulder at Castle Dun na Moor, wondering if she would ever again see its majestic form. She thought it strange how she already looked upon it as home. Then, taking a deep breath, she faced forward, telling herself there was no going back.

She was on her way to London.

"We'll camp here tonight," Miles announced, evaluating the wooded clearing as satisfactory.

Faith gave an audible sigh of relief. They had been riding for hours, with only a few stops to break the monotony. Sliding off the horse, she vigorously rubbed the kinks out of her back.

Miles instructed her and Shaun to begin gathering wood for the fire while he, Furlong and Father Michael fed and watered the horses. Wearily, Shaun and Faith wandered about picking up twigs and sticks until enough wood and kindling had been collected. Kneeling down beside the pile, Shaun scraped together the flint and stone until a spark lit. Holding it carefully to the kindling, he blew on it until a warm blaze burst forth.

Thankful for the warmth, Faith unrolled her bedroll, and she and Shaun sank down on it with a small groan. Furlong, Miles and Father Michael joined them shortly, pulling out a packed meal of bread, cheese and a flask of wine.

They sat companionably about the blaze, eating and passing around the flask. When they had finished the meal and the leftovers were packed away Shaun began to tell a preposterous tale about how he had single-handedly fought off seven English soldiers during a skirmish. The men roared with laughter, and even Faith could not help but smile at the dwarf's animated storytelling.

Yet her thoughts often strayed to her husband, her gaze lingering on his face as the firelight danced off the edges of his square jaw, now covered with a day's beard. Studying his firm, sensual mouth, Faith felt the stirrings of attraction begin

in her stomach. Never before had she felt such an unquench-
able desire for a man.

When it came time to sleep there was an awkward moment
when they were deciding where to lay out their bedrolls. Shaun
insisted that she have the safest and most comfortable position
near the fire, while the men spread out around the camp for
protection. Swallowing her disappointment that she would not
be able to share the comfort of Miles's arms, Faith graciously
accepted the dwarf's offer. Lying down on the bedroll, she
covered herself with a thick woolen wrap before closing her
eyes and hoping for sleep. But her body ached for the reassuring feel of Miles stretched out beside her. She had already
grown accustomed to having him near.

She heard the low murmur of his voice and knew he was
talking softly with Furlong. She had seen them huddle together
when she lay down on the bedroll. She wondered what they
were planning, what strategy they were mapping out for the
following day.

Yet for the first time Faith didn't mind that she was no
longer in control of every aspect of her life. Trusting didn't
come easy, but when it came it was beautiful.

With that thought on her mind and a smile on her lips, Faith
finally succumbed to the warm folds of sleep.

Faith wasn't sure what awakened her, but she suddenly sat
up, disoriented and confused. Her hair tumbled about her
shoulders in disarray as she sleepily regarded the campsite and
slowly got her bearings.

Furlong was sitting not far from the fire, cleaning a knife
with what looked like an old rag. He looked up at Faith as she
ran her fingers through her tangled hair.

"Is everything all right, lass?" he asked softly.

She nodded. "I'm fine, Furlong. I . . . I just couldn't sleep.
What are you doing awake?"

He shrugged. "Just watching things. Go back to sleep."

Faith slid out from beneath the warm wrap. "I will. I just
need a moment of privacy in the trees. I'll be back shortly."

She carefully slipped into the forest. Lifting her skirts, she
quickly took care of business before her body began shuddering from the cold. Quietly, she made her way back into camp,

Julie Moffett

passing a large tree where a dark form slept sitting up. She was nearly past him when his arms unexpectedly shot out, grabbing her about the knee. Faith only had time to gasp in surprise as she fell against his body.

"Hush, lass, 'tis only me," Miles whispered, opening his blanket and wrapping it around her. "I'm sorry to startle ye, but I didn't wish to wake the others." Taking hold of her hips, he guided her into a sitting position on his lap, where she sat straddling him, face to face.

"Miles," she whispered, color flooding her cheeks. "What if someone sees us?"

He bent to nuzzle her neck. "So what if someone does? Ye are my lawful wife, after all. All day long I've been thinking about ye, aching to hold and touch ye." His lips moved to nuzzle the fragile skin behind her ear, and Faith felt a flooding sensation of heat envelop her.

"Miles," she protested weakly. "Furlong is expecting me back any moment. If I don't come, he'll worry something has happened to me."

"Curse Furlong," he mumbled into her neck.

Unable to help herself, Faith shuddered with pleasure as his warm hands slid beneath her gown and traveled up the back of her thighs and buttocks. His large body radiated heat, and in only moments Faith felt the chill leave her body. As she gave a small sigh of contentment, Miles's hands traveled to the edge of her chemise, where he softly stroked the soft skin of her back. He kept up his gentle ministrations, rubbing the aches and kinks out of her lower back and buttocks. The rough stubble of his beard tickled her cheek as his hot breath fanned the side of her neck. Faith trembled in anticipation as she felt his hardness press into her thigh.

He placed light kisses along the length of her neck and shoulders until Faith gripped his shoulders, pulling him closer. "Miles," she whispered, her hands slipping beneath his shirt to caress the hardened muscles.

He nibbled on the lobe of her ear. "Could you be *very* quiet, lass?" he murmured.

Faith pulled back, looking at him in astonishment. "Me?" she whispered heatedly. "Are you implying that . . ."

Laughing softly, Miles's mouth closed over hers, hot and

332

hungry. His tongue sought hers, relentlessly stroking and teasing until Faith felt dizzy from excitement. Clinging tightly to him, she wound her fingers in his hair, keeping his mouth melded to hers.

His thumbs hooked under the edge of her chemise, lifting it so his hands could slide around to the front, cupping her warm, soft breasts in his hands. Dragging his mouth away from hers, he began to tease her tender nipples with the pad of his thumbs. When she could stand his sweet torment no longer, his hands began pushing her skirts up about her hips.

Feverishly, Faith fumbled beneath the heavy wrap, her fingers tangling in the drawstring at his waist. With a small tug she set him free, and was rewarded with the small moan that was wrung from his throat.

"And you said I had to be quiet," she whispered indignantly into his ear, and then stiffened as his fingers slipped in beneath her petticoats and found the warm portal he had been looking for. Her nails dug into his shoulders as his fingertips began to stroke the nub inside her.

"Oh God, Miles," she breathed, throwing her head back, letting her hair spill back over her shoulders. "I think . . ."

"For once, don't think, Faith," he murmured. "Just enjoy."

A fierce, erotic heat built inside her until she thought she might burst. "Please," she begged. "Now."

His own desire raging, Miles quickly moved her legs around his waist and wound his hands in her silky hair as if to keep her in place. Reaching down, Faith guided him through the layers of clothes and the undergarment she still wore until, with a ragged breath, he drove into her with one powerful surge. She stifled the moan that rose to her lips by pressing her mouth tightly against his neck.

Slowly, silently, Miles began to thrust inside her. Faith met his every movement, squeezing her surprisingly strong thighs around him. Swimming through a fog of passion and desire, Faith reached her release only moments before she felt Miles shudder deep within her. For a time they said nothing, simply sharing the deep contentment that flowed between them.

Then, ever so gently, Miles cupped the back of her head, holding her face toward him. His mouth brushed lightly against her lips, feather soft.

333

"Madlise," he whispered quietly.

She smiled, touching the hair at his temple. "Can I stay here for the rest of the night?"

He sighed with regret. "Nay, lass, 'tis time for me to relieve Furlong. Now, let's adjust that gown o' yours, and I'll see ye back to your bedroll before Furlong wakes the camp to look for ye. Altho' somehow . . . I fully expect he's known all along where ye've been."

Chapter Twenty-nine

Faith dutifully followed Miles across the swaying deck of the English frigate, shielding her eyes from the blinding sun. She tried to look as aristocratic as possible, but found herself lurching sideways like a drunken sailor every time the ship bumped against the dock. She fought back her panic with a valiant effort, although she was certain the vessel would tip over at any moment, flinging her headfirst into the water.

A small, hysterical hiccup escaped her lips. Oh God, why hadn't airplanes been invented yet? If the ship crashed into the rocks or sank in a storm, she would live out her worst nightmare by drowning in the murky waters of the Irish Sea. The water would swirl around her nostrils and the air would be sucked out of her lungs as she sank lifeless to the bottom of the sea, her body never to be found. . . .

"Are ye all right, me lady?" a concerned voice inquired, gripping her arm and steadying her. "Yer face looks a bit gray."

Snapping out of her horrid daydream, Faith looked into the face of a grizzled deckhand who had been introduced to her by the captain as Wood. As Faith studied the English sailor now, she thought the nickname rather suited him. Deep lines stretched across his tan, weathered skin, creating an uncanny resemblance to an old, sun-bleached piece of driftwood. His body, however, seemed at odds with the image, appearing lithe and agile.

"Yes, I'm fine, thank you," Faith replied, managing a weak smile. "I just seem to be having a little trouble with my footing."

"It takes a bit of time to get accustomed to the movement o' the ship," Wood answered apologetically in his heavy Cockney accent. "But never ye fear, I'll help ye along."

Glancing over at Miles, Faith felt unreasonably cranky that

he did not seem to have the same problem with walking as she did, although he single-handedly carried the group's supplies with no way to brace himself. From time to time he groaned for effect as he carried them, having informed the captain that they were all the Lady Woodsworth's personal belongings. Faith pursed her lips at his antics but said nothing, knowing that excessive luggage and a poor, overburdened servant was what was expected from a lady of her stature.

They finally came to a stop in front of an opening in the deck at which hung a rickety rope ladder. Calling out a warning below, Miles heaved the bundles down the hold and then began to descend the ladder. Faith watched him disappear into the darkness, trying valiantly not to heave at the unfamiliar and unpleasant scents that wafted up from below.

"Come down, my lady," she heard Miles call up to her.

Faith looked doubtfully at the ladder. It appeared to be old and mildewed and not terribly sturdy. Surely they couldn't expect her to climb down to the hold below while she was dressed in full garb, including the hated corset and several layers of petticoats.

"I don't think so," Faith replied, chewing her bottom lip nervously. "Isn't there a set of stairs or something?"

"Now don't be afeared, me lady," Wood said, flashing her a grin full of rotten and missing teeth. " 'Tis a good, strong rope, that is. Your man is already at the bottom, ready to catch ye if ye slip."

Swallowing her doubt, Faith turned and bravely stepped down on the first rung. The corset seemed to tighten about her middle, cutting off the blood supply to her brain and making her dizzy. For a moment she simply clung to the ladder, fighting back the waves of fear that swept over her. Then, cautiously, she descended, stopping only once when her foot slipped off the ladder. She stifled a scream and was greatly relieved when she felt Miles's reassuring hand on her ankle. He steadied her until she reached the bottom. Wood lithely followed her down.

"This way, me lady," he said, sweeping out an arm toward a narrow corridor. "We've arranged something special for ye . . . and the father."

Faith turned and looked up as Father Michael carefully descended into the hold, his own breath coming in fearful snatches. Faith felt a kindred spirit with the priest, suspecting that he had either developed a fear of heights or had a sudden attack of claustrophobia. Looking about at the small, dank room where they now stood, Faith didn't hold it against him one bit. She was feeling rather faint herself.

"That is most kind of you," Faith said weakly to the old sailor, wondering if he could tell she was breathing only through her mouth.

"I do have a question for ye, if I may," Wood said, leaning close and lowering his voice confidentially. "I can't see why a fine lady like yerself would want Irish servants and a popish cleric as companions on your journey to London. Them priests are privy to the devil's secrets, ye know, and the Irish can't be trusted. I urge ye to beware."

Remembering her status, Faith drew herself up to her full height, looking down at Wood with icy disdain. "Sir, my husband's death was quite sudden and unfortunate. I am bereaved and unwell. I want only to get home as quickly as I can and with as much privacy as can be afforded to me. I've known the father and these servants for some time and consider them tolerable companions—at least until we arrive in London. Now, I suggest that you show me to my cabin at once, for I am feeling rather faint."

The old sailor muttered something inaudible and pushed past Miles, heading down a dark corridor. Taking a deep breath, Faith raised her head haughtily and marched after him. Miles flashed her a grin as she passed. Fleetingly, she wondered how Shaun and Furlong were doing abovedeck. The two were undoubtedly receiving whatever tasks would be assigned to them for the duration of the trip. Miles had earlier explained to her that as servants they would be required to participate in some of the duties on the ship in order to earn their meals. Faith had reluctantly agreed, unhappy that the men would be pressed into hard labor while she and Father Michael whiled away the hours in the relative comfort of a cabin. Unfortunately, she saw no other way.

Wood stopped abruptly in front of a small door, opening it for her. Peering over his shoulder, Faith looked into the smallest cabin she had ever seen. A bunk had been nailed to one side of the wall and covered with a threadbare mattress and a quilt. Thankfully it was clean, but the remaining space in the cabin provided barely enough room for one person to stand.

"This be yer cabin," Wood said to her with obvious pride. "I've something down the corridor a little smaller for the father, but still quite comfortable. I'll let yer manservant get ye settled." Motioning to Father Michael, the two of them disappeared down the dark hall.

Faith stepped into the cabin, turning to face Miles. "My God, I've never seen anything so tiny."

"Hoping for more, were ye?" Miles asked, quirking a dark eyebrow.

"Good God no, I'm not complaining. I'm just wondering that, if this is considered luxury, in what kind of filth will you sleep?"

Miles handed her the pouches, which she pushed beneath the bunk. " 'Tis only for a few days. We've survived much worse."

Faith turned around in the small space, looking at him with a sad smile. "I'll miss sleeping with you, Miles."

He ducked his head and squeezed into the tiny space, one leg and a hip remaining outside the door. Leaning over, he brushed a kiss across her lips. "Pluck up, lass, 'tis only for a few days. Just stay to your cabin and we'll be in London soon enough. One o' us will bring your meals every day. Keep the door bolted and don't open it for anyone unless ye hear four slow raps on the door. I'll try to make certain one o' us sleeps outside your door at night."

She nodded and he kissed her again quickly and fervently. Giving her a grin, he backed up too fast, rapping his head sharply against the doorframe. Cursing, he rubbed his skull, ducking out of the room.

"Are you all right?" Faith asked in concern.

He nodded ruefully. "Aye, 'tis no' much that can hurt this head o' mine. Shut the door now, lass," he instructed her. "And mind my words."

Giving him a tremulous smile, Faith shut the door and bolted it, listening to his footsteps echo as he walked down the ship's corridor. She sat down on the sagging mattress, trying to calm her nerves. How did she ever imagine she could have done this on her own?

Sighing, she put her head in her hands. The longer she thought about the situation, the more her doubts began to assail her. Was she doing the right thing by risking the lives of those she loved on the prospect that Paddy O'Rourke was really in London, plotting an assassination attempt on Cromwell? What if he decided to carry out his attempt one year from now, or six months from now? Perhaps she had been all wrong about him.

She shook her head determinedly. No, historical events were being put into motion too quickly. Paddy O'Rourke knew what she did about history. In just a few short months the English Parliament would behead their own king, and Cromwell would move into an enviable position of power. Paddy would certainly act before that happened. As a professional, he wouldn't act hastily either, but rather take the time to stalk and study his intended target. That gave her the time she needed to find him.

But would she find him in time to stop him? And if she didn't, what would that mean for her and the future as she knew it?

Taking a deep breath, Faith pressed her fingertips to her temples, as if to will the doubts away. How had so much come to rest on her shoulders? Why was she so duty-bound to try to stop it?

"I took an oath in my time to people who trusted me," she whispered softly to the small cabin. She had a responsibility, a duty to make certain that Paddy O'Rourke was not left running loose in this century, armed with twentieth-century knowledge and technology. Even though it was tempting to forget her old life and joyfully accept her new one, she knew deep down that she could not do it. The price was too high. She would never be able to live with herself or her conscience if she didn't try to stop O'Rourke.

"Another character flaw, Worthington," she muttered darkly to herself. "A bloody rotten conscience that refuses to be quieted."

Yet her vow had not included putting others at risk, especially people she cared about. But that was exactly what she had done.

Worriedly, Faith shut her eyes, lying back on the uncomfortable mattress and ignoring the painful stab of the corset in her ribs. As there was little else she could do, she began to pray that no one got hurt.

The journey to London was blessedly uneventful. Faith believed it to be some kind of miracle, but remarkably she was not stricken with seasickness. Unfortunately, the same was not the case with Father Michael, who was deathly ill, his face turning a strange green color and his stomach unable to hold down much of anything he ate or drank. Faith spent most of her time in his cramped cabin, nursing him and helping him lean over the bucket. Miles and the other men checked in on them with surprising regularity, emptying the bucket and bringing them fresh water. Although they seemed cheerful enough, Faith could see from the circles under their eyes that they were weary, undoubtedly from the heavy work required of them abovedeck. Thankfully, none of them seemed to suffer from the seasickness that plagued the priest.

The meals that came her way were barely edible, although Faith did not complain. Twice she declined offers to dine with the captain, pleading weariness and illness; he did not bother her after that. At night she passed on hoarded pieces of bread or cheese to whomever was sleeping outside her door, knowing that the men's meals would surely be even worse than hers and Father Michael's. On a few occasions she managed to garner a quick and comforting kiss from Miles, but he never lingered, fearing discovery.

Several days later, when Shaun finally came to tell her and Father Michael that they had reached London, Faith let out a small whoop of joy. As the good father blessed the dwarf for his good news, Shaun cheerfully picked up the bucket with the remains of the priest's lunch and headed abovedeck.

"Thank God, we've finally arrived," Faith breathed with heartfelt relief, arranging the pillow comfortably behind Father Michael's head. "I thought we'd never reach land again."

He smiled weakly, giving her hand a squeeze. "Nor did I, lass," he agreed fervently. "Nor did I."

Chapter Thirty

Being able to witness London as it existed in the seventeenth century was both a shock and a fascination to Faith. Her first good look at the city was from the upper deck of the ship as they approached the dock. The entire wharf was alive with hundreds of people, milling about and talking and shouting. Some were pushing three-wheeled carts and peddling goods, while some women preened and waved gaily to the incoming sailors, who whistled and whooped appreciatively in response.

As they prepared to leave the vessel, Faith apologized profusely to the captain for refusing his invitations to dine, but thanked him for an enjoyable trip. Insisting that her servants would be able to secure her a carriage, she permitted Miles and the others to ease her into the noisy crowd, thankfully leaving the captain and his crew behind. Once away from sight of the vessel's crew, Miles quickly distributed the pouches before dragging Faith into a nearby alley, behind a stack of mildew-covered crates.

"What in the world are you doing?" she asked him in astonishment as he fumbled with one of the pouches.

"Ye must change your gown, lass. We'll need to secure a room at the local inn. 'Twould raise too many questions for a lady o' your breeding to be seen at such a place, so ye'll have to become a commoner."

"What?" Faith said in horror. "You want me to change clothes right here in this alley?"

" 'Tis little time for arguing, lass. Father Michael is also changing his garments. 'Twill no' do to have a Catholic priest wandering the docks o' London either. Furlong and Shaun are standing guard. Here are your traveling clothes. They look worn enough to suffice." He thrust the gown at her before turning his back and folding his arms against his chest.

Faith looked in astonishment at his back and then at the

341

garments in her hands. "Oh, all right," she said, weighing the favorable prospect of removing the corset against the unfortunate reality of having to do it in a cold, stench-filled alley. "But if you want me to do it quickly, I'll need some help with these hooks."

Mumbling something unkind about women's clothing, Miles helped her free herself from the gown. Faith carefully lifted it over her head and handed it to Miles, who folded it and put it away in the pouch. Then she held out her corset, offering him some salty advice on where he could stick that hated object. He chuckled but returned it to the pouch as well. Pulling on her traveling gown, she had Miles fasten the hooks before he threw a warm cloak over her shoulders.

" 'Tis already growing cold," he said, gently, fastening the cloak at her throat. "I'm sorry to have to make ye do this here."

"It's all right, Miles. As is becoming maddeningly apparent, you're often right."

He brushed a kiss across her forehead. "Well, at least tonight we will be sleeping together."

"We will?" Faith asked, her eyes brightening.

"Aye, but 'twill come at a price. Ye'll have to speak as little as possible, lass. 'Twill be no secret that ye're my wife. In fact, 'twill help me protect ye from unwanted attention from the sailors and other ruffians, but 'tis most unusual for a Englishwoman to marry an Irishman, even if she is a commoner. And your speech is far too cultured and educated for a common lass, so the less ye say, the better."

Faith could see the wisdom in his reasoning and nodded. "Agreed. What next?"

Slinging the pouch over his shoulder, he guided her back to the entrance of the alley, where Furlong, Shaun and a newly plain-clothed Father Michael stood waiting. The priest gave her a grin. He still looked rather pale, and his eyes were weary and surrounded by dark circles, but he was beginning to look much more like himself.

"So, what do ye think, lass?" he asked, turning around slowly for her inspection. He was dressed in a pair of dark brown breeches, a white linen shirt and a matching brown jacket. A hat with a small feather sat jauntily on his head.

"I picked it out for the father myself," Shaun said proudly, puffing out his chest.

Faith smiled at both of them. "I think, Father, that you look less green than you did on the ship. Brown seems to be your color."

The priest laughed. "Aye, but my legs still feel wobbly, as if the ground is moving beneath me."

"They call those sailor legs, Father," Furlong said with a grin, patting the priest on the back. " 'Twill take a wee bit o' time getting used to standing on solid ground."

"Bless the Lord that I'm yet alive," the priest said, crossing himself.

All of them laughed before Miles turned to Furlong. "Have ye seen an inn that looks suitable?"

Furlong pointed down the street at a dingy building. "I walked past it a few minutes ago. 'Tis called the Docksbury Inn. I've been watching the patrons come in and out. Seems like it will suit us very well."

Miles nodded. "All right. Let's ye and I have ourselves a look. The rest o' ye wait here." Miles and Furlong strode down the busy street before disappearing into the building. After some time the two emerged, motioning for the rest of them to follow.

"I've secured us two rooms," Miles said when the group was together again. "One for me and my wife, the other for my brother and two cousins. At first the innkeeper didn't want to give the rooms to 'Irish rabble,' as he put it, but a wee bit more o' silver changed his mind. We're paid up for a week."

"Thank God," Faith said with relief as they entered the inn.

The extra silver also entitled them to a hot meal and a healthy supply of ale. Although the food was not as tasty as the meals Molly prepared back at Castle Dun na Moor, it was an enormous improvement over the paltry fare on the ship. As the group ate hungrily, Faith took the opportunity to study their surroundings. The inn was cozy with a blazing fire, and several capable women kept the mugs brimming with ale and the patrons supplied with food. The customers seemed to be mostly sailors, who guzzled the ale, accompanied by ladies of questionable reputation who sat on their laps giggling. There were a few other people present who looked as if they had worked an honest day of labor and were simply having a meal with their friends or family. Faith assumed that these people were the other boarders.

When the meal was finished Faith was relieved that Miles had no desire to linger and chat. Bidding the others good night, he led her up the rickety steps to their room. Compared to the tiny cabin where Faith had just spent several uncomfortable days, this room seemed palatial. A fire was already blazing in the small hearth and a basin of water sat on a tiny table that was grouped with two wooden chairs. A white chamber pot rested in a far corner, above which was a grimy window overlooking the street. It permitted a small amount of light into the room, and Miles walked over to it, opening it and inspecting the view below.

"This room will suit us well," he commented softly.

Pushing aside the leather pouches, Faith sank down on the bed, not caring that the covers were anything but clean. "It's perfect, Miles. Anything is better than that ship."

Shutting the window, he joined her on the bed. It creaked loudly as he settled his large body onto the frame. "Ye know, ye held up well," he said putting his arms behind his head. "For a lass frightfully afraid o' the water, ye have the stomach o' a sailor."

Faith grimaced. "My nerves were in shreds the entire time. How is it that you managed to have no problems?"

"Och, 'tis no' my first time on a ship, lass. I've been to Scotland several times wi' my da when I was a lad. Twice Shaun and Furlong came wi' us. 'Twas Father Michael's first voyage, though."

"Scotland?" Faith asked with a raised brow. "What took you to Scotland?"

"Och, my father wished to gain support from the Scottish Catholics to form an Irish confederacy. Unfortunately, 'twas yet another failed attempt to rid ourselves o' the English."

"So that is your connection to King Charles," Faith said in surprise, rolling over on her stomach to face him. "As King Charles signed a secret pact with the Scots, I presume it was your Catholic connections there that have you working for the king."

Miles nodded, reaching out to touch the curve of her cheek. "Aye, 'tis so."

"And that is why you are corresponding with the Marquis de Ormonde. You are coordinating strategy with him to surround Cromwell's troops once they arrive in Ireland."

"How do ye know about the marquis?" Miles asked in surprise.

Faith's cheeks reddened slightly. "I overheard you talking about it with Furlong the night of my ill-fated escape from the castle."

Miles laughed. "By all the saints, ye are sharp. 'Tis odd, but I never saw myself talking politics wi' a woman, let alone my wife." For a moment, a strangely melancholy look came over his face.

"What is it, Miles?" Faith asked quickly, wondering if he was regretting his hasty decision to marry her. "I'm sorry if I disappoint you. Do you wish you had never married me?"

With an angry growl he abruptly rolled over, pinning her to the covers beneath him. "Never. Don't ever think such a thing, Faith. 'Tis just that your wit is so keen, I sometimes forget with whom I'm talking. I'm no' used to it in a lass. But I find myself liking it. I never thought I could share myself wi' a woman in such a manner."

Faith closed her eyes, the invisible hand clutching her heart easing. "I'm sorry to have put you in a position of dividing your loyalties."

He nodded, his eyes dark and serious. "Aye, 'tis no' an easy task. Yet even ye admit that King Charles will no' survive to fight Cromwell. 'Tis destiny, is it no'?"

She sighed. "Yes. The English Parliament will behead King Charles and Oliver Cromwell will become Lord Protector of Scotland and Ireland. A terrible battle over Ireland does occur. But what I haven't told you is that Cromwell eventually dies, presumably of a deadly case of malaria that he contracts while on conquest in Ireland. Fitting justice, I suppose. His son, Richard, will prove too weak to hold power. Eventually King Charles's son is restored to the throne."

Miles cupped the sides of her face in astonishment. "The prince will be restored to the throne?"

"Yes, your struggle on behalf of King Charles will not be

Julie Moffett

in vain, though that doesn't change the outcome of all the other terrible things I told you about the fate of Ireland. But you should also know that in my time Ireland is an independent country. That, too, is Ireland's destiny. Hard won, yes, but perhaps all the more savored.''

"Will ye tell me more o' your time, Faith?" he asked her quietly.

She nodded. "If you wish." Her hand stole up behind his neck, pulling his mouth toward hers. "But first a kiss. I've missed you, Miles."

He grinned, lowering his head and meeting her lips hungrily. Finally he pulled away with a groan, drawing his shirt over his head with one hand and tossing it carelessly to the floor. "I'm afraid history will have to wait. And ye said I was insatiable. Are all wenches as lusty as ye in the twentieth century?"

"The perfect topic for your first lesson about my time," Faith replied, laughing and fumbling for the ties on his breeches. "Female sexuality in the nineteen nineties."

Faith awoke in the dark, shivering. Miles had stolen most of the quilt, leaving her entire backside bare to the cool air. Even so, the quilt was mostly bunched beneath his large form. His legs and buttocks were partially exposed and one arm was flung over the side of the bed. She tried vainly to tug some of the quilt from beneath his heavy body, but the material wouldn't budge. Pushing against his shoulder, she tried to roll him over, but his only response was a loud snore.

Sighing, she sat up in bed, reaching for the closest available garment. Miles's shirt was thick and scratchy but warm, and she pulled it tightly around her body. Across the room, she could see no fire in the hearth and the embers appeared cold. Deciding she definitely needed some warmth, she stood, Miles's shirt falling to the top of her knees. The wooden floorboards were like ice beneath her feet as she padded quietly to the fireplace.

"Oh, what I wouldn't do for a pair of warm, woolly slippers and a match," she muttered, kneeling by the hearth. Deftly she arranged some kindling before picking up the stone and flint. After striking the flint several times unsuccessfully she

346

managed to produce a spark that finally ignited the kindling. When a steady flame began to appear she blew gently, adding a small log and waiting until it caught fire.

"I'm no' used to sleeping wi' anyone."

Faith turned quickly to see Miles sitting up in the bed, apologetically holding up a corner of the quilt. He looked incredibly sexy with his bare chest and tousled hair. Stretching his legs out in front of him, he yawned widely.

"It's all right," Faith replied. "It was just a bit cool and I decided to rekindle the fire."

Miles patted the bed invitingly. "If I promise to share the quilt, will ye come back to bed?"

"How do I know you will be true to your word?"

"I'll prove it to ye," he said, crooking his finger at her. "Come here."

Taking two running steps, she bounded onto the bed. "Hmm, your side is nice and warm," she agreed, snuggling up against him under the quilt.

He took her icy hands in his, rubbing them vigorously. "I've never seen a lass wi' such cold hands and feet. Are all lassies born like this in England?"

"Well, I could ask if all Irish are born with internal heaters. Half of you lay uncovered on the bed and yet you still radiated heat, as if it was summer outside."

Miles chuckled, kissing the top of her head. "Och, hot blood runs through Irish veins. 'Tis why we are so passionate and fierce, is it no'?"

Faith laughed, reaching up to cup his cheek. "You're impossible, Miles O'Bruaidar."

He rubbed his beard-roughened cheek against her hand before loosening himself from their embrace and slipping out of the bed. Picking up a candle, he strode stark naked across the room and knelt before the fire, lighting the wick.

"What are you doing?" Faith asked in astonishment.

"I have something to show ye," he said as the glow of the candle lit his features. After placing the candle in a silver holder on the table, he lifted one of the pouches onto a chair and rummaged around in it. "Och, here it is." He turned toward her, holding up the slim object.

347

"The book of poems," Faith said in wonder. "You brought it all this way with you?"

He nodded. "I thought we might have time for another one o' our reading lessons. That is, if ye are no' too weary and still wish to teach me."

Faith smiled. "Come to bed, Miles. And bring that candle with you."

Grinning, he returned to the bed, handing her the book and candle. After lowering himself onto the creaking bed, he put his arm around her, pulling her close.

Faith leaned her head on his shoulder. "What would you like to read?" she asked, handing him the candle.

Miles thought for a moment and then smiled dreamily. " 'The Coolun.' "

"The what?"

" 'The Coolun.' 'Tis the name o' a poem about a bonny lass with fair locks and a sweet mouth." Grinning, he leaned over, nuzzling her neck.

Faith giggled as his whiskers tickled her skin. "You wicked creature. Are we going to read or are you thinking of something else?"

Miles lifted his lips from his ministrations. "Can we do both?" he asked hopefully.

Faith playfully swatted at the roving hand that was slowly moving up the length of her thigh. "Not at the same time. We need to give reading our full concentration."

When she heard him give an exaggerated sigh of disappointment she laughed. "It is possible that a reward could be arranged, but only for the student who performs in an exemplary manner."

Eagerly, Miles leaned forward. "I think I could be a very good pupil," he said in his thick brogue.

Laughing, Faith opened the book and flipped through the pages until she found the poem she was looking for. "Oh, here it is. 'The Coolun.' Bring the light closer." Miles held the candle over the page. "Now watch my finger," she instructed. "I'll put it under the words as I read them, just like last time."

Snuggling closer into the crook of his arm, she began to read softly.

A Double-Edged Blade

In Bal'nagar is the Coolun:
Like the berry on the bough her cheek;
Bright beauty dwells forever
On her fair neck and ringlets sleek;
O', sweeter is her mouth's soft music
Than the lark or thrush at dawn,
Or the blackbird in the greenwood singing
Farewell to the setting sun.

Miles lifted a strand of her hair, letting it fall through his fingers. " 'Twill always remind me o' ye, Faith," he said softly. "My wife with the pale hair and sweet mouth."

Faith smiled, feeling strangely close to tears. Turning, she pressed a kiss into his bare shoulder. "You've made me the happiest woman in the world," she whispered. "How can I ever repay you for all you have given me?"

"Och, I could think o' a way or two," he said, teasing gently. "But mayhap first another lesson o' the letters, wife. I wouldn't want it said that I didn't fairly earn my reward."

Laughing softly, Faith took the candle from him and handed him the book. "Agreed. Do you remember how we did it last time? Recite the poem slowly, and I'll place your finger beneath the words as you say them. Look for words that you say more than once; those are the easiest to remember. Are you ready?"

Miles grinned, leaning over the book. "Och, I'm always ready, lass. 'Tis the creed o' the Irishman; didn't ye know?"

Long after the lesson had finished and the candle had been extinguished, Faith lay comfortably in Miles's arms, listening to the wind howl outside their window. She had never felt such peace and contentment as she did at this moment. Every fiber in her being told her that being with this man was right, that her love for him was genuine.

She cuddled closer, feeling one of Miles's hands steal beneath the curve of her waist, the other one coming to rest lightly on her right buttock. Faith leaned her head against his chest and listened in wonder to the steady thump of his heart.

"Faith?"

"Mmm."

"We've yet to talk about what we shall do wi' this Padriac O'Rourke once we find him. Do ye wish me to kill him?"

Faith lifted her head sharply. "Good God, no, Miles. I think we should take him back to Ireland and the stone circles so I can return him to our own time to face the justice he deserves."

"Just how do ye plan to get him back to Ireland, lass?"

"I would presume the same way we got here—by ship and disguise."

"And what disguise would O'Rourke wear?"

Faith shrugged. "He could be a prisoner of some kind. We'll tell the crew that he is being returned to Ireland to face justice for his crimes. We'll keep him gagged most of the time so he can't speak out."

Miles sighed. "And who are we to be, lass? An English lady and four Irishmen, trying to return a bound and gagged prisoner to Ireland without proper papers? We'd no' get off the docks before we ourselves were arrested. Nay, Faith, I'd recommend another way. We'll travel to Scotland. A friend o' mine can get us passage across the Irish Sea on a vessel where there will be no questions."

"This friend of yours; can he be trusted?"

"Aye, he can."

She thought for a moment. "Then we'll do it your way. I just don't want anyone to get hurt."

Miles tightened his arms around her. "I think ye should know, lass, that if this O'Rourke even hints at raising a hand against ye again, I'll kill him. As it is, I should kill him now for what he did to ye at the lake."

Faith laid a gentle hand on his chest. "He's more afraid of being captured alive, I think. He knows what awaits him if I return him to our own time. He is a hunted man, Miles. A man who kills for his cause, often indiscriminately. Traveling back in time has made no difference; he will continue to kill even here if I don't stop him."

Miles was silent for a long moment. "Ye'll have to take him back through the stone circles, will ye no'? He'll no' be able to go alone."

Faith hesitated and then sighed. "I won't lie to you. No, I can't send him back alone. I'll have to go with him. I suppose

I'll have to tie him up so that if he regains consciousness before me, he won't be able to move."

"How can ye be certain that this . . . travel . . . will work?"

"I don't know for certain. I only know that I have to try."

"And if something happens to O'Rourke and he doesn't make it back to Ireland, will ye still return to your own time without him?"

She didn't answer for so long, Miles leaned down, lifting her chin with his finger. "Faith?"

"I don't want to," she finally whispered. "For the first time in my miserable life I've found happiness. How can I give it up? How could I bear to leave you?" Her voice broke. "I love you so much, Miles. But if I stay, I'll be acting as selfishly as Paddy O'Rourke. I may not set out to change history, but my mere presence in this time may do just that. Do I dare risk that?"

"I would keep ye sequestered at Castle Dun na Moor," Miles said quickly. "We won't travel from Ireland; we won't visit friends. We'll live our lives in seclusion if we must."

"And what if we have children, Miles? Shall we keep them equally isolated?"

Miles closed his eyes, a deep sigh escaping his lips. "I don't want ye to leave, Faith." He paused, listening to the high-pitched wail of the wind. "Do ye know what it feels like to finally meet someone wi' whom ye can be yourself? To Shaun, Furlong and my other men, I'm their leader. To Molly I'm a son, and to Father Michael a soul to be nurtured and saved. Ireland owns the part o' me called the Irish Lion, and people I don't even know look to me for guidance." His voice dropped to a whisper. "But when I'm alone wi' ye I am no more than the man I really am. If ye left me, Faith, a part o' me would be gone forever."

Emotion clogged up so tightly in Faith's throat that she thought she wouldn't be able to speak. "I'm sorry," she managed to choke out. "I never wanted to hurt you."

Miles exhaled, drawing her close to his chest and stroking her hair softly. "I know, lass. Forgive me for speaking o' it."

"No," Faith said, pressing her cheek against his chest. "I ask you to forgive me, Miles. I've known from the beginning what would be the consequences of loving you. I just couldn't help myself.''

He brushed a kiss across her forehead. "Don't be sad, lass. Ye've given me a lifetime o' love in just a few short days. If that is all there is to be, then I'll no' say that I regret it."

"Nor will I," she agreed, closing her eyes. "Nor will I."

Chapter Thirty-one

After six long days in London the group settled into a routine. Miles, Shaun and Father Michael spent the days and nights roaming the city, discreetly inquiring about the whereabouts of Paddy O'Rourke. Day after day they came home empty-handed and discouraged. Faith was relegated to staying close to the inn under the watchful eye of Furlong. Once a day she was allowed to go to the market but was forbidden to exchange more than a word or two with the vendors. It was not at all what she had envisioned as her role in the capture of Padriac O'Rourke, but she tried to console herself with the knowledge that Miles and the others had her best interests at heart. Still, as someone who was used to having things under her own control, it wasn't an easy pose for her to assume. She took solace in Miles's arms as they read together or made love each night. Unfortunately, despite their continued efforts, they seemed no closer to finding Paddy O'Rourke than when they arrived.

On the sixth evening of their stay at the Docksbury Inn Faith and Furlong were supping alone at a table near the fireplace. Faith had just finished a delicious meat pie and was sipping her wine when a young boy appeared at her side, startling her from her thoughts.

"Madame," he said urgently, tugging at her elbow, "there's a man outside wishing to speak wi' ye. He's says he's got information ye be seeking."

Astonished by the lad's sudden appearance, Faith turned slightly in her chair to look closely at him. He appeared to be no more than seven or eight and rather small for his age, clad in a pair of worn and filthy breeches, a torn shirt and a vest. His eyes were huge, appearing almost monstrously large given his thin, sallow skin and sunken cheeks. Faith thought him to be one of London's unfortunate street urchins.

"Well now, lad," Furlong said, reaching across the table and taking the boy by the arm. "Why don't ye tell me again what ye want wi' the lady?"

Dutifully, the boy came around the table to stand next to the hawk-nosed Irishman. "A man paid me a ha'penny to tell the lady he 'as information she wants. That's all I know, I swear on me soul."

Faith exchanged a glance with Furlong before the stout man came to his feet. "Why don't ye show me where this man is, lad? I'll get whatever information the lady needs."

The boy shrugged and weaved his way across the dim room as Furlong reached for his cloak. "Stay here," he said to Faith in a low voice. "I'll see what this is all about."

Faith nodded, watching the Irishman cross the room and go out the door. Picking up her goblet, Faith continued to sip the wine, watching the door for Furlong's return. When she was certain a half an hour had passed and the Irishman still had not appeared she began to get worried. Anxiously, she stood and threw her cloak around her shoulders. She would not sit here all night, waiting and worrying.

Reaching under her cloak, she felt the reassuring weight of the dagger Miles had given her as a wedding present. She would be ready for trouble should it come looking for her. Taking a deep breath, she made her way among the mostly drunk patrons before stepping out into the cool night.

It was windy, in fact; unusually chilly for London in early September. As Faith exhaled, she could see her breath in a puffy white cloud. Taking another step away from the inn, she peered into the gloom. The glow of the candles in the windows provided only a little light, as did a few of the torch-lit lanterns that sparsely lined the cobblestoned street.

"Furlong?" Faith hissed into the darkness, taking another step into the street. The immediate area was uninhabited except for a lone street vendor farther down the street, who was pushing his cart home. Wondering where Furlong could have gone, Faith cautiously made her way toward a nearby alley, her hand gripping the hilt of her dagger.

"Furlong?" she called out again as she reached the entrance of the alley louder this time. "Are you in there?"

There was a rattle from behind a set of crates. Pulling the

dagger from beneath her cloak, Faith held it out in a defensive position as she warily circled the crates. Peering around the wooden edges, she screamed as a black cat hurled itself from behind the boxes and hit her squarely in the chest before skidding between her legs and into the freedom of the street. The dagger flew from her hand, clattering on the stones.

"Christ, an alley cat," she said in disgust, trying to catch her breath. "I was scared out of my bloody wits by a stupid cat."

She stooped to retrieve her dagger when a pair of hands unexpectedly seized her from behind. Gasping, she tried to whirl around, but her captor wrenched her elbow firmly behind her shoulder blades. Before she could scream, another hand clamped itself immovably over her mouth. Faith gagged at the putrid smell of onions and fish.

"Be still," a coarse voice warned her as she struggled fiercely. "I have no scruples about hitting a lady." As if to prove his point, he gave her a hard slap behind the ear.

As he momentarily lifted his hand from her mouth, Faith screamed bloody murder. He retaliated by plastering his palm across her open mouth, effectively cutting off the scream and her breathing at the same time. "Stupid wench," he grunted.

Furious, Faith kicked him hard in the shins and was rewarded when he yelped in pain. She cursed the heavy skirts and petticoats which prevented her from being more effective with her legs and hampered her movements.

"I said cease your struggle," he growled, letting out a stream of curses. When she did not comply he twisted her wrist until Faith could feel tears form in her eyes. He dragged her, still kicking, deeper into the shadows of the alley. At some point he finally stopped, thrusting her up against the wall and pressing his elbow beneath her neck. From a back pocket he pulled a wicked-looking knife and held it firmly to her cheek.

"Now, I'm telling ye to cease your struggle and your screams or I'll cut ye up like a Christmas goose and have ye for me supper. Do ye hear me?"

Faith nodded, not daring to speak, the blade cool against her cheek. Slowly, the man moved his elbow from her neck and stepped aside.

In his place another dark shadow stepped forward, a heavy

cloak swirling about his legs, a candlelit lantern swinging from his hand. "Well, well, what have we here?" a voice asked in cool amusement. "How fascinating to see you again, Mistress Worthington; or should I now say Madame O'Bruaidar?"

Faith gasped, the sound echoing against the cobbles of the alleyway. "Bradford," she breathed. "What in the devil are you doing here?"

He stepped closer, raising the lantern closer to her face, as if to assure himself that it was really her. "I could ask the same of you," he said, studying her. "You look a bit peaked, my dear. I don't think marriage suits you."

"Go to hell, Bradford. What do you want from me?"

"Why, your husband, of course," he replied, looking slightly taken aback at her language. "So you were working for the Irish all along. How curious of him to follow you here to London. What little adventure are you two up to now?"

"It's none of your bloody business. How did you know we were here?"

He laughed, the light making his face seem as pale as a ghost. "It was quite by accident. I left for London the day after your little escape from the gallows. I had to learn more about you. I'd only been here a few days when an acquaintance of mine . . ." he paused, glancing diffidently at the man who had abducted her, ". . . heard there were some Irishmen down by the docks asking unusual questions about Oliver Cromwell, among other things. Naturally, my curiosity was piqued."

"Naturally."

"I took it upon myself to investigate. You can imagine my astonishment when I discovered that it was O'Bruaidar, accompanied by his lovely new English bride. So I set myself a little trap and waited for the bait. That's you, my dear."

"Fascinating," Faith said derisively. "Where's Furlong? Did you harm him?"

Bradford wrinkled his nose distastefully. "Are you referring to that rather odious man with the enormous nose? No, I haven't harmed him . . . yet. But it can be arranged." He walked over to a prone form and held the lantern above it. Faith inhaled sharply as she saw it was Furlong, apparently unconscious.

"If you've hurt him . . ." Faith warned, taking a step toward Bradford.

Bradford's villain stepped forward, waving the knife under her nose. "Easy now, my lady," he warned, his mouth twisting into a crooked smile.

"As you can clearly see," Bradford said calmly, "you are in no position to make threats. Now, we shall just move along and I'll send a messenger to O'Bruaidar requiring that he turn himself in. If he refuses, I will be forced to dispose of his wife . . . in a most callous manner, of course."

"You bastard," Faith hissed, furious that she had allowed herself to fall into Bradford's trap, and even more distraught that she had placed Miles's life in danger. "That's blackmail."

"Indeed it is, my dear. Indeed it is."

Ignoring her curses, Bradford grabbed her arm while the ruffian picked up Furlong's body and slung it over his shoulder. "Shall we be on our way, madame?" Bradford inquired politely.

"You won't get away with this," Faith warned. "Miles will discover what you are plotting, and he won't fall so easily into your trap." Yet even as she said the words she knew them to be false. Miles would give his life for hers; he had said so himself.

As they moved silently down the alleyway, Faith contemplated her chances for escape. They appeared slimmer with each passing minute. With a sinking heart, she knew that she could not leave Furlong alone in Bradford's clutches. She was reduced to fantasizing about strangling Bradford with her bare hands when an enormous figure unexpectedly jumped in front of them. Bradford went flying backward with a single grunt and she fell to her knees with a bone-jarring thud. Before the lantern crashed to the ground, pitching them all into darkness, Faith saw a flash of sandy blond hair and a white smile.

"What the devil?" she heard Bradford's thug shout. Then she heard a sharp crack, which Faith desperately hoped was a fist crashing into the ruffian's jaw. Crawling on her hands and knees, she headed in the direction in which she thought Furlong might be.

"Hold it right there, lassie." A pair of large hands grabbed her by the shoulders, hauling her to her feet. "Where do ye think ye are goin'?'' The voice had a heavy Scottish burr and Faith prayed it was a friendly one.

"My friend. I think he's hurt."

The hands on her shoulders were lifted and she heard the man fumbling around in the dark. "I've found him. Come on, lass. Hold on to my cape and I'll get us safely out o' here."

Reaching out toward the voice, Faith's fingers closed around a scratchy wool material. Holding on for dear life, she let the man lead her from the alleyway.

When they reached the street in front of the inn Faith got her first good look at her rescuer. He was an enormous man, easily equal to Miles in size, with a thick mop of sandy blond hair and a handsome face. Although he had Furlong slung over his broad shoulder, he seemed to carry the stout man with apparent ease. Beneath the heavy cloak, which hung open, Faith could see he was dressed in the Scottish fashion, with a long plaid shirt of dark green and red belted at the middle and exposing his bare knees to the cool wind. He wore thick wool kneesocks and a pair of flat sandals. Having never seen a man dressed in such a way outside of history books, Faith could only stare in wonder.

"Never met a Scotsman, have ye?" he asked in an amused tone.

"Not quite like you," Faith answered honestly.

Smiling, the man hoisted Furlong from his shoulder, laying him out on the cobblestones. "Furlong," he uttered in astonishment. "What the devil are ye doing here?"

Furlong moaned, seeming to come around. His eyes fluttered open, and for a moment he simply stared at the enormous Scotsman. Then, emitting a grunt, he pushed himself up, cradling his head between his hands. "Ian Maclaren, is it ye or am I dreaming? Christ, was it ye who hit me?"

"Nay, no' me," the Scotsman replied. "Come around now, man; we've got to see the lass to safety."

Remembering what had happened, Furlong lifted his head, looking about wildly for Faith. "Where is she?" he barked.

Faith kneeled beside Furlong. "I'm here. Are you all right? We were nearly captured by Nicholas, but this kind gentleman saved us. I'm afraid I have yet to be properly introduced, although he appears to be acquainted with you.''

The Scotsman gave her a wide smile. ''Aye, but I am. The name is Ian Maclaren, my lady. I'm an old friend o' the family. Ye may consider me at your service.''

Chapter Thirty-two

"We can't go back to the Docksbury Inn," Faith said as Ian helped Furlong to his feet. "Bradford knows we are staying there. We must warn the others."

Ian frowned, looking at Furlong. "What others?"

"Miles, Shaun and Father Michael," Furlong said, rubbing the back of his neck.

"By the Holy Rod o' Christ," Ian exploded, "have ye people lost your senses? What in God's name are ye doin' in London?"

Furlong dipped his head toward Faith. "Ian, this is Miles's wife."

"This is Arabella Dunbar?" Ian said in astonishment, his burr deepening.

Faith put her hands on her hips. "Hardly. The name is Faith Worthington."

Ian looked at her as if properly scandalized. "But she's an English lass," he exclaimed in shock, looking at Furlong for corroboration.

"Oh for Christ's sake, it doesn't mean I'm diseased," Faith said, bristling. "Look, I know you are fascinated by this rather strange turn of events, but can we discuss it at a later time? We have more pressing matters on our hands right now. We need to find Miles and the others before Bradford and his accomplice come around, and we must find another place to stay."

"Ye can stay wi' me," Ian said firmly, apparently swallowing his misgivings and taking charge of the situation. "Let's first fetch the supplies from your rooms, and then I'll show ye to the inn where I am stayin'. I'll double back to wait for Miles and the others. This Bradford fellow didna get a good look at me, so he'll no' recognize my face if he dares to come around again."

Furlong nodded and Faith took a worried glance over her shoulder at the dark alley. A sparkle of something winked crookedly at her in the dim light from the street.

"Wait; my dagger," she said, running to the crates and retrieving the knife. She thrust it into the folds of her gown as she returned to the men.

"Come on, lass," Ian warned as he took her elbow firmly in his hand. " 'Tis no' a night to tarry."

"No, it's not, indeed," Faith agreed fervently as the three of them entered the inn.

The night air was bone-chilling. Miles pulled his cloak tighter about his neck as he walked briskly down the dimly lit street. Frowning, he glanced over his shoulder at the dwarf who hiccuped loudly and staggered a bit as he walked.

"Are ye going to tell us, Shaun, what took ye so long, or will ye make us guess?" Miles snapped irritably. He was in an increasingly foul mood. He and Father Michael had waited in the freezing cold for more than an hour before the small man finally appeared. "The father and I almost left without ye."

The priest nodded emphatically in agreement. "Aye, Shaun, 'tis hardly a night to stand out in the cold."

"Sorry," Shaun mumbled apologetically, pulling down his cap over his frigid ears. "I didn't intend on being late, but I did come upon something o' interest today."

"Something other than a full tankard o' ale?" Miles asked wryly.

Shaun hunched his small shoulders against the cold. "Aye, something other. I discovered a man selling magic trinkets down by the dock. He's a swindler, o' course—the English know naught o' magic—but after I bought a little something from him he traded me for a wee bit o' gossip. Seems he has seen a big red-headed Irishman. Says he took note o' the man because he spoke strangely, even for an Irishman. Keeps mostly to himself and doesn't seem overly familiar wi' the coin either."

"Could it be the O'Rourke we seek?" Father Michael asked.

Shaun shrugged. "Possibly. He says he's seen the Irishman

working at unloading crates from the English vessel *Lady-hawke* and thinks he resides somewhere down near the ship. I took the man to supper and bought him ale, hoping to get more, but he knew little else. I suppose it's worth a look on the morn.''

Miles grudgingly slapped the dwarf between the shoulder blades. "Good work, Shaun. 'Tis the first bit o' encouraging information we've found yet. I'll have myself a look at *Lady-hawke* on the morn.''

The dwarf nodded and the three fell silent, walking briskly toward home. They were almost at the inn when a bulky figure abruptly stepped from an alley, blocking their way. Snapping his head up, Miles drew his sword, thrusting the unarmed priest behind him. Shaun also pulled his sword from the scabbard, holding it warily in front of him.

"Who goes there?" Miles called out.

"Lower your swords. 'Tis an old friend," came the reply as the figure stepped beneath the light.

At once Miles saw the plaid shirt, bare knees and blond hair. "Saints above," he exclaimed, sheathing his sword. "Ian Maclaren. What in God's name are ye doing in London?"

Ian moved closer, lowering his voice. "I could ask the same o' ye, man, but later. 'Tis no' safe for ye to return to the inn.''

Miles frowned. "What happened?"

"Nicholas Bradford.''

Miles swore, trying to push past the Scotsman. "Damn ye, Ian, get out o' my way. My wife is in there.''

Ian placed one hand on Miles' shoulder, preventing him from passing. "Nay, no' any more. She and Furlong are safe in my care. A lot has happened since ye've been gone today, my friend.''

Miles reached up to his shoulder and gripped the Scotsman's hand so tightly that Ian winced. "Is she all right?" he asked, a rising note of panic tinging his voice.

Ian nodded. "She's well. But let's no' talk here. 'Tis far too dangerous. We must make certain we are no' being followed.''

Miles nodded tersely and the four men melted into the shadows. None of them saw the fifth dark shadow turn and disappear into the darkness.

A Double-Edged Blade

* * *

"How is she?" Ian asked Miles as he joined him at the end of a long table. The tavern had long ago emptied out and just the two of them remained. A fire still burned in the hearth and Ian added a few more logs to keep it going. The two of them gravitated toward it for both warmth and light.

"Sleeping like a babe," Miles said softly. "I didn't have the heart to waken her."

"Shaun and the others should be settlin' in as well. I rented another room for the rest o' us."

Miles reached across the table to clasp Ian's hand. "Thanks, friend. Tell me what happened."

Ian tersely recounted the story of hearing Faith's cry and following her into the alley. "Made quick work o' this fellow Bradford and his friend, I did. But I had no notion that the lass was your wife, nor did I know that Furlong was wi' her until I saw him clearly in the light. He took quite a blow to the back o' the head but seems more embarrassed that he was jumped from behind than hurt."

Miles swore softly under his breath. "Bradford is a black-hearted bastard. I'd have put an end to him long ago if he'd fight me like a man. Did he harm my wife?"

"I think he only scared the wits out o' her. Ye'll have to tell me more about this bonny wife o' yours; she's a fiery lass. She swore at Bradford as if he were the devil incarnate himself."

Miles smiled in spite of himself. "Thank God ye are here, Ian, but what in the devil are ye doing in London?"

He shrugged nonchalantly. "Och, a wee bit o' work for the king."

Miles placed his thick forearm on the table, leaning forward. "Spying," he said, lowering his voice. "On Cromwell."

Ian nodded. "Aye, 'tis true. And 'tis exactly why I was comin' to the Docksbury Inn. I heard whispers about town that there were a couple o' Irishmen down at the wharf asking unusual questions about Cromwell and a mysterious red-headed man. I never expected it to be ye. What in God's name are ye doing here, Miles? Ye are supposed to be in Ireland, gathering support for King Charles among the Irish noble-men."

363

Miles sighed deeply. "I know, and I've done as ye've asked. But a lot has changed since we last talked, Ian."

Ian raised an eyebrow speculatively. "Including an English wife?"

"Aye, like an English wife. But she's no spy and I haven't gone back on my word to aid King Charles."

"Then why the devil have ye risked coming here?" Ian exclaimed heatedly. "Christ's wounds, man, have ye lost your senses? Given your situation, do ye think it wise to walk into the center o' London and boldly start asking questions about a member o' parliament?"

"I thought I was being discreet."

Ian snorted. "Discreet? An impossible feat in London. 'Tis naught in this city that doesn't reach the ears o' the Parliament. 'Tis no wonder Bradford found ye wi' such ease. God's teeth, man, this isn't Ireland, ye know."

"Aye, 'tis no'," Miles agreed whole-heartedly. "This city is the most miserable pesthole I've ever seen. How can people live like this?"

"First time in London, is it?"

"Aye, and the last, I hope."

Ian sighed. "We are talkin' in circles, Miles. Ye still haven't told me what ye are doin' here. What could be more important than actin' as the king has bidden ye?"

Miles put up his hands. "Look, Ian, I can't explain it to ye. 'Tis no' because I don't trust ye, 'tis only because 'tis too complicated to understand. But we've been friends for a long time, and I ask ye to trust me. I will tell ye that I'm here to find a man, an Irishman by the name o' Padriac O'Rourke. He cannot be allowed to stay in London. I can't explain further, but 'tis very important that I find him."

"And this is worth riskin' your life and the life o' your wife and friends?"

Miles exhaled a deep breath. "Aye, 'tis so."

Ian studied his face for a long moment. "Then tell me what ye know about this man and I'll help ye find him. None o' ye can risk being seen about the streets. Bradford and others will undoubtedly be lookin' for ye."

" 'Tis dangerous, Ian."

"Aye, from your secrecy I would suppose so. But the

sooner I get ye back in Ireland, the better I'll feel.''

"Ye are a good friend.''

"Dinna flatter me so. Besides, it gives me the opportunity to pay ye back for all the favors I owe ye.'' Ian grinned, leaning over the table. "But ye know, Miles, I never expected ye o' all people to take an English wife. Do *Sassenach* lassies have a secret that would reform a Scottish rogue like me?''

Miles laughed. '' 'Tisn't a lass in all o' England or Ireland who could reform a blackguard like ye, Ian. But keep your hands off my wife, Maclaren, or *I'll* be reforming *ye,* one piece at a time.''

Chapter Thirty-three

"Ian thinks he has found your Padriac O'Rourke," Miles exclaimed excitedly to Faith as he burst into their room.

Faith quickly laid aside the book of poems and rose from her chair by the hearth. "He's seen him?" she asked, her blue eyes flashing.

"Aye. This morn' Ian got himself some work on the frigate *Ladyhawke* to try and find him. He's a big man with red hair, but he's clean-shaven and calls himself Donald. But Ian says he's heard him talking and that his speech is strange."

"It's got to be O'Rourke," Faith breathed. "I knew he'd be here."

Miles shrugged. "Possibly, but we need ye to confirm his identity before we try to capture him."

Faith nodded. "How shall we go about it?"

"We'll need to disguise ye and get ye down to the docks to get a close look at him."

Faith thought for a moment. "I can hide my hair under a kerchief, add a little Cockney to my accent and pretend to be selling some kind of wares. A bit of dirt on my face and a few more rips to my traveling gown should do the job."

"Ye are no' going alone," he said firmly.

"Well, you certainly can't accompany me," Faith protested, putting her hands on her hips. "You stand a good half meter over most Englishmen, and you are far from inconspicuous even in disguise. Bradford and O'Rourke would recognize you instantly. Father Michael would be a much better choice and should be able to blend in well enough with the other townsfolk with a little dirt added to his clothes."

"No," Miles said fiercely. "Father Michael is a man o' the cloth, forbidden to harm another. He'll no' be able to protect ye. Furlong would be a better choice."

"Bradford has had a good look at Furlong," she shot back.

"It would be too dangerous to put the two of us together again. Besides, I don't need protecting; I'm just going to have a look at the man in broad daylight. There will be hundreds of people milling about. O'Rourke won't even notice me." When she saw his frown deepen, she crossed the room and put a hand on his arm. "There is nothing to be concerned about, Miles. I won't even get near him. I promise."

"Every time ye tell me no' to worry I get this odd ache in the bottom o' my stomach."

She smiled. "Well, I'm giving you my word that I won't do anything foolish. Trust me, will you?"

Miles sighed, crossing the room and sitting on the edge of the bed. "I still don't like it. All right; I'll permit Father Michael to accompany ye, but I'll have Shaun following at a distance, just in case."

"Then tell him to make it a grand distance. The last thing we want is to draw attention to ourselves and put O'Rourke on guard."

"The last thing *I* want is for ye to get hurt," Miles said emphatically.

Faith joined him on the bed, leaning over to kiss him on the cheek. "I'll be just fine. Remember, O'Rourke doesn't even know for certain whether you were able to save me at the lake. He probably thinks I'm dead and won't be expecting to see me."

"God's wounds," Miles exploded, throwing up his hands. "Must ye remind me o' what that bastard did to ye?"

Faith slipped her arms around his neck. "I love you, Miles, but I really can take care of myself. Everything will be just fine. When do we get started?"

"This afternoon," Miles said, gripping her shoulders between his large hands. "Just promise me again ye'll be careful."

"I promise," she said softly. "I'll get one good look at him and leave. That will be enough. I give you my word."

Faith walked along the wharf, holding a hand to her lower back to compensate for the heavy wooden box that was strapped around her shoulders and held out in front of her. Her pale hair had been tightly braided and thrust beneath a greasy kerchief, her face liberally smeared with dirt and grime until she had to physically restrain herself from rubbing it off. Her traveling gown had been ripped in a few more places until the men were satisfied with her disguise. Father Michael, too, had been dirtied up a bit, but his eyes still twinkled merrily and his cheeks were as ruddy as ever, despite the appalling grime.

"I wish I could carry that for ye, lass," he whispered to her as they walked past a crowd of street urchins who ran past her, peeking into her box to see what goodies she was carrying.

"Fish," one of the boys announced, wrinkling his nose in distaste at the stench before darting off.

Faith, too, felt like wrinkling her nose. The fish had been Miles's idea, certain the smell would keep all but the most determined customers away. So far he had proved to be right.

"Oh, it's not so bad," Faith said halfheartedly to the priest. "It looks heavier than it really is."

Father Michael looked at her doubtfully but said no more. Instead, he shielded his eyes with his hand and peered off into the distance. "*Ladyhawke* is ahead," he murmured. "I think I can already see the top o' Ian's big head. He's lifting a crate onto the ship. He said he'd try to stand near the Irishman so we would know where to look. Are ye ready, lass?"

Faith shifted the box onto her hip. "I'm as ready as I'll ever be. Let's go."

Determinedly they headed for *Ladyhawke*'s berth. Twice Faith stopped to have interested customers inspect what she was carrying, all the while looking over her shoulder at the ship.

"I can see Ian now," she whispered to Father Michael. "And that must be the man they think is O'Rourke."

Although the Irishman had his back to her, the hair was the right color, and Faith thought he was certainly big enough to be Paddy O'Rouke. She needed him to turn around so she could see his face.

"Damn, he won't turn around," she muttered. "We'll have to get a bit closer." Taking a quick step forward, she collided unexpectedly with a drunken sailor who was weaving unsteadily across the dock. Fish went flying everywhere, causing the sailor to lose his footing and end up sprawled in front of her. Faith simply stared at him in shock.

"Wretched filthy peddler," the sailor shouted at her in a slurred voice as he rose, swaying, to his feet. "You didn't watch where you were going. Now look at me. My garments are ruined and I smell like rotten fish. I'll teach you a lesson, I will."

Before either Faith or Father Michael could react, the sailor balled his fist and swung directly at Faith. Fortunately, his reflexes were impaired from the alcohol, and the blow only glanced off her jaw. But the force of it was enough to send her slamming hard into Father Michael. With a loud thump, the priest flew back, landing squarely on his derrière.

Furious at the unprovoked violence against her person and the priest, Faith lifted the wooden box over her head just as the sailor rushed at her again. Balling her fist, she swung at him, connecting solidly with his jaw. At first the sailor seemed startled. Then his eyes rolled back in his head. He teetered sideways and toppled over onto the deck, face first.

The clatter of footsteps sounded as the curious gathered around them on the deck. Father Michael gasped in horror, hastily coming to his feet. Grabbing her arm, he dragged her away from the sailor. The buzz about the woman who had just clocked a sailor had reached a dull roar by the time they had exited the dock.

Twisting around, Faith dared a glance over her shoulder, where Ian stood deathly still next to a tall redheaded man. For a startled moment Faith's eyes met those of Paddy O'Rourke. Her heart sank to her feet. From the way he was staring at her, totally stunned and with an open mouth, it was obvious he had recognized her.

"How could ye let this happen?" Miles roared at Father Michael. The priest nervously twisted his hands in front of him.

"I'm sorry, Miles. It all happened so quickly."

"Oh, stop it," Faith said irritably, grabbing the grimy kerchief off her hair and tossing it onto the bed. "It wasn't his fault, Miles. The sailor took a swing at me. He was completely sotted. There was no way to anticipate his actions."

"Did ye have to fight back?" he asked, glaring at her.

"What did you want me to do? He hit me first."

For a moment she thought Miles might throttle her, but instead he swore softly, taking two long strides across the room and back again. "God's wounds," he finally exploded. "I should never have agreed to let ye do this."

"Well, it happened," she snapped back crossly, "and arguing about it won't change anything."

Miles scowled at her ferociously before resuming his pacing. "All right. Putting aside the spectacle ye made at the docks, did ye manage to get a look at the man next to Ian? Is he the man ye seek?"

Faith nodded in confirmation. "Yes, he's Paddy O'Rourke, all right. But I fear he may have recognized me. We'll have to move at once."

"Ye aren't moving anywhere," Miles said, his voice raising a notch. "Ye will stay right here in this room until we return. Do ye understand?"

"Now look here . . ." Faith started to protest heatedly.

"Is that understood?" Miles thundered so loudly that even Father Michael looked taken aback.

Faith crossed her arms against her chest, feeling unreasonably defensive. "Oh, all right. It's understood."

"Come, Father," Miles said, motioning to the priest. "We've got work to do." He opened the door and the priest exited. For a moment Miles stood in the doorway, glaring back at Faith as she stood alone in the middle of the room, dirt still streaked across her cheeks.

"Ye are no' to leave this room for any reason," he instructed. "Bolt the door when I'm gone."

"I will," she promised. "Miles . . . wait. I'm sorry."

He exhaled a deep breath. "Ye could have been hurt, Faith. 'Tis what makes me angry. I wasn't there to protect ye."

"I'm fine," she said, her voice shakier than she had intended. "I'm far more concerned about you. O'Rourke is a very dangerous man, and we should assume he still has the weapon I told you about. He won't hesitate to kill."

Miles's face was grim. "I'll be careful, lass."

Faith suddenly threw herself across the room and into his arms. "God, Miles, I don't know what I'd do if anything happened to you."

"Hush, lass," he said, pressing a warm kiss on the top of

her head. "We'll be back before nightfall. Pack up our things and be ready to go. We'll leave for Scotland as soon as we have him."

She nodded and pulled away. Miles leaned over and gave her a tender kiss on the mouth. "Be good for once, wife," he admonished before leaving the room and shutting the door behind him. "And don't leave this room."

Chapter Thirty-four

Faith packed all their belongings except the book of poems, which she now held in her hand. She wished she had the patience and concentration to read, but she couldn't keep from constantly jumping up to look out the window to see if the men had returned. An hour earlier the innkeeper had provided a little distraction by bringing her food and a bottle of wine, but she couldn't bear to eat and had managed to swallow only a little of the wine. Nothing seemed able to take her mind off the waiting and the worry.

For the hundredth time that night she rose from her seat at the hearth and went to look out the window. Darkness had already fallen on the city and the men had yet to return. Fear and apprehension swept through her. What in God's name was taking them so long? Had something gone wrong?

A sharp rap on the door jolted Faith from her thoughts. With a small cry, she flew across the room. "Oh God, Miles," she exclaimed, drawing the bolt and throwing open the door, "I've been worried sick about you and—"

Her words died a painful death as she saw the hulking form of Paddy O'Rourke standing in the corridor, aiming the sleek twentieth-century handgun at her midsection. He was clean-shaven, as she had seen him at the docks, with his flaming red hair cropped close to his head. With a brutal shove he pushed his way into the room, slamming the door behind him.

"Worried about me, were ye?" he sneered.

"How did you find me?" Faith asked, her mouth bone dry.

"Well, I must say ye gave me quite a shock today when I saw ye on the dock. So O'Bruaidar managed to fish ye from the lake, did he? Ye have the most uncanny luck to survive, lass. However, I'm afraid that luck has just run out."

"What . . . what did you do with the others?" she asked faintly, afraid of what he might answer.

"Nothing yet. Thanks to ye, they are hunting me. I barely escaped."

Her breath came out in a rush of relief. "How did you find me so quickly?"

"Ye aren't the only one who has people working for ye. I paid an urchin to follow ye from the docks. Traced ye right here to this inn, he did. A couple o' innocent questions to the innkeeper downstairs and here I am. Rather simple, wouldn't ye say?"

"Appallingly so."

"Ye've become quite a nuisance, ye know. Did ye really think ye could stop me?"

Faith raised her gaze from the barrel of the gun to look Paddy squarely in the eye. "Yes, and I still do. Your plans aren't going to work, O'Rourke. Killing me will do little besides enrage those who are helping me. They won't give up until they find you."

Paddy laughed. "It hardly seems likely that your friends will dare to remain long in England. It's no secret that O'Bruaidar is a wanted man."

"How do you know that?" Faith asked in surprise.

"I overheard Donagh talking about it while I was at Castle O'Rourke. Seems O'Bruaidar is quite a thorn in the English side. How did ye manage to get an Irish rebel to betray his country and help ye? Sleep wi' him, did ye? Teach him a few tricks o' the women o' our time?"

Faith frowned in disgust. "You have a filthy mouth and an even more disgusting mind. Miles is no traitor, unlike your beloved ancestor. Did you know that Donagh O'Rourke sold out to the English? That's why your bloody castle exists in our time."

"That's a lie," Paddy growled. "Everyone knows he was an Irish patriot."

Faith laughed. "Christ, don't be so naive, O'Rourke. He was informing on Miles to the English. I know because an English officer at the garrison in Drogheda told me so."

"That's not true," Paddy thundered, taking an angry step forward and forcing Faith back toward the hearth. "Donagh fought against the English. 'Tis well documented in our time. The English lied to ye, lass."

Faith took another step back, bumping into the table. The bottle of wine wobbled precariously. Putting her hands behind her as if to steady herself, she let her fingers close around the glass neck.

"Oh, and did Donagh lie to me too?" she asked. "He himself told me that he had cut a deal with the English to preserve his property in exchange for informing on Miles. Your upstanding ancestor personally took me to Drogheda and delivered me into the hands of the garrison commander. In the process he killed an unarmed Irish boy who tried to stop him. A fine patriot he was."

"Damn you, woman, I'll not stand here and listen to your lies."

"Why? Don't like what you hear? The O'Rourke family tree isn't turning out to be very noble, is it?"

His face turned purple with rage. "I want you to know that killing you is going to be a pleasure."

"Going to save your bullets again?"

Grimly, Paddy tucked the gun into the belt at his waist. "Aye, I am. But this time, no drowning. I'm not taking any chances that you might miraculously survive again."

As he stepped forward, Faith lifted the bottle from behind her back and brought it against the side of his head with a fierce crack. He roared in pain as red wine and glass flew in every direction about the room. While he was off balance, Faith gave him a violent push backward, grabbing for the gun at his waist.

Dazed, Paddy managed to clutch the sleeve of her gown as he toppled heavily to the floor, bringing her down with him. Faith landed on top of him in a tangle of skirts and petticoats, all the while clawing frantically for the gun. To her dismay, O'Rourke proved to be remarkably alert for a man who had just had a bottle cracked across his skull. Cursing, he pushed her off his body and rolled to his side in front of the hearth, gun still in hand.

Panting, O'Rourke came to his feet, eyeing her warily. He rubbed the side of his skull gingerly, frowning when his fingers came away sticky with blood and wine.

"Ye'll pay for that, lass," he growled.

Faith didn't answer and instead frantically searched the

room for a weapon with which to defend herself. A glint on the mantel caught her eye over Paddy's shoulder. With a sinking heart she realized that she had left her dagger lying there. She had no chance of getting past O'Rourke to seize it. It might as well have been on the moon.

Paddy must have seen the expression of despair on her face, for he smiled. "Well, lass," he said softly. "It looks like ye are finally out o' tricks."

Miles hurried up the stairs of the inn, frustrated with the unfortunate turn of events. They'd nearly caught O'Rourke at the inn where he had been staying, but he had somehow managed to slip though their fingers. The men decided to split up, and Miles's search had brought him back near the inn where Faith was waiting. On an impulse he decided to check on her.

"Faith," he called out softly through the closed door. When no one answered he pushed down on the latch, frowning when it clicked open. "Damnation, woman, I told ye to draw the—"

His words broke off as he caught sight of the broad, red-headed Irishman with his hands around Faith's throat. She was bent nearly backward over the small table, her eyes glazed. Fury choked him as he hurtled himself toward O'Rourke with an agonized cry.

"Not a step closer or she dies," Paddy warned.

Miles froze in midmovement, fearing that the Irishman had already been true to his word. Faith lay deathly still. Then he caught sight of the faint rise and fall of her chest, and his heart began to beat again.

"Drop your sword, O'Bruaidar," Paddy instructed. "Drop it or I'll finish her off."

Miles's hand grasped the hilt of his sword so tightly that his knuckles went white. His rage flared once and then settled into a hard, cold ball in the pit of his stomach. "Damn ye, O'Rourke," he managed to say between clenched teeth. "Let her go."

"I said drop your sword," O'Rourke repeated. When he made no move to comply, Paddy's hands began to tighten on Faith's throat. "Well, lass, it's a pity, but it looks like your friend puts little value on your life."

Julie Moffett

"He's . . . my . . . husband," Faith managed to whisper hoarsely, her blue eyes lifting to meet Miles's. The reprieve had apparently permitted her lungs to fill with air, and briefly, she returned to her senses. As she stared at him, Miles could read the silent plea in her gaze.

Don't give in to him.

"The plot thickens," O'Rourke chortled. "Imagine that, a British agent marrying an Irish rebel. Fascinating turn of events. Have ye changed your mind and decided to stay in this time?"

"No," Faith answered weakly. "You and I . . . we have to go back. We don't belong here."

Paddy laughed. "Well, I'm afraid to disappoint ye, but I'm not returning, lass. However, if your husband here doesn't relinquish his sword immediately, I'm afraid ye won't be going anywhere either." He pressed his fingers against her neck so tightly that she gasped for air, hitting his arms ineffectively.

"Stop!" Miles commanded, drawing his sword from its scabbard. With a flick of his wrist he tossed it to the floor.

O'Rourke nodded with satisfaction. "Better. Now kick it under the bed."

Miles booted the sword and sent it sliding under the bed. "I've done what ye've asked, O'Rourke. Now let the lass go."

Paddy loosened his grip long enough to pull her upright and in front of him. His beefy forearm still gripped her about the neck. "One snap is all it would take to end her life," he warned Miles.

"If ye kill her, ye'll never get out o' here alive," Miles said quietly. "I give ye my word on that."

"Oh, ye give me your word, do ye?" Paddy sneered. With his other hand he reached into his belt and pulled out his gun. "Ever seen anything like this, Irishman? Well, it could kill ye before ye could bloody well blink. And quietly, too, so no one will come running to your defense. Ye risked a lot for the Englishwoman. Was she really worth it?"

"Release her," Miles said calmly. "Let's settle this between the two o' us."

"Why are ye so eager to protect her?" Paddy asked. "What did she tell ye? That she's a witch who flew in from the twentieth century? That she has the Sight? That she's a fairy lass come to guide ye to fame and fortune?'' He laughed, pleased with his humor. ''Or did she tell ye nothing at all? She certainly couldn't have told ye who I plan to kill. Ye may be a fool, but ye're still an Irishman, after all.''

''She told me the truth,'' Miles replied calmly. ''That ye both came here from the twentieth century. And I know ye mean to kill Cromwell. She told me everything.''

Paddy's eyes narrowed in surprise. ''I see that she did. And she must have been quite convincing to make you believe such a tale. Did she also tell ye just what Cromwell does to Ireland, or did she fabricate some heroic tale for the blackhearted bastard?''

''I know Cromwell marches across both Scotland and Ireland and there is terrible destruction and pain.''

'' 'Terrible destruction and pain'?'' Paddy laughed. ''Is that all? Christ, didn't she tell ye about the massacres at Drogheda and Wexford, and how thousands o' innocent women and children were slaughtered there? And she undoubtedly told ye about the thousands o' Irish priests and Catholics who were hunted and executed in the name o' God on behalf o' this man.''

The corners of Miles's mouth tightened as he looked to Faith for confirmation. ''Is it true?'' he asked her softly.

She nodded, clutching Paddy's beefy forearm as it tightened around her neck. ''Yes, Miles. I won't lie to you. But it's also true that in time Ireland becomes an independent state with its own government and laws.''

''That isn't true,'' O'Rourke shouted. ''Ye bloody English bastards won't let go o' Ireland entirely. We deserve vengeance for what you have done to us.''

''For God's sake, O'Rourke,'' Faith whispered, ''must you speak only of revenge? Peace may finally be at hand. Would it hurt to listen?''

''Listen to what?'' shouted O'Rourke. ''The lies o' the English? Never. Peace wi' the English is nothing less than treason.''

''Maybe you haven't noticed,'' Faith said quietly, ''but people are tired of the killing and violence. Irish and English mothers no longer wish to weep over their children's bodies. Even the Church condemns the violence. Peace is a laudable goal and you know it. It always has been. We have to learn to put the hate behind us and live together.''

''I've heard enough. Let her go, O'Rourke,'' Miles commanded.

Paddy flashed an angry glance at Miles. ''Ye of all people should support what I am doing, O'Bruaidar. Walk out of here now and let me finish what I came to do. Let me kill that bastard Cromwell and save Ireland from hundreds of years of terrible misery. I can do it.''

''And who will ye kill next to fit your grand vision o' Ireland?'' Miles replied softly. ''Faith is right; ye can't change history to suit your whims, no matter how noble the cause. 'Tis impossible to judge the consequences o' killing Cromwell now, if 'tis no' meant to be. No matter how much I may want it myself, I won't let ye do it.''

''Sure, and ye are in a fine position to stop me,'' Paddy said scornfully. ''Protect this English lass if you must, but I'm afraid your refusal to cooperate will force me to cut short your rather interesting career as an Irish rebel.'' His finger tightened on the trigger.

Faith sank her teeth into his arm just as he fired. Paddy's aim wavered and the gun went off, sending the bullet thudding into the wooden wall above Miles's head with a loud thwack.

Miles dove for Paddy before he could get off another shot, sending them all crashing to the floor. Twisting loose from Paddy's grip, Faith rolled away from the men, cutting the palm of her left hand on the shattered glass from the bottle. Rising to her knees amid tangled skirts, she saw the men struggle fiercely for the gun that O'Rourke still held clenched in his hand.

Dazed and short of breath, she pushed herself determinedly to her feet, even though blood dripped onto her gown. The room swayed sickeningly about her. She took a deep breath, staring at the men and trying to clear her vision. Paddy had somehow rolled on top of Miles and was furiously fighting to gain control of the gun. One hand was choking the breath out of Miles while the other was slowly wrenching the gun toward his chest.

''No,'' Faith cried, turning and groping madly along the mantel with her right hand. She didn't think twice as her fingers closed around the dagger. As soon as the weapon was in her grip, she fell upon Paddy, thrusting the dagger into his back with all her might.

For a moment both men froze, and Faith fell to the floor in a crumpled heap. There was no sound except the muted crackle of the fire in the hearth. Then a shot went off and O'Rourke fell directly on top of Miles. The two men lay in a tangled heap on the floor, neither of them moving.

Emitting a strangled moan, Faith pushed herself onto her hands and knees. She crawled toward the men, tears streaming down her face. "Oh my God," she sobbed. "Miles, are you all right?"

When there was no answer hysteria swept through her. "Miles," she shouted. *"For God's sake, Miles!"*

"Hush, Faith," came the muffled reply. "I'm all right. Just let me get this cursed gun from his grip."

She heard him swear before the gun slid past her, hitting the wall with a crack. With a grunt, Miles managed to push Paddy's body off him and rise to his feet. His shirt was torn and covered in blood and glass, but he was alive.

"Are you shot?" she asked worriedly.

"Nay. He missed." Kneeling over O'Rourke, he pulled the dagger from the body and held it up to the light. It was bent at an odd angle, as if it had struck a bone.

Faith could only stare in horror and shock. "My God," she whispered. "The blade bent when I killed Paddy O'Rourke."

Misunderstanding the source of her shock, Miles knelt down beside her. " 'Tis all right, love. Ye are safe."

"No, you don't understand. I bent the blade. How can that be possible?"

"I don't know, lass. I only know that ye are alive and Paddy O'Rourke is dead."

She buried her head in his chest, overcome by all that had happened to her. "I killed a man," she whispered. She felt no joy or satisfaction in the knowledge that she had put an end to the life of this hardened assassin. Instead she felt only a deep-seated nausea that she had been forced to take the life of another human being.

"He would have killed us both," Miles said quietly. "Ye did what was necessary to survive."

"Yes . . . I suppose I did," she said as her entire body began to tremble. "But I didn't want to kill him—only return him to my time, where he could face the punishment he deserved."

Miles cupped her face with his large hands. "I won't lie to ye, lass, and say I understand exactly what we've done here or what it means. Nor will I blame O'Rourke for his passion for Ireland and his desire to kill Cromwell. But I do know I wasn't going to let him harm ye again." He pulled her tightly against his chest and they sat in silence, clinging to each other. Finally Miles rose, pulling her to her feet.

"Our task is done," he said quietly. "May I suggest we clean ourselves and bury the body? Then let's take his god-forsaken gun and get the devil out o' this miserable pesthole. I'm afraid I haven't found London very hospitable."

Faith pressed her cheek against his. "By all means, Miles," she whispered fervently in his ear. "Let's go home."

Chapter Thirty-five

Castle Dun na Moor
April 30, 1649

"Are ye certain ye must do this?" Miles asked for the hundredth time.

Faith sat on the edge of the bed, clasping her hands tightly in front of her. By the light of the candle and the dim glow of the fire, he could see her face was drawn and gray.

"I've had nearly seven months to think about it," she said quietly. "I don't *want* to go back; I *must* go back. Every day in this time that passes with me in it makes it more likely that I might inadvertently change events. I can't even fathom how much damage I may have done already. I can no longer just think about myself and my happiness. There is more at stake."

Miles anxiously paced back and forth across the room. "Why tonight?" he protested. "There's a cold rain and the sky is dark and threatening."

"It's May Eve," she replied quietly. "It's the same night I arrived, exactly one year ago. I don't know if it means anything, but it is as good a time as any."

"But today is your birthday."

She nodded. "Yes, I know. It's always been a day of monumental changes in my life."

He exhaled in frustration, resuming his pacing. "Ye don't even know if this time travel will work. It could be dangerous."

She lifted her hands helplessly. "I have to try, Miles. If I don't, I will never have peace of mind."

"Must you really go? Naught in history has changed so far," he countered, kneeling in front of her. "As ye predicted, King Charles was beheaded by the Parliament and the war in

Scotland is o'er. Ireland has readied her forces and is preparing for the English."

"Yes," she said softly. "Cromwell is coming." Reaching out, she rested an unsteady hand on his shoulder. "Do you know how often I dream of that, Miles? I don't know what will happen to you. If Cromwell or his forces harm you or anyone at Castle Dun na Moor, it will be my fault. I could have let Paddy O'Rourke stop him."

"Don't," Miles commanded, gripping her cold hand tightly. "Ye said that we all must live with what will be. I've no wish to die, but I'm no' afraid o' death either."

Faith slid from her perch on the bed to wrap her arms around Miles's neck, her body pressing against his. "But I'm afraid for you. For all of you," she whispered. "You are my family. If only you would heed my advice and pack up and move West to Connemara. The English forces largely leave that region alone. You'd be safe there."

Miles pulled away from her gently. "I'm no' going to run from the English. Ye know that, lass."

Tears filled her eyes. "Yes, I know that. Damn you, Miles O'Bruaidar, for being so honorable."

He caught a tear with the pad of his thumb. "Must we truly sacrifice ourselves for this history o' yours? What if 'tis already too late and we've changed something irrevocably?"

She exhaled a deep and unhappy breath. "So far, Miles, we've been lucky. Donagh O'Rourke is dead but has a son to carry on the O'Rourke line, thus securing the family legacy. As Bradford doesn't know what happened to Donagh, he may still be true to his promise to preserve O'Rourke Castle. And now that King Charles is dead and Bradford has thrown his support behind Cromwell, he doesn't dare touch me in case I have been working for Cromwell all along. As a result he'll not harm you either. Thank God, decidedly little has changed so far."

"Except that I've fallen in love wi' ye and ye are my wife, Faith."

She swallowed back a flood of tears. "If I stay, I'll be no less selfish than Paddy O'Rourke. Don't you see? I killed him rather than let him change history. How could I pardon myself by staying in this time and being happy?"

Miles swore, wanting to crush her to his chest and insist that she stay. But with the passing months he had seen her grow thin, pale and quiet. He knew that she could not reconcile her happiness with the knowledge of the dangers of living in a time where she felt she did not belong. Deep in his heart he knew that if he forced her to stay, she would slowly wither away, ravaged by the guilt that plagued her. Closing his eyes, he drew her to him, pressing a soft kiss to her hair.

"I know ye must go, lass," he whispered, surprised at how shaky his voice had become. "And I gave ye my word that I'd no' stop ye. But before ye go . . . let me love ye one last time."

Not trusting herself to speak, she simply pressed herself against him. Cradling her gently, Miles lifted her up onto the bed. Her pale hair splayed across the quilt, candlelight flickering on her features. She was crying in earnest now, silent tears slipping from the corners of her luminous blue eyes and falling to the bedcovers.

"Hush, Faith," he whispered. "I don't want ye to weep." He proceeded slowly, removing her clothing with care and tenderness. "I love ye," he whispered as he undressed himself and settled onto the bed beside her. "Don't ever forget that."

He touched every part of her body, from the flat plane of her stomach to the sweet curve of her breasts. He tasted the saltiness of her skin, mixed with the tears that fell from her eyes.

"Ye are so beautiful," he said in wonder as he lifted the pale strands of hair that spilled across his bare chest. "I want to remember ye just like this."

Rolling her over onto her back, he kissed her mouth, throat, shoulders and breasts. Faith watched his dark head as it moved down to her stomach. His mouth touched her skin with such reverence that she thought her heart would break.

He finally entered her, bringing her to the peak of sensation again and again, holding himself back. Finally she wound his fingers in her hair, pulling him close and urging him on.

"Together," she said softly. "I want us to do this together."

He yielded and together they reached the edge of passion.

Faith remembered calling his name once and hearing the echo ring in her ears.

For a while they simply lay unmoving, Miles's body resting on top of hers. Her arms wound around his waist, holding him tightly. She could feel the rapid beat of his heart against her chest and the warm stickiness of their lovemaking between her legs. They were still connected as one, his pulse pounding a beat through the fragile thread that bound them. At last he rolled free, slipping his arm beneath her head and pulling her close. His breath was warm on her cheek.

Faith closed her eyes, willing away the suffocating pain in her heart. "There is a poem that Fiona and I used to recite to each other when we were children," she said. "But I think it is fitting for you, too." Softly she recited,

> *"My husband for always,*
> *Naught can us part.*
> *My husband forever,*
> *One bond to one heart."*

At that instant she knew that no matter the time in which she lived, she would never be able to cut the cord that bound her to him.

"For always and forever, husband," she murmured.

Miles reached out, cupping her cheek. "Promise me something," he said quietly. "Promise me that no matter what happens, someday, somewhere, we'll be together again."

Faith felt a single tear slip down her cheek. "I promise," she whispered fiercely. "Even if it's only in my dreams, I promise you, Miles."

They dressed and stood awkwardly in the center of the room. Miles finished buckling his belt and looked at her.

"Ye'd best fetch your cloak," he said softly.

Swallowing the grief that strangled the breath in her throat, Faith moved to the wardrobe and pulled out her heavy cloak. With one last look about the room, she threw it over her shoulders and followed him out the door.

They rode without escort, two riders on a single horse. Miles held a small brush torch that lighted the path as they made their way through the dark forest. Faith sat behind him in the saddle, her arms wrapped around his waist, her cheek pressed against his back. They didn't speak as he gently guided the horse with a firm press of his thighs.

A light drizzle fell, not enough to douse the torch, but enough to add to the deepening gloom of the night. Each thump of the horse's hooves beat a painful tune as they neared their destination. She heard the gurgling sound of a brook, and Miles pulled back on the reins as they entered the clearing. The stone configurations were barely visible.

"The Beaghmore Stone Circles," she breathed softly. She had an odd sense of déjà vu—as if her life had come full circle.

Miles dismounted and reached up to help her out of the saddle. "O'er there is where I found ye lying on the ground."

She nodded, barely trusting herself to speak. Turning to the horse, he reached into the pouch and pulled out a white bundle. "Your things," he said, unrolling the linen strip. "Including Paddy O'Rourke's gun."

Faith looked at the objects, marveling that they actually looked foreign to her. Had she really been in this time an entire year?

"I'm sorry ye don't have your clothes," he said apologetically. "I mean, from your time."

"It's all right," she replied, taking the flashlight and the compass and rewrapping the rest of the objects into the bundle. "I'll think of some plausible explanation for this gown."

He nodded, looking away. "What do ye do now?"

Faith lifted her shoulders helplessly. "I honestly don't know. I suppose I'll go stand by the circle where you found me and wait. I remember there was a humming sound, and my compass went haywire. I think those were the signals for the opening of the time portal." She glanced down at the compass. The arm pointed north.

"Aye," he said doubtfully.

They fell silent for a moment before Faith cleared her throat. "Miles," she said, her voice wavering, "will you tell the others good-bye for me? I couldn't bear to do it myself."

"I will," he answered simply.

She swallowed hard, fighting for control. "Will you also tell them . . ." she started, and then stopped to push down the lump in her throat. "Tell them how much they mean to me. Molly, Shaun, Patrick, Furlong and Father Michael . . . they've become the family I always wanted."

"I'll tell them, Faith, altho' I think they already know how ye feel about them."

She closed her eyes against the tears, but a few slipped past her anyway. "What about you, Miles?" she asked softly. "Will you ever forgive me for leaving?"

He stepped forward, taking her face gently between his hands. "I don't blame ye for doing what ye must. Just as ye will no' blame me for staying at Castle Dun na Moor and living out the life to which I was destined."

She put her arms around his neck, pressing her tearstained face into his neck. "I'll miss you so much," she whispered.

"Och, ye'll undoubtedly be better off without my hormones," he said, forcing a light tone. "And I'll have Father Michael continue the lessons ye started. I'll even learn how to write my name."

She smiled through her tears. "That would be wonderful."

"*Madlise*," he breathed into her hair. " 'Tis time." Looking down, he gently pried her arms loose from around his neck. "Ye must go, Faith. I fear 'tis close to midnight."

They stood in silence, hands linked, facing each other. Finally Miles lifted her fingers to his lips, gently kissing the *claddagh* ring she still wore on her finger.

"Remember our union," he said softly. "For if we canno' be together in this time, I believe there is another place and time where we can renew our vows to one another."

Faith nodded, not able to speak. Gently, Miles gave her a push toward the stone circles. "Go now, love. If ye linger but a moment longer, I'll no' be able to let ye go."

Hot tears blurring her vision, Faith turned and walked blindly toward the circles. When she reached the site she flicked on the flashlight and swept the beam of light around the area. A startled gasp broke from her lips.

"Miles," she shouted in panic, dropping the flashlight and stumbling toward him. "Come quickly. Some of the stones at the circle where I came through . . . they're gone."

Chapter Thirty-six

"I can't believe I'm out again on a May Eve," Shaun muttered, clutching his cloak tighter around his neck. The drizzle formed cold droplets that settled uncomfortably on his nose and beard. Wiping them away impatiently, he reached furtively beneath his cloak, as he had numerous times that evening, to touch reassuringly the ring of primrose he carried there. " 'Tis dangerous work we are doing on a night when the fey folk's magic is at their height."

"Hush," Father Michael admonished as he lifted his shovel and dug with renewed vigor into the ground. "Bring the torch closer. I can hardly see."

Dutifully, Shaun carried the torch closer, throwing light over the hole they had already dug. "Just a wee bit more and 'twill be deep enough to conceal the stones," the Father added, breathing heavily.

Sighing, the dwarf put his hand on Father Michael's shoulder. "Let me have a turn at it, Father. This is taking far longer than I expected. We've been at this all day. Dragging the stones from the site to our hiding place here 'twas most difficult. Concealing our trail took even longer. The hour grows late. We must return to the castle."

The priest exhaled wearily, handing over the shovel to the dwarf. "Do ye really think this will work?" he asked, watching Shaun throw a pile of dirt to the side. "I mean, removing the stones from their site and hiding them here?"

"O' course it will. Do ye doubt my knowledge o' magic?"

The priest shifted uneasily on his feet. "I'm talking about more than just magic. These stones were sacred to the Druids. Being a man o' the cloth, I can't say that I agree wi' pagan rituals . . . but disturbing a holy site, even a pagan one, is somehow quite unsettling."

Shaun paused, leaning against the shovel and looking up at

the priest. "Did ye no' agree wi' me that the lass is part o' our destiny?"

Father Michael nodded. "I did."

"Did I no' tell ye that a vision came to me that said the lass should stay; that she belonged here?"

"Ye did. Ye know I have great faith in your dreams, Shaun."

"And did I no' overhear her telling Miles how she came here from another place and time? A place which lay on the other side o' these stones?"

"Aye, Shaun, all ye say is true."

"Then she cannot leave. My vision warned me in no un-certain terms that her fate lies wi' us . . . and wi' Ireland. What we are doing is right. Ye must believe me." With that he turned and resumed his digging.

The priest sighed, watching the hole grow deeper. "May God preserve our souls, but I do believe ye, Shaun. Ye have yet to lead me astray."

The dwarf smiled. "Then let's finish our task and return home. Tonight o' all nights, I don't want anyone to venture out looking for us."

"I've had Furlong question everyone in the castle, and no one admits to being near the site," Miles said to Faith wearily, running his fingers through his dark hair. "Shaun and Father Michael are no' back yet from their trip to the village, but I don't think they'll know much about it either. Shaun wouldn't go near the stones on May Eve for fear of being spirited away by the fey folk, and Father Michael would certainly no' disturb such a sacred site. I myself hadn't been to the place in years until I found ye there."

"The stones—they might have been missing for months," she whispered.

Miles nodded, stopping short of telling her what she had failed to notice in the dark—the stones had been dug up re-cently, and the site meticulously recovered.

"It didn't work," she whispered. "I don't know if the stones are the catalyst or not, but without them I don't think it's going to work."

"I give ye my solemn word that I had naught to do wi' the

disappearance o' the stones. But I won't lie to ye; I'm no' sorry the stones are gone.'' He crossed the room in two quick strides and knelt beside her. '' 'Tis fate that brought ye to me, and now fate has dictated that ye stay. I don't know why, but I damn well will no' question it.''

He felt a clutch in his heart when he remembered how she had stood so forlorn, clutching her compass, waiting for something to happen. When it hadn't he swept her into his arms and back to the castle.

''What will I do?'' she whispered.

''Ye are my wife. Ye'll stay here wi' me. 'Tis time for ye to accept your fate here in this time.''

She exhaled a deep breath. ''I've been thinking of the dagger—the one you gave me for our wedding . . . and the one with which I killed Paddy O'Rourke. Given the mysterious disappearance of the stones, it makes me think that perhaps I was meant to live in this time all along.''

Miles looked down at her hand. The wedding ring he had placed on her finger so many months before gleamed in the firelight. ''Have ye any regrets about us?'' he asked softly.

She looked up at him, startled. ''Good God, no. Marrying you was the best decision I ever made.''

He pressed her hand to his cheek. ''Then ye'll stay here . . . wi' me?''

''Yes.''

He closed his eyes, a look of immense relief crossing his face. ''Ye know, I can't help but be selfish about ye, Faith. I want ye to stay by my side. But ye must no' argue if I eventually decide to send ye and the others away to safety.''

Faith shook her head firmly. ''I'll not leave you, Miles, even for my own safety. We must stay together. I can help you. Remember, I still have a knowledge of the future. I don't want to use it to change history, but I don't have to waste it either. We'll be all right, Miles, as long as we stay together. I'll see to that.''

''I don't want ye to do anything that would make ye unhappy,'' Miles said softly.

''Being without you would make me unhappy. Honestly, I'm relieved to have this horrible decision taken out of my hands. I tried to return to my own time and I couldn't. Unless the stones miraculously reappear, there is nothing else I can do. My conscience is clear."

Miles looked at her worriedly. "Then why do I detect a hint o' sadness in your voice? Did ye wish so much to return to your other life?"

She reached out and placed her hand on top of his. "No. But I can't stop thinking about my cousin Fiona. Knowing that I'll never see her again, I now realize that I never thanked her for all she did for me. She stood by me when no one else would. She was a friend, a confidant . . . a sister. If only there were some way I could let her know I'm all right . . . and so very, very happy."

Miles wound a strand of her pale hair between his fingers. "Ye'll think o' something, Faith. Ye always do."

Her eyes softened as she looked at her husband. "You have remarkable faith in me, Miles. I think that's part of the reason why I love you so very much. No one ever believed in me as you do."

" 'Tisn't hard. Ye are a remarkable woman."

She leaned over and kissed him on the cheek. "I once told Fiona that I sincerely believe we all get what we deserve in life. How did I manage to be so lucky as to find you?"

Miles flashed her a dazzling grin. "Och, Shaun always said ye had the luck o' the saints."

"The saints," Faith murmured. "Perhaps I have them to thank."

Miles leaned forward to nuzzle her neck. "No matter what happens, Faith, I know, here in my heart, that we were meant to be together, regardless of time."

She smiled. "Yes, Miles, together for always and forever," she echoed, pressing her lips against his in a message as ancient as the stones of Castle Dun na Moor.

She knew that tomorrow would come, but for now they were together, and nothing else mattered.

Epilogue

Ah, my Beloved, fill the cup that clears
Today of past regrets and future fears—
Tomorrow? Why tomorrow I may be
Myself with Yesterday's seven thousand years.
        —The Rubaiyat of Omar Khayyam

London, England
August 1, 1997

Fiona slowly turned the key in the lock of Faith's townhouse. She dreaded the task that lay ahead: cleaning out her cousin's belongings and putting the house up for sale.

The door opened and Fiona walked into the foyer. The house smelled musty, and a layer of dust coated the small entryway table. Swallowing back the emotion that rose in her throat, Fiona shook out her raincoat and hung it up on a peg.

For more than a year she had refused to believe that her cousin was gone. Repeated calls and frantic letters to the offices of MI5 had gained her little more than an official statement that the proper authorities were conducting an investigation of their own. Finally, three weeks ago, Fiona had been summoned to MI5 headquarters, where she had been informed that Faith had been declared missing in Ireland and the worst was feared. Intelligence had not been able to turn up a shred of evidence that she was still alive. Instead she seemed to have simply vanished into thin air, never to be seen again. The investigation would continue indefinitely, they said, but they had come to the reluctant conclusion that Faith had regrettably been slain during the mission.

"Regrettable, my foot," Fiona muttered as she walked into Faith's sitting room and turned on the lamp. Papers were still

391

scattered everywhere across the couch and on the floor. The house was its usual mess, just as Faith had left it. In fact, nothing appeared to have been touched since that fateful night before her departure to Ireland, even though Fiona knew full well that the agency had already been to the townhouse, turning it upside down and looking for clues to Faith's disappearance.

Sighing, Fiona bent down, picking up the papers from the floor and stacking them into a neat pile. She had been told that all work-related papers would have to be relinquished to the agency. She didn't feel terribly charitable toward the agency at the moment, but she knew she would do as they asked. If there was any chance that she would ever find out what had really happened to Faith, she would have to cooperate with them.

Standing up, she glanced at the table, noticing the framed picture she had given Faith the last time they had been together. Stepping over a stack of books, she picked up the picture and hugged it to her breast.

"Oh, Faith," she admonished as tears began to fall. "Why did you have to be so bloody stubborn? Why couldn't you have listened to me and become a professor or an advertising executive? No, you had to follow in your father's frigging footsteps . . . a damn fine example he set for you. Now you die without a moment of real happiness in your life. Christ, it's so unfair. You deserved more . . . so much more."

She walked over to the couch and sat down, still clutching the picture. A glint from the diamond on her engagement ring caught her eye and she looked at it through her tears. She had postponed the wedding, waiting until she heard word of Faith. Now the wedding would go forward without a maid of honor. There would be no replacement.

Dabbing at her eyes with the sleeve of her blouse, Fiona stood, wandering over to the hearth. On impulse she picked up the antique dagger from the mantel, the same one Faith had so proudly shown her the last time they had been together. Her heart aching, she let it rest in the palm of her hand.

Sadly, Fiona ran her perfectly manicured nail across the blade, wondering what had caused the iron to bend at such an odd angle and trying to remember what Faith had said about it.

"Whoever the owner was, she appeared to have used it. You can see the tip has been bent back considerably, as if it hit against bone."

Fiona shivered but slipped her hand around the handle, marveling at how snugly it fit.

"You can see there was even some kind of engraving on both sides of the blade. It is unreadable but very unusual for the period. I can't stop wondering who owned it and why she felt compelled to use it."

Peering down at the engraving, Fiona suddenly gasped. Stumbling over a notebook, she made her way to the lamp, her hand trembling. Carefully, she lifted the blade to the light, peering closely at the inscription.

Sisters.

Fiona's mouth opened in surprise. She closed her eyes for a long moment and then opened them again.

The writing was still there.

Stunned, she touched the inscription with her fingernail. Even to an untrained eye such as her own, it was clear the engraving had been made long ago. The last time she and Faith had stood in this very spot, they had agreed that the inscription was unreadable. But now . . . now she could read it, and it seemed to be speaking directly to her.

"What in the world?" Fiona murmured, turning the blade over in her hand.

For always.

A small cry slipped from Fiona's lips as she took a step backward. What she was thinking was impossible, unfathomable. Lifting her head sharply, she looked out of the townhouse window, up toward the faint embroidery of stars. They glittered like diamonds on a black velvet curtain.

"Faith?" she whispered softly. "Where in the devil are you?"

Author's Note

As many of you may not be familiar with Irish history of the seventeenth century, I thought I might add a few historical footnotes.

It is true that King Charles I was beheaded by his own parliament in January 1649. His death order was signed by Oliver Cromwell, among others of the English Parliament. The murder of the king set off a war between England and Scotland that lasted little more than a year and resulted in a punishing defeat for the Scots. The Irish by and large supported Scotland in its fight against Cromwell and the Parliament.

Enraged, Cromwell deployed a huge number of soldiers to Ireland to put an end to the "Irish problem," as he called it. After conquering Dublin he set off to the city of Drogheda, where he laid siege. The governor of Drogheda, Sir Arthur Aston, a brave, crankily tenacious English officer who was fiercely loyal to King Charles and his son, refused to surrender. Aston had lost a leg in the English Civil War and was fitted with a wooden one. When Cromwell finally broke through the lines of the city, Aston was allegedly beaten to death with his own wooden leg.

Cromwell died in 1658, reportedly as a result of a severe case of malaria, which he contracted while on campaign in Ireland. For centuries rumors have abounded that his death was actually an assassination of sorts—the result of a slow poisoning. In fact, Cromwell's chief physician, Dr. George Bates (also the doctor who had served Charles I and would subsequently serve Charles II) admitted on his deathbed that he had indeed poisoned Cromwell, accelerating his death. Some historians, however, discount Dr. Bates's confession, saying it was nothing more than the ramblings of a dying man. Cromwell's son, Richard, ascended to power but proved to be a weak successor. Charles's son was eventually crowned king.

Author's Note

I have a lot of people to thank for their assistance with this manuscript, but for the sake of brevity I will name only a few. Donna Moffett, my mother, and Winifred Braden, my grandmother, faithfully read each chapter as I wrote it, offering valuable advice and suggestions. Also much thanks to my sister and fellow author, Sandra Parks, whose constant encouragement and counsel probably cost her a fortune in phone bills. Lastly, kudos are due to the men and women of RW-L, the marvelous Romance Writers Bulletin Board on the Internet (RW-L@SJUVM.STJOHNS.EDU). Thanks a million for your encouragement and advice—you know who you are! You may also visit my home page on the Internet at http://www.writepage.com/moffettj.htm

I greatly enjoy receiving letters from readers and fellow authors alike. If you would like to write to me with comments or receive my newsletter and a handmade bookmark, please send a self-addressed, stamped, legal-size envelope to: P.O. Box 10001, Alexandria, VA 22310.

The Sorcerer's Lady

DEBRA DIER

Victorian debutante Laura Sullivan can't believe her eyes. Aunt Sophie's ancient spell has conjured up the man of Laura's dreams—and deposited a half-naked barbarian in the library of her Boston home. With his bare chest and sheathed broadsword, the golden giant is a tempting study in Viking maleness, but hardly the proper blue blood Laura is supposed to marry. An accomplished sorcerer, Connor has traveled through the ages to reach his soul mate, the bewitching woman who captured his heart. But Beacon Hill isn't ninth-century Ireland, and Connor's powers are useless if he can't convince Laura that love is stronger than magic and that she is destined to become the sorcerer's lady.

___52305-1 $5.50 US/$6.50 CAN

THE RELUCTANT VIKING
SANDRA HILL

The hypnotic voice on the self-motivation tape is supposed to help Ruby Jordan solve her problems, not create new ones. Instead, she is lulled from a life full of a demanding business, a neglected home, and a failing marriage—to an era of hard-bodied warriors and fair maidens, fierce fighting and fiercer wooing. But the world ten centuries in the past doesn't prove to be all mead and mirth. Even as Ruby tries to update medieval times, she has to deal with a Norseman whose view of women is stuck in the Dark Ages. And what is worse, brawny Thork has her husband's face, habits, and desire to avoid Ruby. Determined not to lose the same man twice, Ruby plans a bold seduction that will conquer the reluctant Viking—and make him an eager captive of her love.

___52297-7 $5.50 US/$6.50 CAN

Dorchester Publishing Co., Inc.
P.O. Box 6640
Wayne, PA 19087-8640

Please add $1.75 for shipping and handling for the first book and $.50 for each book thereafter. NY, NYC, and PA residents, please add appropriate sales tax. No cash, stamps, or C.O.D.s. All orders shipped within 6 weeks via postal service book rate. Canadian orders require $2.00 extra postage and must be paid in U.S. dollars through a U.S. banking facility.

Name_____
Address_____
City_____State_____Zip_____
I have enclosed $_____ in payment for the checked book(s).
Payment <u>must</u> accompany all orders. ❑ Please send a free catalog.
CHECK OUT OUR WEBSITE! www.dorchesterpub.com

DESPERADO
SANDRA HILL

Major Helen Prescott has always played by the rules. That's why Rafe Santiago nicknamed her "Prissy" at the military academy years before. Rafe's teasing made her life miserable back then, and with his irresistible good looks, he is the man responsible for her one momentary lapse in self control. When a routine skydive goes awry, the two parachute straight into the 1850 California Gold Rush. Mistaken for a notorious bandit and his infamously sensuous mistress, they find themselves on the wrong side of the law. In a time and place where rules have no meaning, Helen finds Rafe's hard, bronzed body strangely comforting, and his piercing blue eyes leave her all too willing to share his bedroll. Suddenly, his teasing remarks make her feel all woman, and she is ready to throw caution to the wind if she can spend every night in the arms of her very own desperado.

_52182-2 $5.99 US/$6.99 CAN

THE Last Viking

SANDRA HILL

He is six feet, four inches of pure unadulterated male. He wears nothing but a leather tunic, speaks in an ancient tongue, and he is standing in Professor Meredith Foster's living room. The medieval historian tells herself he is part of a practical joke, but with his wide gold belt, callused hands, and the rabbit roasting in her fireplace, the brawny stranger seems so… authentic. Meredith is mesmerized by his muscular form, and her body surrenders to the fantasy that Geirolf Ericsson really is a Viking from a thousand years ago. As he helps her fulfill her grandfather's dream of re-creating a Viking ship, he awakens her to dreams of her own until she wonders if the hand of fate has thrust her into the arms of the last Viking.

___52255-1 $5.99 US/$6.99 CAN